THERE CAN BE NO DOUBT THAT YOU ARE
IN CONTROL OF CASTLE TRINITY.

"The elves are few, but my troops are many," the ogrillon went on. "I will not fear even a few thousand dead when Shilmista falls under my shadow."

"*My* shadow?" Dorigen asked slyly. For the first time since she'd entered the tent, she saw a hint of trepidation in the ogrillon's gaze.

"You were away on private matters," Ragnor argued, somewhat subdued. "The time had come to attack, and I did. I struck with every soldier I could muster. I led the attack myself and carry the scars of battle."

Dorigen bowed her head respectfully to calm the volatile beast. Ragnor had told her much more than he had intended. With the ogrillon so adamant in his statement that Shilmista would fall under *his* control, and not to Castle Trinity, Dorigen worried just how far Ragnor's newfound independence would take him.

She had no desire to be anywhere near the ogrillon when he decided he didn't need Castle Trinity.

"The Orc King finds Drizzt's whirling scimitar blades tackling both familiar foes and refreshingly ambiguous moral challenges . . . The story line marks the continuation of Salvatore's maturation as a writer, introducing more complex themes into a frequently black-and-white fantasy landscape."

—*Kirkus*

"(R.A. Salvatore) knows how to fashion a story so that you have to keep reading—even if it's two in the morning and you have to get up at five, even though you still have more than a hundred pages to go, and even if you're so tired you have to keep telling yourself you will read only one more page, just one more, and that's all."

—Terry Brooks

R.A. SALVATORE'S
THE CLERIC QUINTET

BOOK I
Canticle

BOOK II
In Sylvan Shadows

BOOK III
Night Masks
May 2009

BOOK IV
The Fallen Fortress
August 2009

BOOK V
The Chaos Curse
September 2009

FORGOTTEN REALMS

R.A. SALVATORE

The Cleric Quintet

BOOK

II

In Sylvan Shadows

Cover Art by
DUANE O. MYERS

WIZARDS OF THE COAST®

The Cleric Quintet, Book II
IN SYLVAN SHADOWS

©1992 TSR, Inc.
©2009 Wizards of the Coast LLC

Published by Wizards of the Coast LLC

FORGOTTEN REALMS, WIZARDS OF THE COAST, and their respective logos are trademarks of Wizards of the Coast LLC, in the U.S.A. and other countries.

Printed in the U.S.A.

Cover art by Duane O. Myers

First Printing: April 1992
This Edition First Printing: March 2009

9 8 7 6 5 4 3 2 1

ISBN: 978-0-7869-5326-4
620-21968740-001-EN

U.S., CANADA,
ASIA, PACIFIC, & LATIN AMERICA
Wizards of the Coast LLC
P.O. Box 707
Renton, WA 98057-0707
+1-800-324-6496

EUROPEAN HEADQUARTERS
Hasbro UK Ltd
Caswell Way
Newport, Gwent NP9 0YH
GREAT BRITAIN
Save this address for your records.

Visit our web site at www.wizards.com

PROLOGUE

Cadderly moved his quill out toward the inkwell then changed his mind and put it down on his desk. He looked out the window at the foliage surrounding the Edificant Library, and at Percival, the white squirrel, tangling with acorns along the rain gutter of the lower level. It was the month of Eleasias, Highsun, the height of summer, and the season had been unusually bright and warm so high in the Snowflake Mountains.

Everything was as it always had been for Cadderly—at least, that's what the young scholar tried to convince himself. Percival was at play in the sunshine, the library was secure and peaceful once more, and the lazy remainder of summer promised days of leisure and quiet walks.

As it always had been.

Cadderly dropped his chin into his palm then ran his hand back through his sandy brown hair. He tried to concentrate on the peaceful images before him, on the quiet summer world of the Snowflake Mountains, but eyes looked back at him from the depths of his mind: the eyes of a man he had killed.

Nothing would ever be the same. Cadderly's gray eyes were no longer so quick to turn up in that boyish, full-faced smile.

With renewed determination, the young scholar poked the quill into the ink and smoothed the parchment before him.

Entry Number Seventeen
by Cadderly of Carradoon
Appointed Scholar, Order of Deneir
4 Eleasias, the Year of Maidens (1361 DR)
    It has been three and a half tendays since Barjin's defeat, yet I see his dead eyes—

Cadderly stopped and scribbled out the thought, both from the parchment and from his mind. He looked again out the window, dropped his quill, and rubbed his hands over his boyish face.

This is important, he reminded himself.

He hadn't made an entry in more than a tenday, and if he failed at his year, the consequences to all the Southern Heartlands could be devastating. Again the quill went into the inkwell.

It has been three and a half tendays since we defeated the curse that befell the Edificant Library. The most distressing news since then: Ivan and Pikel Bouldershoulder have left the library in pursuit of Pikel's aspirations to druidhood. I wish Pikel well, though I doubt that the woodland priests will welcome a dwarf into their order. The

2

dwarves wouldn't say where they were going (I don't believe they themselves knew). I miss them terribly, for they, Danica, and Newander were the true heroes in the fight against the Talonite priest named Barjin—if that was his true name.

Cadderly paused for a few moments. Assigning a name to the man he had killed didn't make things any easier for the innocent young scholar. It took him some time before he could concentrate on the information necessary to his entry, the interview he had done with the interrogating priests.

The clerics who called back the dead man's spirit warned me to take their findings as "probable" rather than exact. Witnesses from beyond the grave are often elusive, they explained, and Barjin's stubborn spirit proved to be as difficult an opponent as the priest had been in life. Little information was garnered, but the clerics came away believing that the evil priest was part of a conspiracy—one of conquest that still threatens us, or so I must assume. That only increases the importance of my task.

Again, many moments passed before Cadderly was able to continue. He looked at the sunshine, at the white squirrel, and pushed away Percival's staring eyes.

Barjin served the goddess Talona, and that bodes ill indeed for us all. The Lady of Poison is a vile deity of chaos, restricted by no moral code. But I am hard-pressed to explain one discrepancy:

Barjin hardly fit the description of a Talonite disciple; he had not scarred himself in any visible way, as priests worshiping the Lady of Poison typically do. The holy symbol he wore, though—the trident with small vials atop each point—does resemble the triangular, three-teardrop design of Talona.

But with this, too, we have been led down a trail that leads only to guesses. More exact information must be gained, and gained soon, I fear.

This day, my quest has taken a different turn. Prince Elbereth of Shilmista, a most respected elf lord, has come to the library, bearing gloves taken from a band of marauding bugbears in the wood. The insignia on these gloves match Barjin's symbol exactly—there can be little doubt that the bugbears and the Talonite priest were allied.

The headmasters have made no decisions yet, beyond agreeing that someone should accompany Prince Elbereth back to the forest. It seems only logical that I will be their choice. My quest can go no farther here; already I have perused every source of information on Talona in our possession—our knowledge is not vast on this subject. And as for the magical elixir that Barjin used, I have looked through every major alchemical tome and have consulted extensively with Vicero Belago, the library's resident alchemist. Further study will be required as time permits, but my inquiries have hit only dead ends. Belago believes that he would learn more of the elixir if he had the bottle in his possession, but the headmasters have flatly refused that request. The lower catacombs have been sealed—no one is to be allowed down there, and the bottle is to remain where I put it, immersed in a font of blessed water in the room that Barjin used to house his vile altar.

The only clues remaining, then, lead to Shilmista. Always have I wanted to visit the enchanted forest, to witness the elves' dance and hear their melancholy song. But not like this.

Cadderly set the quill down and blew lightly on the parchment to help dry the ink. His entry seemed terribly short, considering that he had not recorded anything for many days and there was so much to catch up on. It would have to do, though, for Cadderly's thoughts were too jumbled for him to make sense of them in writing.

Orphaned at a very young age, Cadderly had lived at the Edificant Library since his earliest recollections. The library was a fortress, never threatened in modern times—not until Barjin had come. To the young Cadderly, orcs and goblins, undead monsters and evil wizards, had all been the stuff of tales in dusty books.

It had suddenly become all too real and Cadderly had been thrust into the midst of it. The other priests, even Headmaster Avery, had called him a hero for his actions in defeating Barjin. Cadderly saw things differently, though. Confusion, chaos, and blind fate had facilitated his every move. Even killing Barjin had been an accident—a fortunate accident?

Cadderly honestly didn't know, didn't understand what Deneir wanted or expected of him. Accident or not, the act of killing Barjin haunted the young scholar. He saw the Talonite's dead eyes in his thoughts and in his dreams, staring at him, accusing him.

Outside the window, Percival danced and played along the rain gutter as warm sunshine filtered through the thick leaves of the huge oaks and maples common to the mountainside. Far, far below, Impresk Lake glittered, quiet and serene, in the gentle rays of the summer light.

To Cadderly, the "hero," it all seemed a horrible facade.

ONE

BY SURPRISE

Twilight.

Fifty elf archers lay concealed across the first ridge and fifty more waited behind them atop the second in the rolling, hilly section of the Shilmista Forest known as the Dells. The flicker of faraway torches came into view through the trees.

"That's not the leading edge," the elf maiden Shayleigh warned, and indeed, lines of goblins were soon spotted much closer than the torches, traveling swiftly and silently through the darkness. Shayleigh's violet eyes glittered eagerly in the starlight; she kept the cowl of her cloak up high, fearing that the luster of her golden hair, undiminished by the quiet colors of night, would betray her position.

The advancing goblins came on, their shortbows bent back, arrows poised to strike.

The skilled elves held their longbows steady, not one of them trembling under the great pull of their powerful weapons. They looked around somewhat nervously, though, awaiting Shayleigh's command, their discipline severely tested as orcs and goblins, and larger, more ominous forms, came almost to the base of the ridge.

Shayleigh moved down the line quickly. *Two arrows away and retreat,* she instructed, using a silent code of hand signals and hushed whispers. *On my call.*

Orcs were on the hillock, climbing steadily toward the ridge. Still Shayleigh held the volley, trusting in the erupting chaos to keep her enemies at bay.

A large orc stopped and sniffed the air just ten paces from the ridge. Those in line behind the beast stopped too, glancing around in an effort to discern what their companion had sensed. The porcine creature tilted its head back, trying to bring some focus to the unusual form lying just a few feet ahead of it.

"Now!" came Shayleigh's cry.

The lead orc never managed to squeal a warning before the arrow dived into its face, the force of the blow lifting the creature from the ground and sending it tumbling back down the slope. All across the north face of the hillock, the invading monsters screamed out and fell, some hit by two or three arrows in just the blink of an eye.

Then the ground shook under the monstrous charge as the invading army's second rank learned of the enemy concealed atop the ridge. Almost every arrow of the elves' ensuing volley hit the mark, but it hardly slowed the sudden press of drooling, monstrous forms.

According to plan, Shayleigh and her troops took flight, with goblins, orcs, and ogres on their heels.

Galladel, the elf king of Shilmista, commanding the second line, turned his archers loose as soon as the monsters appeared over the lip of the first ridge. Arrow after arrow hit home. Groups of four elves concentrated their fire on single targets—the huge ogres—and the great monsters were brought crashing down.

Shayleigh's group crossed the second ridge and fell into place beside their companions then turned their longbows and joined in the massacre. With horrifying speed, the valley between the ridges filled with corpses and blood.

One ogre slipped through the throng and nearly got to the elven line—even had its club raised high for a strike—but a dozen arrows burrowed into its chest, staggering it. Shayleigh, fearless and grim, leaped over the closest archer and drove her fine sword into the stunned monster's heart.

Q

As soon as he heard the fighting in the Dells, the wizard Tintagel knew that he and his three magic-using associates would soon be hard-pressed by monstrous invaders. Only a dozen archers had been spared to go with the wizards, and those, Tintagel knew, would spend more time scouting to the east and keeping communication open with the main host than fighting. The four elf magic-users had mapped out their defenses carefully, and they trusted in their Art. If the ambush at the Dells was to succeed, Tintagel and his companions would have to hold the line in the east. They could not fail.

A scout rushed by Tintagel, and the wizard brushed aside his thick, dark locks and squinted with blue eyes toward the north.

"Mixed group," the young elf explained, looking

back. "Goblins, mostly, but with a fair number of orcs beside them."

Tintagel rubbed his hands together and motioned to his three wizard comrades. All four began their spells at about the same time and soon the air north of their position was filled with sticky filaments, drifting down to form thick webs between the trees. The scout's warning had come at the last moment, for even as the webs began to take shape, several goblins rushed into them, becoming helplessly stuck.

Cries went up from several sources to the north. The press of goblins and orcs, though considerable, couldn't break through the wizard's spells, and many monsters were crushed into the webs to gag on the sticky substance and slowly suffocate. The few archers accompanying the wizards picked their shots carefully, protecting their precious few arrows, firing only if it appeared that a monster was about to break loose of its sticky bonds.

Many more were still free, beyond the webbing. Many, many more, but at least the spells had bought the elves in the Dells some time.

Q

The second ridge was given up, but not before scores of dead invaders lay piled across the valley. The elves' retreat was swift, down one hill, over the piled leaves at its base, up another hill, then falling into familiar positions atop the third ridge.

Screams to the east told Shayleigh that many monsters had approached from that way, and hundreds of torches had sprung up in the night far to the north.

"How many are you?" the elf maiden whispered, almost out of breath.

As if in answer, a black tide rolled down the southern side of the second ridge.

The invaders found a surprise waiting for them at the bottom of the small valley. The elves had leaped over the piled leaves, for they knew of the spike-filled pits hidden beneath.

With the charge stalled, showers of arrows had an even more devastating effect. Goblin after goblin died, and tough ogres growled away a dozen arrow hits only to be hit a dozen more times.

The elves cried out in savage fury, raining death on the intruders, but no smile found Shayleigh's face. She knew that the main host, coming in steadily behind the advance lines of fodder, would be more organized and better controlled.

"Death to the enemies of Shilmista!" one exuberant elf screamed, leaping to his feet and hurling his fist into the air.

In answer, a huge rock sailed through the darkness and caught the foolish young elf squarely in the face, nearly decapitating him.

"Giant!" came the cry from several positions all at once.

Another rock whipped past, narrowly missing Shayleigh's cowled head.

$$Q$$

The wizards couldn't possibly conjure enough webbing to block the entire eastern Dells. They had known that from the beginning and had selected specific trees on which to anchor their webs, creating a maze to slow the enemy's approach. Tintagel and his three cohorts nodded grimly to each other, took up predetermined positions at the mouths of the web tunnels, and prepared their next spells.

"They have entered the second channel!" called a scout.

Tintagel silently counted to five then clapped his hands. At the sound of the signal, the four wizards began identical chants. They saw the forms, shadowy and blurred by the web veils, slipping through the maze, apparently having solved the riddle. On came the charging goblins, hungry for elf blood. The wizards kept their composure, though, concentrating on their spells and trusting that they had timed the approach through the maze correctly.

Groups of goblins came straight at each of them, all in a line between the channeling webs.

One after another, the elf wizards pointed out at the enemy and uttered the final syllables of their incantations. Bolts of lightning split the darkness, shooting down each of the channels with killing fury.

The goblins didn't even have time to cry out before they fell, scorched corpses in a sylvan grave.

Q

"It is time to leave," Galladel told Shayleigh, and the maiden, for once, didn't argue. The woods beyond the second ridge were lit by so many torches it seemed as though the sun had come up—and still more were coming in.

Shayleigh couldn't tell how many giants had taken position beyond the ridge, but judging from the numbers of boulders sailing the elves' way, there were several at least.

"Five more arrows!" the fiery elf maiden cried to her troops.

But many of the elves couldn't follow that command. They had to drop their bows and take up swords, for a host of bugbears, stealthy despite their great size, had slipped in from the west.

Shayleigh raced over to join the melee. If the bugbears delayed their retreat even for a short while, the elves would be overwhelmed. By the time she got there, though, the competent elves had dispatched most of the bugbears, with only a single loss. Three elves had one of the remaining monsters surrounded, and another group was in pursuit of two bugbears, heading back to the west. To the side, though, another bugbear appeared, and only one elf, a young maiden, stood before it.

Shayleigh veered straight in, recognizing the elf as Cellanie and knowing that she was too inexperienced to handle the likes of a bugbear.

The young elf fell before Shayleigh got there, her skull crushed by the bugbear's heavy club. The seven-foot, hairy goblinoid stood there grinning with its yellow teeth.

Shayleigh dipped her head and growled loudly, as though to charge. The bugbear braced itself and clenched its wicked club tightly, but the elf maiden stopped and used her forward momentum to hurl her sword.

The bugbear stood dumbfounded. Swords were not designed for such attacks! But if the creature doubted Shayleigh's intelligence in throwing the weapon, or her prowess with such a trick, all it had to do was look to its chest, to the elf's sword hilt, vibrating horribly just five inches out of the bugbear's hairy ribs. The creature's blood spurted across the sword hilt and stained the ground.

The bugbear looked down, glanced up at Shayleigh, and it fell dead.

"To the west!" Shayleigh cried, rushing over to retrieve her sword. "As we planned! To the west!"

She grabbed the bloodied hilt and tugged, but the weapon would not slip free. Shayleigh remained more concerned with the progress of her troops than her own vulnerable position. Still looking back to oversee the retreat, she braced her foot on the dead bugbear's chest and gripped her sword tightly in both hands.

When she heard the snort above her, she knew her folly. Both her hands were on a weapon she could not use, either to strike or to parry.

Defenseless, Shayleigh looked up to see another bugbear and its huge, spiked club.

Q

The wizards, coming in to join their allies, concentrated their magical attacks on the torches of the enemy host beyond the second ridge. Enchanted flames roared to life under the pyrotechnical magic. Sparks flew wildly, burning into any monsters standing too close. Other torches poured heavy smoke, filling the area, blinding and choking, forcing the monsters to drop back or fall to the ground.

With that magical cover holding back their foes, the elves soon cleared the third ridge.

Q

A flash emanated from beside Shayleigh's face, burned her and blinded her. At first, she thought it was the impact from the bugbear's club, but when the elf maiden's wits and vision returned, she still stood over the bugbear she had killed, clutching her impaled sword.

She finally sorted out the other bugbear, its back

14

against a tree, a smoldering hole burned right through its belly. The creature's hair danced wildly, charged, Shayleigh realized, from a wizard's lightning bolt.

Tintagel was beside her.

"Come," he said, helping her tear her sword from the dead monster. "We have slowed the enemy charge, but the great, dark force will not be stopped. Already, our lead runners have encountered resistance in the west."

Shayleigh tried to respond, but found that her jaw would not move.

The wizard looked to the two archers covering his rear. "Gather up poor Cellanie," he said. "We must leave no dead for our cruel enemies to toy with."

Tintagel took Shayleigh's arm and led her off after the rest of the fleeing host. Cries and monstrous shouts erupted from all around them, but the elves did not panic. They stayed with their carefully designed plan and executed it to perfection. They met pockets of resistance in the west, but the broken ground worked in their favor against the slower, less agile monsters, especially since even on the run the elves could shoot their bows with deadly accuracy. Every group of monsters was overwhelmed and the elves continued on their way without taking another loss.

The eastern sky had grown pink with the budding dawn before they regrouped and found some rest. Shayleigh had seen no more fighting during the night, fortunately. Her head ached so badly she couldn't even keep her bearings without Tintagel's aid. The wizard stayed beside her through it all, and would have willingly died beside her if the enemy had caught them.

"I must beg your pardon," Tintagel said to her after the new camp had been set, south of the Dells. "The bugbear was too close—I had to begin the bolt too near you."

"You apologize for saving my life?" Shayleigh asked. Every word she spoke pained the valiant maiden.

"Your face shines with the redness of a burn," Tintagel said, touching her glowing cheek lightly and wincing with sympathy as he did.

"It will heal," Shayleigh replied, managing a weak smile. "Better than would my head if that bugbear had clubbed me!" She couldn't even manage a smile at her statement, though, and not for the pain, but for the memory of Cellanie, falling dead to the ground.

"How many did we lose?" Shayleigh asked.

"Three," replied Tintagel in equally grim tones.

"Only three," came the voice of King Galladel, moving to them from the side. "And the blood of hundreds of goblins and their allies stains the ground. By some accounts, even a giant was felled last night." Galladel winced when he noticed Shayleigh's red face.

"It's nothing," the elf maiden said into his wide-eyed stare, waving her hand his way.

Galladel broke his concentrated stare, embarrassed. "We are in your debt," he said, his smile returning. "Because of your fine planning, we scored a great victory this night." The elf king nodded, patted Shayleigh on the shoulder, and took his leave, having many other matters to attend to.

Shayleigh's grimace told Tintagel that she didn't share Galladel's optimism.

"The outcome," the wizard reminded her, "could have been much, much worse."

From his somber tone, Shayleigh knew she didn't have to explain her fears. They had hit their enemy by surprise, on a battlefield they had prepared and that their enemy had not seen before, and so they had lost only three. All that was true, but it seemed to Shayleigh that those three dead elves held more value than hundreds of dead goblins among the seemingly countless masses invading Shilmista's northern border.

And it was the elves, not the invaders, who had been forced to flee.

TWO

A BOOK WORTH READING

Y ou have met Prince Elbereth?" Headmaster Avery
Schell asked Cadderly as soon as the young scholar
entered Dean Thobicus's office. The headmaster rubbed
a kerchief across his blotchy face, huffing and puffing as
his bloated body tried to pull in enough air. Even before
the advent of the chaos curse, Avery had been a rotund
man. Since having gone on an eating spree along with
several other of the Edificant Library's most gluttonous
brothers, he had become morbidly obese. In the throes of
the chaos curse, some of those priests had literally eaten
themselves to death.

"You must take longer walks each morning," offered
Headmistress Pertelope, a neatly groomed, graying
woman with hazel eyes that still showed the inquisitive
luster of youth.

Pertelope was Cadderly's favorite instructor, a wistful,
often irreverent woman more concerned with common
sense than rules. He noted her long-sleeved, ankle-length
gown, bound tightly at the collar, and the gloves that

she had been wearing every time Cadderly had seen her since the chaos curse. Never before had Pertelope been so modest, if it was indeed modesty that kept her so covered. She wouldn't talk about it, though, to Cadderly or to anyone else. She wouldn't talk about anything that had occurred during the time of the curse. Cadderly wasn't too concerned, for even with the new wrappings, Pertelope seemed her old, mischievous self. Even as Cadderly watched, she grabbed a handful of Avery's blubber and gave it a playful shake to the incredulous stares of both Avery and Dean Thobicus, the skinny, wrinkled leader of the library.

A chuckle erupted from Cadderly's lips faster than he could bite it back. The stares turned grave as they shifted his way, but Pertelope offered him a playful wink to comfort him.

Through it all, Prince Elbereth, tall and painfully straight, with hair the color of a raven's wings and eyes the silver of moonbeams on a rushing river, showed no emotion whatsoever. Standing like a statue beside Dean Thobicus's desk, he caught Cadderly's gaze with his own penetrating stare and held the young scholar's attention.

Cadderly was thoroughly flustered and didn't even notice the heartbeats passing by.

"Well?" Avery prompted.

Cadderly at first didn't understand, so Avery motioned the elf prince's way.

"No," Cadderly answered quickly, "I have not had the honor of a formal introduction, though I have heard much of Prince Elbereth since his arrival three days ago." Cadderly flashed his boyish smile, the corners of his gray eyes turning up to match his grin. He pushed his unkempt, sandy brown locks from his face and moved toward Elbereth, a hand extended. "Well met!"

Elbereth regarded the offered hand for some time before extending his own in response. He nodded gravely, making Cadderly was more than a little bit embarrassed by the easy smile splayed across his own face. Yet again, Cadderly felt out of his element. Elbereth had come with potentially catastrophic news and Cadderly, sheltered for all of his life, simply didn't know how to respond.

"This is the scholar I have told you about," Avery explained to the elf. "Cadderly of Carradoon, a most remarkable young man."

Elbereth's handshake was incredibly strong for so slender a being, and when the elf turned Cadderly's hand over, the young scholar offered only token resistance. Elbereth examined Cadderly's palm, rubbing his thumb across the base of Cadderly's fingers.

"These are not the hands of a warrior," the elf said, unimpressed.

"I never claimed to be a warrior," Cadderly retorted before Avery or Thobicus could explain. The dean and headmaster turned accusing glares back at Cadderly. Even easygoing Pertelope offer him no escape.

Headmaster Avery cleared his throat to break the tension.

"Cadderly is indeed a warrior," the robust headmaster explained. "It was he who defeated both the Talonite priest Barjin and Barjin's most awful undead soldiers. Even a mummy rose up against the lad and was summarily put down."

The recounting didn't make Cadderly swell with pride. The mere mention of the dead priest made

21

Cadderly see him again, slumped against the wall in the makeshift altar room in the catacombs, a blasted hole in his chest and his dead eyes staring accusingly at his killer.

"But more than that," Avery continued, moving over to drape a heavy, sweaty arm over the young scholar, "Cadderly is a warrior whose greatest weapon is knowledge. We have a riddle here, Prince Elbereth, a most dangerous riddle, I fear. And Cadderly, I tell you now, is the man who will solve it."

Avery's proclamation added more weight to Cadderly's shoulders than the headmaster's considerable arm. The young scholar wasn't absolutely certain, but he believed he liked Avery better before the events of the chaos curse. Back then, the headmaster often went out of his way to make Cadderly's life miserable. Under the influence of the intoxicating curse, though, Avery had admitted his almost fatherly love for the young scholar.

"Enough of this banter," said Dean Thobicus in his shaky voice. "We have chosen Cadderly as our representative in this matter. The decision was ours alone to make. Prince Elbereth will treat him accordingly."

The elf turned to the seated dean and dipped a curt and precise bow.

Thobicus nodded in reply. "Tell Cadderly of the gloves, and of how you came to possess them," he bade.

Elbereth reached into the pocket of his traveling cloak—an action that pushed the garment open and gave Cadderly a quick glance at the elf prince's magnificent armor, links of golden and silvery chain finely meshed—and produced several gloves, each clearly marked with stitching that showed the same trident-and-bottle design that Barjin had displayed on his clerical vestments.

Elbereth sorted through the tangle to free one glove, and handed it to Cadderly.

"Such vermin does not often find its way into Shilmista," the proud elf began, "but we are ever alert for its encroachment. A party of bugbears wandered into the forest. None of them escaped with their lives."

None of this was news to Cadderly, of course; rumors had been circulating throughout the Edificant Library since the elf prince's arrival. Cadderly nodded and examined the gauntlet.

"The symbol is the same as Barjin's," he declared at once.

"But what does it mean?" asked an impatient Avery.

"An adaptation of Talona's symbol," Cadderly explained, shrugging to let them know that he was not absolutely certain of that fact.

"The bugbears carried poisoned daggers," Elbereth remarked. "That would be in accord with the Lady of Poison's edicts."

"You know of Talona?" Cadderly asked.

Elbereth's silvery eyes flashed, a moonbeam sparkling off a cresting wave, and he gave Cadderly a derisive, sidelong glance. "I have seen the birth and death of three centuries, young human. I will still be young at the time of your death, though you might live more years than all others of your race."

Cadderly bit back his retort, knowing that he would find little support in antagonizing the elf.

"Do not underestimate that which I, Prince of Shilmista, might know," the haughty Elbereth continued. "We are not a simple folk wasting our years dancing under the stars, as so many would choose to believe."

Cadderly started to reply, sharply again, but Pertelope,

ever the calming influence, moved in front of him and took the glove, shooting him another wink and subtly stepping on the young scholar's toe.

"We would never think so of our friends in Shilmista," the headmistress offered. "Often has the Edificant Library sought the wisdom of ancient Galladel, your father and king."

Apparently appeased, Elbereth gave a quick nod.

"If it is indeed a sect of Talona, then what might we conclude?" Dean Thobicus asked.

Cadderly shrugged helplessly. "Little," he replied. "Since the Time of Troubles, so much has changed. We do not yet know the intentions and methods of the various sects, but I doubt that coincidence brought Barjin to us and the bugbears to Shilmista, especially since each carried not the normal symbol of Talona, but an adapted design. A renegade sect, it would seem, but undeniably coordinated in its attacks."

"You will come to Shilmista," Elbereth said to Cadderly. The scholar thought for a moment that the elf was asking him, but then he realized from Elbereth's unblinking, uncompromising stare, that it had been a command. Helpless, the young scholar looked to his headmasters and to the dean, but they, even Pertelope, nodded in accord.

"When?" Cadderly asked Dean Thobicus, pointedly looking past Elbereth's ensnaring gaze.

"A few days," Thobicus replied. "There are many preparations to be made."

"A few days may be too long for my people," Elbereth remarked, his eyes still boring into Cadderly.

"We will move as fast as we can," was the best Thobicus could offer. "We have suffered grave injuries, Prince.

An emissary from the Church of Ilmater is on the way, to make an inquiry concerning a group of his priests who were found slaughtered in their room. He will demand a thorough investigation, and that too will require an audience with Cadderly."

"Then Cadderly will leave him a statement," Elbereth replied. "Or the emissary will wait until Cadderly returns from Shilmista. I am concerned for the living, Dean Thobicus, not the dead."

To Cadderly's amazement, Thobicus did not argue.

They adjourned the meeting then, on Headmaster Avery's suggestion, for there was an event scheduled in the Edificant Library that day that many wished to witness—and which Cadderly flatly refused to miss for any reason.

"Come with us, Prince Elbereth," the portly headmaster offered, moving by Cadderly's side. Cadderly gave Avery a somewhat sour look, not so certain he wanted the haughty elf along. "One of the visiting priestesses, Danica Maupoissant, of Westgate, will perform a most unusual feat."

Elbereth gave a quick glance at Cadderly, smiled, and agreed. Cadderly knew, to his further dismay, that Elbereth honestly enjoyed the fact that accepting Avery's invitation would bother the young scholar.

They came into the great hall on the library's first floor, a huge, ornately decorated, thick-pillared room lined by grand tapestries depicting the glories of Deneir and Oghma, deities of the building's host religions. Most of the library's priests, of both orders, had turned out. Nearly a hundred men and women gathered in a wide circle around a block of stone supported on cross-legged sawhorses.

Danica kneeled on a mat a few feet from the stone, her almond eyes closed and her arms held out before her and crossed at the wrists. She was a tiny woman, barely five feet tall, and seemed tinier still when kneeling before the formidable, solid block. Cadderly resisted the urge to go to her, realizing that she was deep in meditation.

"Is that the priestess?" Elbereth asked, a tinge of excitement in his voice. Cadderly snapped his head around to regard the elf, noting the sparkle in Elbereth's silvery eyes.

"That is Danica," Avery replied. "She is beautiful, is she not?" Indeed Danica was, with perfect, delicate features and a thick mop of strawberry blond hair dancing about her shoulders. "But do not allow that beauty to deceive you, Prince," Avery went on proudly, as though Danica was his own child. "Danica is among the finest fighters I have ever seen. Deadly are her bare hands, and boundless is her discipline and dedication."

The sparkle in Elbereth's admiring eyes did not diminish; those shining dots of light shot out like tiny spears at Cadderly's heart.

Preparation or no preparation, Cadderly figured it was time to go to Danica. He crossed through the onlookers' circle and knelt before her, reaching out to lightly touch her long hair.

She did not stir.

"Danica," Cadderly called softly, taking her deceptively soft hand in his own.

Danica opened her eyes, those exotic brown orbs that sent shivers up Cadderly's spine every time he gazed into them. Her wide smile told Cadderly that she was not angry about the interruption.

"I feared that you would not be here," she whispered.

"A thousand ogres couldn't have held me from this place," he replied, "not today." Cadderly glanced back over his shoulder at the stone block. It seemed so huge and so solid, and Danica so very delicate. "Are you certain?" he asked.

"I'm ready," Danica replied grimly. "Do you doubt me?"

Cadderly thought back a few tendays, to the horrible day when he had entered Danica's room and found her barely conscious on the floor, after having slammed her head repeatedly against a similar stone. Her wounds were long gone, healed by salves and the magic of the library's mightiest clerics, but Cadderly would never forget how close Danica had come to death, nor would he forget his own terrible feeling of emptiness when he thought he might lose her.

"I was under the curse's influence then," Danica explained, easily reading his concern. "The mist prevented me from attaining the proper concentration. I have studied Grandmaster Penpahg D'Ahn's scrolls . . ."

"I know," Cadderly assured her, stroking her delicate hand. "And I know you're ready. Forgive me my fears. It doesn't mean I doubt you, or your dedication, or your wisdom." His smile was sincere, if strained. He moved near, as if to kiss her, but backed away suddenly and glanced around.

"I-I wouldn't want to disturb your concentration," he stammered.

Danica knew better, knew that his embarrassment alone had pulled him away from her. She laughed aloud, charmed as always by his innocence.

"Do you not find this alluring?" she asked with mock sarcasm to comfort the nervous young man.

"Oh, yes," the young scholar answered. "I have always wanted to be in love with one who could put her head through solid stone."

They shared a laugh then Danica noticed Elbereth and fell silent. The elf prince stared at her with his penetrating gaze, looked right through her, it seemed. She pulled her loose robes more tightly around her, feeling naked under that stare, but she didn't look away.

"That is Prince Elbereth?" she asked with what little breath she could find.

Cadderly considered her for a long moment then turned to regard Elbereth. The gathering be damned, he thought, and he bent back in and kissed Danica hard, forcing her attention away from the elf.

It was Danica, not Cadderly, who was flustered, and Cadderly couldn't be certain if her embarrassment came from the kiss or from her own realization that she had been caught staring a bit too intently at the visiting elf.

"Go back to your meditation," Cadderly offered, afraid of what the growing number of distractions might do to Danica's attempt. He felt childish indeed that he had let his own emotions take precedence at such an important moment. He kissed her again, a light peck on the cheek. "I know you will succeed," he offered, and he took his leave.

Danica took several deep breaths to steady herself and cleanse her mind. She looked to the stone first, the obstacle that stood in the way of her progress as one of the leading disciples of Penpahg D'Ahn. She grew angry at that stone, putting it in the light of an enemy. Then she left it with a final mental threat and turned her attention to the wide room around her, the distractions she had to be rid of.

Danica focused on Elbereth first. She saw the elf prince, his strange eyes still staring her way, and he was gone, a black hole all there was to mark the spot where he'd stood. Avery went away next then those standing beside the portly headmaster. Danica's gaze shifted and locked on one of the many huge archways supporting the great hall. It, too, disappeared into the darkness.

"Phien denifi ca," Danica whispered as another group of people disappeared. "They are only images."

All the room was fast replaced by blackness. Only the block remained, and Cadderly. Danica had saved Cadderly for last. He was her greatest supporter; he was as much her strength as her own inner discipline.

But then he, too, was gone.

Danica rose and slowly approached the stone.

You cannot resist, her thoughts called out to the block. *I am the stronger.*

Her arms waved slowly before her, weaving in an intricate dance, and she continued her mental assault on the stone, treating it as some sentient thing, assuring herself that she was convincing it that it could not win. It was the technique of Penpahg D'Ahn, and Penpahg D'Ahn had broken the stone.

Danica looked beyond the block and imagined her head crashing through the stone and exiting the other side. She studied the depth of the block then mentally reduced it to a parchment's width.

You are parchment, and I am the stronger, she told the stone.

It went on for many minutes, the arm dance, Danica's feet shifting, always in perfect balance, and she softly chanted, seeking complete harmony of body and spirit.

It came so suddenly that the crowd barely had time to gasp. Danica fell forward in two quick steps. Every muscle in her small, finely toned frame seemed to snap forward and down, driving her forehead into the stone.

Danica heard nothing and saw nothing for a long moment. Then there was the blackness of the meditation-dispatched room, gradually fading back into images that the young monk recognized. She looked around her, surprised to see the block lying on the floor in two nearly equal-sized pieces.

An arm was around her, and she knew it was Cadderly's.

"You are now the highest ranking disciple of Grandmaster Penpahg D'Ahn!" Cadderly whispered into her ear, and she heard him clearly, though the gathering had erupted into a wild burst of cheering.

Danica turned and hugged Cadderly close, but couldn't help looking over his shoulder to regard Elbereth. The serious elf prince did not cheer, but stared at Danica with approval in his sparkling silver eyes.

C

Headmistress Pertelope heard the cheering from her room above the great hall and knew that Danica had successfully broken the stone. Pertelope was not surprised; she had seen the event in a dream that she knew was prophetic. She was glad of Danica's continuing success and growing power, and glad, too, that Danica would remain by Cadderly's side in the coming days.

Pertelope feared for the young scholar, for she alone among all the priests at the library understood the personal trials Cadderly would soon face.

He was of the chosen, Pertelope knew.

"Will it be enough?" the headmistress asked quietly, hugging *The Tome of Universal Harmony,* the most holy book of Deneir. "Will you survive, dear Cadderly, as I have survived, or will the callings of Deneir devour you and leave you an empty thing?"

Almost to mock her own claims of survival, the headmistress noticed then that her sharp-edged skin had again sliced several lines in the long sleeve of her gown.

Pertelope shook her head and hugged the book tightly to her fully covered body. The potential for insight and knowledge was virtually unlimited, but so, too, was the potential for disaster.

THREE

INTRIGUE

The wizard Dorigen reached a tentative hand out for the door handle to the chamber of her leader, Aballister. Surprised by her own reluctance to open that door, though she considered the man her mentor, and even once her lover, Dorigen grabbed the handle and walked in.

Aballister sat in his comfortable chair, gazing out a small window at the distant Shining Plains and at the new construction he had ordered begun at Castle Trinity. He seemed a wretched thing to Dorigen, not nearly the vital, powerful wizard who had once so captivated her. Aballister was still powerful, but his strength lay in his magic, not in his body. His black hair lay matted to his head and his eyes, dark before, seemed like empty holes, sunk deeply into his sharp-featured face. Dorigen wondered how she ever could have found him alluring, how she ever could have lain beside that loose-skinned bag of bones she saw before her.

She shook those thoughts away and reminded herself

that Aballister's tutoring had brought her considerable power, and it had all been worth it.

Aballister's imp familiar, a bat-winged creature named Druzil, perched on the desk behind the wizard, posing as a gargoylelike statue. A nervous orc guard stood in front of the desk, unaware that the creature just a few inches away was actually alive.

Dorigen hardly looked at the orc, focusing more on Druzil, a sneaky character Dorigen didn't trust in the least. Druzil had been with Barjin when the priest was defeated at the Edificant Library, though no one in Castle Trinity complained about the imp's apparent role in bringing Barjin down. Few other than Aballister, Dorigen, and the castle's third wizard, Bogo Rath, even knew the imp existed. Aballister had planned to introduce Druzil to the castle's garrison, but Dorigen had managed to change his mind—at least for the time being. Dorigen looked back at the wizard's hollowed face and nearly sneered at the notion of his dangerous arrogance. Aballister had always carefully guarded Druzil, his secret weapon, so why would he suddenly want to give that secret up?

Druzil managed to slip a sly wink at Dorigen without alerting the oblivious orc.

Dorigen replied with a private scowl then turned to Aballister. "You requested my presence?" she asked, sharp and to the point.

"I did," the wizard answered, not bothering to look Dorigen's way. "Aballister," he mumbled to himself, then, "Bonaduce." He considered each word for a moment, then turned to Dorigen, his smile wide. "Or Aballister Bonaduce, perhaps? Do you have a preference, or should I use both names when I claim dominion over the Southern Heartlands?"

"That claim would be premature," Dorigen reminded him. "Our only expedition so far has failed utterly." She studied the orc soldier, no doubt one of Ragnor's personal attendants, then turned to stare back at Aballister, amazed that the wizard would be so brash with his only surviving rival's henchman standing beside him.

"Patience," Aballister said, waving his hand derisively. "Ragnor is on Shilmista's border. When he chooses to march, the elves will be no more."

"The elves are but one our enemies," said Dorigen, again looking toward the trembling orc.

Aballister waited a few moments, seeming to enjoy Dorigen's discomfort, then dismissed the wretched creature. "Get word back to Ragnor that he has our blessings and the blessings of Talona," Aballister said. "And good fighting!"

The orc spun and rushed from the room, slamming the door behind it. Aballister clapped his hands with glee.

"Greetings, Mistress Magic," Druzil slurred his customary title for the female wizard. He unwrapped his leathery wings and stretched since the orc was gone. "And how is your nose today?"

Dorigen winced at the remark. She was a handsome woman—a bit too round for her own liking, perhaps—with fair, if a bit plain features and small but remarkably lustrous eyes the color of pure amber. Her nose was her one weak spot. In her earliest days practicing magic, Dorigen had executed a magically enhanced jump, high in the air. Her landing had been less than perfect, though, for she had overbalanced on her descent, slammed face first into the stone floor, and bent her nose halfway over her cheek. It had never been straight since.

"Greetings to yourself, imp," Dorigen replied. She moved to the desk and began drumming her hand atop it, prominently displaying an onyx ring. She knew that Druzil knew what that ring could do, and he retreated into his leathery wings as though he expected Dorigen to loose its fiery magic at him then and there.

"I need no bickering between my allies," Aballister said, seemingly amused by it all. "I have important decisions before me—such as what to call myself when I have claimed my title."

Dorigen did not appreciate Aballister's overconfidence. "There remains Carradoon, and the Edificant Library," she said. She thought she saw Aballister flinch at the library's mention, but she couldn't be sure. The wizard hid his emotions well in the hollowed features of his drained face.

"The men of Carradoon will surrender without a fight," Aballister replied. "They are fishermen and farmers, not warriors. We must begin our preparations for what is to come after the conquest. Riatavin is not so far away, nor Westgate. We must establish our appearance as orderly and lawful rulers if we are to be accepted by the neighboring realms."

"Aballister the Diplomat?" Dorigen asked. "Orderly and lawful? Talona will not be pleased."

"It was I who met the goddess's avatar," Aballister reminded her.

Dorigen hardly needed the reminder. It was that very meeting that had so changed Aballister, had turned his simple ambitions to excel at his craft into something more dire, more consuming. It was no coincidence that Dorigen had broken off her relationship with Aballister not long after. Aballister had grown even more confident in the past few tendays. Barjin, as head of Castle Trinity's clerical order, had been Aballister's principal rival for control of the ruling triumvirate.

"Barjin is dead, and our clerics are in disarray," Aballister went on. "We cannot know how weakened Ragnor will be from his march through Shilmista. Would you have us begin a larger war so soon after the first conquest is complete?"

"The first conquest has not yet begun," Dorigen dared to say.

Aballister seemed on the verge of an explosion, but he calmed quickly. "Of course," he agreed, seeming in that instant more his old, patient self. "Ragnor is on the edge of Shilmista, though, even now making forays into the elven wood."

"Have you truly considered the implications of his march?" Dorigen asked.

Still sitting on the desk, Druzil sighed and nodded in agreement, as if the imp had been hoping someone would point out the potential problems to the increasingly arrogant wizard.

"Ragnor is powerful," Dorigen began, "and the ogrillon holds little respect for magic-users."

"We could defeat him," Aballister offered.

Dorigen nodded her agreement. "Perhaps," she said, "but what would such a conflict cost Castle Trinity? I know you have shed no tears for Barjin—and rightly so," she added, seeing Aballister's scowl. "But the priest's defeat has cost us dearly. If he and the chaos curse had taken down the Edificant Library, we could march on Carradoon even as Ragnor begins his assault on Shilmista. We cannot, though, not with the library's priests looking over the town. If Ragnor wins in the elven wood without incurring heavy losses, he will gain in prestige among the rabble. He might now be wondering how the neighboring kingdoms might deal with an ogrillon king."

Her blunt words seemed to hit Aballister as if Dorigen had struck him with a mace. He sat very still in his chair, staring straight ahead for some time.

He has known of this threat all along, came an unexpected message to Dorigen's mind. The woman glanced over at Druzil, who peeked at her over his wings.

He has refused to accept it, the imp added, *for he is too immersed in his debate over whether to call himself "Aballister the Beneficent" or "Bonaduce the Conqueror."*

Dorigen could hardly believe that the familiar could be so bold with his master sitting right before him. Though she agreed with the imp, Dorigen was smart enough not to reply. She looked away from the imp and back at the wizard.

"There can be no doubt that you are in control of Castle Trinity," Dorigen offered, "but we must continue with caution, for the seat has been a precarious one. What new cleric will rise in Barjin's place to lead the order? How strong will Ragnor become?"

"And what of Boygo Rath?" Aballister asked slyly, referring to the third and least adept wizard of Castle Trinity, whom both Aballister and Dorigen considered an upstart child. The wizard's real name was Bogo Rath, but Aballister and Dorigen referred to him as Boygo, even to his face. "And what of you?" Aballister added.

"Do not doubt my loyalty," Dorigen assured him. "In your absence, I would indeed have designs on ruling the triumvirate, but I know my betters and have more patience than you believe. As for Boygo. . . ." She let the thought hang with an amused look, as though the notion of the young upstart challenging the likes of Aballister Bonaduce was simply too ridiculous to consider.

Aballister's laughter showed that he wholeheartedly agreed. "The clerics and Ragnor, then," the wizard said, "and neither should pose too serious a threat if we are cautious and attentive."

"Ragnor is a long way from here," Dorigen reminded him, prompting an invitation.

Aballister looked at her carefully for a moment, as though trying to discern her agenda. "Ragnor will not easily accept your presence in his camp," the wizard remarked.

"I do not fear him," replied Dorigen.

She clapped her hands sharply three times. Aballister's door opened again, and in strode a man nearly seven feet tall, with corded muscles obvious under his fine silken clothes. His hair hung, thick and blond, braided down over his shoulders, and his pale blue eyes stared ahead with incredible intensity. Aballister hardly recognized him, except for his bronze skin and the curious tattoo, a polar worm, he wore upon his forehead.

"Surely this cannot be . . ." the wizard began.

"Tiennek," Dorigen confirmed, "the barbarian I plucked from the shadows of the Great Glacier in faraway Vaasa."

"Dear Dorigen," cried the wizard, his tone revealing sincere amazement, but also disdain, "you have civilized him!"

Tiennek growled.

"Perhaps a bit," Dorigen replied, "but I would not destroy Tiennek's spirit. That would serve neither my purposes . . . nor my pleasures."

Aballister's jaw tightened at that remark. Apparently, the image of his former lover in that huge man's arms did not sit well with him, not well at all.

"Impressive," Aballister admitted, "but be warned if you think him a match for Ragnor."

Tiennek growled again.

"Take no offense," Aballister added. The wizard had never been comfortable around Dorigen's dangerous pet. Under the lip of his great desk, he fingered a wand that would blast the barbarian apart if Tiennek even hinted at charging. "Your barbarian companion is powerful beyond doubt, possibly the strongest human I have ever seen," the wizard continued, looking at Dorigen once more, "but still I doubt that any human could defeat Ragnor in single combat. The ogrillon would kill him, and you would have to go all the way back to the Great Glacier to catch yourself another one."

"I, too, have never seen mighty Ragnor bested," Dorigen admitted. "Perhaps you're correct in your assessment, but Tiennek would prove a difficult opponent. Within his breast beats the heart of a warrior of the White Worm, and I have given him much more than that. I have disciplined him so that he might better use those savage powers. Ragnor would find himself hard-pressed to defeat this one, and even more so with me standing beside him." Again she drummed her fingers, displaying her deadly ring.

Aballister spent a long moment considering Dorigen's claims, and Dorigen could see the doubts plainly upon his pale, wrinkled face. In truth, she doubted that Tiennek could stand up to Ragnor as well as she had proclaimed—or that she, for all her magical prowess, could offer much help if Ragnor decided to do away with both of them—but going to Shilmista was simply too important for the success of the campaign for Dorigen to accept such possibilities.

"Ragnor could become too powerful to control," she remarked. "By one count, he has five thousand at his command."

"We have three thousand," Aballister retorted, "a strong defensive position, and the services of three wizards."

"Do you desire that war?" Dorigen asked. "What title would you gain from fighting Ragnor and his rabble?"

Aballister nodded and put his sharp chin in his skinny hand. "Go to him, then," the wizard said. "Go to Shilmista and help our dear Ragnor. He should have a wizard at his side anyway, if he hopes to deal with the elves. I will watch the clerics and prepare for the next step in our conquest."

Dorigen didn't wait around to see if Aballister might reconsider. She bowed and started from the room.

"Dorigen," Aballister called after her. She stopped and clenched her fist at her side, somehow knowing that the wily wizard would throw a new complication her way.

"Take Druzil along with you," Aballister said as she turned back around. "With the imp beside you, you and I can communicate from time to time. I don't like to be left out of so important a matter as Ragnor's progress."

Suspicions concerning Druzil's role in Barjin's death hovered over Dorigen's thoughts, and she didn't doubt for a moment that Aballister was sending the imp along to watch over her as much as Ragnor. But how could she argue? The hierarchy at Castle Trinity was specific, and Aballister ruled the wizard's leg of the triumvirate.

"A wise decision," she said.

More than you believe, came another of Druzil's intrusions.

Dorigen hid well her surprise and walked out of Castle Trinity that very afternoon, Tiennek at her side and the bat-winged imp flapping lazily behind them, invisible through his own innate magic. Dorigen tried to hide her disdain as she passed the workmen building the castle's new walls, fearing that Druzil might already be reporting back to his master.

Dorigen was not pleased by the construction and thought Aballister a fool for ordering it begun. Because of the enclave's secrecy—it resembled no more than a natural outcropping of stone—Castle Trinity had survived unmolested in the otherwise civilized Heartlands for several years. Travelers generally walked right past the hidden castle on the northern slopes of the Snow-flake Mountains without beginning to guess that a wondrous complex of tunnels and chambers lay beneath their feet.

But Aballister was apparently feeling invulnerable. They would need the new walls, he had argued, if the final battles reached their gates. Dorigen favored secrecy, preferred that the fight never got so far north. She guessed, too, Aballister's real motivations.

Again the senior wizard was thinking ahead, beyond the conquest of Shilmista and Carradoon. He didn't really expect to be attacked at the castle, but knew that an impressive stronghold might help in his diplomatic dealings with neighboring realms.

I share your thoughts, came Druzil's not-so-unexpected call. Dorigen turned on the imp, and frantic flaps revealed that he had darted to the side in a wild flurry.

"Apparently you do," the female wizard snarled, "for I was thinking of blasting you from the sky!"

"A thousand pardons," the imp said aloud, landing on the ground before Dorigen, becoming visible, and falling immediately into a low bow. "Forgive my intrusion, but your feelings were obvious. You like neither Aballister's plans nor the way he has behaved since Barjin's demise."

Dorigen did not reply, but purposely kept her features locked in an unforgiving grimace.

"You will come to learn that I am no enemy," the imp promised.

Dorigen hoped he spoke the truth, but she didn't believe him for a moment.

Q

Cadderly knew his time was up as soon as Elbereth and Headmaster Avery entered his room, neither smiling.

"We leave today for Shilmista," Elbereth said.

"Farewell," Cadderly quipped.

Elbereth was not amused. "You will pack for the road," the elf prince ordered. "Carry little. Our pace will be swift and the mountain trails are not easy."

Cadderly frowned. He started to reply, but Avery, seeing the mounting tension between the two, cut him off. "A grand adventure for you, my young lad!" The portly headmaster beamed as he walked over and dropped his heavy hands on Cadderly's shoulders. "Time for you to see some of the land beyond our library doors."

"And what are you packing?" Cadderly asked, his sarcasm unrelenting.

His words stung Avery more than he had intended. "I wished to go," the headmaster replied sharply, rubbing a kerchief over his blotchy face. "I pleaded with Dean Thobicus to let me accompany you."

"Dean Thobicus refused?" Cadderly could not believe the placid dean would refuse any request from one of his headmasters.

"*I* refused," Elbereth explained.

Cadderly, incredulous, stared at him over Avery's shoulder.

"I am Prince of Shilmista," the elf reminded him. "None may enter my domain without my leave."

"Why would you refuse Headmaster Avery?" Cadderly dared to ask, right in the face of Avery's silent but frantic signals for him to let the matter drop.

"As I have told you," the elf replied, "our pace will be swift. Horses cannot carry us through all of the mountain passes, and I fear the headmaster could not keep up. I will not delay my return, and I do not wish to leave an exhausted man in the wild to die."

Cadderly had no rebuttal, and Avery's embarrassed expression pleaded with him not to press on.

"Just you and I?" Cadderly asked the elf, his tone revealing his displeasure at the thought.

"No," Avery answered. "Another has agreed to go along, at Prince Elbereth's request."

"Headmistress Pertelope?"

"Lady Maupoissant."

Danica! The name came like a mule's kick to Cadderly's face. He straightened, eyes wide, and tried to figure out when Elbereth had found the chance to invite Danica along. And she had accepted! Cadderly had to wonder if Danica had known that he, too, would be venturing into the wood before she'd agreed to go.

"Why does that so surprise you?" Elbereth asked, a

slight trace of sarcasm in his melodic voice. "Do you doubt—"

"I doubt nothing where Danica is concerned," Cadderly was quick to reply. His scowl turned to an expression of confusion as he realized the many implications of his claim.

"Easy, lad," Avery said, holding him steady. "Danica agreed to go along only when she learned that you would be accompanying Prince Elbereth."

"As you wish," Elbereth added slyly, and Avery joined Cadderly in scowling at the elf.

"We shall depart presently," Elbereth said, standing impassively, fully composed. His black hair and silver eyes shone in the morning light that streamed through Cadderly's window. "You will come with whatever you have packed, and silently endure any hardships resulting from what you have neglected to take along." The tall, proud elf turned and walked away without another word.

"I'm starting to dislike him," Cadderly admitted, easing away from Avery's grip.

"He fears for his homeland," the headmaster explained.

"He's an arrogant—"

"Most elves are," said Avery. "It comes from living so long. Makes them believe they have experienced so much more than anyone else, and thus that they are wiser than anyone else."

"Have they, and are they?" Cadderly asked, his shoulders slumping a bit. He hadn't considered that fact about Prince Elbereth, that the elf had seen more in his life than Cadderly ever would, and probably would live on long after Cadderly's body was no more than a scattering of dust.

"Some have, and they are indeed wise, I would presume," replied Avery, "but not most. The elves have become increasingly untrusting and xenophobic. They keep to their own, and to their own lands, and know little beyond their borders. I first met Prince Elbereth three decades ago and would guess that I have learned much more than he in that time. He seems much the same as he did then, in face and mind.

"Well," Avery continued, turning for the door, "I'll leave you to your packing. Please don't leave Prince Elbereth waiting too long."

"I wouldn't care to live for centuries," Cadderly remarked just before the headmaster exited the room. "But then," the young scholar continued when Avery turned back to him, "I'm not sure I've begun to live at all."

Avery studied Cadderly for a long while, caught off guard by his unexpected words. He'd certainly noticed a change in Cadderly since the incident with Barjin, but the young scholar knew his last thought had deeply troubled the headmaster. Avery waited a few moments longer then obviously sensed that Cadderly had nothing further to offer, shrugged, and closed the door.

Cadderly sat unblinking on his bed. The world was going too fast for him. Why had Elbereth asked Danica along? Why had it fallen upon him to kill Barjin? The world was going too fast, indeed.

And he was going too slow, he soon realized. He would find enough time on the road for contemplation, but at that moment he had to prepare himself for the journey before Elbereth pulled him out of the library with only the clothes on his back.

He stuffed a pack with extra clothing and his writing kit then placed in his magical light tube, a narrow, cylindrical device, which when uncapped, issued a beam of light that Cadderly could widen or narrow with a turn of the wrist.

Satisfied with the pack, the young scholar donned his blue silk traveling cloak and wide-brimmed hat, banded in red and set with the eye-over-candle holy symbol of Deneir in its center. He took up his ram's-head walking stick and headed for the hall.

At the doorway, he turned back, stopped by the cries of his conscience.

Cadderly looked down at his feathered ring, as if that might offer him some relief from what he knew he must do. The ring's base was circular and hollow, holding a tiny vial of drow-style sleep poison. The point of the tiny dart was a cat's claw, and once fitted into the hollow shaft of Cadderly's walking stick, it became a potent weapon indeed.

But Cadderly couldn't count on that. Using the blowgun required time to set the dart, and he wasn't even certain of its potency anymore. Drow poison didn't last long on the surface world, and though Cadderly had taken great pains to protect his investment, placing the sealed vials into a strong box enchanted with a darkness spell, many tendays had passed since its creation.

Reluctantly the young scholar walked back to the wardrobe and put his hand on the door handle. He looked around helplessly, as if searching for some way out.

Cadderly opened the wardrobe door, picked a wide strap from among dozens of hanging leather ties, and belted it around his waist. It sported a wide, shallow holster on one side, which held a single-hand crossbow of dark elf design. Cadderly took out a bandoleer next, and found some comfort in the fact that only three explosive darts remained. Nearly two score other darts were in the bandoleer—it was designed to hold as many as fifty—but their centers were hollow and empty, not yet fitted with the tiny vials of *oil of impact* that gave the loaded three their wicked punch.

Despite his ambivalent feelings, Cadderly couldn't resist undoing the small leather tie and taking out the crossbow. It was an instrument of beauty, perfectly tooled by Ivan and Pikel. That beauty paled beside Barjin's dead eyes, though, for it was the same weapon Cadderly had used on that fateful day. He had fired at a mummy, trying to destroy the undead monster as it tried to destroy Barjin. One shot had slipped through the mummy's meager wrappings, though, thudding into helpless Barjin's chest as he lay propped against a wall.

Cadderly distinctly remembered the sound as that dart collapsed on the magical vial and exploded, a sharp echo that had followed him every day and every night since.

"Belago asked me to give you this," came a voice from the doorway. Cadderly turned and was surprised to see Kierkan Rufo, tall and tilting, standing in the doorway. Though they had once been friends, Rufo had been avoiding Cadderly the past few tendays.

Cadderly winced as Rufo held out a small ceramic container, for he knew what was inside. Belago's alchemy shop had been blown up during the confusion of the chaos curse, and the alchemist had thought the formula for his oil of impact lost in the flames. Not lamenting the loss, Cadderly had lied and told Belago that he didn't remember where he'd found the formula, but the alchemist, determined to reward Cadderly for his heroics against the Talonite priest, had vowed to recover it.

The same trapped, resigned expression he had worn when retrieving the crossbow crossed Cadderly's face as he took the flask. The container was heavy. Cadderly guessed he could fill perhaps twenty more darts with that amount. He searched for some way out, and even thought of letting the flask slip to the floor, feigning an accident, but reconsidered that course immediately, knowing the potentially catastrophic consequences.

"You are surprised to see me," Kierkan Rufo said in his monotone voice. His dark hair clung tightly to his head, and his dark eyes sparkled like little points of shimmering blackness.

"You haven't been around lately," Cadderly replied, turning his head up to look the taller man in the face. "Are you angry with me?"

"I-I . . ." Rufo stammered, his angular features contorting uncomfortably. He ran a hand through his matted black hair. "The curse affected me deeply," he explained.

"Forget the curse," Cadderly advised him, feeling some sympathy, but not too much. Rufo's actions during the curse had hardly been above suspicion. The tall man had even made advances toward Danica, which the young woman had promptly discouraged— by beating Rufo severely.

"We shall talk more when I return," Cadderly said. "I have no time—"

"It was I who pushed you down the stairs," Rufo announced.

Cadderly's reply caught in his throat, and his mouth hung open. He had suspected Rufo, but never expected an admission.

"Many acted unwisely during the curse," Cadderly managed to say after a long silence.

"It was before the curse," Rufo reminded him.

"Why are you telling me this?" Cadderly demanded, his gray eyes narrowing with mounting anger. "And why did you do it?"

Rufo shrugged and looked away. "That priest, I suppose," he whispered. "The Talonite caught me in the wine cellar while you were looking down the secret stairway to the lower levels."

"Then forget it," said Cadderly with as little anger as he could, "and accept no blame. Barjin was a powerful adversary, with tricks and charms beyond our comprehension."

"I cannot forget it," Rufo replied.

"Then why do you come to me?" Cadderly snapped. "Am I to forgive you? All right, then, I do. You are forgiven. Your conscience is cleared."

Cadderly pushed by, heading for the hall, but Rufo grabbed him by the shoulder and turned him around.

"I cannot ask your forgiveness until I have forgiven myself," he explained, and his wounded expression touched Cadderly.

"We all have cause to forgive ourselves," Cadderly remarked, glancing down at the flask in his hands.

"I wish to come with you," Rufo said.

Cadderly could not reply for many moments. Rufo was full of surprises.

"I must regain my dignity," the man explained. "As with you, I must see this threat, or whatever it may be, through to its conclusion. Only then will I forgive my actions of those tendays ago."

Again Cadderly started to drift toward the hall, but Rufo pulled him back.

"The dwarf brothers are gone," Rufo reminded him, "and the druid Newander is dead. You may need help."

"You're asking the wrong person," Cadderly replied. "Dean Thobicus—"

"Left the choice to Headmaster Avery," Rufo interrupted, "and Avery left it to you. I may go with your permission, so say they, and Prince Elbereth has agreed as well."

Cadderly hesitated and thought it over for just a few moments. After all that had happened, he wasn't certain he trusted Rufo, but he couldn't ignore the pleading look in the repentant man's dark eyes.

"You have virtually no time left to prepare your gear," he said, but Rufo's dark face brightened.

"I'm already packed."

Somehow, Cadderly wasn't surprised.

Elbereth and Danica were waiting for Cadderly outside the library's ornate double doors. There, too, were Avery, Pertelope, and two spare horses—-apparently the headmasters had expected Cadderly to allow Rufo along.

Danica flashed a wide smile Cadderly's way, but it dissipated, her full lips turning down into a scowl, when she saw Rufo coming out the doors on Cadderly's heels.

Cadderly offered only a shrug for an explanation as he mounted the horse next to Danica's.

The monk's visage softened as she watched Rufo fumble with his horse. The man was so awkward, and Danica was not without pity. She nodded Cadderly's way, she too determined that she would put the past behind her and concentrate on the road ahead.

"You will see many sights along the road and in the elven wood," Pertelope said to Cadderly as she moved beside his horse. Cadderly tried not to notice the carefree headmistress's prudish dress, but her long gloves seemed out of place, especially in a summer day's warmth.

"Wondrous sights," Pertelope continued. "I know you will learn more in your short time away from the library than in all the years you have been here."

Cadderly looked at her curiously, not certain of how to take her strange words.

"You will see," Pertelope explained, and she tried hard to hide a chuckle, not wanting to mock the young scholar. "There is more to life than the adventures of others, dear Cadderly, and more to living than reading books.

"But, when you find some empty time out there . . ." she continued, producing a large tome from under her robes. Cadderly knew the book as soon as she handed it to him, for he, like all priests of his order, had studied the work since his first days in the library: *The Tome of Universal Harmony,* the most holy book of Deneir.

"For good fortune?" he asked, still confused.

"For reading," Pertelope replied.

"But—"

"I'm sure you have the work memorized," Pertelope interrupted, "but I doubt you've ever truly read it."

Cadderly wondered if he looked as stupid as he felt. He consciously forced himself to close his hanging jaws.

"Words can be read in many ways," Pertelope said, and she pulled herself up enough to peck Cadderly on the cheek. "That was for good fortune," the headmistress explained, throwing a wink Danica's way.

"I wish I were going with you!" Headmaster Avery cried suddenly. "Oh, to see Shilmista again. . . ." He wiped a kerchief over his eyes and over his chubby face.

"You may not," Elbereth said coldly, tiring of the lengthy farewell. He touched the reigns of Temmerisa, his shining white stallion, and the mighty horse kicked off, a thousand bells jingling with each step. Kierkan Rufo fell in behind the elf and Danica, too, started away.

Cadderly looked from *The Tome of Universal Harmony* to Headmistress Pertelope and smiled.

"Your perceptions of the world will change often as you grow," Pertelope said quietly, so the others couldn't hear her. "And while the words in the book remain the same, your reading of them will not. The Scribe of Oghma's heart is a poet's heart, and a poet's heart drifts with the shadows of the clouds."

Cadderly held the thick book in both hands. His perception of the world, of morality, had indeed changed. He had killed a man, and had somehow found his first adventure beyond the thousands he had read about in books.

"Read it," Pertelope told him gravely. She turned back to the library, hooked Avery by the arm, and dragged him along.

Cadderly's mount took its first step, and the young priest was on his way.

FOUR

INDECISION

Felkin looked around at his eight companions, feeling terribly insecure despite the company. They had come probing deep into Shilmista on orders from Ragnor, the brutish, unmerciful ogrillon. Felkin hadn't questioned the orders, not even to his fellow goblins, thinking that whatever dangers awaited them in the elven forest would be no match for the severity of Ragnor's anger.

Surrounded by the trees of Shilmista, though, Felkin wasn't so sure. They had seen nothing, heard nothing, but every member of the nine-goblin scouting party sensed they were not alone.

They crossed one sandy ridge and came into a deep patch of tall green ferns growing in the shadows of wide-spreading elms.

"What was that?" one goblin croaked, dipping into a defensive crouch and trying to keep his eyes on an elusive, figure darting through the deepening shadows. The group fidgeted nervously, knowing how vulnerable they were.

"Quiets!" Felkin scolded, fearing the noise more than any elf spies.

"What was—?" the goblin tried to ask again, but his words were cut short as an arrow pierced his throat.

The eight remaining goblins scrambled for cover, dropping under the ferns and crawling for the elms. Felkin heard a noise like a snapping stick, and the goblin closest to him soared into the air, kicking and gasping, as a vine noose tightened around his neck.

That proved too much for two of the others. They jumped up and broke into a run for the trees. Neither got more than a few short strides before arrows took them down.

"Where was they?" Felkin called to his companions.

"Left!" cried one goblin.

"Right!" screamed another.

There came a flurry of bow shots, arrows slicing through the ferns and knocking into trees, then all went quiet. The goblin in the air stopped thrashing and began turning slowly with the wind.

Felkin crept over to one of his companions, lying still in the ferns. "Five of usses left," Felkin reasoned. When the other didn't answer, Felkin roughly turned him around.

A green arrow shaft protruded from one of the goblin's eyes. The other eye stared ahead blankly.

Felkin dropped the corpse and scrambled wildly away, drawing several bow shots in his noisy wake. Somewhere to the side, another goblin tried to run and was cut down with brutal efficiency.

"There remain no more than four of you," said a melodic voice in the goblin tongue, but with the unmistakable accent of a female elf. "Perhaps only three. Do you wish to come out and fight me fairly?"

"Me?" Felkin echoed quietly, confused. "Only one elf?" His entire party had been trimmed by a single elf? Boldly, the goblin poked his head above the ferns and saw the elf warrior, sword in hand, standing beside an elm with her bow leaning against the tree within easy reach.

Felkin looked to his own crude spear, wondering if he could make the shot. One of his companions apparently entertained the same notion—the goblin leaped from the ferns and hurled his spear.

The elf, hardly caught unaware, dropped to her knees. The spear flew high. Faster than Felkin could follow, she took up her bow and put two shots into the air. The foolish goblin hadn't even the chance to drop back into the ferns. The first arrow thudded into his chest and the second caught him in the throat.

Felkin looked at his spear again, glad that one of the others had shown him his folly. By his count, only he and one other remained—still two against one if they could get close to the elf archer.

Felkin heard someone call his name, and he recognized the voice of Rake, a fine fighter. "How many of usses?"

"Two!" he replied, then he called to the elf. "Two of usses, elf. Will you puts your nasty bow down and fights us fair-like?"

The elf leaned her bow back against the tree and took up her sword. "Come on, then," she said. "The day grows long and my supper awaits."

"Yous is ready, Rake?" Felkin cried.

"Ready!" the other goblin eagerly replied.

Felkin licked his cracked lips and set his floppy feet for a good start. He'd send Rake into action against the elf and use the diversion to run away into the forest.

"Ready?" he called again.

"Ready!" Rake assured him.

"Charge!" came Felkin's cry, and he heard the rustle as Rake, far to his right, leaped from the ferns.

Felkin, too, leaped up, but ran off to the left, away from the elf. He looked back once, thinking himself clever, and saw that Rake had similarly retreated to the right. The elf, wearing an amused smile, took up her bow.

Felkin put his head down and sprinted into the shadows, running as fast as his spindly goblin legs would carry him. There came a distant *twang* of a bowstring and Rake's steady stream of curses. Felkin's hopes returned with the knowledge that the elf had gone after his companion.

There came an agonized scream, and Felkin knew he was alone. He ran on, not daring to slow. Only a few moments later, Felkin thought he heard a rustle behind him.

"Don't kills me! Don't kills me!" Felkin cried pitifully, breathlessly, over and over. Panicking, he looked behind him once again—and turned back just in time to see that he had veered straight into an oak tree.

Felkin went down in a heap, folding neatly into a leafy crook between the huge roots at the great tree's base. He didn't hear the footsteps pass him by, a few strides to the side. He didn't hear anything at all.

Q

"Are you in contact with Aballister?" Dorigen asked Druzil, seeing the imp in a contemplative stance.

Druzil laughed at her. "Why?" he asked, feigning innocence. "I have nothing to tell him."

Dorigen closed her eyes and muttered a short chant, casting a simple spell that might allow her to confirm Druzil's claim. When she looked at the imp again, she seemed satisfied.

"That's good," she muttered. "You aren't a familiar in the accepted sense of the word, are you, dear Druzil?"

Again the imp laughed in his raspy, breathless voice. "Truly you err, Mistress Magic," Druzil replied, wondering if Aballister had arranged a little test of fealty. "I am loyal to he who summoned me from the torments of the Abyss."

Dorigen was unimpressed, and Druzil didn't push it. Rumor had it that he'd helped kill Barjin, but in truth the imp had considered joining the cleric and abandoning Aballister all together. Then Barjin's grand designs had come crashing down.

The rumors worked in Druzil's favor, though. They made upstarts such as Dorigen treat him with a bit of respect and kept Aballister from discerning what had really transpired in the catacombs of the Edificant Library.

"We work for a single cause," Dorigen said, "a cause given to us by Talona. All the Heartlands will fall to Castle Trinity, have no doubt, and those who stand beside us shall profit greatly—but those who stand against us shall suffer even more."

"You make a threat?" The imp's simple question nearly knocked Dorigen over.

Dorigen took a moment to collect her thoughts then replied, "If you believe so. Should it be?" She seemed more unsure of herself than Druzil had ever seen her.

"I am loyal to my master," Druzil said again, "and now to you, the wizard my master has bade me travel beside."

Dorigen relaxed a bit. "Then let us travel," she said. "The sun is rising, and we're still several days from Shilmista. I don't like the prospect of having Ragnor stomping about uncontrolled." She called Tiennek, who was gathering water from a nearby stream, and took up her walking stick.

Druzil wholeheartedly agreed. He gave a lazy flap and landed on Dorigen's shoulder then folded his leathery wings around himself to shield him from the sun. He liked his position. On a journey with Mistress Magic, he could see the progress of Castle Trinity's conquest, and even more importantly, in Shilmista he would be out of Aballister's reach.

Druzil knew that Cadderly, the young priest who had defeated Barjin, was Aballister's deserted son, and Aballister knew that he knew. The web of intrigue seemed to be tightening around Aballister, and the imp refused to be choked by its strands.

Q

"One of them got away," Shayleigh reported to Tintagel when she returned to the new elven camp, "but eight others are dead."

The elf wizard nodded, having heard similar reports all day. The enemy had backed off after the slaughter in the Dells, and now sent small probing groups—mostly goblins—deeper into Shilmista. "Perhaps it is good that one escaped," the elf wizard offered, the corners of his blue eyes turning up in a smile. "Let it return to its foul brethren and tell them that only death awaits them under Shilmista's boughs."

Shayleigh, too, managed a smile, but there was worry reflected in the elf maiden's violet orbs. The enemy scouting parties were being slaughtered, but the fact that their leader seemed to easily accept the losses only heightened Shayleigh's belief that a huge force indeed had found its way into Shilmista's northern reaches.

"Come," Tintagel said. "Let us go to the king and see what plans he has formulated."

They found Galladel alone in a clearing beyond a shielding wall of thick pines, pacing nervously. The elf king motioned for them to join him then brought his slender hand up to stroke his raven-black hair, still vibrant and thick, though Galladel had lived many centuries. He stopped his hand when he saw that it was trembling, and dropped it back to his side. He glanced at Shayleigh and Tintagel to make sure that they had not seen.

"The slaughter of goblins continues," Tintagel announced, trying to calm the nervous king.

"For how long?" Galladel retorted. "The reports, sightings—so many sightings of monstrous scum in our fair wood!—have continued to come in."

"We will beat them back," Shayleigh pronounced.

Galladel appreciated his fine young commander's confidence, but in the face of the emerging force against him, it seemed only a minor thing.

"For how long?" he asked again, less sharply. "This black tide has rolled over the northern reaches. Our enemy is cunning."

"He sends his troops to be massacred," Tintagel argued.

"He bides his time," the elf king countered. "He sacrifices his weakest fodder to keep us busy. Damn this waiting game."

"Something will happen soon," Shayleigh said. "I can

feel the tension. Our enemy will soon reveal himself in full."

Galladel looked at her with curiosity, but knew better than to dismiss the elf maiden's intuition. Shayleigh had been the one to argue for, and to organize, the ambush in the Dells, having read the enemy's initial probing actions perfectly. Certainly the king was glad to have her at his side, especially with Elbereth, his son and closest advisor, in the east, trying to gain some insight from the priests of the Edificant Library. Galladel had ordered Elbereth not to go, but lately his commands carried little weight with his headstrong son.

"Soon," Shayleigh said again, seeing that the tension was near to breaking Galladel.

"They are marching now," came a chirping voice from the side. Both Galladel and Shayleigh turned and eyed a large oak tree.

They heard tittering laughter. Thinking to defend her king, Shayleigh drew her slender sword and advanced. Tintagel took up a position to the side, producing a spell component from his pocket, ready to strike at a moment's warning.

"Oh, don't tell me you haven't heard the warnings of the trees!" came the voice, followed by a movement around the back of the tree. A pixie-featured woman, her skin as tan as the oak's bark and her hair as green as the great tree's dark leaves, peeked out from around the thick trunk.

Shayleigh's sword went back into its scabbard. "We have heard nothing but the dying gasps of intruders," the elf maiden said, her voice as cold as her eyes.

"Who is it?" demanded Galladel.

"A dryad," Shayleigh replied. "Hammadeen, I believe."

"Oh, you remember me!" chirped Hammadeen, and she clapped her delicate hands together. "But you just said you can feel it!"

The dryad's abrupt change of subject left the elf maiden bewildered. "I feel what?" she asked.

"The excitement in the air!" cried Hammadeen. "It's the talk of the trees that you hear. They're afraid, and so they should be."

"What nonsense is this?" growled Galladel, moving to join Shayleigh.

"Oh, no, not nonsense!" replied Hammadeen, suddenly sounding distressed. "They're marching in force, too many for the trees to count. And they have fire and axes! Oh, the elves must stop them—you must."

Shayleigh and Galladel exchanged confused looks.

"Listen!" cried the dryad. "You must listen to—"

"We are listening!" roared a frustrated Galladel.

"To the trees," Hammadeen explained. Her voice diminished—and her body seemed to, as well—as she blended into the oak. Shayleigh rushed over, trying to catch the dryad or at least follow her, but the elf maiden's reaching hands found only the rough bark of the wide oak.

"Dryads. . . ." Shayleigh remarked, her tone less than complimentary.

" 'Listen to the trees,' " spat Galladel. He kicked dirt at the base of the oak and spun away.

Shayleigh was surprised by the intensity of the king's disdain. It was said that the trees of Shilmista had often spoken with the forest elves, that once the trees had even uprooted and walked to fight beside Dellanil Quil'quien, an elf hero and king of times long past. That was only legend to young Shayleigh, but surely aged Galladel, a direct descendent of Dellanil's, had lived in those times.

"We know now that our enemy is on the move again," Shayleigh offered, "in great numbers. And we know from where they will come. I will arrange another surprise—"

"We know only what a dryad has told us!" yelled Galladel. "You would risk our entire defense on the fleeting words of a dryad, by nature a creature of half-truths and insidious charms?"

Again the elf maiden was taken aback by Galladel's unwarranted anger. The dryads most certainly weren't enemies of the elven host, and could well prove valuable allies.

Galladel took a deep breath and seemed to calm himself, as though he, too, realized his misplaced wrath.

"We have only the word of Hammadeen," Shayleigh offered, "but I do not doubt that our enemy is on the march. There are many defensible ridges between here and the northern reaches. It would seem prudent to begin preparations even without the dryad's warning."

"No," Galladel said. "We will not go out to meet the enemy again. We will not catch him so unaware again, and the result could be disastrous. Our powers are greater near the center of the forest, and there we may more easily elude this great force, if indeed it is coming."

"If we run, we give them miles of the forest to destroy," Shayleigh growled. "Shilmista is our home, from the southernmost tree to the northernmost tree!"

"Daoine Dun is not so far," Tintagel offered as a compromise. "The caves there offer us shelter, and certainly the hill figures prominently in our power."

Shayleigh considered the suggestion for a moment. She would have preferred taking the offensive again, but she knew well that Galladel would not give in to her reasoning. Daoine Dun, the Hill of the Stars, seemed a reasonable compromise. She nodded to Galladel.

The elf king didn't seem convinced. "There are better choices more to the south," he said.

Shayleigh and Tintagel exchanged fearful glances. Both wished that Elbereth had not gone away, for the elf prince was more attuned to their way of thinking, more determined to preserve what little remained of Shilmista's glory. Perhaps Galladel had lived too long; the burdens of rulership over the centuries could not be underestimated.

"Our enemy numbers in the thousands, by every report," Galladel snapped at them, apparently sensing their heartfelt disapproval—for his decision and for him. "We number barely seven score and hope that our courage alone will turn aside that black tide. Do not confuse courage with foolishness, I say, and I am still your king!"

The younger elves would have lost the argument then, except that cries rang out in the elven camp beyond the pine grove.

"Fire!" the shouts proclaimed.

One elf rushed in through the trees to report to his king. "Fire!" he cried. "Our enemy burns the forest. In the north! In the north!" The elf turned and fled back through the natural barrier.

Galladel turned away from Shayleigh and Tintagel, ran a shaking hand through his raven-black hair, and muttered several silent curses at Elbereth for going away.

"Daoine Dun?" Tintagel asked.

Galladel waved a resigned hand the wizard's way. "As you will," he offered listlessly. "As you will."

Q

When Felkin opened his eyes again, he had to squint against the morning sunlight. The forest around him was deathly quiet, and a long time passed before the goblin mustered the nerve to crawl out of the leaves. He considered going back to check on his companions then snorted the thought away and made off with all speed for Ragnor's camp on the forest's northern borders.

Felkin felt a bit relieved a short while later, when he heard the hacking of axes. The sky lightened in front of him, the thick canopy thinned, and he came out of the trees suddenly, only to find himself immediately surrounded by Ragnor's elite guard, a contingent of eight huge and hairy bugbears.

They looked down at poor, shivering Felkin from their seven-foot height. Evil, yellow-eyed gazes bored into the goblin.

"Who're you?" one of the creatures demanded, poking a trident against the goblin's shoulder.

Felkin winced from the pain and fear, nearly as terrified of bugbears as of the elf he had left behind. "Felkin," he squeaked, bowing his head submissively. "Scout."

The bugbears murmured something in their own guttural tongue then one of them prodded Felkin even harder and demanded, "Where're the others?"

Felkin bit his lip to prevent crying out in pain; revealing weakness would only inspire the cruel monsters to greater acts of torture. "In the forest," he whispered.

"Dead?"

Felkin nodded meekly, then he felt as if he were flying as one bugbear grabbed him by the scraggly hair and hoisted him high off the ground. Felkin's skinny arms flapped as he tried to secure a supporting hold on the bugbear's sinewy arm. The merciless creature carried him by just the hair all the way across the large encampment. Felkin continued to gnaw on his lip and fought back tears as best he could.

He determined their destination to be a large, hide-covered tent. Ragnor! The world seemed to spin around to the quivering goblin. He knew that he was fainting and hoped he would never wake up.

He did awaken, though, and wished that he'd stayed in the forest and taken his chances with the elf.

Ragnor didn't seem so imposing at first, sitting behind a large oaken table across the tent. Then the ogrillon stood, and Felkin whined and crawled backward across the ground. A prod from a trident forced him back to his place.

Ragnor was as tall as the bugbears and twice as wide. His features were those of an orc, mostly, with a snout resembling a pig's nose and one tusklike tooth protruding from his bottom jaw, over his upper lip. His eyes were large and bloodshot, and his brow heavy, always crinkled in an ominous glare. While his features were orc, his body more resembled his ogre ancestors, with thick, powerful limbs, corded muscles, and a barrel-like torso that could stop a charging horse dead in its tracks.

The ogrillon took three heavy strides to stand before Felkin, reached down, and easily lifted the goblin to his feet.

"The others are dead?" Ragnor asked in his throaty, commanding voice.

"Elveses!" Felkin cried. "Elveses killed 'em!"

"How many?"

"Lots and lotses!" Felkin answered, but the ogrillon didn't seem impressed.

Ragnor put a single large finger under Felkin's chin and lifted the goblin to his tiptoes. The ugly orc face with evil-smelling breath moved just an inch from the goblin, and Felkin thought he would faint again—though he realized that Ragnor would skin him if he did.

"How . . . many?" Ragnor asked again, slowly and deliberately.

"One," squeaked Felkin, thinking the better of adding that it was a female. Ragnor dropped him to the floor.

"An entire patrol cut down by *a single elf!*" the ogrillon roared at the bugbears. The hairy monsters looked around at each other, but didn't seem overly concerned.

"You send goblins and orcs," one of them remarked.

"I first sent bugbears!" Ragnor reminded them. "How many of your kin returned?"

The embarrassed bugbears mumbled excuses in their own tongue.

"Send bigger scouting groups?" the bugbear spokesman offered a few moments later.

Ragnor thought it over then shook his huge head. "We cannot match the elves with such tactics—not in the woods. We have the advantage of numbers and strength, but that's all in this cursed forest."

"They know the ground well," agreed the bugbear.

"And I don't doubt they have spies all around us," added Ragnor. "Even the trees I don't trust!"

"Then how do we proceed?"

"We continue our march," the frustrated ogrillon growled. He grabbed Felkin by the throat and pulled him off the ground, again close to Ragnor's ugly face.

"The elves know their forest, so we will *destroy* their forest," the ogrillon growled. "We will force them out in the open ground and crush them!" Too excited by his own words, Ragnor's hand jerked. There came a loud *crack,* and Felkin twitched violently then was still.

The bugbears looked on in amazement. One of them chuckled, but bit it back quickly. Too late; the other bugbears burst out in laughter, and their mirth increased tenfold when Ragnor joined in, giving the goblin a shake to make sure it was dead.

FIVE

FIRST CONTACT

Cadderly sat in the dim light of the dying campfire, a line of tiny vials on the ground before him, paralleling a line of empty crossbow darts. One by one, he took the vials and carefully dripped in a few drops from the flask that Kierkan Rufo had delivered to him.

"What is he doing?" Elbereth asked Rufo as they stood on the edge of the firelight.

"Making darts for his crossbow," the tall man explained. His face seemed even more angular, almost inhuman, in the flickering shadows.

Elbereth studied the diminutive weapon, resting on the ground at Cadderly's side, and the elf's expression was hardly complimentary.

"That is a drow device," he spat, loudly enough for Cadderly to hear. Cadderly looked up and knew the elf prince was about to put him on trial.

"Do you consort with dark elves?" Elbereth asked.

"I've never met one," Cadderly answered, thinking, but not adding, that if Elbereth's arrogance exemplified

71

the good side of the so-called People, he most certainly would have no desire to meet one of the bad side!

"Where did you acquire the crossbow then?" Elbereth pressed, as though he was just looking for a reason to begin an argument with Cadderly. "And why would you wish to carry the weapon of such an evil race?"

Cadderly picked up the crossbow, somehow comforted in the fact that it had brought Elbereth some grief. He understood that Elbereth provoked him simply out of general frustration, and he certainly sympathized with the elf's worries for Shilmista. Still, Cadderly had his own concerns and was in no mood for Elbereth's continued insults.

"It was fashioned by dwarves, actually," he corrected.

"Nearly as bad," the elf snipped without hesitation.

Cadderly's gray eyes were not as striking as Elbereth's silvery orbs, but his glare more than equaled the elf's in intensity. In a fight of weapons, of course, Elbereth could easily cut him down, but if the elf prince launched more insults Ivan and Pikel's way, Cadderly had every intention of pummeling him with his fists. Cadderly was a fine wrestler, having grown up among the clerics of Oghma, whose principal rituals involved weaponless combat. While Elbereth was nearly as tall as the six-foot scholar, Cadderly figured he outweighed the slender elf by at least seventy pounds.

Apparently understanding that he had pushed the young scholar as far as he could without starting a fight, Elbereth did not continue, but neither did he blink.

"The perimeter is clear," said Danica as she came back into camp. She looked from Elbereth to Cadderly and saw the obvious tension. "What happened?"

Elbereth turned to her with a warm smile that bothered

Cadderly more than the uncompromising glare the elf had given him.

"A discussion of the young scholar's unusual cross-bow, nothing more," Elbereth assured Danica. "I do not understand the value of such a puny weapon—nor the honor of its heritage."

Danica sent a sympathetic look Cadderly's way. If the young scholar was vulnerable about anything in the world, it was the crossbow and the memories it inevitably conjured.

"I killed a man with this," he growled.

Danica's look turned to one of horror, and Cadderly realized how stupid that proclamation had been. What a ridiculous and disgusting thing to brag about! He knew he had laid himself open to the elf, for Cadderly would find no courage to back up his bravado.

But the elf, looking from Cadderly to Danica, chose to discontinue the discussion. "It is my watch," he said, disappearing into the darkness.

Cadderly looked at Danica and shrugged an apology. The young woman sat across the fire from him, wrapped herself in a heavy blanket, and lay down to sleep.

Cadderly considered the crossbow, feeling that it had betrayed him once again. He wished he'd been more attentive in his combat studies at the library. If he had been, perhaps he wouldn't need to carry the unconventional weapon. But while the other clerics had practiced with the mace, quarterstaff, or club, Cadderly had concentrated on his spindle-disks—twin disks joined by a connecting bar, on which was tied a slender cord—a useful enough weapon for felling small game and an enjoyable toy to put through a variety of mesmerizing tricks, but hardly a match for a sword.

Cadderly's hand went unconsciously to the disks, which were looped on his belt. He'd used them in battle a couple of times—had dropped Kierkan Rufo when the man, under the chaos curse's influence, had come after Cadderly with a knife. Even against the tiny blade that Rufo had carried, Cadderly won only because his opponent was distracted. A single lucky throw had saved him.

Cadderly considered his walking stick as well, with its sculpted ram's-head handle and smooth-bored interior. It was an expensive item and well balanced, and Cadderly had used it, too, in battle. Danica had told him that such a small staff—she called it a bo stick—was a favorite among monks in her mother's ancient homeland of Tabot. Cadderly was barely skilled with it. He could twirl it and thrust it, even parry basic attacks, but he wouldn't want to test his talents against a seasoned fighter like Elbereth, or any monster, for that matter.

Resigned, the young scholar filled another vial and carefully snapped it into place in the hollow of a dart. He slipped the loaded dart into a loop on his bandoleer; that made twelve.

In the first few fights at least, Cadderly might show as well as Elbereth. The young scholar hated that that fact mattered to him, but he couldn't deny that it did.

The eastern fringes of Shilmista were not too far from the Edificant Library, and even crossing the rough mountain trails the travelers could have seen the forest on their second day out. Shilmista was a long wood, though, running one hundred and fifty miles from north to south, and Elbereth wanted to come out of the mountains nearer the forest's center, where the elves made their homes.

For several more days, the four companions walked up, down, and around high peaks and through steep valleys. It was summer, even in the mountains, and the air was warm and the sky blue. Each turn in the trail promised a new majestic view, but even mountain scenery became somewhat dull to Cadderly after several straight days.

Often during this quiet time, Cadderly took *The Tome of Universal Harmony* from his horse's pack. He didn't read it, though. He was too agitated by the trials ahead and Elbereth's growing relationship with Danica—the two got on famously, swapping tales of places Cadderly had never seen—to concentrate properly.

On the fifth day, they came at last to the western ridges. Looking down, they could see the dark canopy of Shilmista, a peaceful and quiet cover for the mounting tumult beneath the thick boughs.

"That is my home," Elbereth announced to Danica. "There is no place in all the world to match Shilmista's beauty."

Cadderly wanted to rebuff him. The young scholar had read of many wondrous lands—magical lands—and by all accounts, Shilmista, though a fitting wood for elves, was nothing extraordinary. Cadderly had the foresight, though, to understand how pitiful he would sound in making such a claim, and the common sense to anticipate Elbereth's angry reaction. He kept his thoughts to himself and resolved to point out Shilmista's weak points to Danica later.

Though the path had become clear and smooth enough for riding, the steep decline and winding turns forced the party to continue walking the horses. As they came to the lower foothills, mountain stone gave way to earthen ground, and walking their mounts proved a fortunate thing. From the back of Temmerisa, his great stallion, Elbereth would not have noticed the tracks.

He stooped low to examine them and said nothing for a long while. Cadderly and the others could guess the source of those markings from the elf's grim expression.

"Goblins?" Danica asked finally.

"Some, perhaps," Elbereth replied, his gaze drifting back to his precious forest, "but most are too big to have been made by goblins."

The elf took out his longbow and handed the reigns of his horse to Kierkan Rufo. He then motioned for Danica to give her mount over to Cadderly.

The young scholar wasn't thrilled with acting the part of a page, but he couldn't argue against the value of having Danica and Elbereth with their hands free, ready to meet any sudden attacks.

Elbereth took up the lead, pausing often to study new tracks, and Danica fell into line at the rear of the party, watching in all directions.

They came back into the tree line and grew even more cautious Shadows loomed all around them, possible hiding spots for monsters setting an ambush. They crossed in and out of the gloom, moving under thick trees one moment and coming suddenly into the open sunlight the next as the trail wound across wide stones.

Temmerisa's thousand bells tinkled suddenly with the steed's nervous movement. Elbereth went on his guard, crouching low and looking all around. He moved across the trail, slipped into concealment amid a tumble of boulders, and peered down at the mountainsides below.

Danica and Cadderly joined him, but Rufo stayed back with the horses, seeming ready to spring upon his roan mount in an instant and fly away.

"The trail doubles back on itself down below," the elf explained in a whisper. His observations were evident to Cadderly and Danica, for the trees and brush were not thick below them and the looping road was clearly visible. Elbereth seemed intent on one huge maple tree, its thick branches overhanging the road.

"There!" Danica whispered, pointing to the very same tree. "On the lowest branch above the road."

Elbereth nodded gravely, and Danica blew a quiet whistle.

Cadderly watched them in confusion. He, too, peered intently at the tree, but all he saw were thick, overlapping leaves.

"The limb bends under their weight," Elbereth remarked.

"Whose weight?" Cadderly had to ask.

Elbereth scowled, but Danica took pity on Cadderly and continued to point out what she had noticed until he at last nodded in recognition. Several dark forms crouched together on that branch, high above the road.

"Orcs?" Danica asked.

"Too big for orcs," reasoned Elbereth. "Orogs."

Danica's delicate features crinkled with confusion.

"Orogs are kin to orcs," cut in Cadderly, beating the elf to the explanation. Orogs were uncommon, but Cadderly had read about them in books. "Larger and stronger than their pig-faced cousins. It is believed that they originated—"

"What do you think they're waiting for?" Danica

interrupted before Cadderly could make a complete fool of himself.

"Us," Elbereth said. "They have heard our horses, perhaps seen us on the open expanses of the higher trails."

"Is there another way around?" Cadderly knew the question sounded ridiculous even as he asked it. Danica, and especially Elbereth, had no intention of going around the monsters.

Elbereth considered the terrain straight from his position. "If I pick my way down the mountainside while you continue along the trail," he reasoned, "I may be able to take a few of them down with my bow." The elf prince nodded in affirmation of his own plan. "Come then," he said, "we must get the horses moving again before the orogs grow suspicious."

Danica turned and started back to Rufo, but Cadderly was struck with an idea. "Let me go," he offered, a smile widening across his face.

Elbereth regarded him curiously, and even more so when Cadderly took out his tiny crossbow.

"You believe you can inflict more damage with that than I with my longbow?" the elf prince asked.

"Wouldn't you prefer to fight them on the ground?" Cadderly replied, grinning Danica's way. Elbereth, too, looked to the woman, and she nodded and smiled, trusting in Cadderly and knowing that playing a role in the fight was important to the young scholar.

"Go along the trail," Cadderly told them. "I shall meet you at the tree."

Elbereth, still not convinced, turned back to study the young scholar. "Your hat and cape," the elf said, holding out his hands.

Cadderly's pause displayed his confusion.

"Blue is not a forest color," Elbereth explained. "It shows in the daylight as clearly as a fire in the dark of night. We will be fortunate if the orogs have not already spotted you."

"They haven't," Danica insisted, realizing that Elbereth had made that last statement only to belittle Cadderly.

The scholar untied his short cape and handed it and the hat to Elbereth. "I'll see you at the tree," he said finally, trying to appear confident.

His firm jaw weakened as soon as the others moved out of sight. What had he gotten himself into? Even if he managed to get down the steep slope without breaking his neck and causing enough noise for all the orogs in the Snowflake Mountains to hear, what would he do if they noticed him? What defense could Cadderly present against even a single opponent?

He shook the dark thoughts away and started down, having no other choice, he believed, if he wished to hold any honor at all in Danica's almond eyes. He stumbled and tripped, stubbed his toes a dozen times, and set several stones skipping down, but somehow managed to get level with the giant maple apparently without disturbing the ambush-intent monsters. He crawled into a crevice between two sharp-edged rocks a short distance from the side of the trail. He could see the orogs clearly then; nearly a dozen crouched side by side on the low branch. They held nets, spears, and crude swords, and it wasn't difficult for Cadderly to discern their tactics.

The monsters went quiet. At first, Cadderly feared he had been discovered, but he soon realized that the orogs continued looking up the trail. He knew that his friends would arrive soon.

He loaded the crossbow, taking care to move the small crank slowly and smoothly so that it wouldn't make any noise. Then he leveled the weapon—but where to shoot? He could probably knock an orog out of the tree, maybe even kill one if his aim or his luck was good enough. His earlier boasts seemed so foolish now, with the danger so very close and the responsibility fully on his shoulders.

He had to go with his original plan. Elbereth and Danica were counting on him to get the monsters out of the tree. He took aim, not at any of the monsters, but at where the thick branch joined the trunk. It was not a difficult shot with the accurate crossbow, but would the explosive suffice? Cadderly took out a second dart, just in case.

The orogs shifted nervously; Cadderly could hear the plodding hoofbeats down the trail.

"Deneir be with me," the young scholar mumbled, and he squeezed the crossbow's trigger. The dart floated in, struck the branch, and collapsed on the vial, and the ensuing explosion shook the tree violently. Orogs grabbed on—one tumbled from the branch—and Cadderly, to his relief, heard a loud cracking noise. The young scholar sent another dart looping in.

The branch blew apart. An orog screamed as its ankle got hooked on the jagged break, the skin tearing off the side of its leg as it fell.

Danica and Elbereth, upon their horses, were barely thirty feet from the tree when the orogs tumbled out. Elbereth, concerned, glanced sidelong at the young woman, for only one of the monsters seemed injured and the others were well armed.

"There are only ten of them!" Danica cried, reaching down to pull a crystalline-bladed dagger from a boot sheath. She laughed wildly and spurred her horse ahead. Temmerisa, bearing the elf, charged right behind.

Q

Danica came in hard and fast on the closest three monsters. Just before she reached them, she rolled off the side of her horse, caught a handhold on the saddle's cinch, and pulled herself under the horse, straight through the beast's legs. The horse blasted through the stunned orogs, all of them expecting Danica on the wrong side.

Danica hit the ground running, used her momentum to leap into a spin, and connected on the closest orog with a circle kick that snapped the creature's neck and sent it tumbling away.

Her wrist flicked as soon as she got her bearings, launching the dagger point-over-hilt. It spun several times, a glittering sliver in the sunlight, before burying itself hilt-deep in the second orog's face.

The third monster heaved its spear and drew out a crude sword. Its aim had been perfect, but Danica was too quick to be taken by such a clumsy weapon. She sidestepped and threw out a forearm parry that sent the spear flying harmlessly wide.

The orog came in unconcerned, and Danica nearly laughed at how defenseless she must have appeared to the six-and-a-half-foot, two-hundred-pound monster. Slender and pretty, she barely topped five feet, with unkempt locks flying wildly about her shoulders and eyes that sparkled, to the unknowing observer, with childish innocence.

Blood quickly replaced drool on the orog's hungry lips. It stepped in and reached for Danica with its free hand. She caught it with a lightning-quick jab that took out two of its front teeth. Danica jumped back, bouncing on the balls of her feet and feeling good about the beginning of the battle. It had taken just a few heartbeats, but two monsters lay dead or dying and the third stood teetering and trying to shake the stars out of its vision.

Elbereth's charge was even more straightforward and more brutal. He led with a single bow shot, catching a monster in the shoulder. Then, drawing his sword and slipping his arm through the leather straps of his shield, the elf trusted in his disciplined steed and crashed right into the main group of orogs. His magical blade glowed with a bluish flame as he hacked at the monstrous throng. He took several quick hits from the orogs' crude weapons, but his fine shield and finer armor deflected the blows.

More deadly were Elbereth's thrusts. The unarmored orogs simply couldn't afford to swap blows with the elf. The closest monster, the one with the arrow in its shoulder, learned that well when Elbereth responded to its spear thrust by lopping off its head.

Temmerisa reared and danced about, keeping in perfect balance and harmony with the elf prince. One orog slipped behind the shining white horse, its spear held high for a throw that would have taken Elbereth squarely in the back. Temmerisa kicked with both hind feet, connecting on the orog's chest and launching it many yards away. The broken monster crumpled to the ground, gasping futilely with lungs that had collapsed.

Elbereth's battle would have been a rout then, for only two monsters remained—and one of those could barely stand, leaning against the huge tree with one of its legs torn apart—but when the limb had broken, a single orog had managed to keep a handhold in the tree. Grasping a net in its free hand, the monster swung out on the higher branch and timed its leap perfectly, coming down on the slender elf's back and bearing Elbereth to the ground under it—and under the net.

A deceptively swift sword cut forced Danica to hop and throw her head backward. She knew that a monster as powerful as an orog could not be taken lightly, but she found herself distracted, for off to the side, Elbereth had gone down and Kierkan Rufo had not yet entered the fray. Just as unnerving to the young woman, two of the orogs had fled toward Cadderly.

Another slice made Danica drop almost to the ground, and a third sent her rolling to the side. The orog, confident again, advanced steadily.

It swung again, but Danica, instead of backing away, charged straight ahead. She caught the orog's sword hand in her own and stepped toward it, hooking her free forearm so forcefully around the orog's extended arm that she heard the monster's elbow snap. Fierce Danica barely gave the monster time to cry in pain. Still holding fast to its sword hand, she whipped her other arm back, free of the monster's, and threw her elbow up and out, slamming the creature in the nose.

Danica's elbow came back tight to her side and her backhand went snapping out, scoring another solid hit. When the arm recoiled, still before the orog had time to react, Danica straightened her hand tightly and chopped across the orog's throat.

She dipped under the monster's trapped arm. Her grip turned the muscled limb half a circuit as she passed under it, and Danica turned to face the creature.

The weakened orog reached for her, but Danica paid the lame attempt no heed. Her foot shot up under the orog's reach and slammed the monster in the chin, then again, and a third time, in rapid succession.

"Cadderly," the monk breathed, looking down the trail. The two fleeing monsters must have been close to her beloved.

Q

Cadderly, acting on pure instinct, didn't hesitate to consider the moral consequences in the least as the first orog bore down on him, pointedly shifting its course when it noticed him lying between the stones.

An exploding dart abruptly halted its charge.

The monster's surprised roar came out as a wheeze, for the dart had put a hole cleanly through one lung. Stubbornly the monster came on, and Cadderly shot it again, in the belly.

The orog doubled over, growling in agony.

"Die, damn you," Cadderly moaned when it straightened and came on again. His third shot blew off the top of the orog's head.

Cadderly himself was having trouble finding his breath, and his revulsion turned to stark horror when he looked up to see the second orog towering over him, straddling the stones with its very big sword angled to split Cadderly in half. There was no time for another dart, the young scholar knew, so he grabbed his walking stick and tossed it up to the monster.

The orog's face contorted in confusion as it batted the walking stick aside, but Cadderly's ruse was not without purpose. In the split second the orog's attention was stolen, Cadderly turned himself around and rolled to his back, looking up to the orog's backside. He curled up in a ball, hooking his calves behind the orog's knees and straightened and pulled with all his might.

For a long moment, nothing happened, and Cadderly thought that he must look ridiculous indeed, as though he were straining against an immovable object. Then the orog did fall forward, but not heavily, and with no damage done. Cadderly scrambled forward over the orog's back, and he hooked one arm around the orog's thick neck and pulled for all his life.

Undaunted, the creature stood back up, taking Cadderly with it. It looked around for its sword, which it had dropped in the fall, then spotted the weapon and made for it.

Cadderly realized that the monster could easily jab the weapon behind it, right into his vulnerable torso. Frantic, the young scholar considered letting go and making a run for cover, but he knew he would never get out of the monster's reach in time.

"Fall, damn you!" Cadderly growled, tightening and twisting his arm.

The orog, to Cadderly's astonishment, dropped its sword back to the ground. As though it had noticed the choke hold for the first time, the monster's thick hands came up to grab at Cadderly's arm, but by that time, there remained little strength in them.

Eyes closed, Cadderly desperately held on, still pulling with all his might.

Finally, the orog tumbled to the ground.

The last orog, near the tree, favored its right foot. It wanted to go with its two companions, one lying atop the netted elf and the other waving a sword menacingly and looking for an opening, but the creature winced whenever its toe came near the ground. The beast looked up and saw the flesh from its leg hanging grotesquely from the jag on the broken tree branch.

Cursing its luck and ignoring the burning agony, the stubborn creature hopped on its good foot out from the maple's wide trunk.

Right into Kierkan Rufo's path.

Rufo rode one horse and held the other beside it, and his charge came powerfully, if a bit late. The man hadn't meant to run the orog down with his own horse—he had purposely placed the riderless steed closer to the tree— but the orog's unexpected movement had put it right between both horses.

The monster got tangled in the worst possible way and was stepped on several times, but when the horses passed, it was still alive, lying helplessly on its back. Its spine was crushed, leaving it staring straight up at the dripping meat of its own ripped leg.

The riderless horse crossed the broken branch without trouble, but Rufo's horse, stumbling from the tangled orog, flipped headlong, sending the man on a long, bouncing roll. Rufo spat dirt, shifted, and sat looking back at the battle.

His attack did much to aid Elbereth's cause, for one of the three orogs moving to engage the elf was down and a second had broken away from the fray.

It seemed little comfort to poor Rufo, though, for the orog had only run because it had spotted an easier target: Rufo. It charged down the trail, its huge sword waving and its tongue hanging hungrily between broken yellow teeth.

Danica, over to the side, reacted. She snapped off one more kick, which sent her orog's head jerking backward, then broke free of the monster. She hesitated, glancing at Elbereth, but apparently figured that the elf had the situation under control, and ran after the orog approaching Rufo.

Elbereth squirmed around to face the heavy orog. He worked his hand to his belt, using his other arm to keep the ugly monster's snapping mouth from biting at his face. The elf prince's arm moved in three rapid jolts, the orog heaving with each. The fourth time, Elbereth held his arm tight against the monster and began twisting his wrist back and forth.

The monster rolled off the elf's slender stiletto and thrashed in the road, trying to hold its entrails inside its opened belly.

In a single movement, the agile Elbereth slipped out from under the crude net and came up to his knees. Merciless and grim-faced, he whipped his dagger into the squirming orog's leg so that it couldn't run while he retrieved his sword.

Danica was swift, but the orog's lead was too great. Rufo pulled his mace from his belt and tried to stand. He was less skilled with weapons than even Cadderly and couldn't hope to hold out for long. Even worse, Rufo's ankle, twisted in the fall, would hardly support him, and he fell back on the seat of his pants. The orog was almost upon him, and he seemed certain he was about to die.

The orog's head jerked suddenly to the side, though, and half of its face blew off, showering Rufo and Danica, as she rushed in, with blood and gore.

Rufo and Danica stared at each other in disbelief for a moment then turned in unison to the side, to see Cadderly standing between the rocks, crossbow in hand and a horrified expression splayed across his face.

SIX

THE QUALITY OF MERCY

Cadderly stood perfectly still for a few moments, too immersed to even notice his two friends' approach. All of his thoughts were focused on what had just occurred, on what he had just done. Three orogs lay dead by his hand, and worse yet, he had killed one of them with his bare hands.

It had been so easy, Cadderly hadn't even thought about what he was doing, had moved solely on instinct. He had even killed the orog that ran down the road toward Rufo, nowhere near Cadderly. The orog was there, in his crossbow sights, then it was dead.

It was too easy.

Not for the first time in the last few tendays, Cadderly questioned his purpose in life, the sincerity of his calling to the god Deneir. Headmaster Avery had once called Cadderly a Gondsman, referring to a sect of inventive priests who showed little moral guidance in forming their dangerous constructions. That word, "Gondsman," hovered over the young scholar like the dead eyes of one of his victims.

Cadderly came out of his trance to see Danica standing beside him, wiping her face, and Kierkan Rufo holding Cadderly's wide-brimmed hat and nodding with appreciation. Cadderly shuddered as Danica wiped blood from her fair cheek.

Can she really wash that blood away? he wondered. And will I ever cleanse my own hands?

An image of beautiful Danica covered in gore flashed across his psyche and Cadderly felt as if the world had been turned upside down, as if the lines of good and evil had flip-flopped and blurred together to become a gray area based purely on primal instincts.

After all, they could have avoided that tree, could have avoided the slaughter entirely.

Sympathy was plain on Danica's face. She took the hat from Rufo and handed it to Cadderly then she offered her arm. The shaken young scholar took both without hesitation. Kierkan Rufo again nodded grimly at him, a gesture of thanks, and it seemed to Cadderly as though Rufo understood his inner turmoil.

They headed back to the maple, Danica and Cadderly arm in arm, just in time to see Elbereth smash in the skull of a writhing orog. The elf prince unceremoniously tore his stiletto out of the creature's leg.

Cadderly looked away, pushed Danica from him, and was sure he would vomit. He eyed the elf prince for a moment with a grave stare then turned and walked from the scene. He moved parallel to Elbereth, but didn't look at him.

"What would you have me do?" he heard an angry Elbereth call out.

Danica mumbled something to the elf that Cadderly

couldn't hear, but Elbereth wasn't finished with his tirade.

"If it were *his* home . . ." Cadderly heard clearly, and he knew that Elbereth, though talking to Danica, was directing the remark his way. He looked back to see Danica nodding at Elbereth, the two exchanging grim smiles then clasping hands warmly.

The world had turned upside down.

A sound by the maple caught his attention. He saw another orog, lying still and staring upward. Cadderly followed its gaze up to the broken tree limb, to the piece of dripping flesh. Horrified, the young scholar rushed to the creature's side. It took him a moment to realize that the creature still drew breath, its chest moved so slowly, its breathing shallow and uneven. Cadderly pulled the eye-above-candle emblem, his holy symbol, from the front of his hat and fumbled with a pouch on his belt. He heard the others moving behind him, but paid them no heed.

"What are you doing?" Elbereth asked him.

"He's still alive," Cadderly replied. "I have spells that—"

"No!"

The sharpness of the retort did not strike Cadderly as profoundly as the fact that it had been Danica, not Elbereth, who snapped at him. He turned slowly, as if he expected to see a horrid monster looming over him.

But it was just Danica, Elbereth, and Rufo; Cadderly hoped there remained a difference.

"The creature is too far gone," Danica said, her voice quiet.

"You shall not waste your spells on the likes of an orog!" Elbereth added, and there was nothing at all quiet about his sharp tones.

"We cannot leave it here to die," Cadderly shot back, fumbling again with his pouch. "Its lifeblood will drain out into the dirt."

"A fitting end for an orog," Elbereth replied.

Cadderly looked at him, still surprised by the grim elf's lack of mercy.

"Go, if you will," Cadderly growled. "I am a cleric of a merciful god and I'll not leave a wounded creature like this."

Q

Danica pulled Elbereth away. They had much to do before they could leave, in any case. A lot of their equipment lay scattered, weapons buried in orog flesh, and one horse, the one that had stumbled over the broken branch, needed tending.

Elbereth understood and honored the young woman's feelings. Cadderly had fought well—the elf couldn't deny that—and they could prepare to leave without his assistance.

Back up the trail, Elbereth retrieved his dropped bow. As he began to sling it over his shoulder, he heard a gasp from Danica, picking up her pack just a few feet from him.

Elbereth spun to her then turned immediately to where she was looking.

Black smoke rose over Shilmista's northwestern edge.

Q

Oblivious to the distant spectacle, Cadderly worked furiously to stem the flow of blood from the orog's torn leg. Where to begin? All the flesh of the outside half of the leg, from ankle to mid thigh, had been ripped away.

Furthermore, the creature had suffered a dozen other severe wounds, including broken bones, from being run down by Rufo's horse. Cadderly had never been overly proficient at his priestly studies, and clerical magic was not easy for him. Even if he was the finest healer of the Edificant Library, though, he doubted he could do much for the broken creature.

Every so often, a drop of blood plopped beside him from the hanging skin. A pointed reminder, Cadderly believed, falling rhythmically, like a heartbeat. Then it stopped. Cadderly took great pains not to look up.

The least he could do was comfort the doomed creature, though that hardly seemed sufficient in the face of his actions. He pulled in a piece of the broken branch and propped it under the orog's head. Then he went back to work, refusing to consider the beast's nature, refusing to remember that the orogs had planned to kill him and the others. He wrapped and tied, plugged holes with his fingers, and was not disgusted by the blood on his hands.

"Young scholar!" he heard Elbereth say.

Cadderly looked to the side then fell back and cried out, seeing a drawn bow leveled his way.

The arrow cut right by his chest—Cadderly felt the windy wake of its rushing flight—and it dived into the wounded orog, catching the monster under the chin and driving up into its brain. The creature gave one violent jerk then lay still.

"We have no time for your folly," Elbereth snarled.

The elf prince stormed past the stunned man, not taking his glare off Cadderly until he reached the wounded horse.

Cadderly wanted to cry out in protest, wanted to run

over and strike Elbereth in the face, but Danica was beside him, calming him and helping him to his feet.

"Let the matter drop," the young woman almost pleaded.

Cadderly turned on her, but saw only tenderness in her clear brown eyes and pursed lips.

"We must leave at once," Danica continued. "The forest is burning."

With his already bloodied sword, Elbereth finished off the doomed horse. Cadderly noted the elf's sad expression and the gentle way he completed the grim task, and noted too that the elf cared more for the horse than for the orogs.

It had been Cadderly's mount, and when they left, Cadderly was the one walking, refusing offers from both Danica and Rufo to share their steeds, and not even answering Elbereth's offer that the elf prince would walk and Cadderly ride.

Cadderly looked straight ahead, every step, refusing to acknowledge his companions. In his silent vigil, though, the battle replayed in his head, and Barjin's dead eyes stared at them all from above that battlefield, forever judging.

They entered the thick boughs of Shilmista at twilight, and Elbereth, despite his desire to find his people, quickly moved to set up camp.

"We will leave before dawn," the elf explained. "If you wish to sleep, do so now. The night will not be a long one."

"Can you sleep?" Cadderly snarled at him.

Elbereth's silver eyes narrowed as the young scholar approached.

"Can you?" Cadderly asked again, his voice growing

dangerously loud. "Does your heart cry at the deeds of your bow and sword? Do you even care?"

Danica and Rufo looked on with alarm, almost expecting Elbereth to kill Cadderly where he stood.

"They were orogs, orc kin," Elbereth reminded him.

"Without mercy, how much better are we?" Cadderly growled in frustration. "Do our veins run thick with the same blood as orcs?"

"It is not your home," the elf replied. His voice filled with sarcasm. "Have you ever had a home?"

Cadderly did not reply, but he did not, could not, ignore the question. He really didn't know the answer. He had lived in Carradoon, the town on Impresk Lake, before going to the library, but he remembered nothing of that distant time. Perhaps the library was his home.

"If your home was in danger, you would fight for it, do not doubt," Elbereth continued. "You would kill whatever threatened your home, without mercy, and would hold no lament for its death."

The elf stared into Cadderly's gray eyes for a few moments longer, awaiting a reply, but got none. Then Elbereth was gone, disappeared into the forest gloom to scout the perimeter of their camp.

Cadderly heard Danica's relieved sigh behind him.

Exhausted, Kierkan Rufo tumbled down and was snoring almost immediately. Danica seemed to have the same idea, but Cadderly sat before the low-burning fire, wrapped in a heavy blanket. Its thickness did little to warm the chill in his heart. He hardly noticed when Danica came over to sit beside him.

"You shouldn't be so . . . troubled," she offered after a long silence.

"Was I to let the orog die?" Cadderly asked.

Danica shrugged. "Orogs are vicious, evil things," she said. "They live to destroy, and further no cause beyond their own vile desires. I do not lament their deaths." She glanced sidelong at Cadderly. "Nor do you.

"It's Barjin, isn't it?" Danica asked him, her voice full of pity.

The words stung. Incredulous, Cadderly turned on Danica.

"It was never about the orog," Danica continued undaunted. "The fury of your movements as you tended the creature was not befitting any kin of orcs. It was guilt that drove you, memories of the dead priest."

Cadderly's expression didn't change, though he found it difficult to dispute Danica's claims. Why had he cared so deeply for the orog, a notorious villain that would have torn the heart from his chest if given the chance? Why had that wounded orog evoked so much pity in him?

"You acted—you *fought*—as the situation demanded," Danica said, "against the orogs and the priest. It was Barjin, not you, who caused his death. Lament that it had to happen at all, but accept no guilt for what you could not control."

"What's the difference?" Cadderly asked.

Danica draped an arm around his shoulders and moved close. Cadderly could feel her breath, hear her heartbeat, and see the moisture on her full lips.

"You must judge yourself as fairly as you judge others," Danica whispered. "I, too, battled Barjin, and would have killed him if given the opportunity. How would you look upon me if that had come to pass?"

Cadderly had no answer for that.

Danica leaned closer and kissed him then hugged him tightly, though he hadn't the strength to respond. Without another word, she moved back to her blanket and lay down, offering him a parting smile before she closed her eyes and gave in to her weariness.

Cadderly sat for a while longer, watching her. She understood him so well, better than he understood himself. Or was it just that Danica understood the wide world in ways the sheltered Cadderly couldn't? For all his short life, Cadderly had found his answers in books, while Danica, worldly wise, had searched out her answers through experience.

Some things, it seemed, could not be learned simply by reading about them.

Elbereth came back into camp a short while later. Cadderly was down, but not asleep, and he watched the elf. Elbereth rested his bow against a log and unbelted his sword, placing it beside his bedroll. Then, to Cadderly's surprise, Elbereth went over to Danica and gently tucked her blankets around her shoulders. He stroked Danica's thick hair a moment then walked back to his own bedroll and lay under the myriad stars.

For the second time that day, Cadderly didn't know what to think, or how to feel.

SEVEN

PRAGMATIC MAGIC

W hat have you learned?" Tintagel asked Shayleigh when he found her atop Daoine Dun, the Hill of the Stars. Another day neared its end in Shilmista, another day of hit and run battles against the overwhelming force of invaders.

"Fifty goblins were killed in one fight," Shayleigh replied, but there was no smile on her face, fair and undeniably beautiful even though one side remained bright red from Tintagel's lightning bolt of a few days earlier. "And a giant was brought down in another. We suffered a few wounded, but none too seriously."

"That is good news," the elf wizard said, his smile intentionally wide in an effort to cheer the young maiden. It was a meager attempt, though, for Tintagel knew as well as Shayleigh that victory or defeat could not be measured by counting dead bodies. The enemy forces had indeed, as Hammadeen had told them, taken to the march, and for all the devastation the elves were handing them they slowly but steadily progressed through beautiful Shilmista, scarring the land as they passed.

"They have taken a hundred square miles," Shayleigh said. "And they are burning the wood in the northwest."

Tintagel, for all his strained optimism, understood that Shayleigh was not alone among the elves in her growing despair.

"The night will be clear and dark, for the moon is new," the elf wizard offered, trying to sound hopeful and lifting his light blue eyes heavenward. "Might King Galladel call for *Daoine Teague Feer?*"

"The Star Enchantment?" Shayleigh echoed softly in the common tongue. Without even considering the motion, she ran her slender fingers through her hair—and her face crinkled in disgust, for her golden locks were matted with blood and grime. Shayleigh felt dirty, as did many of Shilmista's elves. The woodland folk had a way of countering those negative thoughts, though, with a cleansing of body and soul, an ancient ritual of rejuvenation: *Daoine Teague Feer.*

"Let us go to Galladel," Shayleigh said, hope and excitement in her melodic voice for the first time in many days.

They found the aged king in one of the caves along the side of the hill that had become the elves' sanctuary. From that cave, Galladel directed scouting missions, coordinated patrol times, and gathered war parties. It was a heroic task, surely, for the elf king had to keep in mind which of his people were experienced fighters and which were novices, and ensure a proper blend in each party. Even more complicated, many of the elves had been injured and required rest.

As soon as they entered the torchlit cave, both Shayleigh and Tintagel recognized how heavy Galladel's burden had become. His once-straight shoulders sagged and circles lined his eyes.

"What do you want?" the elf king snapped. He threw his hands out to the side, unintentionally knocking several scrolls from the chamber's main table. Obviously embarrassed, Galladel's visage softened and he reiterated his question in a quieter tone.

"The moon is new," Shayleigh said, hoping the hint would be enough.

Galladel just stared at her blankly, though. He seemed to grow angry, as if the two were wasting his precious time.

"The sky is clear," added Tintagel. "A million stars will show themselves to us, lend us their strength for the morrow's fight."

"*Daoine Teague Feer?*" Galladel asked. "You wish to dance and play?"

"It is more than play," Shayleigh reminded him.

"The millions of stars will not complete my million tasks!" cried the frustrated elf king.

Shayleigh had to bite her lip to keep from responding. She and a dozen others had offered to assist the king in his planning when they weren't out on patrol, but Galladel had taken it all on himself, called it his duty despite the obvious fact that he could not carry the burden alone.

"Forgive me," the king said quietly, seeing Shayleigh's wounded expression. "I have not the time for *Daoine Teague Feer*. Perform the celebration in my absence?" he offered.

Shayleigh was not ungrateful, but the king's request was impossible. "Only one of the ruling line may perform *Daoine Teague Feer,*" she reminded Galladel. The look on the elf king's face explained much to Shayleigh and Tintagel. Galladel was old and tired, and made no secret of the fact that he no longer held much faith for Shilmista's ancient magic. *Daoine Teague Feer* was indeed just play to him, a dance with little value beyond its immediate enjoyment. If taken from the king's disbelieving perspective, then, what did it matter who led the celebration?

Still, Shayleigh couldn't hide her frown. Her king had grown pragmatic, even humanlike, and she hadn't the courage to blame him. When she was but a child, only a short two centuries past, a thousand elves had danced in Shilmista. The whole forest, from north to south, echoed with their unending song. But those days seemed far removed. How many of Shilmista's children had passed to Evermeet, never to return?

Tintagel tapped the maiden on the elbow and nodded to the exit. "You are due on patrol," the elf wizard whispered to prompt her along.

Shayleigh had the presence of mind to dip a bow as she left, but Galladel, already back to poring over the many parchments, didn't even notice.

C

A mood of similar frustration gripped the invaders' camp as twilight descended over Shilmista.

Ragnor's march was making gains, but those gains came painfully slowly, and at incredible expense. The elves fought better than the ogrillon had expected. He thought he would be more than halfway through Shilmista already, but his forces had put only ten, maybe fifteen of the hundred and fifty mile expanse behind them—and they hadn't even secured their rear flank. Ragnor feared that his troops were looking more to their sides, for fear of concealed archers, than ahead to conquest.

Better news came from the flanks, where resistance had been minimal. Orogs and orcs, running in the foot-hills of the Snowflake Mountains, had passed Shilmista's halfway point, and a tribe of goblins out on the plains to the west had nearly entered the southwestern pass around the forest, where they would set up camp and discourage any reinforcements from the city of Riatavin.

But Ragnor knew he didn't have the numbers to sur-round the forest, and if the elves continued to hold him off at the present rate, they would surely find allies before the ogrillon claimed Shilmista for Castle Trinity. And what of the coming winter? Even cocky Ragnor didn't believe he could hold the goblinoid rabble at his side when the first snows fell. Time worked against him, and the elves intended to fight him every step of the way.

If the ogrillon had any doubts of the elves' intent, he had the proof right before him. Looking out across a steep valley and a rushing river, Ragnor watched the latest skirmish. A mixed group of goblins, orcs, and a few ogres had been surprised by a band of elves. Ragnor's troops had been crossing a field, approach-ing a thick grove, when a hail of arrows had sent them scrambling for cover. From so far back, the ogrillon had no idea how many enemies his forces faced, but he suspected that the elves were few. Few, but undeniably effective, for the orcs and goblins had not come out of hiding, and those few brave or stupid ogres who had rushed the tree line had gone crashing down with a score of arrows in each of their bodies.

"Have you sent the giant and a band of bugbears?" the ogrillon snapped at his closest lieutenant, a weak but cunning goblin.

"Yesses, my general," the goblin replied, cowering, and with good reason. Ragnor's first few "closest advisors" numbered among the dead, though none of them had gotten anywhere near an elf.

Ragnor glared at the goblin and it cowered even lower, nearly rubbing its belly on the turf. Fortunately for the pitiful creature, the ogrillon had other business on his mind. Ragnor looked back out to the distant battle scene, trying to figure how long it would take his giant to get across the river and within boulder-throwing range.

Another anguished cry split the morning air as yet another monstrous soldier caught an elven arrow. Ragnor reflexively swung his hand out to the side, catching his advisor with a backhand slap that sent the goblin tumbling away.

"That should inspire loyalty," came a woman's voice from behind.

The ogrillon spun to see the wizard Dorigen. A bat-winged imp sat on her shoulder, and a burly human stood at her flank.

Ç

"What are you doing here, wizard?" the ogrillon spat. "This is not your place, nor the place of your favored boy!" He eyed Tiennek dangerously and Dorigen feared she might already have to intervene between the two.

"Well met to you as well," the wizard replied. She hadn't expected a warm reception from Ragnor; he was smart enough to understand that Aballister had sent her to spy on his progress, as well as his ambitions.

Ragnor took a threatening step Tiennek's way, and Dorigen wondered if she had anything in her magical repertoire that could stop the monstrous general if she had to. She fingered her onyx ring, considering the time it would take for her to loose its fiery fury, and the potential for that fury to stop the brutish ogrillon.

"I'm here because I was told to be here," she said. "You've been out of Castle Trinity for many days, Ragnor, but you seem to still be stumbling about the woods with few clear gains to show for our considerable expense." Ragnor backed off a bit and Dorigen hid her smile, amazed at how easily she had put the powerful beast on the defensive. Her conclusions had been no more than an educated guess—she had no way of knowing how Ragnor's battle plan was progressing—but the ogrillon's reaction had confirmed that she wasn't far off the mark.

"We're . . . concerned," Dorigen continued, mellow and nonthreatening. "The summer is nearly past, and Aballister wants to take Carradoon before the first snow."

"So he sent you," huffed Ragnor, "thinking that you might help poor Ragnor?"

"Perhaps," Dorigen purred.

"You need the help," Druzil added then dropped back under his bat wings to escape the ogrillon's glare.

"I need no weakling wizards in my camp," Ragnor growled. "Be gone, and take Aballister's bat and your boy with you." He turned back to the valley and the river, and tried to look busy.

"Then all goes well?" Dorigen asked, using the most innocent tones she could muster, cocking her head coyly.

When Ragnor didn't react, Dorigen got more direct after selecting the components for a defensive spell from one of her deep pockets, in case the ogrillon seriously objected.

"You're stopped, Ragnor," she declared. "Admit it, before you fall like Barjin did."

The ogrillon spun on her, but she did not relent.

Did you have to make that reference? Druzil asked telepathically, for the imp most certainly didn't like the way Ragnor was looking at him.

"And have you come to bring that about?" Ragnor spat.

"I have come as an agent of Talona, to aid an ally," Dorigen insisted. "Even one too foolish to accept the help he needs."

Dorigen looked past the ogrillon to the distant valley and the battle that was not going Ragnor's way. She waved her hand and chanted, and a block of shimmering, flickering blue light appeared before her.

Ragnor took a tentative step backward. Dorigen handed Druzil over to Tiennek, took one step forward into the light, and was gone.

After barely a heartbeat to consider his new position, Druzil dived into the portal behind her.

Ragnor spun about and saw a similar field of blue flickering beyond the river. It diminished as soon as Dorigen stepped through, Druzil again on her shoulder.

"I don't like elves," Druzil whispered as he faded into invisibility. "Nasty creatures!"

Dorigen paid him no heed, except to offer a scowl to let him know that she had wanted him to remain with Tiennek. Dorigen had no time to worry about the bothersome imp, though. She studied the battle, trying to get a perspective on what was happening around her. She saw orcs and goblins far ahead of her, crouched behind fallen logs, small ridges—anything they could find to shelter them from the tree line. Other monsters lay dead or dying, some of the ogres covered with arrows. Dorigen followed Druzil's lead and became invisible, not trusting the range of fine elven bows.

Even with the masking spell, Dorigen dared not approach the trees. Elves, being magically inclined, had a natural sense for such magic. Dorigen considered her options for a moment then fumbled about in the many pockets of her robes.

"Damn!" she growled. Then, with sudden insight, she reached up, felt for Druzil, and tore a bit of fur from the joint at the base of the imp's wing. The movement, offensive in nature, forced the wizard back to visibility.

"What are you doing?" Druzil demanded, shifting about and digging his claws into Dorigen's shoulder. He, too, became visible, only to fade away a moment later.

"Sit still!" Dorigen commanded.

She felt the tuft for a moment, hoping it would suffice. The spell called for bat fur, but the wizard couldn't seem to find any among her components at the moment, and she had no time to go hunting bats. Dorigen found some natural cover behind a tree and prepared herself.

For several moments, for this spell was not a quick and easy one to cast, the wizard went through the designated motions, chanting softly. Another goblin died in that time, but Dorigen considered it a minor loss in light of the coming gains.

Then it was done and an eyeball hovered in the air a few feet ahead of Dorigen. It became translucent almost immediately, and following Dorigen's mental commands, floated off toward the tree line.

Dorigen closed her own eyes and saw through the detached orb. It made the trees and flitted about, looking this way and that, floating the length of the elves' line. Dorigen kept it moving swiftly, but even so, several elves stiffened and looked around nervously as it passed.

Dorigen soon came to the conclusion that all of the elves—not a substantial number—were above the ground in the trees. The greatest factor working against the orcs and goblins was their own fear. A bold charge would dislodge the few elves from their tenuous positions.

"I must begin the charge," the wizard whispered.

She chose as her target a large elm in the center of the elves' line. The detached eyeball floated in so that the wizard could make a count of her intended victims. One maiden, golden haired and with striking violet eyes, turned, following the floating orb's path.

Dorigen released her thoughts from the eyeball, pulled a different component from her robe, and began another spell.

"Down! Down!" she heard the distant elf maiden cry. "Wizard! They have a wizard! Get down!"

Dorigen moved her next spell along with all the speed she could muster. She saw a slender form drop from the distant tree, then another, but she hardly cared, for her spell was done and the rest would not escape.

A tiny ball of fire flew from Dorigen's fingers, making great speed for the tree. Dorigen had to stand partly in the open to direct its course, but she knew the elves would be too busy to bother with her.

The ball disappeared into the elm's boughs. In the blink of a magical eye, the great tree became a fiery torch.

The savage flames quickly consumed all the fuel that the elm, and the elves in its boughs, could offer. Branches crackled and tumbled down beside the charred bodies and blackened suits of fine mesh armor.

Dorigen aimed her next spell at her own troops.

"Do not hesitate!" she roared in a magically enhanced, thunderous voice. *"Charge them! Kill them!"*

The sheer power of her command, a voice as great as a dragon's roar, sent the orcs and goblins scrambling toward the tree line. A few died from random bow shots, but most tore right into the brush. They found only one living elf to hack, a pitifully wounded creature at the base of the ruined elm. Near death even before the goblins arrived, he offered only minor resistance. The goblins took him apart with wicked glee.

Just as satisfying, the monsters recovered bodies—the first enemy bodies they had seen since the start of the campaign—of charred and blackened elves.

Gratified by their whoops of joy, Dorigen turned, conjured another extradimensional door of shimmering light, and stepped through, back to the high ground beyond the river.

"I believe they killed one wounded elf," the wizard said, walking by the stunned ogrillon. "Foolish. He might have made a valuable prisoner. You should better control your bloodthirsty troops, General Ragnor."

Ragnor's sudden burst of laughter turned her around.

"Have I welcomed you to Shilmista?" the ogrillon offered, his tusk-adorned smile stretching from ear to ear.

Dorigen was glad she had improved the surly monster's mood.

EIGHT

QUIETLY

The forest was eerily still. No birdcalls greeted the dawn, and no animals scurried through the thick branches overhead. Elbereth glanced back to the others every few steps, a look of dread on his face.

"At least there aren't any battles in the area," Danica offered, her voice a whisper, but still seeming loud in the quiet wood.

Elbereth moved back to join them. "The paths are clear, but I fear to ride," he whispered back. "Even leading the horses at so slow a pace, their hoofbeats can be heard many yards away."

Cadderly snapped his fingers then cringed at the sharp sound. Ignoring the surprised looks from Danica and Rufo, and a scowl from Elbereth, the young scholar pulled his pack from Temmerisa, the horse he'd been leading. The bells had been removed, muffled with clothing, and packed away in saddlebags.

"Wrap them," Cadderly said, producing a thick woolen blanket. The others didn't seem to understand.

"The hooves," Cadderly explained. "Rip the blanket into strips . . ." His voice trailed off as he locked gazes with the stern elf. Elbereth eyed him curiously—Cadderly thought he noted a flash of admiration in Elbereth's silver eyes.

Without another word, Elbereth pulled out his knife and took the blanket from Cadderly. In a few moments, they were moving again, the hoofbeats still audible, but muffled. When Elbereth looked back again and nodded his approval, Danica nudged Cadderly and smiled.

They stopped for a short rest late that morning, far from the wood's eastern edge. Still the forest was quiet; they had found no sign of anyone, friend or foe.

"The People will fight in quick skirmishes," Elbereth explained. "We are not numerous enough to afford the losses of a strategic battle. They will move swiftly and silently, striking at the enemy from afar and disappearing when he moves against them."

"Then we don't have much chance of finding them," said Danica. "More likely, they'll find us."

"Not so," the elf explained. "They have horses to tend, and undoubtedly—" the next words came hard for him—"wounded who will need to rest in a secure place. Shilmista was not caught defenseless, no matter how sudden the attack was. We are not many, and not allied with any great powers, but we of Shilmista have rehearsed our home's defense since the first elf walked into this wood many centuries ago."

Elbereth picked up a twig and drew a rough map of the forest on the ground. "By the location of the rising smoke, the fight is up here," he said, pointing to the northern section.

"Then we need not muffle the horses," Rufo put in,

"and we might ride instead of walk." The man's suggestion met with only tentative acceptance.

"We are near the center of the wood." Elbereth went on, leaving Rufo's thoughts hanging unanswered for the moment. "The first defensive camp would have been here, just south of a defensible region known as the Dells." Again the elf seemed to fight past a lump in his throat. "I would presume that camp has been deserted by now."

"And the next?" Cadderly asked. He thought Elbereth might need a moment to recover.

"Here," the elf said, indicating an area not too far from their present position. He looked up to find a break in the trees then pointed out a fair-sized hill poking out of the green canopy several miles to the north.

"Daoine Dun, Hill of the Stars," the elf prince explained. "Its sides are thick with pine and blocked by tangled dusk-wood to the north and west. There are many caves, easily concealed, and some large enough to stable horses."

"How long to get there?" Danica asked.

"Faster if we ride," said Rufo.

"Before we decide to ride," Cadderly cut in, drawing Elbereth's attention before the elf had time to answer Rufo, "explain to me why the wood is so quiet?"

"It hangs thick with dread," Danica agreed.

Elbereth nodded. "I think it better that we walk. Even so, we can make Daoine Dun soon after sunset. I will go first, far in front."

"And I'll keep to the side of the trail," offered Danica, "concealed in the brush." She looked at Cadderly. "You can lead two mounts."

Cadderly's nod set them off again, plodding slowly, as quietly as possible, through the forest. Rufo, pausing to rub his feet every so often, was obviously not happy to be walking again, but he didn't complain with anything more than the occasional sour look sent Cadderly's way.

When the sun began its western descent in earnest, Danica whispered for Cadderly and Rufo to hold the horses still. Both were amazed at how close the woman actually was to them, for though the brush beside the path was thick and tangled, they hadn't heard a sound of her passing in quite some time.

Elbereth came rushing back, motioning for the two men to lead the horses off the path.

"Goblins," the elf explained when they were all under thick cover. "Many of them, spread out east and west. Their eyes are on Daoine Dun, but they have archers posted along the way."

"Can we go around them?" Cadderly asked.

"I do not know," the elf answered. "Their line is long, I believe, and to pass beyond them we will have to go far from the road, among tangles that our mounts may not be able to cross."

Danica shook her head. "If their line is long," she reasoned, "then likely it's not too deep. We could charge right through them."

"And the archers?" Rufo reminded her.

"How many are along the road?" Danica asked Elbereth.

"I saw two," the elf replied, "but I believe there were others, at least a few, hidden in the brush."

"I can get them," the woman promised.

Elbereth started to protest, but Cadderly grabbed his elbow. The young scholar's nod took the bite from the elf's argument.

Danica drew a rough sketch of the road in the dirt. "You take a position here," she explained. She gave Elbereth a wink. "Be ready with your bow!" she offered, pointedly including the elf in her plans.

She remained cryptic, though, completing the plans by stating, "When you hear the jay, charge on." With no reply forthcoming, and not wanting to waste a moment, Danica started off along the edge of the trail.

"I will catch you as I pass," Cadderly promised her back.

Elbereth and Cadderly took up positions near a bend in the road that allowed them to watch the distant goblins, while Rufo stayed back with the three horses, ready to spring ahead at the elf's call. Elbereth, keen-eyed and attuned to the forest, pointed out Danica's progress as the young woman made her silent way through the bushes on the right side of the road. Barely visible even though she had just set out, Danica soon disappeared all together, not a single shaking twig to mark her movement.

There came a sudden rustle beside the goblins. Elbereth leveled his bow, but Cadderly put a hand on the elf's arm, reminding him to keep patient. Apparently the movement had been more obvious to Cadderly and Elbereth than to the two goblin sentries on the road, for the monsters did not even turn toward it.

All was quiet again for moments that seemed like days to the nervous companions.

"Where are you?" Cadderly whispered to the empty path ahead, trusting in Danica's skills but fearful nonetheless. He held his small crossbow, cranked and ready, and had to remind himself several times, as he had reminded Elbereth, to have patience and trust in Danica. "Where are you?"

As if in reply, Danica shot up behind one of the goblin guards. Her arm flicked then she reached around the goblin's head, put her hand over its mouth, and pulled it down into the bushes.

The other guard slumped to its knees, clutching at the dagger embedded deeply in its chest.

The cry of a jay sounded almost immediately, and Elbereth echoed it back to Rufo. In a heartbeat, they were up and riding, with powerful Temmerisa easily outpacing the lesser mounts.

To the left of the road, an archer popped up, but Elbereth was quicker on the draw and the goblin went down in a heap.

Two other archers appeared from the brush farther down the road. Danica noticed them and rushed ahead. She spun to the side, dodging one arrow, and stopped her spin perfectly to continue her charge then dived flat to her belly to avoid another arrow. She never slowed through the evasive movements, and the goblins didn't have time to ready their bows again before Danica leaped at them, turning flat out and horizontal in midair to knock both of them to the ground.

His blue silk cape flying behind him, Cadderly put his head down, held on to his wide-brimmed hat, and spurred his horse on, desperate to get beside Danica. He could see the bushes shaking with the struggle. A goblin arm shot up, holding a sword, then chopped down wickedly.

"No!" Cadderly cried.

The same sword reappeared above the brush—but in Danica's hand. When it descended, a goblin squealed in agony.

Elbereth's mount reared as it passed the wounded guard on the road. The elf finished the monster off with his sword then bent low in his saddle to retrieve Danica's valuable dagger. A goblin rushed out from the brush on the other side, intent on the elf, but Kierkan Rufo—or more accurately, Kierkan Rufo's horse—promptly ran the creature down.

Danica was back to the edge of the road, crouching low and waiting for Cadderly to get to her. Another goblin appeared, rushing toward her with sword drawn.

Cadderly's wide-brimmed hat flew off, bouncing behind his neck at the end of its tie and flying with his silken cape. He drew his loaded crossbow and tried to get a shot at the creature. Frustrated by the bounce of the horse's gallop, he spurred his mount on, thundering right up behind the goblin. The goblin turned, growled, and waved its sword.

It never got the chance to use it. Just a couple of feet away, Cadderly let the dart fly. Another long horse stride took him right by the goblin, within the creature's sword reach, but the goblin was in the air, flying away into the brush, already dead.

Cadderly hadn't escaped unscathed, though. So close to his target, the flash of the exploding dart burned and blinded him, and he nearly lost his seat. Then Danica was up behind him, guiding the horse back to the center of the path and holding Cadderly steady.

Elbereth and Rufo were right behind; hoots and calls went up all around them.

"Ride on!" the elf prince cried, rearing and spinning Temmerisa around. His great bow twanged again, then again, each shot sending another enemy to the grave.

Rufo's horse, with just one rider, got a few paces ahead of Cadderly's, making Cadderly and Danica the prime targets for those goblins springing from the brush along the road. A few clumsily thrown spears bounced harmlessly short, one arrow whistled by, and another came in, straight for Cadderly's back.

Danica noticed it at the last instant and threw her arm up to block.

"What?" came Cadderly's alarmed cry.

"It is nothing!" Danica replied. "Ride on!" She figured it wasn't the time to show Cadderly the arrow sticking through her forearm.

A few more strides and they were running free. Then came Temmerisa, as fast as an arrow. In a heartbeat, Elbereth was beside them again, grim-faced but unhurt.

When they had put half a mile behind them, they slowed their pace and dismounted. It was then that they noticed Danica's wound.

Cadderly nearly fell over, seeing the bloody arrow shaft protruding from both sides of Danica's delicate limb. Elbereth rushed over to her, spurring the young scholar to do the same.

"It's not serious," Danica said to calm them.

"How can you say that?" came Cadderly's retort.

He went back to the horse to retrieve his pack and returned bearing bandages and a jar of salve. By the time he was back beside her, Danica had pulled the arrow all the way through and was deep in concentration, using her meditative powers to gather the strength she would need to battle the pain.

Cadderly tried not to disturb her concentration as he gently wrapped the wound. Danica's mental powers were truly amazing. Cadderly had once seen her force a two-inch sliver from her leg without even touching it with her hands, using nothing but sheer concentration and muscle control. He did the best he could in wrapping the arm, but hesitated, a trapped expression clouding his face.

"What is it?" Elbereth demanded.

Cadderly ignored him and summoned the courage to call upon Deneir. He muttered the chants of minor healing prayers, one after another, though he wasn't well-versed in the art and didn't know how much good he was doing.

Reluctantly, for he had hoped to save his curative spells for himself, Kierkan Rufo came over to join him.

Before Rufo could begin to work on the arm, though, Danica opened her eyes. "That will not be necessary," she said to the sharp-featured priest, her eyes glazed and a look of sincere contentment on her smooth face.

Elbereth and Cadderly both started to protest, but then Cadderly looked more closely at the wrapping and realized that the wound had already stopped bleeding. He couldn't be sure if his spells or Danica's own concentration had stemmed the flow, and he honestly didn't care either way.

"We must continue," Danica said, her voice almost sleepy, "as before, with Elbereth in front and me to the side."

Elbereth protested. "I will take the lead," he agreed, "but you will stay with the others and the horses. We are not so far from Daoine Dun. If that is my people's camp, I do not believe we will encounter any more enemies between here and there."

Cadderly was surprised when Danica failed to argue. He knew then that her wound was much more serious and painful than she had let on.

They walked on into the twilight, when the wood, shrouded in deepening gloom, took on an even more ominous appearance to Cadderly. He grew alarmed as Elbereth disappeared from sight, slipping suddenly into the trees. Soon, though, the elf was back on the path and approaching, two other tall, grim-faced elves beside him. He introduced them as his cousins and was glad to report that his people had indeed set camp on the Hill of the Stars, just a mile north.

One of the elves accompanied them the rest of the way; the other went back to his watch.

Their escort told Elbereth of the battles; Cadderly saw the elf prince grimace as the other elf described the last skirmish, wherein a wizard had appeared and turned a tree to flames.

"Ralmarith is dead," the elf said, "and Shayleigh—"

Elbereth spun on him and grabbed him by the shoulders.

"She lives," the elf said, "though she is sorely wounded, and sorely wounded, too, is her heart. She was the last to leave Ralmarith and had to be pulled away."

Elbereth was not surprised. "She is a loyal friend," he agreed.

Elbereth went first to find Shayleigh when they reached Daoine Dun, though word was quickly—and often—passed to him that his father, the king, wished to speak with him.

Cadderly was amazed at how easily the elf prince seemed to ignore that request and follow his own agenda. It reminded the young scholar somewhat of himself on one of the many occasions he had avoided a summons from Headmaster Avery. Cadderly dismissed the thought quickly, not yet comfortable with any comparisons between himself and the arrogant, unmerciful Elbereth.

They found the wounded maiden on a cot in a small cave that had been set up to care for the injured. She was heavily bandaged in several places but didn't seem so bad off to Cadderly—until he looked into her eyes. There loomed a sadness unlike anything the young scholar had ever seen.

"We left Ralmarith," the maiden whispered, her voice choked, as soon as Elbereth moved beside her. "They killed him, hacked his body . . ."

Elbereth tried to calm her. "Ralmarith walks in Arvandor. Do not fear for him."

Shayleigh nodded but had to look away.

They sat in silence for some time then another elf entered and moved to tend Danica's injured arm. The stubborn monk politely refused, but Cadderly nudged her hard and reminded her that the dressing had to be changed. With a defeated sigh, Danica moved off with the elf.

"When will you be back in the fight?" Elbereth asked Shayleigh.

"Tomorrow," the maiden said.

"That is good," said Elbereth. "Rest well this night. Tomorrow we shall fight together, and together avenge Ralmarith!" He took a step toward the entrance.

"You are leaving?" Shayleigh asked, alarmed.

"There are goblins to the south," Elbereth explained. "I believe they intend to surround the hill. We cannot allow that." He looked over at Danica. "She will remain beside you," he said to Shayleigh. "A fine warrior and ally for our struggle."

"Are you going after the goblins tonight?" Cadderly asked Elbereth. "The day would seem more favorable. Goblins don't fight well in sunlight."

"This is Shilmista," Elbereth reminded him, as though that fact alone explained everything. The elf prince stood tall and straight, his jaw firm, his silver eyes narrowed and stern. "The goblins shall die, day or night."

"I'll go with you," Cadderly offered.

"I will not have you," Elbereth replied. "You are *n Tel'Quessir*—not of the People—and will not be able to see in the darkness." Of Shayleigh he asked, "Where is Tintagel?"

"With your father," Shayleigh replied. "We have called for *Daoine Teague Feer,* but Galladel has refused thus far."

Elbereth considered that news for a few moments but had no time to worry about it. He swept out of the tent, telling Cadderly and Rufo to rest easily and find a fine meal.

Scant moments later, fifty elves set out on the goblin hunt, Elbereth leading upon Temmerisa, and the wizard Tintagel at his side. They returned at middark, reporting a hundred goblins slain and scores more sent running. Not a single elf had been wounded.

Q

Cadderly was too excited to sleep, weary though he was. He had read much about elves over the years, but had met only a few—and those only at the library. Something about being in Shilmista, on a hill under the stars, surrounded by elves, transcended the experience of reading about the People. There was a flavor, an eldritch aura, that mere words, however well constructed, couldn't hope to capture.

He wandered the camp, greeted at every turn by smiles on otherwise grim faces, noting the rich colors, even in the quiet darkness, of the elves' hair and eyes. Those stirring in the camp were too busy to be disturbed, so he didn't bother introducing himself, just tipped his wide-brimmed hat and wandered past.

He had known from the moment he'd left the Edificant Library that the journey would change his life, and he had feared that. He feared it still, for already the world seemed a wider place—more dangerous and more wonderful all at once.

And what of Elbereth? Cadderly didn't like the elf or the way the elf treated him, but instincts told him differently, told him of the elf's honor and loyalty.

When his thoughts inevitably turned to Danica, he found a rocky seat on the north side of the hill and dropped his chin into his hands. Danica, it seemed, held no reservations concerning Elbereth. She had accepted the elf prince as friend and companion. That fact bothered Cadderly more than he cared to admit.

Cadderly sat for a long while, long after the war party had returned. In the end, he resolved nothing.

NINE

DAOINE TEAGUE FEER

Many elves' eyes had opened wide when Elbereth entered the encampment escorted by three humans. Few *n Tel'Quessir* came to Shilmista, especially with battle raging. Another set of eyes opened wider still, though, yellow eyes sown with tiny red capillaries.

Druzil nearly fell out of his perch, high in a thin blueleaf tree overlooking the camp, when he saw Rufo, Danica, and especially Cadderly. The imp recognized the young scholar at once and instinctively rubbed the remnants of a bruise on his flank where Cadderly had once popped him with a poisoned dart.

Druzil felt suddenly vulnerable, despite the fact that he was invisible and in a tree too weak-limbed for even the lithe elves to climb. He hadn't approached the camp too closely, fearing that the elves would discover him, but with that devilish young man about, the imp wondered what distance might be safe.

Druzil sent his thoughts back to Dorigen, who awaited his return about a mile to the north. Druzil let the wizard see through his eyes as he followed Cadderly's progress through the camp.

What is he doing here? Druzil demanded, as though he expected Dorigen to know.

He? came her incredulous thoughts. *Who is he?*

The young priest! the imp shot back. His thoughts almost screamed that Cadderly was Aballister's son, but Druzil deflected that notion, preferring to hold that bit of news until he could watch Dorigen's expression.

He is from the Edificant Library, the one who defeated Barjin, the imp continued.

From the long pause that followed, Druzil could tell that Dorigen had caught on to his sense of urgency. The imp recalled the battle in which Cadderly had brought him down with a dart coated in sleep poison. Druzil thought he sensed Dorigen's amusement when she shared that memory—he had to let her deep in his thoughts to allow her to see what he saw—and he sent a stream of curses her way.

Another thought struck Druzil and he looked around the camp, searching for the two dwarves that had accompanied Cadderly on that previous occasion. They were nowhere to be found, though, and Druzil hoped they were dead.

Who are the others? Dorigen asked, growing impatient after silent moments had passed.

The girl was with the priest then, though I do not know what role she played, the imp explained. *The other . . .* Druzil paused, recalling the description Barjin had given him of the fool who had initially aided the Talonite priest's cause: angular and tall, and walking with a slight tilt to his stance.

Kierkan Rufo, Druzil decided, figuring there couldn't be

another at the library who so accurately fit Barjin's description. Dorigen didn't press him further, so Druzil decided to be blunt with the wizard. *I wish to be gone from here.*

Around him, the camp seemed to come alive with activity, elves running about and shouting that Prince Elbereth had returned.

Come to me, Druzil, Dorigen bade, apparently seeing the imp's wisdom.

She didn't have to ask twice.

Q

"I requested your presence some time ago," Galladel said when Elbereth finally walked into his chamber. "In times of peace, I can overlook your irrespon—"

"A force of goblins had set up to the south of Daoine Dun," Elbereth interrupted. "Would you rather I had allowed them to fortify and entrench? They are gone now, and the way is clear if we are forced to flee—as I suspect we might if rumors of the approaching northern force are true."

The news took the momentum from the aged king's ire. He turned to the many scrolls strewn across the wide stone table.

"I will need your assistance," he said. "The patrols need to be coordinated. We must keep count of weapons and food." He roughed the papers around a bit, just to show his obvious displeasure.

Elbereth watched his father with growing concern. There was something too restrictive about Galladel's movements and tactics, something too humanlike for the younger elf's liking.

"The forest is our home," Elbereth said, as though that remark alone explained his disrespect.

Galladel glared at him, suspecting he had just been insulted.

"We must be out fighting," Elbereth continued, "freely, as our instincts and the trees guide us."

"Our attacks must be planned," the older elf argued. "Our enemy is many times stronger than we, and well organized."

"Then awaken the wood," Elbereth said.

Galladel's silver eyes, so similar to his son's, widened in disbelief.

"Awaken the trees," Elbereth said again, more firmly. "Call up the allies of our past, that together we might destroy those who have come to conquer Shilmista."

Galladel's soft laughter mocked him. "You know nothing of what you speak," he said. "You talk of the task as though it were a foregone event, easily manifested. Even in the older days, when I was a young elf, the trees would no longer come to the king's call."

Elbereth had only made the remark to draw a response from his weary father. When he saw the sadness creep into Galladel's eyes, he came to doubt his own wisdom.

"The ancient magic is gone, my son," Galladel continued, his voice subdued, "as faded as the days when the world belonged to the fey races—legends for fireside tales, but no more. We will win this war, but we will win it with blood and arrows."

"Yet you have sent emissaries to the Edificant Library, begging aid?" Elbereth asked.

Galladel paled. "I sent you," he replied.

"I was sent to gather information. I knew nothing of the start of a war," Elbereth argued. He knew he was right, but knew, too, that his father's patience had worn thin. "We must ask for aid from the library, and the legion of Carradoon should be called up as well."

"Send the emissary," Galladel replied absently, exhausted. "Go now. I have much to prepare."

"There is one other matter," Elbereth pressed.

The king gave him a sour look, as though he understood what was coming.

"Some of the People have requested *Daoine Teague Feer*," Elbereth said.

"We have no time—" Galladel started to protest.

"We could not spend our time in any better pursuit," the younger elf insisted. "Our People carry many wounds. They wear the blood of enemies and friends alike. They see the smoke of their burning forest and find goblins and orogs in every direction. Blood and arrows, yes, but battles are fought with emotion, my father. They are won by those willing to die if that must be, and by those eager to kill. Our spirits will carry us where your scrolls—" he waved a hand derisively at the stone table—"cannot!"

Galladel neither blinked nor made any move to reply.

"*Daoine Teague Feer* will lift those spirits," Elbereth said more quietly, trying to bring the conversation back to a reasonable level.

"You are of noble blood," answered Galladel, an unmistakable edge of anger and disappointment to his voice. "*You* perform the ceremony." He looked back to his scrolls then, taking particular interest in one and purposely avoiding lifting his eyes his son's way.

Elbereth waited a few moments, torn between what he knew was right and the fact that his actions would wound his father. Galladel's invitation to perform

Daoine Teague Feer was wrought of sarcasm, and if Elbereth went through with the ritual, his father certainly would not be pleased. But Elbereth, for all his loyalty to Galladel, had to follow his heart. He left the small cave to find his ceremonial robes and tell the others to find theirs.

Q

"Aballister's *son?*" Dorigen could hardly believe the news

"I fought him in the library," Druzil rasped, not liking the taste of the bitter words, "as I showed you when we communicated from afar. He is a trickster—take heed! And he surrounds himself with powerful friends."

"Does Aballister know of him?" Dorigen asked, wondering what intrigue might be swirling around her. Was Aballister perhaps in contact with the young priest in those fateful moments that lead to Barjin's demise?

Druzil nodded, his tall, doglike ears flipping forward. "Aballister learned of Cadderly when the priest fought Barjin," he explained. "Aballister was not pleased to find Cadderly in the library. He will be most upset to learn that the trickster now aids the elves."

A hundred possibilities whirled through Dorigen's mind then, of how she might gain the upper hand in the conflict against the elves, and in her own struggles within the hierarchy of Castle Trinity.

"You're sure this Rufo is the fool Barjin spoke of?" she asked.

"I am," Druzil lied, hoping that his guess was correct, but not daring to disappoint Dorigen when she was so excited. He studied her amber eyes, sparkling dots straddling the bridge of her disfigured nose.

"Go back to the elves," Dorigen commanded. She had to lift her voice over Druzil's whine to complete her orders. "Arrange a meeting with this Kierkan Rufo. If he was Barjin's fool, then he will be mine as well."

Druzil groaned, but flapped his wings and obediently started off.

"And Druzil," Dorigen called, "I trust that you will make no contact with Aballister, or that, if you do, nothing of this will be mentioned."

Druzil nodded. "What would be my gain?" he asked then continued on his way.

Dorigen considered the question carefully, and she knew that the best way to trust the imp was to keep him well advised. Indeed, what would be Druzil's gain in telling Aballister of the latest events? Dorigen clapped her hands. Unlike the imp, she was not sorry that the young scholar and his friends had come to help the elves. With Ragnor and his huge force finding a foothold in the forest, and with her beside them, Dorigen believed Shilmista's fate sealed anyway, and she resolved then to add to her personal gains at the expense of Aballister's son.

Q

"Tonight," Elbereth whispered into the wounded maiden's ear.

Shayleigh stirred and opened a tired eye.

Cadderly and Danica watched from across the cave, Cadderly still thinking that Shayleigh would have been better off left in the strange meditative state that passed for sleep among the elves. He had protested that the wounded elf needed her Reverie, but Elbereth had waved his doubts away, assuring Cadderly that *Daoine Teague*

Feer would do much more to improve Shayleigh's health and strength than any amount of meditation.

"Tonight?" Shayleigh echoed, her voice melodic even through her drowsiness and pain.

"Tonight we gather strength from the stars," Elbereth replied.

Shayleigh was up in a moment, to Cadderly's surprise. Just the mention of *Daoine Teague Feer* seemed to pump new vitality into the elf maiden. Elbereth bade Danica to help Shayleigh dress, and he and Cadderly exited the cave.

"Do we get to watch this celebration?" Cadderly asked. "Or would you prefer privacy?"

Elbereth's answer surprised him.

"You have become a part of our struggle," the elf prince replied. "You have earned the right to partake of this ritual. The choice is yours."

Cadderly understood the honor that had just been given him and his companions, and he was truly overwhelmed and amazed. "Forgive my arguments against disturbing Shayleigh," he said.

Elbereth nodded. "Your concern for my friend did not escape me." Elbereth glanced back at the cave, his expression grim. "Our enemies have found a powerful ally," he said. "This wizard must not be allowed to appear on any other battlefield."

Cadderly understood the proud elf's meaning and intentions, and he was not the least bit surprised by Elbereth's ensuing vow.

"When the celebration is complete and the People are prepared to take up the fight, I will hunt the wizard, whose head shall avenge Ralmarith's death, and Shayleigh's wounds.

"Go now and find Kierkan Rufo," Elbereth instructed. *"Daoine Teague Feer* will begin atop the hill as soon as the others are gathered."

Q

Cadderly, Danica, and Rufo sat to the side of the gathered elves, talking quietly among themselves. Cadderly told them of Elbereth's vow to go after the wizard, and again was not surprised when Danica vowed that she would hunt beside the elf.

More and more elves gathered atop the hill until nearly all the camp was there—the guards had decided to rotate their watch so that all might enjoy the celebration for at least a while—with the notable exception of King Galladel. Elbereth gave apologies for his father, explaining that the king had many duties to attend to and would come out later if he found the time. Whispers around Cadderly and Danica told them the elves doubted the truth of that explanation and hinted that the king hadn't come out because he thought the whole thing a waste of time.

As soon as the ceremony began, any doubts those whispers had placed in the young scholar's mind washed away.

All the elves rose up and formed a circle atop the hill. Hands were offered to the visitors. Rufo declined immediately, seeming uncomfortable. Danica looked to Cadderly with a wishful smile, and he nodded for her to go, but said that he would rather watch the beginning, at least, from the side. He took out his writing kit and his light tube, and smoothed a sheet of parchment in front of him, determined to prepare a firsthand account of the rarely seen ritual. He took care, though, to shield the light. Somehow it didn't seem fitting, magical though it was, to intrude on the starlight of the enchanted forest.

The elven song began slowly, almost as a spoken chant. The elves, and Danica, lifted bowls to the sky and began to walk the circle. Their walk became a dance, their chant a melodic song. Though he couldn't understand all of the words, the emotions evoked by the song affected Cadderly as much as any of the elves. Sad and sweet at the same time, and edged by the experiences of centuries long past, the Song of Shilmista offered the elven experience more fully than any book ever could. Cadderly came to understand that the elves were a people of feeling, a race of aesthetics, spiritual and at one with their natural surroundings, even more so than the humans who dedicated their lives as woodland priests. Cadderly thought of the three druids who had come to the Edificant Library not so long ago, particularly Newander, who had died at Barjin's hands.

He thought of Pikel, who longed to be a druid, and knew then, with a touch of sadness, that the dwarf, however unlike his gruff and pragmatic kin, could never achieve that spiritual calling.

The song went on for a long while and ended gently, becoming a walk and a chant then fading away as subtly as the setting moon. The elves and Danica still stood holding their bowls to the sky, and Cadderly wished he had joined them from the start. He diligently kept to his recording, though when he looked at the parchment he wondered whether his god would have preferred him to write about *Daoine Teague Feer* or experience it.

Elbereth, splendid in his purple robes, moved to the closest elf and took the bowl. He began a quiet chant to the heavens, to the millions of stars that dotted the night sky, then he reached into the bowl and threw its contents heavenward.

The glitter of stardust filled the air, descending over the targeted elf. His eyes sparkled, his rich golden hair seemed to shine more brightly, and when the stardust settled, he stood perfectly still, glowing with inner contentment.

Cadderly could hardly find the words to describe the transformation. He sat dumbfounded as Elbereth moved around the ring, repeating the ceremony. Most dramatic was the change that came over Shayleigh. Before the stardust descended over her, she had hardly been able to stand and had seemed more concerned with keeping her balance than in the precise movements of the dance.

Cadderly had seen many healers at work in the Edificant Library, experienced clerics with powerful spells, but he didn't think any of them could match the healing that took place in Shayleigh. Her dazzling smile returned, and even the blood washed from her hair. Her burned face regained the tanned, creamy complexion of her fey kin.

Elbereth went to Danica last, and though the stardust did not affect her as it had affected the elves, the woman seemed comforted and pleased. She stared at the elf prince with sincere, unblinking admiration.

A twinge of jealousy shot through Cadderly, but he found that he could not sustain it. Unexpectedly, Elbereth took a bowl from another elf and came over to him. Cadderly looked to where Rufo had been seated, excited, but the man was gone.

"You wished to record the ceremony," the elf prince

said, towering over Cadderly, "and watch from afar, that you might better understand it."

"That was my mistake," Cadderly admitted.

"Stand, *Sha'Quessir,*" Elbereth bade, using the Elvish word for "elf friend," and Cadderly slowly rose to his feet.

Elbereth looked around to his People, all nodding, and to Danica, who smiled with anticipation. The prince began the chant and sprinkled the stardust.

From inside the shower, the view was even more glorious. Cadderly saw a million stars reflected a million times. They reached out to him, communicated to him a sense of universal harmony. He thought, for that too-short moment, that he saw the world as an elf saw it, and when it was over he found himself looking at Elbereth in the same appreciative way that Danica had.

Never again would Cadderly feel jealousy toward his wonderful new friend, he vowed, and his sudden determination to save Shilmista was no less than that of any elf in the forest.

C

Kierkan Rufo wandered down the side of Daoine Dun, secure that no goblins would stray too near the enchanted mound that night. The elven celebration had meant little to him. Like King Galladel, he considered it a waste of time. All Rufo wanted was to be out of the forest and back to the security of the Edificant Library. He was never a warrior by choice, and had no intention of dying to save someone else's homeland.

He thought himself incredibly stupid then, for giving in to his guilt and offering, even begging, to go along with Cadderly.

"Greetings, Kierkan Rufo," said a raspy voice behind him.

Rufo spun to see a grotesque, dog-faced and bat-winged imp staring at him from a perch on a branch just a few feet away. Instinctively, the tall man backed away and looked for an escape route, but the imp stopped him short.

"If you try to flee or call out, I will kill you," the creature promised. It looped its barbed tail, dripping venom, over its shoulder in prominent display.

Rufo steadied himself and tried to appear unafraid. "Who are you?" he demanded. "And how do you know my name?"

"I am Druzil. A mutual friend once told me your name," the imp replied. "I never forget names, you see. They are so important in choosing future allies."

"Enough of your riddles!" snapped Rufo.

"As you wish," said the imp. "My mistress wishes to meet with you—to the benefit of both."

"The wizard that's taken the field against the elves?" Rufo reasoned. "If she wishes parley with—"

"She wishes to meet with you," Druzil interrupted, "and only you. If you do not agree, I am instructed to kill you, but you shall agree, shan't you? What have you to lose? My mistress will not harm you in any way, but the gains. . . ." He let the implication hang, a teasing glimmer in his rodentlike, black eyes.

"How do you know my name?" Rufo asked again, intrigued, but not yet convinced of anything.

"Meet with my mistress and find out," the imp replied. "Tomorrow night, soon after sunset, I will come for you. You need not pack, for you will be returned to the elves' camp long before dawn. Are we agreed?"

Rufo hesitated, looking at the poison-tipped tail. To his horror, Druzil gave a flap of leathery wings, and before Rufo could even react, landed upon his shoulder. Rufo nodded weakly, having little choice but to agree with the poisonous stinger so close to his exposed neck.

Druzil eyed him for a while then grabbed him by the front of his tunic and tossed out a threatening snarl. The imp locked Rufo's stare with his own, purposely keeping the man's gaze high.

"If you don't come along tomorrow, or if you tell anyone of this meeting, you will become my mistress's primary target," Druzil warned. "Do not doubt that she will see to your death before your friends can find her, Kierkan Rufo!" The imp laughed its wicked, rasping laugh then was gone, fading away to nothing.

Rufo stood there, alone on the trail, for some time. He considered going immediately to tell Elbereth and the others, to surround himself with the elven host, but Rufo feared magic-users and had no desire to cross an imp, a creature that no doubt had allies on the dreaded lower planes. The priest went to his cave instead of the elves' camp and tried to lose himself in sleep.

He twisted and turned on his blankets, never noticing the tiny amulet that Druzil had pinned to an inside fold of his tan tunic.

TEN

BETRAYED

The elves' camp was astir the next morning, the revitalized elves eager to engage their enemies. Cadderly, Danica, and Rufo tried their best to keep out of the way as the fair folk rushed about, resupplying their patrol groups with rope and arrows.

"I'm going with Elbereth on his hunt," Danica informed her two friends. "Wizards aren't as much of a threat to one of my training."

"You don't even know if Elbereth is going at all," Cadderly retorted. The elf prince and his father were engaged in a terrible argument, in the cave right in front of them.

"Elbereth will go, as he promised," remarked Shayleigh, who, looking much better than she had before *Daoine Teague Feer,* approached the trio. "Just as he went in to King Galladel to argue the value of last night's celebration. The whispers say the king was not pleased that Elbereth presided over *Daoine Teague Feer.*"

As if to accentuate the maiden's point, several loud

shouts echoed out of the cave. Shayleigh shook her head and walked away. She couldn't go out on patrol quite yet, but those tending her agreed that she would not be much longer in healing.

Cadderly considered the noise from the cave in light of Shayleigh's words. He knew Danica wouldn't listen to him. The monk was as headstrong as he.

"If you're going then so am I," the young scholar said.

Danica scowled at him. "You're not trained in stealth," she said. "You'll hinder us at least, even endanger us."

"Priests have measures to counter a wizard's powers," Kierkan Rufo reminded her.

Danica balked. "You intend to go as well?"

"Not I," Rufo assured her. "I didn't come here to do battle, and the elves will be better for it if I don't."

His admission did little to diminish Danica's scowl. Her continued dislike of the man was obvious.

"I will do what I must," said Cadderly. "By word of Dean Thobicus, I am the leader of our party. If you choose to go with Elbereth, I will not stop you, but I must go beside you."

"I am not of your order," she reminded Cadderly, "nor am I bound to the commands of your library's dean."

"To disobey Dean Thobicus could prevent you from ever returning there," Cadderly warned, "which would prevent you from resuming your studies of Penpahg D'Ahn."

Danica's glower intensified, but she gave no retort.

Elbereth came out of Galladel's chambers then, his face flushed with anger. He mellowed when he saw Danica and the others, and came straight over to join them.

"Your father is not pleased with you," Danica remarked.

"He never is," said Elbereth, managing a weak smile, "but we share respect, and do not doubt our love."

"Will you to join a patrol, then?" Danica asked.

"I will scout alone," the elf prince replied, looking to the dark forest spread below them. "I must find and destroy the wizard before more harm is done."

"You will not be alone," said Danica.

Elbereth understood her intent as soon as he looked into her brown, almond-shaped eyes. He did not appear pleased.

"Danica and I wish to go with you," Cadderly explained, and many expressions crossed Elbereth's face as he considered the unexpected request.

"I will not be riding," the prince said at length, "and I expect to pass far beyond the closest lines of goblins."

"More the reason to have companions," said Cadderly.

"Perhaps," the elf admitted, eyeing Danica more carefully. Elbereth certainly couldn't deny the young woman's value if it came to battle. "And none of my own People might be spared," he said, "but I can offer no g—"

"We need no guarantees," Cadderly assured him. "We understand the dangers." The young scholar flashed his boyish smile at Elbereth then to Danica. "Consider it repayment for *Daoine Teague Feer.*"

That thought touched Elbereth, and he soon agreed that the two could accompany him. He told them that an elf warrior would also leave for the Edificant Library, an emissary asking for aid, and that they or Rufo were welcome to go along with that elf if they so chose.

"You have heard our choice," Danica insisted.

"And . . . and I cannot go," Kierkan Rufo stammered, coming back over when he heard his name. "Back to the library, I mean."

Danica looked at the man curiously, thinking it would be more in Rufo's character to simply run away. Cadderly congratulated his fellow priest on his brave decision to remain in Shilmista. Danica was too suspicious to agree.

In truth, Rufo would have liked nothing better than to go back with the elf emissary, but he dared not miss a certain meeting he had arranged the previous night.

Q

"A wise decision," the imp said, again from behind, when Rufo came down from the hill shortly after sunset.

Rufo spun on him angrily. "You left me with little choice," he growled, his volume causing Druzil to look around nervously.

"Follow!" the imp commanded, thinking it prudent that they get as far from the enchanted hill as possible.

He led Rufo through the dark trees to the appointed meeting place with Dorigen. Rufo was obviously surprised to find a woman before him, a not-unattractive woman, though she was older than he and sported a severely crooked nose.

The wizard and Rufo stared at each other for a long while, neither moving to begin the conversation. Finally, Rufo could bear the suspense no longer.

"You called me out here," he protested.

Dorigen let her stare linger a bit longer, let Rufo shift uncomfortably from one foot to the other several times before offering any explanation.

"I need information," she eventually replied.

"You would ask me to betray my companions?" Rufo asked, trying to sound incredulous. "Perhaps I should go back—"

"Don't sound so surprised," Dorigen scolded. "You understood the purpose of this meeting before you ever agreed to it."

"I only agreed because I was left with no choice," Rufo argued.

"You are left with no choice again," Dorigen said. "Consider yourself my prisoner, if that might ease your pitiful conscience. I need information, Kierkan Rufo, he who aided Barjin. . . ."

Rufo's eyes widened in disbelief.

"Yes, I know who you are," Dorigen continued, apparently thinking she'd gained the upper hand. "You were Barjin's pawn, and so you shall be mine!"

"No!" Rufo roared, but when he turned to leave, he found himself facing Druzil's poison-tipped tail. The angular priest's bluster flew away in the blink of an eye.

"Do not be angry, dear man," Dorigen purred. "I have done you a favor, though you do not yet understand that. The forest is doomed, and so, too, are all who fight beside the elves."

"Then why do you need me?" Rufo asked.

"That does not concern the war," Dorigen replied. She paused for a moment to discern how she might explain without giving away too much. "Consider it a personal matter, between me and those who accompanied you to Shilmista."

"The elf prince?" Rufo asked.

"Perhaps," Dorigen answered slyly, thinking it best that Rufo be kept guessing. Not wanting to lose momentum, she pressed on again, her amber eyes flickering with growing delight. "It doesn't matter. I offer you survival, Kierkan Rufo. When I claim victory, your life will be spared. You might even find a place among my ranks of advisors."

Rufo appeared intrigued, but not convinced.

"And if the elves should somehow escape, and your friends along with them," Dorigen added, "then none will know of your deceit, and you will emerge with nothing lost."

"And if I refuse?"

"Must I go into the unpleasant details?" Dorigen replied, her voice so calm and even-toned that it sent shivers up Rufo's spine.

"Oh, I might not kill you now," Dorigen continued. "No, it would be a sweeter thing to see you dishonored for your aid of Barjin and he chaos curse, to lay public those deeds you committed in the library's cellar." Dorigen obviously enjoyed the way Rufo squirmed, and she gave Druzil an approving nod for supplying her with such valuable information.

"How do you know about that?" Rufo asked.

"I am not without my sources," Dorigen stated. "And do not think that your torment shall end with disgrace," she went on, her voice taking a distinctly malign edge. "After your humiliation has ebbed, I will have you killed . . . in time. Consider the life you will lead if you disappoint me now, Kierkan Rufo. Consider years of looking over your shoulder for assassins."

Rufo again shifted from foot to foot.

"And know that your grave will not be sanctified by the Edificant Library, for certainly your indiscretions with Barjin shall come out in full—and I will see to it that they are not easily forgotten—to dishonor you even in death."

The weight of the threat lay heavy on the guilt-ridden man, both because of the deadly imp just a few feet behind him and the fact that he was indeed vulnerable to the wizard's accusations.

"But let us not focus on such unpleasantness," Dorigen offered. "I require very little of you, and you may go on your way, secure that whatever the outcome of this war, you will be safe."

Rufo could hardly believe the words as they escaped his thin lips. "What do you wish to know?"

Q

Cadderly felt clumsy, crunching through the brush beside the stealthy Danica and Elbereth. He didn't regret his decision to accompany them, though, and neither of them gave more than a slight frown at the young scholar's loudest crackles.

They had passed several goblin and orc encampments, the creatures sleeping under the light of day, with the exception of a few bleary-eyed guards. Elbereth's planned destination was the same grove in which the wizard had appeared, where Ralmarith had been killed. The elf prince hoped he could pick up the villain's trail from there.

He never would have imagined that finding the wizard could be so easy.

They had believed their progress exceptional, for they had moved unhindered long after dusk. The forest grew quiet around them as they rested.

Too quiet.

Elbereth sat regarding his sword. "I had thought to bloody it before now," he whispered to the others. "I did not expect that the resistance would be so meager. Perhaps our enemies are not as many as we have been led to believe."

Cadderly had a sickening thought. "Or perhaps—" he began, but never got the chance to finish the sentence.

Elbereth, detecting movement in the thick brush to the west of their hasty camp, motioned for silence and crept away.

Danica, too, went on the alert, only she crouched low and turned toward the snap of a twig in the shadows to the east.

"I have a bad feeling. . . ." Cadderly remarked under his breath. He quickly loaded a dart on his crossbow and took up his spindle-disks in his other hand.

"Ogres!" cried Elbereth. Cadderly spun to see the elf engaged with two of the gigantic creatures.

Danica disappeared into the brush back to the east, forcing Cadderly's attention that way. He turned again just in time to see an ogre bearing down on him, a net held wide in its long arms. Ten ogre strides away, the monster lurched as Danica burst out of the brush and rammed her shoulder against the inside of the monster's knee.

Cadderly heard the crack of the huge bone, but the ogre remained standing, though dazed—until Danica came charging back in, leaped high in the air, and double-kicked it in the chest. It flew down into a patch of brambles.

Danica had no time to finish it off. A group of orogs appeared, and orcs beside them. Danica went into a fighting fury, spinning and kicking as the creatures flowed around her.

An orc was the first to get to Cadderly. The young scholar leveled his crossbow to blast it away, but wisely decided to hold that shot until sheer desperation forced it. As the orc came in slowly, measuring its enemy,

Cadderly set his spindle-disks spinning down to the length of their string.

Cadderly was not well-versed in the Orcish tongue, but had picked up a few words and phrases from his readings.

"Watch!" he said to the orc, trying to sound excited, and he sent the disks into a wide, looping circuit.

The orc did watch, almost mesmerized.

Cadderly snapped the disks back into his hand, continued his arm's circular motion to confuse the stupid monster, and waded ahead a long stride.

The orc's head went back up, expecting the disks to go flying up into the air.

Cadderly snapped them straight out instead, where they slammed under the orc's raised chin and into the creature's throat. The creature went down on its back, clutching at its crushed windpipe.

Cadderly had barely registered that the orc was down when he heard a rush behind him. He spun and fired his crossbow point blank into an orog that had charged in to tackle him. The dart hit the mark and exploded, but the heavy creature slammed into Cadderly anyway and bore him to the ground.

Cadderly struggled and thrashed for many moments before he realized that the orog's chest was blown wide open and that the creature was quite dead.

Q

Elbereth spent a long time parrying, keeping out of the huge ogres' tremendous reach and the paths of their monstrous clubs. For some reason, the monsters seemed to be only half-swinging, as though they didn't want to crush the elf completely.

Elbereth wasn't about to let them hit him in any case.

An orc sprang up from a bush to the side, just a couple of feet from Elbereth, and readied to throw a net. Elbereth was quicker, though, and his side-cut opened a gash in the monster's face and sent it tumbling.

The battle had begun in full behind the elf—he heard one of Cadderly's darts go off—and he knew that he could afford no more delays. He waited for the exact moment then charged between the ogres, slashing and sticking as he passed.

More harmful to the beasts, though, were their own clubs. They turned to swipe at the elf, but couldn't match his quickness and wound up slamming each other instead. One of the unfortunate ogres caught its companion's club in the head as it bent low to grab the elf. It spun two full circles before winding down to the ground.

Elbereth was back on the other before it could recover from the force of the clubbing and the shock of downing its companion. The elf leaped right up the creature's chest and drove his sword hard into its neck. The magical blade bent as it slipped into the thick hide, but its steel proved stronger than ogre flesh.

The doomed monster did manage to slap Elbereth from it before it died, sending the elf flying into the brush between two wide elms. Elbereth was not badly hurt, but he knew he was in trouble. He looked up to see the tree full of waiting orcs. He scrambled as the first of the monsters dropped on him.

Q

Danica met the monstrous charge head-on, though she feared straying too far from Cadderly, still back in the original camp, and Elbereth, all the way over to the other side. She kicked one orc in the throat and took another down with three quick punches to the face.

There were too many targets.

Danica blocked one orog club between crossed arms and quickly snapped her arms back out wide, tearing the weapon from the monster's grip. Her foot came straight up, catching the orog under the chin and launching it head-over-heels backward. Another orc rushed in from the side, and Danica, frantically turning, sent her foot flying out to meet it.

A club smashed into her back, blasting her breath away. Danica resisted the urge to fall and stubbornly turned to meet this newest orc attacker, but an ogre crashed out of the brush suddenly and locked its huge hand on her head, twisting her neck dangerously to the side.

Danica started to counter, but the orc's club hit her again then orogs grabbed her arms and pressed against her.

She thought her head would burst as the ogre's great hand clenched and twisted some more.

Q

Warm blood dripped over Cadderly's face and neck. By the time he was able to push his way out from under the dead orog, he was drenched with the gruesome stuff. He scrambled to his feet and loaded another dart.

A large group of orogs, orcs, and a single ogre approached from the east. Desperate, Cadderly didn't know who to shoot first. Then he saw the ogre's cargo: Danica, held firmly by the head, with two orogs loosely holding her arms. The ogre eyed Cadderly and gave a quick twist, and Danica's face contorted in pain.

"Enough!" roared an orc from behind the lead rank. The creature moved cautiously around its ogre companion. "Surrender or me ogre breakses the girl's neck!"

Cadderly wanted to swing his bow around and destroy the arrogant orc, but he couldn't deny Danica's predicament. He looked to his love helplessly. He thought of his ring and poisoned dart but dismissed the notion. He didn't even have his walking stick and doubted that the dosage on the tiny cat's claw would even affect the large ogre.

Then another thought came to him.

Danica eyed him curiously then flashed him a wistful smile, and Cadderly knew she understood.

Slowly, Cadderly lowered the crossbow toward the ground. It swung back up suddenly and the young scholar fired the dart into the ogre's shoulder. The ogre hardly flinched at the explosion, but Cadderly knew he had hurt the creature badly.

Q

Danica knew it, too, could tell from the way the monster's grip suddenly loosened. She dipped free, snapping her arms from her orog captors as she continued to drop. Her crouch brought her to the ground before she reversed her momentum and leaped straight up.

The stunned orogs stared dumbfounded as the powerful monk soared into the air, rising above them. They had only barely begun to react when Danica kicked out to the sides, each foot smashing an orog in the face and sending it flying away.

Danica hit the ground and whirled, punching straight out at her shoulder level, which was the same level as the wounded ogre's groin. The monster bellowed and went back on its heels, and ferocious Danica pounded it again.

"Stop them!" the orc to her side screeched. Another explosion sounded and the monster fell silent—several feet from where it had been standing.

Q

Cadderly wondered if their last ploy had been worth it as he watched Danica batter the ogre's midsection. Would death be preferable to capture at the hands of such vile monsters?

Orogs came at the young scholar slowly, fearing his deadly crossbow. Cadderly knew he was doomed, though he didn't even realize that Elbereth was no longer fighting and a host of orcs was rushing in from behind.

He felt a hot explosion as a club slammed against the back of his neck. His last sensation was the taste of dirt in his mouth.

ELEVEN

THE TROUBLE WITH TRAPS

The goblin kept its back pressed against the tree for a very long time, not even daring to breathe. A dozen of its companions lay dead, their lives snuffed out in the blink of an eye, it seemed. The frightened goblin heard the steadily diminishing screams of its only living companion, the terrified creature putting more and more distance between itself and the site of the massacre.

Finally, the remaining goblin mustered the courage to slip out from behind the tree. It peeked around the trunk's huge girth, and looked at its hacked and battered companions.

No sign of the murderous monsters.

The goblin crept out a bit farther and glanced all around.

Still nothing.

Still hugging the trunk, it moved around one more step.

"I knowed ye was there!" cried a yellow-bearded dwarf.

The goblin fell back and looked up to see a swiftly descending double-bladed axe.

Q

That business finished, the dwarf turned around to see how his brother was doing.

The last living goblin screamed, running full speed away from them, knowing that the dwarf with the nasty club was just a few steps behind.

"Oo oi!" the dwarf answered happily.

With another pitiful scream, the goblin made straight for a row of enormous bluetop trees, thinking it might find an escape route through the massive trunks and thick roots. It saw, then, a beautiful human female, tan-skinned and with green hair, beckoning it her way. The woman pointed to the side, revealing a tunnel leading right into one tree.

With no other options, the goblin asked no questions. It bent its gruesome head low, ran full speed, and hit the tree like a ram. The little creature bounced back two steps, perhaps still not understanding that the tunnel was no more than a dryad's illusion. Blood flowed from a dozen gashes on the goblin's face and chest. It nearly swooned, but stubbornly held its footing, stupid thing.

The dwarf, lowering a club that more resembled a tree trunk, never slowed. The club hit the goblin, and the goblin hit the tree again, with considerable weight behind it. That impact hurt less than the last, though, for the wretched creature was dead before it realized what had happened.

Pikel Bouldershoulder spent a moment considering the squashed object between his club and the great bluetop, honestly wondering how it once might have resembled a living goblin.

Then the dwarf looked over to Hammadeen and gave a resounding, "Oo oi!"

The dryad blushed in response and disappeared into the grove.

"Ye hit 'im hard," Pikel's brother, Ivan, remarked a bit later. The yellow-bearded dwarf held his great axe over his shoulder with an impaled goblin still stuck to one blade.

Pikel regarded it curiously and scratched at his green-dyed hair and beard. Unlike his brother, who tucked his long beard into his belt, Pikel pulled his back over his ears and braided it, along with his hair, down his back.

Ivan heaved the impaled goblin over his shoulder and let it fall in front of him. "Hit mine hard, too," he explained.

He put one foot on the dead monster's shoulder, spat into both of his gnarly, calloused hands, and clenched the axe handle tightly. Bone crackled as the dwarf tugged at the axe.

"Didn't want to wait and do this back there," he explained between grunts. "Thought ye might be needin' me help."

"Uh-uh," Pikel replied, shaking his head and looking to the spattered goblin still stuck against the tree.

Ivan finally wrenched his axe free. "Messy things," he remarked.

"Another battle mars the forest just a few miles west," came the melodic voice of Hammadeen.

Ivan shook his head in disbelief. "Always another battle!" he growled at the dryad then he looked at Pikel. "Bloody life, this druid thing."

"Doo-dad!" Pikel howled.

"We ain't found a day's quiet since we came to this stinking—" he glanced at Hammadeen and winced— "this pretty forest."

Pikel shrugged, offering no other explanation. Indeed, the dwarf brothers had discovered one fight after another since their arrival in Shilmista more than a tenday before. Not that they minded, given the nature of their opponents, but even Ivan was beginning to worry about the sheer number of goblinoids and giant-kin in the supposedly peaceful wood.

The dryad put her ear and gentle hands against the oak's rough bark, as though listening to the tree. "The fight is just ended," she announced.

"Elves win?" asked Ivan. "Not that I'm caring!" he quickly clarified. Ivan was not fond of elves. They were too fanciful and scatterbrained for his dwarven sensibilities.

"Eh?" Pikel prodded, nudging his brother hard in the arm as though he had just caught Ivan in a rare moment of compassion.

"They're a better lot than orcs," Ivan admitted, "but I've no heart for sharing a meal with either breed!"

Pikel joined in with his gruff chuckle, then they both turned on Hammadeen.

"Well, did they win?" Ivan asked again.

The dryad drew a blank and somewhat worried look, having no answers.

"Me guess's that we should go and see what we can do," Ivan said. "We got the one body away from them under the burned tree—even an elf deserves better than to be served up on a goblin's dinner table!"

When they finally reached the battlefield, Pikel

was the first to spot a victim: a slashed orc lying in a thick bush.

"Oo!" the dwarf squealed with delight when he got to the body and found four other orcs in similar states.

"Oo!" he howled even more enthusiastically when he spotted two dead ogres a few paces away, one with its throat pierced and the other with its head caved in.

"Someone did some fine fightin'," Ivan agreed, circling wide around the field. He saw a dead orc and a dead orog lying beside what looked to be a small campsite, but continued on around the camp to an area that apparently had seen even more action.

Two orogs lay dead, their heads twisted almost all the way around to the back, and several orcs and orogs were strewn about the ground a short distance from them. Ivan spent a while inspecting the creatures and their curious wounds. None had been slashed by sword or pierced by spear or arrow, and even the killing, crushing blows didn't resemble any mace or hammer marks the dwarf had ever seen. Also, the way the two orogs had died, their necks snapped in a strikingly similar fashion, hardly seemed the work of an elf.

Pikel's call turned his brother around. Pikel was in the campsite, holding high the head and chest of the dead orog and pointing to the creature's scorched wound. Only one weapon Ivan had ever seen could have caused that mark. He glanced back at the two dead orogs, an image of Danica suddenly coming to his mind.

"Wizard's work," Ivan offered hopefully, moving to join his brother. "Or . . ."

That last thought was answered soon enough as Pikel dropped the orog, leaped over to some brush, and produced a familiar ram's-head walking stick.

"Uh-oh," said Pikel.

"Dryad!" Ivan bellowed.

"Quiet would serve better in the dangerous forest," Hammadeen offered as she appeared from a tree behind the dwarf. She gave Ivan a wink and a wistful smile.

"None o' yer charming stuff!" the dwarf yelled at her, but even gruff Ivan mellowed when Hammadeen's disarming smile became a frown. "This is too important," Ivan explained. "Who fought the fight?"

The dryad shrugged.

"Well, ask yer trees!" roared the dwarf. "Was it elves or humans?"

Hammadeen turned around for just a moment then announced, "Both."

"Where'd they go?" Ivan asked, looking all around.

Hammadeen pointed to the northeast. Ivan and Pikel ran off at once, Ivan begging the dryad to lead them.

They were relieved when they caught up to the party and found Cadderly and Danica still alive, though badly beaten. Danica was held suspended from the ground by two ogres holding a large stick tied across her shoulders and along the back of her neck. The giant monsters showed the woman plenty of respect, keeping far from her, even though her arms and legs were securely bound. One of them limped badly, and the other was all scratched and bruised. The dwarves could easily guess that the ogres had found the misfortune of tangling with Danica back in the camp.

Cadderly came next, walking with his hands tied behind his back, a hood over his head, and four orogs surrounding him and prodding him every step. Last in line was an elf being dragged by a host of orcs, his ankles bound to a plank.

"Too many," Ivan muttered, and indeed, no fewer than twenty formidable monsters surrounded their helpless friends. He looked at his brother and smiled. "We need to set us a trap."

"Oo oi," Pikel agreed.

They ran off, circling far ahead of the caravan. Some time later, they stopped in a small clearing. Ivan glanced around and scratched at his beard.

He looked up a thick-limbed elm to a tumble of boulders a short distance away then back down the path to where the caravan would make its approach.

"If we can get a few of them rocks up the tree. . . ." the dwarf mused. His dark eyes sparkled, and he slammed his hands together twice in rapid succession. *"Thump! Thump!* And two less ogres to fight."

"Uh-oh," Pikel whispered, rolling his eyes around.

A chuckle from the boughs showed that the dryad saw the same disastrous possibilities as the doubting dwarf.

Ivan had no time to hear any protests. He pulled his brother along and together they managed to roll one large rock under the overhanging limb. Ivan scratched his yellow beard and considered how they might get the boulder up the tree, for at its lowest point, the branch was still eight or nine feet from the ground—and it was the lowest branch in the elm.

"Ye pick up the stone and get on me shoulders," Ivan said. "Stick it in the crook and we'll climb up and sort it out later."

Pikel eyed the stone and the branch with doubt, and shook his head.

"Do it!" Ivan commanded. "Ye wanna see Cadderly and Danica served up for ogre snacks?"

Grunting and groaning every inch, Pikel managed to heave the two-hundred-pound rock up to his chest. Ivan dropped his deer-horned helmet to the side, stepped up behind Pikel, and dipped his head between his brother's legs. The mighty dwarf heaved with all his might, finally bringing Pikel unsteadily into the air.

"Put it up! Put it up!" Ivan begged between grunts. In the wavering seat, Pikel couldn't hope to get the stone far enough from his body to clear the thick branch.

"I'll take a run at it," Ivan offered, seeing his brother's dilemma. He swerved back a few steps from the tree then charged ahead, hoping his momentum would aid Pikel.

Pikel heaved mightily, pushing the stone out to arm's length, then slammed into the branch. Oblivious to his brother's sudden dilemma, Ivan continued on, stretching poor Pikel to his limit. The rock went atop the branch and rolled over, dropping straight at Ivan's head.

"Oops!" came Pikel's warning. Ivan managed to get his arms up to deflect the bomb, but he went sprawling anyway, leaving Pikel hanging from the branch by his fingertips.

"Oooooo!" Pikel wailed, and he fell, his landing cushioned by Ivan's chest.

Unseen but not unheard, Hammadeen's titters didn't do much to improve Ivan's mood.

When they had recovered a few moments later, they next tried using their ropes to coax the boulder up. It slipped out of their noose a few times—until they got the hang of properly tying it—and bounced once off Ivan's foot. They nearly had it to the branch when the rope snapped.

Pikel wagged his head and looked nervously back down the path, thinking that their time was just about up.

"Ye're the druid!" Ivan growled at him. "Tell yer tree to bend down and pick the damned thing up!"

Pikel put his hands on his hips and scowled fiercely.

Ivan put his fist in Pikel's eye.

Pikel grabbed the hand and bit Ivan's knuckle.

They rolled around on the dirt, pinching, biting, kicking—whatever worked—until Ivan broke off, a grin of inspiration spread across his thick-skinned face.

"I get ye up the tree and toss ye the rock!" he beamed.

Pikel looked around then grinned, too.

Boosting Pikel up was not a problem, but the stubborn rock proved a different matter. As strong as he was, Ivan couldn't hope to heave the boulder high enough for Pikel to catch it. Growing as frustrated as his brother, Pikel turned around, hooked his stubby legs at the knees over the branch and reached down as far as he could.

The rock hit him square in the face and chest, but he managed to hold his precarious perch, though he had no idea of how he was going to right himself with the heavy stone.

Ivan called out support, urging his brother on. He realized—too late—that he had wandered directly under his brother.

Pikel had just about turned upright when his legs let go. Ivan managed a single desperate step before his brother and the boulder buried him.

Hammadeen's laughter echoed louder.

"That did it!" Ivan bellowed, hopping to his feet. He grabbed the stone and tried to pry it away from Pikel, who just lay there, saying "Oo," over and over and clutching the rock like it was some dwarf baby—and in truth it somewhat resembled one.

Then Ivan had the stone. He charged the tree and hurled it at where the limb met the trunk. It bounced off, but Ivan scooped it back up and heaved it again, and again, and again after that.

Pikel just sat in the dirt, watching his brother in disbelief.

Then, amazingly, the stone wedged into the crook and held, and Ivan turned around triumphantly.

"They'll get here soon," he observed, gathering the rope. "No time for another rock."

"Phew," Pikel remarked under his breath.

They looped the rope over the branch and started up, one on either side. Pikel, less armored and less heavily supply-laden than his brother, gained a quick advantage then put his sandal on Ivan's shoulder—waggled his smelly toes in his brother's face—and pushed off. His momentum carried him the rest of the way, and he pulled himself over and sat up, forgetting to keep his weight on the rope. He watched, mesmerized, as it flew by, and Ivan plummeted back to the dirt.

The yellow-bearded dwarf sat up, spitting twigs and pebbles and scolding himself for not knowing better.

"Oops," Pikel offered.

"Tie off the rope!" Ivan growled.

Pikel considered the task and the consequences of letting his angry brother get near him then shook his head.

"Tie it off!" Ivan roared. "Or I'll cut the tree down!"

He picked up his axe and took a stride toward the thick trunk before Hammadeen appeared between him and his target.

"Do not do that," the dryad warned.

Of more concern to Ivan was his brother, the would-be druid, who had slid down the branch near the crook and the heavy rock's precarious perch. Ivan had no doubt that if he went to chop at the tree, Pikel would drop the stone on his head.

Ivan crossed his burly arms in front of his chest and stood staring up at Pikel. Finally, the seated dwarf relented and tied off the rope, motioning for his brother to climb up. Soon then they sat together on the branch, Ivan impatient and uncomfortable, but Pikel, thinking his perch very druidlike, quite content.

"What are ye laughing about now?" Ivan demanded of the pesky dryad some time later. Hammadeen appeared on a branch above them, pointing to the north.

"The ogres did not come this way," she said.

Sure enough, peering through the trees, Ivan and Pikel could just make out the distant commotion of the prisoner caravan, some distance north and moving away.

Pikel looked to Ivan, then to the rock, then back to Ivan, a sour expression on his cherubic face.

"Shut—" Ivan started, but he stopped, noticing some movement in the not-too-distant brush.

A moment later he made out an orc, foraging through the trees, cutting pieces of kindling with a long knife. Ivan considered the creature's path and realized it would pass not too far from the trap.

"Get it over here," he whispered to Pikel.

His brother squeaked and poked a finger into his own chest.

"Yeah, yerself!" Ivan whispered harshly, and he slapped Pikel on the back of his head, dislodging him from the branch.

"Oooooo!" Pikel wailed before hitting the ground with a thud.

Ivan paid his brother no heed. He was more concerned with the orc, who had noticed the noise. The creature crept in slowly, knife held ready.

Pikel rolled around for a moment then glared up at Ivan, but kept enough wits to move to the clearing's far side. He turned his back to the approaching orc, put his hands in his pockets, and began to whistle nonchalantly.

The orc slipped up to the tree trunk, oblivious of Ivan holding the rock above its head. One step out, then two, then it broke into a run.

Then it was dead.

Ivan looped the rope and swung down. He slammed a heavy boot atop his squashed victim, pounding a hand triumphantly against his barrel-like chest. "I telled ye it would work!" he proclaimed.

Pikel looked at the crushed orc then up at the branch, an amused expression splayed across his face. Ivan knew what his brother was thinking: that it would have been much easier just to walk over and put an axe through the orc's thick head.

"Don't ye say a word!" Ivan growled. Fortunately, Pikel never had trouble following that particular command.

"I think we can get the rock back in place," Ivan started, looking back to the crook. "If I can—"

Pikel ran him down, and the fight was on. Quite unknown to the wrestling dwarves, another orc was nearby, collecting wood. It came to the clearing, noticed its squashed companion, and considered the titanic struggle. It looked at its meager knife then shrugged and moved along, thinking that some sights were better forgotten.

TWELVE

UNDER GUARD

"adderly." The word came from a great distance, from beyond the edge of the young scholar's consciousness. "Cadderly," it came again, more insistent.

Cadderly strained to open his eyes. He recognized the voice, and he recognized the caring eyes he found himself looking into, rich brown and exotic. Still, it took him a while to remember the woman's name.

"Danica?"

"I feared you would never awaken," Danica replied. "That bruise on your neck is wicked indeed."

Cadderly didn't doubt that. Even the slightest shift of his head hurt him. He gradually came back to consciousness, to see that they were in a tent fashioned from animal skins. Cadderly's hands were tightly bound behind his back and Danica's behind hers. Danica sat with Cadderly's head and shoulders gently propped on her lap. No guards were in sight, but Cadderly heard the guttural grunts of orcs and orogs outside, and that noise led him to recall the battle, and the last desperate act in which he had blasted the ogre's shoulder.

"They didn't kill us?" he asked, confused.

He wriggled his hands around and could feel that he still wore his feathered ring.

Danica shook her head. "They were under orders not to, I must assume—strict orders," she replied. "The orc that struck you was punished by the orogs for hitting you so hard. They all feared you would die."

Cadderly considered that news for a moment, but couldn't understand why it would be so.

"Elbereth?" he asked, panic coloring his voice.

Danica looked beyond the young scholar, to the back of the tent. With some effort, Cadderly managed to shift around for a glance as well. Elbereth, the elf prince, seemed far removed from royalty at that moment. Dirty and bloodstained, he sat with his head down, his arms tied to his knees. One eye was bruised so badly it wouldn't open.

He must have sensed the stares and looked up.

"I caused our capture," he admitted, his choked voice barely more than a whisper. "It was I they sought, an elf prince to ransom."

"You cannot know that," Danica offered, trying to comfort the distraught elf.

There was little conviction in the young woman's voice, though. Elbereth's guess seemed logical. The elf put his head back down and did not answer.

"Orogs. . . ." Cadderly muttered, trying to jog his memory.

He had read several passages concerning the brutes and searched his memory for answers. A prince's ransom made some sense, but what of he and Danica? Had they, perhaps, been taken prisoner to be sacrificed in some horrible ritual? Were they to be the meat of an orog's dinner? Neither explanation offered much solace, and Cadderly nearly jumped upright when the flap of the tent was thrown aside.

It was no orog that walked in from the dusky light, but a man, great and tall, bronze-skinned and golden-haired. A tattoo of some strange creature was centered on his forehead, between his ice-blue, piercing eyes.

Cadderly studied him intently, thinking that the tattoo—Cadderly recognized it as a remorhaz, a polar worm—should tell him something.

The huge man walked over to Danica and gave a leer that sent shivers through her spine and evoked silent rage in Cadderly. Then, casually, with the slightest flick of his muscled arm, he tossed the young woman aside. With one hand and similar ease, he grabbed the front of Cadderly's tunic and hoisted the young scholar to his feet.

"White Worm," Cadderly muttered, unconsciously thinking aloud, the words brought on by the man's sheer size. He was nearly a foot taller than Cadderly's six feet, and easily a hundred pounds heavier, though there wasn't a bit of softness on his mighty frame.

The bronze-skinned giant's frown quickly became a threatening scowl aimed at Cadderly. "What do you know of the White Worm?" he demanded, his voice edged by the hint of an accent from a distant land.

It was Cadderly's turn to frown. The big man's command of the language seemed too smooth and unaccented for the young scholar's budding theory to be correct. Also, the man's clothes were richly made, of silk and other fine materials, cut as a king might wear them, or a servant of a king's court. The man seemed quite comfortable in them—too comfortable, Cadderly noted, for a barbarian.

"What do you know?" the man demanded, and he lifted Cadderly from the floor again with one gigantic hand.

"The painting on your forehead," Cadderly gasped. "It's a remorhaz, a white worm, an uncommon beast, even in the northern reaches, and known not at all among the Snowflake Mountains and the Shining Plains."

The large man's scowl did not relent. He eyed Cadderly for some time, as if waiting for the young priest to elaborate on his explanation.

There came a rustle from the door, and the giant promptly lowered Cadderly to the floor. In walked a black-haired woman, a wizard, judging from the robes she wore. She reminded Cadderly somewhat of a younger Pertelope, except that her eyes were dots of amber, not hazel, and she wore her hair longer and less tended than the neatly groomed Pertelope. And while Pertelope's nose was arrow straight, the wizard's had obviously been broken and forever bent to the side.

"Welcome, dear Cadderly," the wizard said, her words drawing surprised looks from both Cadderly and Danica. Even Elbereth looked up. "Have you enjoyed your visit to Shilmista? I know Kierkan Rufo longs for home."

Danica sucked in her breath at the mention of Rufo. Cadderly turned to her, anticipating her anger and trying to diffuse it for the time being.

"Yes, I know your name, young priest of the Edificant Library," the woman continued, reveling in her superior position. "You will come to understand that I know many things."

"Then you have me at a disadvantage," Cadderly dared to remark, "for I know nothing of you."

"Nothing?" The woman chuckled. "If you knew nothing of me then surely you would not have come out to kill me."

Cadderly and Danica could not manage to stifle gasps, their astonishment plain on their faces.

Cadderly heard Danica mutter, "Rufo."

"I do not wish to die, you must understand," the wizard said sarcastically.

Not as Barjin died, rang a voice inside Cadderly's head. He glanced around at Danica then realized that the words had come to him telepathically. The unexpected connection to the slain priest brought a thousand questions rushing through Cadderly's thoughts. He settled them quickly, though, asking himself if someone, or something, had actually communicated with him, or if that inner voice had been his own, reasonably placing the wizard in the same conspiracy as the slain priest.

Cadderly looked the wizard over, up and down. Her dress was unremarkable enough, certainly not as ornamented as Barjin's clerical robes had been. The young scholar strained his neck, trying to get a better view of the wizard's rings. She wore three, and one of them appeared to hold an insignia.

The wizard smiled at him, drawing his eyes to hers, then pointedly slipped her hands into her pockets.

"Always curious," she mumbled, but loud enough so Cadderly could hear. "So similar to that other one."

The way she spoke surprised Cadderly.

"Yes, young priest," the woman continued, "you will prove a valuable well of information."

Cadderly wanted to spit on her foot—he knew that his dwarf friend Ivan would have without a second thought—but he couldn't muster the courage. His sour expression revealed his feelings, though.

That disdainful, uncompromising expression gave way to despair when the wizard took her hand back out of her deep pocket. She held something, something terrible by Cadderly's estimation.

She leveled Cadderly's deadly crossbow, cocked and loaded with an explosive dart, at Danica. Cadderly didn't breathe for what seemed like days.

"You will do as I command you," the wizard said, glaring at Cadderly, her visage suddenly icy and removed. "Say it!"

Cadderly couldn't say anything past the lump in his throat.

"Say it!" the wizard cried, jerking the crossbow Danica's way. For a heartbeat Cadderly thought she had pulled the trigger, and he nearly fainted away.

"I will do as you command!" he cried as soon as he realized that the bow hadn't fired.

"No!" Danica shouted at him.

"A well of information," the wizard said again, her lips turning up in a comfortable smile. She turned to her bronze-skinned soldier. "Take him."

Stubborn Danica was up in a flash, cutting between Cadderly and the huge man. She tugged at her ropes, but was unable to get her hands free and settled instead for kicking.

The big man's agility and quick reactions surprised the monk. He was down in a crouch even as Danica's foot flew up, and he caught her leg cleanly. A subtle twist of his powerful arms sent Danica off balance, gritting her teeth in pain. The huge man tossed her aside, again with no more than a casual flick of his hands.

"Enough!" the wizard commanded. "Do not kill her."

She gave Cadderly an awful smile and said, "Fear not, young priest, I will not kill those who allow me to control you like a puppet. Ah, to have my prize, and an elf prince thrown into the package by sheer chance! Yes, I know of you, too, Elbereth, and do not doubt that you shall be reunited with your 'People' soon. You are much too dangerous a prisoner for me to keep." The wizard snickered again and added, "Or at least, your head will soon be reunited with your father."

Her words renewed Elbereth's futile struggling with his tight bonds. The wizard laughed aloud, mocking him. "Take him!" she said again to the warrior, indicating Cadderly.

The huge man grabbed Cadderly quickly, before Danica could react, and wrapped him in a tight headlock, the great man's other hand waving ready in case the fiery woman decided to come back for more.

"Stay back!" Cadderly called out meekly, and Danica did, for she saw that the warrior could snap Cadderly's neck with ease.

"Stay back," the huge man echoed. "Come only when you are summoned." The manner in which he spoke, through a lascivious grin, renewed the shivers along the young woman's spine.

Behind the huge man, the wizard frowned, and both Cadderly and Danica were quick to understand the jealousy behind that look.

At the wizard's snapping command, two orogs took up positions inside the tent as she and her giant lackey departed with Cadderly in tow.

The camp itself struck Cadderly as out of place from the moment he was half-dragged, half-carried outside. Even in the fading daylight he could see that beautiful Shilmista had been scarred and torn, with trees that had lived a hundred years ripped down and broken apart. It was an odd feeling for the young scholar, something he hadn't expected. He himself had used firewood back at the Edificant Library, had plucked a flower from the roadside to give to Danica without a second thought. But there was a majesty about Shilmista that Cadderly had never known, a raw and natural beauty that even the print of a boot seemed to mar.

Watching filthy orogs and orcs milling about the forest pained Cadderly's heart. He recognized many of the creatures, mostly from wounds—such as the limp one ogre exhibited and the heavy bandage on its shoulder. The monster noticed Cadderly, too, and its scowl promised death if the thing ever got its hands on the young scholar.

The wizard's tent was on the far side of the camp. While on the outside it seemed a normal animal skin canopy, the inside revealed that the wizard enjoyed her niceties. Plush cloth covered the one table and the four chairs around it. The bed was thick and soft—no blanket on the ground for her—and a silver serving set was perched upon a cart off to the side.

The bronze giant roughly sat Cadderly in one of the chairs.

"You may leave us, Tiennek," the wizard said, taking a seat opposite the young scholar.

Tiennek didn't seem overly pleased by that idea. He scowled at Cadderly and made no move toward the flap.

"Oh, be gone!" his mistress scolded, waving her hand. "Do you believe I cannot protect myself from the likes of this one?"

Tiennek bent close to Cadderly and issued a threatening growl then bowed low to his lady and departed.

Cadderly shifted in his seat, letting the wizard know that his bindings were uncomfortable. The time had come for him to take command of his own situation, he decided, to let his enemy understand that he was not some coward she could do with as she pleased. Cadderly wasn't certain he could hold up that facade, especially not with Danica and Elbereth's lives hanging so tenuously before him. But that facade, he realized, might be the only thing that kept them all alive.

The wizard considered him for a long while then muttered some words under her breath. Cadderly felt the ties around his wrists being undone, and soon his aching arms were free.

His first thought centered on his feathered ring. If he could manage to get the cat's claw out and stick the wizard. . . .

Cadderly dismissed that notion. He didn't even know if the drow sleep poison was still active. If he made his attempt and failed, he had no doubt that the wizard would punish him severely—or, more likely, punish his helpless friends.

"He is cultured beyond what one would expect from a barbarian," the young scholar said, thinking to catch the wizard off her guard.

The wizard's chuckle mocked him. "Deductive, as I expected," she said, more to herself than to Cadderly. Again her tone gave Cadderly pause.

"The, uh . . . The marking on his forehead, I mean,"

Cadderly stammered, trying to regain his composure. "Tiennek is of the White Worm Tribe, the barbarians who live under the shadows of the Great Glacier."

"Is he?" the wizard purred, leaning forward in her chair, as if to better hear Cadderly's startling revelations.

Cadderly realized that it was useless to continue.

The wizard fell back comfortably in her seat. "You are correct, young priest," she said. "Amazingly so. Few from the Heartlands would recognize the remorhaz at all, let alone connect the marking to an obscure barbarian tribe that never ventures south of the Galena Mountains. I congratulate you as you have congratulated me."

Cadderly's eyebrows rolled up with curiosity.

"Tiennek's mannerisms are indeed an aberration," the wizard explained, "far from what one would expect from the savage warriors of the White Worm."

"You taught him that culture," Cadderly added.

"It was necessary if he was to properly serve me," the wizard explained.

The casual conversation put Cadderly at ease enough to offer a prompt. "Does he properly serve his lady . . . ?"

"Dorigen," the wizard said. "I am Dorigen Kel Lamond."

"Of?"

Again came that mocking chuckle. "Yes, you are inquisitive," she said, her excitement mounting. "But I have dealt far too long with one too much like you for your words to entangle me." She calmed, putting the conversation back into a casual air. "So many things have happened so quickly, and Cadderly Bo—" Dorigen paused and smiled, seeing his reaction. It was true,

Dorigen realized, the young priest did not know his heritage, or even his family name.

"You will pardon me," Dorigen went on. "For all my knowledge, I fear I know not your surname."

Cadderly slumped back, knowing Dorigen had lied to him. What was the significance of that single syllable the wizard had uttered? he wondered. Did Dorigen know of his parentage? Determinedly, Cadderly resolved not to play her mocking game. To do so would put Dorigen in an even higher position of authority, something he and his friends could not afford.

"Cadderly of Carradoon," he answered curtly. "That is all."

"Is it?" Dorigen teased, and Cadderly had to concentrate hard to hide his interest.

Dorigen broke the ensuing silence with a heartfelt laugh. "Let me answer some of your questions, young priest," she said, and she tapped her shoulder, or rather, she tapped something invisible that was perched upon her shoulder.

Druzil, the imp, faded into view.

So they were connected! Cadderly realized, recognizing the imp, the same imp who had poisoned Pikel back in the library's catacombs. There could be no doubt. Barjin and Dorigen had come from the same place, the same enigmatic cabal. Cadderly understood then that the silent voice he had heard back in the other tent was the imp's. He looked to Dorigen's delicate hand and the signet ring, recognizing it at least, when he realized what should be upon it: The trident and bottle design, the variation of Talona's holy symbol that had so quickly become a mark of disaster to the library.

"Greetings again, young priest," the imp said in his raspy voice. Druzil's forked tongue flicked, lizardlike, between his pointed yellow teeth, and he leered at Cadderly as an ogre might stare at a piece of roasting mutton. "You have been well, I presume?"

Cadderly didn't blink, refused to show any weakness. "And you have recovered from your flight into a wall?" he replied.

Druzil growled and disappeared from view.

Dorigen laughed again. "Very fine," she congratulated Cadderly. "Druzil usually is not so easily intimidated."

Still Cadderly didn't blink. He felt an intrusion in his mind, an empathic bond he knew was coming from the imp.

"Let him in," Dorigen instructed. "He challenges you. Do you fear to learn who is the stronger?"

Cadderly didn't understand, but still determined not to reveal any weakness, he closed his eyes and lowered his mental defenses.

He heard Dorigen chanting softly, heard Druzil snicker, then felt the energy of a magical spell fall over him. His mind became a tangible blackness, as though he had been mentally transported to an empty place. Then a light, a glowing and sparkling orb, appeared in the distance, floating toward him.

His mind watched the orb curiously as it neared, not understanding the danger. Then it was upon him, a part of his thoughts, burning him like a flame. A thousand fiery explosions went off inside his brain, a thousand searing blasts of agony.

Cadderly grimaced, thrashed in his seat, and opened his eyes. Through a dark cloud he saw the wizard, and

IN SYLVAN SHADOWS

the imp, seated, smiling, on her shoulder. The pain intensified, and Cadderly cried out and feared he would fall unconscious—or dead, and he almost wished he would.

He closed his eyes again, and tried to concentrate and find some way to relieve the agony.

"Push it away," came a distant voice that Cadderly recognized as Dorigen's. "Use your will, young priest, and push the fire away."

Cadderly heard her and understood her words, but he could hardly find his focus through the pain. He took a deep breath and slammed his fists on the table before him, determined to distract himself from the ball of fiery light.

Still it burned. He heard Druzil snicker.

Cadderly mentally reached for his meditation techniques, tried to blot out the light as he could blot out the material world, bit by bit.

It would not go away. Druzil snickered again.

Anger replaced the vacuum of meditation, destroyed any serenity the young scholar had managed to create. The light became his enemy, and he convinced himself that it would turn on Danica after it devoured him.

"No!" Cadderly growled, and suddenly the ball was moving away, out of the void he had entered. It wavered for many moments then slipped beyond Cadderly's awareness. The pain was no more, and Druzil no longer snickered.

Cadderly realized that there was another void, another hole of blackness beyond his own, and he knew instinctively that it belonged to the imp, to the one who had forced the pain upon him. His anger did not relent, and the ball of sparkling light moved toward the other blackness.

"Enough!" he heard Druzil cry, to which Dorigen merely laughed.

Cadderly forced the orb into Druzil's thoughts. The imp squealed out, and that only prompted Cadderly on. He would show no mercy. He would hold the fire in Druzil's mind until it burned the imp away to nothing!

Then it was over, abruptly, and Cadderly found himself seated at a table opposite Dorigen and Druzil, the imp reeling, his bulbous eyes promising death to the young scholar.

"Excellent!" Dorigen cried, clapping her hands together. "You are powerful indeed if you can defeat Druzil, who is practiced in the game. Perhaps even more powerful than your—" She stopped and tossed Cadderly a teasing stare. "You will do well beside me."

Again the young scholar would not play along. "I do not serve Talona," he announced, and it was Dorigen's turn to try to hide her surprise. "I never shall, whatever the price."

"We shall see," Dorigen replied after a short pause. "Tiennek!"

The barbarian was upon Cadderly in an instant, fiercely tugging his arms behind his back and retying his hands so tightly that the cords cut into his wrists. The young scholar was hoisted into the air and carried away.

Cadderly struggled to sit up when the barbarian dropped him back in his tent. Tiennek offered one more leer Danica's way before he departed.

"What happened to you?" Danica asked when the barbarian was gone. She shuffled over to Cadderly, resting her head against his.

Cadderly, still overwhelmed and with too many questions whirling about in his thoughts, did not answer.

Danica sent a concerned look Elbereth's way.

"Alas, for my studies," the woman lamented.

Cadderly looked at her in disbelief.

"Physical suspension," Danica explained. "If I could achieve that state, slow my heart so that its beating could not be detected. . . ."

Cadderly's incredulous stare did not diminish.

"But I cannot," Danica said, lowering her eyes. "That feat is beyond me."

Her declaration rang ominously for the prisoners, a general sound of doom. Cadderly, too, allowed his head to bow.

"I shall kill that wizard," Cadderly heard the elf vow.

"And I, her giant lackey," Danica added, a ring of determination returning to her voice. That thought did little to comfort Cadderly, though, given his new insight concerning Tiennek.

"He is of the White Worm," Cadderly said, turning to Danica.

She shrugged. The words meant nothing to her.

"A barbarian tribe of the North," Cadderly explained. "Savage, living—surviving—in brutal conditions. And Tiennek—that is his name—is of Kura-winther, their elite warriors, unless I am mistaken."

Danica looked at him curiously, and he realized that his words still meant little to her.

"Fear him," Cadderly said grimly. "Do not underestimate his prowess. Kura-winther . . ." he said again, closing his eyes to recall all he had read of the White Worm Tribe. "To get the marking upon his forehead,

Tiennek would have had to kill a polar worm, a remorhaz, single-handedly. He is an elite warrior of a tribe of warriors." Cadderly's expression, sincerely terrified, unnerved Danica more than any words ever could.

"Fear him," Cadderly said again.

Q

"There's the camp," Ivan whispered to Pikel, "though I'm not fond of fighting orc-types in a dark, foresty kinda night."

Pikel wagged his head in agreement. Dwarves were more accustomed to the blackness of a deep cave, a much different situation than the starlit forest.

"We could get after them just afore the dawn," Ivan offered, talking as much to himself as to his brother. "Yeah, that'd do fine. But there's too many. We can't just go walking into them. We're needing a plan."

"Uh-oh."

Ivan glared at his doubting brother, but his expression lightened considerably when a thought came to him. He pulled his deer-antler helm from his head, fished a small hammer from one impossibly deep pocket, and began chipping away at the lacquer holding one of the antlers firmly in place.

Pikel wagged his head fearfully and tried not to watch.

Ivan had done well in making the helmet, and it was a long time before he had the lacquer cleared enough to unscrew the antler, and even then, he had to fight with the firm hold of his own setting. He got it free, finally, and handed it to Pikel, putting the now-lopsided helmet back in place on his hairy head.

"When we go, ye hold it up atop ye and keep close by me," Ivan instructed.

Pikel prudently waited for Ivan to take up a more distant spying position before uttering "Uh-oh" again.

Somewhere unseen in the shadows of the trees behind him, Hammadeen tittered.

THIRTEEN

It was a dreamless sleep, where sheer exhaustion over-ruled the tumult of Cadderly's emotions. That deep slumber made it all the more shocking to the young scholar when Danica's cry shattered his serenity.

Cadderly jerked to a sitting position and made out a hulking form bending over Danica. He knew at once that it was Tiennek who'd come calling, and he prayed that the barbarian hadn't been in the tent very long.

Cadderly started toward his love, but found his wrists roughly grabbed and jerked painfully high behind him.

"If she fights, break the priest's arms," Tiennek said, and Danica, with one look Cadderly's way, stopped her struggling.

Tiennek heaved the young woman over his shoulder and started out, flanked by two orogs. The third beast, giving one final, painful tug on Cadderly's arms, soon moved to follow. Cadderly stood up behind the orog, but the beast spun and smacked him to the floor.

The world became a blur of pain and irresolvable confusion. Cadderly noticed Elbereth, still seated at the back of the tent, struggling fiercely but futilely. The elf's wrists were bound so tightly around his knees that he could not even begin to stand.

Growling, on the very edge of control, Cadderly started up, but the orog kicked him in the ribs and sent him crashing down again. He looked around, at his feathered ring, a cask on the side of the room, Elbereth, but had no recourse. Danica was gone, and in peril, and Cadderly had no way to fight back.

"No!" he snarled, drawing another kick from the orog. "No! *No!*" Like a man gone mad, Cadderly repeated the word, ignoring the outraged orog's kicks.

"No! No! No!" But for all Cadderly's stubbornness and anger, his words rang hollow, a puny retaliation.

Q

Danica didn't bother struggling atop Tiennek's huge shoulder. She would bide her time, wait for an opportunity when she would have the bronze-skinned man alone—at least she hoped she would have Tiennek alone.

Tiennek's obvious intentions revolted her, but the thought that orogs would be present was too much for her to bear.

Tiennek's tent was the third largest in the encampment, centered at the back side of the camp and doubling as a warehouse for the enemy troupe. The blond-haired barbarian, to Danica's profound relief, told his flanking orogs to remain on guard outside then pushed his way past stacked barrels and boxes to a pile of blankets and furs in the center of the room. An oil lamp burned low in one corner, and the smell of meat was strong in the air.

Tiennek lowered Danica to her feet, more gently than the young woman expected. He stared into her almond eyes and stroked her strawberry blond hair.

Play along, Danica told herself, against every instinct in her body.

"Untie me," she whispered to her huge captor. "It will be better for both of us."

Tiennek's huge hand slid over Danica's smooth cheek, barely touching her, but sending shivers through her in spite of her revulsion.

"Untie me," she whispered again.

Tiennek laughed at her. His gentle touch became an iron grasp on her face, nearly snapping her jaw apart. Danica jerked back from him, got free for an instant, but was then pulled back, and the barbarian tugged at a clump of her thick hair.

"You think me a foo—" He stopped abruptly as Danica's knee slammed into his groin. She'd had to hop off the ground to even reach her target.

Tiennek grimaced for just a moment then flung Danica backward. She managed to keep her balance and snapped a kick into the man's rock-hard belly as he stalked her.

Tiennek, his face locked in a murderous stare, didn't seemed to notice the kick, but Danica could tell from his slight limp that her first attack had done some damage.

Danica went for his knee, but she had to stop and dodge instead as Tiennek launched a heavy punch for her face. She was able to duck aside, awkwardly, but the agile barbarian's second hand came in more quickly, clipping her on the cheek.

The tent spun, and Danica was down to her knees. Tiennek had her and could do as he pleased with her, she knew. There was nothing she could do against such a mighty warrior with her hands bound behind her back. Danica tugged at her cords, ignoring the burn of rough rope on her wrists, and savagely fought to free herself.

Many moments passed, and Danica could feel warm blood on her hands. Why hadn't Tiennek continued his assault?

Danica dared to look over her shoulder, to see the giant limping away. That initial knee strike she had launched against him had apparently changed his lewd intentions, for the time being, at least.

The barbarian called a huge orog into the tent and gave it orders to watch Danica, but not to touch her unless she tried to escape. If she did, Tiennek explained, looking pointedly at Danica as he spoke, the orog could do whatever it wanted with her.

Tiennek eyed Danica slyly. "Give me your weapons," he commanded the orog. The creature balked and put a hand defensively over its sword.

"Give them!" Tiennek growled. "That one will take them from you and kill you with them, do not doubt." The orog continued to snarl, but it handed over its sword and the long dagger from its boot.

Then the bronze-skinned man was gone, and the orog cautiously stalked over to stand beside Danica, its breathing coming in short, hopeful gasps. "Make a break, pretty one," it whispered under its stinking breath, thinking that his guard duty might turn out to include a bit of unexpected fun.

"Could you help me to my feet?" Danica asked after some time. She suspected that Tiennek would return before dawn, before his mistress realized what had happened, and knew that sunrise was not too far away.

The orog reached down and grabbed her by the hair, pulling her roughly to a standing position. "Ye likes that better?" it growled, again putting its stinking breath in Danica's face.

Danica nodded and told herself that she must act then, or never. She hoped she had loosened her bindings enough, prayed that she had, for the consequences of failure were too wretched for her to even imagine.

The young woman called upon all her discipline in that critical moment, mustering her courage. She dropped toward the floor, feigned that she was falling. The orog instinctively started down to catch her, but Danica's legs coiled under her and she sprang past the surprised beast. She bent her knees up to her chest and whipped her bound hands down under her feet. Even as she descended, she launched her first attack, snapping one leg out straight to drive her foot under the orog's chin.

The creature gasped and fell back. Danica was standing again, still bound, but with her hands were in front of her. The orog, stunned but barely hurt, whooped and charged back in. Danica slowed it considerably with a straight kick to the chest and another to the knee. She clenched her hands together and smacked the monster across the face, twice. Growling with every movement, her motions became a blur—kicking, kneeing, punching—and the orog could only hold its arms across its face and try to cover up.

The vicious attack abruptly ceased and the orog moved, just as Danica had expected, to the offensive. The creature lunged awkwardly for her, but caught only air as Danica took a quick step back. Before the overbalanced monster could recover, Danica attacked. She dived right over the orog's shoulder, turning a somersault as she went and hooking her bindings around the monster's thick neck.

The orog bent backward under the brutal pull; a man's neck would have snapped under the great strain. Danica realized quickly that she couldn't hope to hold on long enough to choke such a thick-skinned, hard-muscled monster. Already the orog had begun to recover and had grabbed at Danica's wrists, tugging and loosening the choking cords from around its neck.

Danica saw her chance slipping away. She scanned the orog, but found no weapons. She scanned the room, but nothing presented itself as a club or knife. Then a desperate plan came to her. She reversed her grip, going along with the orog's pull and turning to face the creature as it tugged. Predictably, the orog swung around.

Danica caught its lumbering swing and yanked it along then dropped and twisted, flipping the orog over her. Danica dived with it, guiding its descent, plopping it head-down in an open water barrel. The monster disappeared up to its waist and Danica jumped atop it, threw one leg between its flailing legs and hung on for all her life.

The creature was much stronger than she, but Danica called upon powers that the orog couldn't begin to understand. She locked her legs inside the rim of the barrel and clamped her hands vicelike on its rim for further support. The orog's hands came up over the lip and it pulled mightily, but Danica held her position, using her stiffened legs as a wedge to prevent her from being dislodged.

The monster's thrashing battered and bruised her, but she reminded herself that it would not last long.

Still, it seemed like a day passed to the weary, beaten woman as the orog fought wildly, trying to get its head up above the water. A knee bloodied her nose, a foot scraped across the side of her head so wickedly that Danica had to wonder if her ear had been torn off.

Then it stopped.

Almost surprised, Danica held her seat for many moments longer, just to make sure. When she realized that Tiennek might soon return, and she crawled off the barrel. Soaking wet, tears in her eyes, and blood running freely from her nose, she discerned which side of the tent would provide the best exit and rushed over, biting at her bindings as she went.

Q

The orc rubbed its bleary eyes and looked to the east, hoping the dawn would come quickly and end its tedious watch. South of the creature's position, in its watch direction, was a field of tall grass, sparsely dotted by occasional trees.

The dawn's light was not nearly in full, and the orc heard a distant rustle before it noticed the antlers moving steadily through the grass. At first, the creature lifted its spear, thinking a fine venison dinner had walked right up for the slaughter. Then the orc blinked and rubbed its eyes again, wondering how any deer with such a large rack could be small enough to be concealed by grass no more than three feet high.

The antlers came gliding on, still a fair distance away. They neared the trunk of a twisted apple tree, then the orc blinked again as the antlers passed by the barrier, one on either side.

"Molargro," the orc called to its orog watch chief.

The large and ugly orog, warming his gnarly toes by the campfire, cast the sentry an indifferent look then turned away.

"Molargro!" the orc called again.

The orog reluctantly rose and came over, not even bothering to put on his worn and tattered boots.

"Deer," the orc explained when the orog arrived, pointing to the approaching antlers, not so distant anymore.

"Deer?" Molargro questioned, scratching his huge head. "Bah, ye're a stupid one," the orog said a moment later. "What kinda deer says, 'Ooooo'?"

Both the orog and the orc crinkled their faces in confusion. They glanced back toward the approaching antlers and asked in unison, "Ooooo?"

They got their answer a heartbeat later, at the end of Ivan's great axe and Pikel's tree-trunk club.

Q

Crawling along the brush on the camp's perimeter, Danica had nearly reached the prisoners' tent when the cries of alarm rang out. At first she assumed that Tiennek had found the dead orog, but then she heard, "Oo oi!" above the commotion, followed by a heavy thud and the grunt of a wounded ogre.

"How?" Danica wondered, but, having no time to figure things out at that moment, she stood and ran the rest of the way, carefully slipping in under the loosely tied skins of the tent sides. She stopped halfway in and scrambled to the side, behind some piled crates, as Tiennek and an orc rushed in through the tent flap.

"Take the human to Dorigen!" the barbarian commanded, indicating Cadderly. Tiennek drew Elbereth's finely crafted sword from his belt and grinned wickedly. "I will deal with the elf."

Danica's first reaction, as Cadderly was whisked away, was to slip back out, encircle the tent, and go to his aid. She had to resist those urges, though, for Tiennek's intentions concerning Elbereth were painfully obvious. The barbarian took a long stride toward the elf, but then, in the blink of an eye, Danica was between them.

"Flee!" she heard Elbereth say at her back. "I accept my doom. Do not die for me."

Tiennek's shock disappeared in the heartbeat it took him to conjure his mocking smile. "The orog is dead?" he asked, showing little concern. He nodded as though he was not the least bit surprised.

Danica's visage didn't soften, nor did she move from her defensive crouch. Tiennek brought the sword her way.

"A great loss, I fear," he said. "My dear lady, I could have shown you pleasures you cannot imagine."

"I am not your lady!" Danica growled, and she kicked him in the chest, driving him back a step.

"A great loss," the barbarian said again, a bit breathless but otherwise appearing unshaken. He pulled a small net from his belt, holding it wrapped around his free hand.

Danica circled cautiously, understanding the potentially disastrous consequences of getting a kicking leg entangled in that net. She looked for openings, weaknesses, but saw none. The giant barbarian held the elf's slender sword as though it had been designed for him; his balance remained perfect as he executed the circles to keep in step with the young woman.

Danica rushed forward and started to kick then dropped to the floor and swept both legs across Tiennek's ankles. The barbarian got one foot clear of the move, but stumbled as Danica's flying feet clipped his other foot. He caught his balance quickly and leaned back in, meaning to hack at the prone woman while waving the net to keep her kicks away.

Danica was not so foolish as to continue her offensive move, though. She was back up and balanced before Tiennek took his first chop.

"I am the stronger," the barbarian teased. "Better armed and at least equally skilled. You cannot hope to survive."

Danica had trouble convincing herself that the big man was not speaking the truth. She'd hit him with several solid shots, but he'd barely flinched. She saw his obvious comfort in handling a sword and had already felt his iron grip.

He came straight at her then, in a vicious flurry, thrusting and chopping, weaving the net deftly around his flying blade.

Danica dodged and dived, and deflected one thrust aside, though she gashed her arm in the process, and finally wound up in full retreat.

"Flee!" Elbereth cried, struggling futilely with his tight bonds. He rolled and kicked, and pulled his arms until they bled, but the stubborn ropes would not relax their painful grip.

Danica was glad that Tiennek continued his pursuit of her. The barbarian could have turned around and easily finished Elbereth before she ever got close enough to interfere.

"He will die after I have defeated you," Tiennek explained, as if he had read her thoughts. "After he has watched. After I have taken you!"

Elbereth's groan brought another smile to the cruel barbarian's lips.

Tiennek charged again, but Danica was not caught off her guard. She lifted a foot, as if to kick straight out at her attacker, but kicked to the side instead, snapping the large tent's center support. The roof drooped in around them, defeating Tiennek's attack.

The barbarian thrashed around to get the drooping skins high enough in case Danica charged him, but the young woman was not to be seen.

"A worthy chase!" Tiennek howled, refusing to be intimidated. "And a prize worth catching." He stalked off, pushing the hide roof from his path.

Danica easily could have slipped away and out of the collapsed tent, but that would have left Elbereth helpless. The barbarian, fearless and thinking the fight no contest, was making no secret of his whereabouts. And Danica, desperate for something to equalize the lopsided contest, determined to use that against him.

Q

"Ye got that one!" Ivan bellowed, pointing to a fleeing orc.

Pikel stepped out from behind a tree, right into the orc's path. Holding his club in both hands by its slender, tapered end, the dwarf leaned into a swing that blasted right through the miserable creature's blocking arm and hit its head with enough force to snap its scrawny neck.

"Oo oi!" the happy dwarf squealed to his brother.

"Behind ye," Ivan replied, and Pikel spun, crunching an orc's head between his flying club and the tree.

Bellowing advice to his brother did nothing to hinder Ivan's own ferocious attacks. He stood atop the felled ogre's back, chopping at the orogs and orcs encircling him. The ogre wasn't quite dead yet, and every time it groaned or stirred a bit, Ivan made a point of stomping hard on the back of the monster's fat head.

Sheer viciousness replaced finesse as the dwarf held several monsters at bay with deadly chops of his mighty axe. One orc managed to get up on the ogre behind Ivan, clubbing the dwarf solidly on the back of his head.

Ivan laughed at it then sent it flying away with a cut that drove one side of his double-bladed axe halfway through the creature's ribcage.

C

Tiennek stopped his thrashing and shouting and stalked slowly, easing the fallen roof out of his way. "I am not a weakling fighter of civilized lands," he said. "I am Kura-winther!"

He sensed a bit of movement, a shift in the fallen tent, off to the side, and he took one small step that way. He raised one hand up high so that the roof would not sag, and bent as low as he could.

He saw Danica's legs under the low skins a few feet away. The game was over, Tiennek decided, knowing that he was needed in the battle outside.

"I know your tricks!" he cried, and he heaved at the roof and charged Danica's way, sword leading. Tiennek grinned with the knowledge that his long reach would give the woman no opportunity to parry or counter.

What confident Tiennek didn't know was that Danica had grabbed the broken bottom half of the center pole, a crude spear that was longer than his sword.

Tiennek's eyes widened in disbelief as he impaled himself on Danica's set weapon.

"Some of my tricks, perhaps," the woman said, showing

no remorse for the man's demise. She drove the pole deeper and twisted it.

Elbereth's sword fell from Tiennek's outstretched arm. The net in his other hand hung loosely. He dropped to his knees, and Danica released her grip.

The spear propped Tiennek up, supported him in that kneeling position, and the tent roof descended over him, a fitting death shroud.

Q

Danica didn't hesitate. Poor Elbereth, sitting blindly in the back of the collapsed tent, would simply have to wait. The young woman got her bearings and crawled and scrambled her way into the open air.

Morning had dawned and orogs and orcs were scattering and howling in chaos, with the exception of one group putting up a fair fight against the Bouldershoulder brothers, who stood back-to-back atop the felled ogre. Cadderly was off to the other side, still being pulled along by the orc.

Danica ran after her love then skidded to a stop as the wizard appeared beside the tent Tiennek had used. The woman made several gestures, held something Danica could not discern in one outstretched hand, and uttered a triggering incantation.

Danica's instincts sent her diving between two trees just as the wizard's lightning bolt went off. The blast split one of the small trees and rebounded into the other, scorching it just above the sprawled woman's head. Danica was up and running in an instant, but soon, too, came the wizard's second spell.

Sticky filaments filled the air, descending around Danica and catching hold of the trees, the shrubs, anything at all, to form a thick web. Danica scrambled every which way, using her speed and agility to stay one step ahead of the quickly forming trap.

Then she was clear of the tangle, though a bit to the side of her original course, and the wizard was not so far away. She heard a flap of wings, but saw nothing. The imp became visible right in her path, and its barbed tail shot at her shoulder.

The wound was minor, just a scratch, but the sudden tingling numbness and the burn in Danica's arm told her that the imp had indeed poisoned her. She slumped back against a tree, the creature hovering in front of her, smiling wickedly and wagging his tail as though it meant to lash at her again.

Q

Cadderly's thrill at seeing Ivan and Pikel unexpectedly rushing to his aid was tempered by the fact that the dwarves were fully engaged and would not have the opportunity to prevent the orc from getting him to Dorigen. The creature's grip on Cadderly's arm was unrelenting, though the monster was looking more at its comrades' fight than to its prisoner.

"No one but me. . . ." Cadderly muttered under his breath. He saw an opportunity to pull away as the orc released its grasp for just an instant.

But it passed without Cadderly mustering the courage to make the attempt. He heard a blast to the side and saw Dorigen loosing some thunderous wizardry, though at what target he could not discern.

Another chance presented itself when they neared the fire. Cadderly rose to the test. He stumbled and dropped at the orc's feet, groaning and feigning injury. When the startled creature reached for him, Cadderly swung his legs inside the orc's, hooked it behind the knees, and heaved with all his strength. The startled orc tumbled headlong past him. Not a pretty maneuver, perhaps, but effective—and even more so since the campfire burned low just a few feet away. Sparks flew when the orc hit the embers. It came up shrieking and screaming, smacking at the sparks that had caught hold on its clothing.

Cadderly struggled to his feet and dived against the creature's back, knocking it into the fire once again. The orc came up on the other side, running away and paying no more heed to the young scholar.

"Well done, lad!" Cadderly heard Ivan cry, and he turned just in time to see the dwarf cleave an orog nearly in half with a mighty overhead chop. Cadderly was feeling good about his trickery, but for all he'd accomplished, he still found himself in the middle of a battlefield, unarmed, with his wrists bound behind his back. He scooted off to the quietest side and fell for cover behind a water trough.

Q

Danica turned her thoughts inward, and personified the poison as a tiny, devilish thing biting her shoulder. Her muscles became her tools, flexing and tightening, turning to drive the insinuating intruder back toward the wound.

The poison devil was a stubborn one, gnawing and burning, but Danica possessed determination far beyond that of an ordinary human. Her muscles worked intricately, shifting the poison to one side then back an inch. She pictured the open wound as a doorway, and working relentlessly, finally drove the fiend through.

Waves of dizziness rolled over her when she opened her eyes. She saw the imp again, still wagging its deadly tail, but wearing an expression that was considerably less cocksure. Danica followed the creature's surprised gaze to her own shoulder, to the black liquid that had poured from her wound to roll down her arm.

The imp's tail whipped back and shot forward, but Danica's attack, a straight-ahead punch, came quicker, sending the hovering imp spinning head over heels.

Danica moved to give chase, but had to brace herself against a tree for a moment to stop from falling over. She saw the wizard scoop up the stunned imp and begin casting yet another spell. The woman held her closed fist out toward the monk, an onyx ring clearly visible on one finger.

Danica forced herself forward, ignored the dizziness, and focused on reaching the wizard.

The woman uttered a few quick incantations and a shimmering blue light appeared in front of her, and she and the imp stepped through and were gone.

C

The six remaining orogs had no desire to continue their combat with the brutal dwarves. They took flight together, Ivan and Pikel right on their heels. The monsters took to the trees as soon as they crossed the clearing, figuring that the armored dwarves would have a harder time climbing.

Ivan and Pikel stopped at the trunk. Pikel hopped about, trying to reach a branch to pull himself up, but Ivan had another course in mind. He dropped the head of his great axe between his feet, spit into both his hands, then took up the weapon and stalked in for the trunk.

"Uh-uh," Pikel, the would-be druid, growled, wagging his head and throwing his short arms wide around the precious trunk.

"What? Have ye gone bats?" Ivan cried. "There's damned big orcs up there, me brother. Damned big!"

"Uh-uh." There was no compromise in Pikel's tone.

The discussion was resolved a heartbeat later, when Cadderly spotted a shimmering field of blue in the distance and saw Dorigen step out and begin casting a spell toward the camp.

" 'Ware the wizard!" the young scholar cried.

Pikel just managed to reply, "Eh?" before the spell went off, engulfing the tree, and the dwarves, in a ball of flame.

Cadderly leaped up from the trough and rushed over.

Pikel emerged from the carnage first, his clothes and face blackened with soot and his beard singed and sticking wildly every which way. Ivan came up behind him in a state of similar dishevelment. Worse off were the orogs, toasted in the branches of the leafless, charred tree.

"Boom!" the druid-minded dwarf said. Ivan toppled face down in the dirt.

Cadderly started for him, but Pikel stopped the young scholar with an outstretched hand, pointing back toward the large tent at the rear of the compound, and to Danica, stumbling out of the brush.

Cadderly ran to her side while Pikel saw to his brother.

Danica's face seemed too pale, too delicate, and Cadderly nearly screamed in rage. Danica assured him that she was all right—or that she would be—but then she collapsed against him and seemed on the verge of losing consciousness.

Riddled with guilt, the young scholar wondered how in the Nine Hells he had gotten her into such an awful setting, into the middle of a war.

FOURTEEN

REVELATIONS AND RELUCTANT ALLIES

Cadderly saw the black liquid oozing from Danica's wound and grew doubly concerned. He had seen the imp's sting fell Pikel, and the dwarf would have died if it hadn't been for a druid's healing magic. How could a human survive a poison potent enough to overpower a dwarf?

Danica's arm continued to twitch, and still more of the evil substance flowed out, mixing with her blood. Her breathing came slower, alarming Cadderly until he realized she was using a technique to keep herself calm. Then she opened her eyes and smiled at him, and he knew, though didn't understand how, that she would be all right.

"A wicked sting," she whispered. "And the burn. . . ."

"I know," Cadderly replied. "Rest easily. The battle is won."

Danica's eyes looked past Cadderly and she couldn't suppress a chuckle. Cadderly turned and saw Ivan and Pikel, both covered head to toe in soot, rushing around the camp, searching the bodies of dead monsters.

Danica sat up, took a deep breath, and shook her head vigorously. "The poison is no more," she announced, her voice suddenly solid again. "I have defeated it, forced it from my body."

Cadderly couldn't begin to express his amazement. He shook his head slowly and made a mental note to question Danica on how she had overcome the deadly substance. But that would wait for another, more peaceful time. Cadderly had other concerns.

"Dorigen got away," he said. Danica nodded and began working at the bindings on his wrists.

"You do not understand," Cadderly continued, building himself into a minor fit of frenzy. "She has my crossbow. The weapon has fallen into the hands of an enemy!"

Danica didn't seem overly concerned. "We're alive, and free again," she said. "That's all that matters. If you get into a fight again, you'll find a way to win without that weapon."

Danica's confidence in his ingenuity touched Cadderly, but she had missed his point. It wasn't for himself that he was frightened.

"She has the crossbow," he said again. "And the explosive darts."

"How many?"

Cadderly thought for a moment, trying to recall all those he had used and all the ones he had continued to make during his stay in Shilmista.

"Six, I believe," he said then he sighed with relief as he remembered another important point. "But she doesn't have the flask containing more of the potion. I left that back at the elven camp."

"Then fear not," Danica said, still not understanding his concern.

"Fear not?" Cadderly echoed, as though his worries should be plain to see. "She has it—don't you understand the implications? Dorigen could copy the design, unleash a new . . ." He stopped, unable to penetrate the frown on Danica's face. She pointed behind him and he looked again over his shoulder.

Not even the dwarves were there. Cadderly didn't understand.

"The tree," Danica explained. "Look at the tree."

Cadderly did as instructed. The proud elm, just moments before lush and vibrant in its late summer colors, remained only a charred and blackened skeleton. Small fires burned in several nooks. Waves of rising heat distorted the air above and around the tree. Heaped, blackened forms of the dead orogs seemed to meld together with the dark limbs.

"Do you believe that a wizard who could wreak such sudden and terrible destruction would be impressed by your tiny crossbow?" Danica reasoned. "In her eyes, would the bow be worth the expense?"

"Dorigen raised it against you," Cadderly argued, but he knew before Danica even scowled at him that the wizard had threatened her with the bow only to further weaken Cadderly's resolve.

"Your bow is a fine weapon," Danica said, "but one that a wizard of . . . Dorigen's? . . . power does not need."

Cadderly couldn't argue against that logic, but he was not comforted. Whatever the outcome, he couldn't ignore the fact that a weapon he had designed might be used against an innocent, perhaps even against someone close to him.

Again the crossbow was a symbol of the insanity around him, the rushing violence that he could not control and from which he could not hide.

Q

The haul was a bit meager by Ivan's standards, and the stubborn dwarf refused to yield until he had searched every inch of the camp. He sent Pikel to a tent across the way while he moved to the collapsed one that Cadderly and Danica had exited.

He slapped at the fallen skins with his free hand and used his axe to hold enough of the roof up so that a monster wouldn't crash into him. He came upon a big human's body first, still kneeling, propped by the crude spear

"I bet that hurt," Ivan said, seeing the gruesome wound. He didn't know whether the man had been friend or foe, so he didn't go out of his way to search the body. Ivan did scoop up the fine sword that lay beside the dead man's hand, though, muttering, "Ye won't be needin' this," almost apologetically as he pressed farther under the fallen canopy.

"Another one," the dwarf said in surprise, nearly stepping on another prone form. "And still alive," he added when the wounded creature snarled and wriggled away.

Ivan's expression turned sour when he saw it was an elf, not an orc, but his disdain didn't outdo the antipathy plainly exhibited on the elf's face.

"You have my sword," the elf said, staring hard into the dwarf's dark eyes.

Ivan looked down to his belt. "So I do!" he replied, making no move toward the sword or the elf.

The elf waited as patiently as he could for a long moment then said, his voice trembling with anger, "I am still bound."

Ivan looked at him long and hard, finally bobbing his hairy head. "So ye are!" the dwarf agreed, and he walked away.

He nearly bumped into Cadderly and Danica back outside the tent.

"Where's Elbereth?" Cadderly asked, surprised that Ivan had come out alone.

"What's an Elbereth?" the dwarf asked in reply.

Cadderly wasn't in the mood for bantering. "Ivan!" he shouted.

The dwarf's eyes widened, two shining orbs in the middle of his blackened face. "That's a fine 'well met,' ye ungrateful—"

"All of our thanks," Danica interrupted, relieved to see the dwarf but also wanting to calm the increasingly volatile scholar. She stepped over and threw a huge hug around the dirty dwarf, even kissing him on his hairy cheek—and leaving a clean spot in the soot.

"That's better," Ivan said, an inevitable tenderness emerging in his normally gruff voice as he looked at Danica.

"Now, where is Elbereth?" Danica asked.

Ivan poked his thick thumb back over his shoulder. "If Elbereth is an elf, I'd say he's in a foul mood, that one," he explained.

Danica started for the collapsed tent, and Cadderly, too, but Ivan stomped a boot on the young scholar's foot, holding him in place.

"I still ain't heard a word of thanks from yer mouth," the dwarf growled.

Cadderly's expression was warmly sincere. He bent over quickly and kissed Ivan's other cheek, sending the dwarf in a sputtering tirade across the compound.

"Durned fool boy!" Ivan growled, wiping at the wet mark. "Durned fool!"

Cadderly enjoyed a much-needed smile at the spectacle, but the young man's relief was short-lived. Danica pulled him under the tent and led him to Tiennek's body. She lifted the hide roof to make sure that Cadderly had a good view of the corpse.

"Slain at my hands," Danica announced, no pride evident in her voice. "I killed him, do you understand? I did as I had to do, as the barbarian forced me to do."

Cadderly shuddered but didn't get Danica's point, if there was any.

"Just as you did with the Talonite priest," she said, putting it more bluntly.

"Why do you bring Barjin into this?" Cadderly demanded, horrified. That too-familiar image of the dead priest's eyes came at him from the depths of his subconscious.

"I never bring Barjin into it," Danica corrected him. "You do." She went on quickly, cutting short Cadderly's forthcoming protest. "You bring Barjin with you wherever you go," she explained, "a ghost that haunts your every thought."

Cadderly's expression reflected his confusion.

"As with the wounded orogs back in the foothills," Danica said, her tone softening. "Leave dead Barjin behind. I beg you. His death was brought about by his own actions. You did only as you had to do."

"You don't regret that you killed this man?" Cadderly asked, almost accusingly.

"I regret that it had to happen," Danica snapped, "but I know that if I were given the chance to do it again, Tiennek would be dead exactly as he is now. Can you say differently about Barjin?"

Cadderly thought back to the events in the Edificant Library's catacombs. They seemed as if they had happened just that morning and had occurred a hundred years before, all at the same time. Cadderly had no answer to Danica's disturbing question, and she didn't wait for any, remembering that Elbereth, bound and probably humiliated, awaited his rescue. Cadderly followed at Danica's heels, his eyes locked on dead Tiennek until the drooping roof put the barbarian out of sight.

Elbereth didn't blink through the long moments it took Danica and Cadderly to free him. He would not show weakness openly, would not reveal the humiliation in his helplessness and capture. Only anger shone in the elf's silver eyes and showed in the set of his angular jaw. When he was free, he rushed from the collapsed tent, tearing through the skins with fury.

Ivan and Pikel stood beside the flap to Dorigen's tent. Ivan fingered Danica's crystal-bladed daggers, admiring the golden tiger hilt of one and the silver dragon hilt of the other. Pikel held a thick purple robe while trying futilely to get Cadderly's spindle-disks to spin back up into his chubby palm. At the dwarves' feet lay Cadderly's pack and walking stick.

It wasn't hard for Cadderly and Danica to guess where Elbereth was heading.

"My sword!" the elf prince shouted at the dwarf.

Elbereth threw his slender hand out Ivan's way. When Ivan didn't immediately react, Elbereth grabbed the sword right from Ivan's belt.

"Skinny thing anyway," Ivan remarked to Pikel. "Probably break the first time I hit something with it."

In the blink of an eye, Elbereth had his sword tip against Ivan's thick throat.

"And ye're welcome," came the dwarf's reply.

"Uh-oh," remarked Pikel.

"Ye keep playing like that, and ye're going to get hurt," Ivan added, locking stares with the silver-eyed elf.

It went on for a long, uncomfortable while, a battle of wills that teetered on the brink of violence.

"We have no time for this," Cadderly said, going to inspect his pack. *The Tome of Universal Harmony* was there, to his relief, as was his light tube. All his belongings remained, in fact, with the notable exception of his crossbow.

Danica's approach was more straightforward. She casually pushed Elbereth's sword aside and stepped between the elf and the dwarf, alternately shaming each of them with her uncompromising glare.

"Haven't we enough enemies?" the woman scolded. "An army of monsters surrounds us, and you two think to do battle with each other?"

"I have never seen much difference between an orc and a dwarf," Elbereth spat.

"Oo," answered a wounded Pikel.

"Ye view yer betters in a similar light, then," Ivan fought back.

"Oo," said Pikel, regarding Ivan with admiration.

Elbereth drew in his breath. Danica could see his grip tighten on his sword.

"They saved us," Danica reminded Elbereth. "Without Ivan and Pikel, we would remain Dorigen's prisoners—or we would be dead."

Elbereth scowled at the notion. "You would have defeated the barbarian in any case," he argued, "then we would have been free."

"How many orogs and orcs would have come to

Tiennek's cries if the dwarves had not held them in battle outside our tent?" Cadderly interjected.

Elbereth's scowl did not diminish, but he did slide his sword into its sheath. "When this is over. . . ." he warned Ivan.

"When this is over, ye're not likely to be around," Ivan huffed back, and the smugness of his tone suggested that he knew something the others did not.

He let them wait a while before offering an explanation.

"How many kinfolk ye got, elf?" he asked. "How many to fight against the army that's come to yer wood?"

"Two more now," Cadderly replied.

"If ye're talking of me and me brother, then ye're talking nonsense," Ivan said. "I'm not about to die for the likes of some elves."

"It's not just for the elves, Ivan," Cadderly explained. He looked around at all of them to get their attention. "This battle—this war—goes beyond Shilmista."

"How can you know that?" Danica asked.

"Dorigen serves Talona," Cadderly replied. "We suspected that from the gloves Elbereth took from the bugbears before we ever came here. Now the connection is undeniable." He looked at Pikel. "Do you remember the imp that stung you?"

"Oo," answered the dwarf, rubbing his shoulder.

"That very imp was with Dorigen in her tent," Cadderly explained. "She and Barjin have come from the same source, and if they have attacked the library and now the forest, then . . ."

"Then all of us are in danger," Danica finished for him, "and the headmasters' worst fears shall be realized."

"So, you and your brother will fight," Cadderly said to Ivan. "If not for the elves, then for everyone else from Carradoon to the library and the rest of the Southern Heartlands."

Ivan's dark eyes narrowed, but he said nothing to refute the young scholar's logic.

"This would seem the place to begin," Cadderly went on, determined to forge an alliance. "We cannot allow our enemies a hold in Shilmista, and the Boulder-shoulder brothers' help would go far in accomplishing our tasks."

"All right, elf," Ivan said after looking to Pikel for confirmation. "We'll help ye out, ungrateful though ye're sure to be."

"Do you believe I would accept—" Elbereth started, but Danica's glare stopped him short.

"Fight well, then," Elbereth said instead. "But do not doubt, dwarf, that when this is ended, you and I will speak again about our meeting in that tent."

"Ye won't be here," Ivan said again.

"Why do you keep saying that?" Cadderly asked.

"Because I seen the enemy, lad," Ivan answered, "hundreds of 'em, I tell ye. Ye think the elves'll beat that number?"

Elbereth shook his head and turned away.

"There," Ivan said, pointing to a tree where he had spotted the elusive Hammadeen. "If ye don't believe me, then ask the faerie-thing!"

Elbereth did just that, and when he returned from his private conversation with Hammadeen, his face was pale.

"We cannot stay here, in any event" Danica said, trying to shake the elf from his concerned state. "Do we go after the wizard?"

"No," Elbereth replied absently, his eyes looking to the distant south. "They have fought at the Hill of the Stars. I must go to my People."

"It would be a better course," Cadderly agreed. "Dorigen is too dangerous. She has spies . . ." He stopped to consider Danica, who was mouthing their missing companion's name and pounding a fist into her hand. Cadderly didn't indicate his agreement, though. He refused to believe that Kierkan Rufo, for all his faults, willingly would have given information to the wizard.

But Cadderly had to admit that, lately, he simply didn't know what to believe.

Q

Dorigen approached Ragnor's camp tentatively, not certain how the volatile ogrillon would act since the battle had taken such an unexpected twist. She had been absent, away hunting Cadderly and his friends, when Ragnor had launched his attack on the elven camp. Even without her help, though, the ogrillon had routed the elves and driven them miles southward.

Dorigen cursed her own stupidity. She had supplied Ragnor with the elves' position. She should have foreseen that the cocky brute would move against them, particularly if she wouldn't be around to share in the victory.

Dorigen found herself in an awkward position, for while the ogrillon's moves had met with success, Dorigen's had met with disaster. But she went to see Ragnor anyway. Her magical energies were all but exhausted and she needed Ragnor even if he did not need her.

"Where are my soldiers?" was the first thing the burly ogrillon barked at her when she entered his tent. Ragnor looked around slyly to his elite bugbear guard, realizing that it was the first time he had seen Dorigen without her barbarian escort. "And where is that slab of flesh you keep at your side?" he asked.

"We have powerful enemies," Dorigen answered and countered all at once, raising her voice loud enough to silence the bugbear chuckles. "You should not be so smug in your temporary victory."

"Temporary?" the ogrillon roared, and Dorigen wondered if perhaps she had pushed the ogrillon too far. She half expected Ragnor to rush over and tear her apart.

"Two score of the elves fell," the ogrillon went on. "Six I killed myself!" Ragnor displayed a gruesome necklace featuring twelve elf ears.

"At what cost?" Dorigen asked.

"It doesn't matter," Ragnor replied, and Dorigen knew by the way Ragnor winced that the elven camp had not been easily overrun. "The elves are few, but my troops are many," the ogrillon went on. "I will not fear even a few thousand dead when Shilmista falls under my shadow."

"*My* shadow?" Dorigen asked slyly. For the first time since she'd entered the tent, she saw a hint of trepidation in the ogrillon's gaze.

"You were away on private matters," Ragnor argued, somewhat subdued. "The time had come to attack, and I did. I struck with every soldier I could muster. I led the attack myself and carry the scars of battle."

Dorigen bowed her head respectfully to calm the volatile beast. Ragnor had told her much more than he had intended. He mentioned that she was away, but she hadn't told him that she would be far from camp. For some reason, Ragnor had chosen that time to attack, without Dorigen to help him. With the ogrillon so adamant in his statement that Shilmista would fall under *his* control, and not to Castle Trinity, Dorigen worried just how far Ragnor's newfound independence would take him.

She had no desire to be anywhere near the ogrillon when he decided he didn't need Castle Trinity.

"I go to my rest," she said, bowing again. "Accept my congratulations on your great victory, mighty General."

Ragnor couldn't hide his thrill at hearing those words. Figuring that was a good note on which to depart, Dorigen left the tent, thinking it strange that a merciless brute such as Ragnor could be so easy a mark for flattery.

"He got scared," Druzil remarked from his perch on Dorigen's shoulder soon after the wizard had departed the tent. The imp materialized. "He feared that you would control the battle and that he would not be needed."

"Let us hope he still believes that I can be of some use to him," Dorigen replied. "He will not be pleased to learn how many of his soldiers I have lost."

"Do not mention them," Druzil suggested. "I don't believe Ragnor can count anyway."

Dorigen turned her head sharply to face the imp. "You will never underestimate the ogrillon again," she growled. "Any mistakes could bring a swift end to our lives."

Druzil snarled and grumbled but did not argue. "What are your plans?" he asked after a long enough while for Dorigen to cool down.

Dorigen stopped her march to consider the question. "I will see where I may be of use," she answered.

"Have you given up on Aballister's son?" The imp sounded surprised.

"Never!" Dorigen snapped. "This Cadderly of Carradoon is a dangerous one, as are his friends. When this fight is over, whatever path Ragnor chooses, young Cadderly will prove valuable." Her eyes narrowed as though she had reminded herself of something important.

"You can still contact Kierkan Rufo?" she asked.

Druzil chuckled, the rough laugh sounding almost like a cough in his raspy little voice. "Contact?" he echoed. "Intrude upon would be a better description. Kierkan Rufo wears the amulet. His mind is mine to explore."

"Then hear his thoughts," Dorigen instructed. "If Cadderly returns to the elven camp, I wish to know."

Druzil muttered as usual and faded away, but Dorigen, too engrossed by the intrigue unfolding around her, paid his complaints little heed.

Q

"Afore ye set yer sights on going back to the hill," Ivan said gruffly, "me brother and me has got something ye should see."

Elbereth eyed the dwarf with curiosity, wondering what cruel surprise Ivan had in store for him. But when they at last arrived at the dwarves' small camp, just a mile or so out of their way, Elbereth cast a surprised look Ivan's way. Buried under a cairn of piled rocks lay a partially burned elf body, which Elbereth knew at once was Ralmarith's, his friend who had been slain in the enemy wizard's initial attack.

"How did you come by this?" the elf demanded, his voice a mix of suspicion and relief.

"Took it from the goblins," Ivan said, taking care to keep all hints of sympathy out of his gruff voice. "We figured that even an elf deserved a better resting place than a goblin's belly."

Elbereth turned back to Ralmarith's body and said no more. Danica moved and knelt beside him, putting an arm over his slender shoulders.

"Them two're a bit friendly, eh?" Ivan said to Cadderly, and the young scholar had to bite his lip to hold back his thoughts—indeed, to force them from his mind. He had to trust in Danica, and in their love, he knew, for their situation was too dangerous to allow for any rifts between he and Elbereth.

Danica nodded Ivan and Pikel's way more than once, trying to prompt the elf to offer some thanks. Elbereth did not respond, though. He just whispered his farewells to his friend and carefully repacked the cairn, leaving Ralmarith's body to the forest the slain elf so loved.

Shilmista was strangely quiet as the five companions made their stealthy way toward Daoine Dun. They stopped once for a short break, with Elbereth heading off to scout the area and see if he might find Hammadeen or some other woodland being to gather some information.

"You must forgive Elbereth," Cadderly said to Ivan, taking the opportunity to try to play peacemaker.

"What's an Elbereth?" Ivan asked snootily, not looking up from his work resetting the antler in his helmet. The dwarf grimaced and tightened the screw as much as he could, since he had no lacquer to reinforce the fit.

"He is the Prince of Shilmista," Cadderly went on, wincing at, but otherwise ignoring, the dwarf's unyielding stubbornness. "And Shilmista might prove the cornerstone to support our struggles."

"I'm not for giving much hope to our struggles," Ivan replied grimly. "Yer handful of elves won't do much against the army that's walked in."

"If you really believed that, you would not have agreed to come along," Cadderly reasoned, thinking he had found a chip in the dwarf's iron facade.

The incredulous grin Ivan gave stole that thought away. "I'm not for missing a chance to bash a few orc brains," the dwarf retorted. "And yerself and the girl needed me and me brother."

Cadderly couldn't compete with Ivan's seemingly endless surliness, so he walked away, shaking his head at Danica and Pikel as he passed them. A few moments later, Elbereth came back to the camp and announced that the path to the hill was clear.

Q

Daoine Dun was not as Cadderly remembered it. The once beautiful Hill of the Stars lay blasted and blackened, its thick grasses trampled under the charge of monstrous feet and its lush trees broken or burned. Even worse was the stench. Flocks of carrion birds flew off at the companions' approach. The dead—a fair number of elves among them—had been left out to rot.

Even Ivan had no comment in the face of Elbereth's shock. Indeed, Ivan called Pikel to the side, and together they began to dig a common grave.

The elf prince wandered back and forth across the battlefield, checking the bodies of his kinfolk to see if he could determine which elves had fallen. Most had been mutilated, though, and the stoic elf just shook his head sadly at Danica and Cadderly as they followed him through his silent vigil.

They buried the fallen elves, Danica offering her thanks to the dwarves, though stubborn Elbereth would not, then they searched the whole hill. Elbereth kept to the trees, seeking to learn more of what had happened and where his friends and enemies might have gone. Ivan and Pikel led the search of the caves. In one they found the half-eaten bodies of several horses, though, fortunately, Temmerisa was not among them.

In another chamber, in the cave that Galladel had used as his own, they made what Cadderly considered a remarkable discovery. Several books and scrolls were strewn about the floor, as if the elf king had hurriedly departed, quickly selecting what he should take with him and what to leave behind. Most of the writings were meaningless notes, but in one corner Cadderly found an ancient tome, bound in black leather and bearing the Espruar runes for the letters "D," "Q," and "q." Cadderly took up the book in trembling hands, suspecting its contents. He gingerly undid the snap and opened it.

The ink was faded and the page was filled with many symbols that Cadderly could not understand. It bore the name Cadderly expected to see, though: Dellanil Quil'quien, the long-dead king of Shilmista and one of the forest's legendary heroes.

"What have you found?" came Elbereth's call from the cave entrance. He stood beside Danica; Ivan and Pikel had moved on to the next hole.

"Your father would not have left this intentionally," Cadderly explained, turning and displaying the black-covered tome. "It is the book of Dellanil Quil'quien, a priceless work."

"I am surprised my father brought it along at all," Elbereth replied, "but I am not surprised that he left it behind. The book holds little value for him. Its writings are arcane, using many symbols that we of Shilmista can no longer comprehend. The book holds nothing for us. Take it back to your library if you desire."

"Surely you err," Cadderly said. "Dellanil Quil'quien was among your greatest heroes. His feats, his magic, could prove critical examples at this dire time."

"As I have told you," replied Elbereth, "we can no longer even read the work. Nor can you. Many of the symbols have not been used for centuries.

"Come now," Elbereth bade the two humans. "We must move on. Even as we speak, my People may be in another battle, and I do not wish to remain at this scarred place any longer than is necessary." The elf walked out into the afternoon sunlight.

Danica waited by the entrance for Cadderly. "You're keeping the book?" she asked, seeing him placing it in his pack.

"I don't agree with Elbereth's estimation of its value," Cadderly replied. "There may be something in Dellanil's writings that will help us in our fight."

"But you cannot even read it," Danica said.

"We shall see," Cadderly replied. "I've translated many works back at the library. Now, at least, I have a task that I am prepared to handle—as you might, when you are faced with hand-to-hand combat."

Danica nodded and said no more. She led Cadderly out of the cave and down to where the elf prince waited for the dwarves to complete their search.

For Cadderly, the book came as a godsend. He really didn't believe, didn't dare to hope, that he would find something important in the work, even if he could manage to translate the strange runes. But just working toward the common goal of saving the forest while using his unique skills added a bit of spring to the young scholar's steps.

Most important of all, finding and working with the book of Dellanil Quil'quien would somewhat remove Cadderly from the violence. He longed for that time past, before Barjin had come to the Edificant Library, when adventures were found only in the words of ancient books.

Perhaps the work would block the harsh realities that had so suddenly surrounded the young scholar.

FIFTEEN

AIMING HIGH

We can get around them by shifting a mile to the east," Danica explained when she rejoined the others in the small evergreen grove they had taken as shelter. "The enemy line is less deep there. We'll be beyond them before they ever realize we've passed."

The plan met with approval from Cadderly, but Ivan and Pikel didn't seem too pleased to learn that they'd marched that far and might not even get the chance to crunch an orog's skull. The companions had journeyed several miles from Daoine Dun without incident, though signs of the enemy's passing—hack and scorch marks on almost every tree—were painfully obvious. At last the companions had found the enemy along a rushing river, in a line that seemed to span the forest's width. Elbereth's people had apparently made a stand at the river and were encamped beyond its protective banks.

Elbereth didn't immediately embrace Danica's plan. He, too, had gone scouting, and while Danica had found a potential break to the east that might get them to the elven camp, the elf prince had found something that might alter the entire battle's course.

A short distance west of their position, on a high ridge above the river and overlooking the lands to the south, lay an enemy camp dotted with tents—the only tents Elbereth had seen.

"I've found their leaders' camp," Elbereth explained to Danica. "Or so I believe."

"Well guarded, no doubt," Cadderly had to put in, especially when he saw a gleam in Danica's almond eyes.

"Perhaps," Elbereth answered, hardly paying any heed to the worried young scholar, "but no more than any other position in the enemy's lines."

"Except the break that Danica has found," Cadderly replied, his desire to be rejoined with the elven host without further combat obvious in his almost frantic tone.

"Not to fear," Ivan whispered to Cadderly. "Me brother and me can be making our own breaks."

"What say you, Danica?" Elbereth asked. Cadderly wasn't certain he liked that the elf prince, who always seemed to value nothing but his own opinions, had asked for Danica's approval. "If we can get to the enemy leader, we may be able to change the course of the war," Elbereth added before the woman gave her answer.

Danica's wry smile revealed the adventurous woman's answer before she opened her mouth to reply. "It seems a desperate course," she began, but her tone reflected no fear. "A desperate course for a desperate situation."

"Oo oi!" Pikel heartily agreed. Cadderly gave the dwarf a frown that stole his widening smile.

Elbereth quickly knelt and cleared away some pine needles. He took up a stick and drew a map of the ridge.

"There are only five of us," Cadderly reminded them, though no one was listening.

"I have heard that the leader's name is Ragnor," Elbereth began, "a monstrous beast, an orc-ogre half-breed, my scouts believe, marked by a tusk protruding over his upper lip."

"Wonderful," Cadderly muttered grimly, and Ivan paid enough attention to kick him in the shin.

"If Ragnor is at the camp, we can expect he will separate himself from us behind whatever monstrous guards he can muster."

"Wonderful," Cadderly said again. Danica elbowed him hard in the ribs. The young scholar began to get the feeling that he wouldn't even make it to the enemy camp if he kept commenting.

"And what monsters did ye see?" asked Ivan, leaning closer than anybody toward the crude map.

Elbereth seemed surprised by the dwarf's interest. "Bugbears, mostly," the elf answered. "Actually, I would have expected more powerful guards, ogres at least, and perhaps a giant or two."

Cadderly winced but held his tongue. The orogs, large and powerful, had come as a shock to him, and the ogres' sheer size had nearly made him swoon. What would be his reaction, he wondered, if he found himself facing a true giant?

"Can you be certain, then, that this is the leader's camp?" Danica asked.

Elbereth thought for a moment then shook his head. "It is an assumption," he admitted. "I saw no other tents anywhere along the line, just crude lean-tos of twigs. And this particular ridge is most favorable for the enemy leader to keep a watch on the action to the south."

"Maybe it's Dorigen's camp," Cadderly put in.

"Either way," Ivan boomed, slapping his great axe against his hand, "we'll give the scum a thing or two to think about!"

Again, Elbereth was surprised by the dwarf's interest. "I do not know how we might best approach," the elf admitted. "If we sneak in as close as we can, perhaps we will discern the appropriate attack route."

"In what order?" Ivan asked.

Elbereth looked at him blankly.

"As I thought," remarked the dwarf. "Ye're more for working on yer own than to leading a fight. Step aside, elf. I'll give ye a plan!"

Elbereth neither moved nor blinked.

"Listen, ye stubborn son of a willow tree," Ivan growled, poking a stubby finger Elbereth's way. "I know ye're doubting me friendship—and ye should be, for I'm not calling ye friend. And when the fightin's done, yerself and me have a date. Don't ye hope for a moment that I'm forgetting that! And I'm not caring a thing for yer 'People,' or yer stinking wood, neither!"

Pikel's growl slowed Ivan's budding momentum.

"Well, me brother likes yer wood," Ivan said to calm the savage would-be druid. He spun back on Elbereth. "For all yer suspicions, though, don't ye be doubting me friendship to Cadderly and Danica. If they're to go in, then me and me brother are fighting aside them, and I'm betting that me axe takes more heads than yer skinny sword!"

"We shall learn the truth of that boast," Elbereth said, his silver eyes narrowed. His grim expression did not relent, but he shifted away from the map, giving the dwarf full access.

Ivan bent low over the sketch, grunting and pulling at his still sooty beard. "How deep's the river beyond the ridge?" he asked.

"To my waist, perhaps," the elf replied.

"Hmmm," mumbled the dwarf. "And the drop's a bit high to take that course. We'll have to hit 'em hard and get quick to the east, to where yerself—" he pointed to Danica—"saw a way through."

"Our lives are not important," said Elbereth. "If we can kill the enemy leader, whether or not we escape is of no concern."

Cadderly's mouth dropped open.

"Yer own life's not important," Ivan agreed, "but the rest of us would prefer to keep our skin, thank ye."

Cadderly's sigh sounded clearly like a note of gratitude to Ivan.

"But if we can hit them hard and fast enough, we'll get our way back out," Ivan went on. "We'd be better off if ye had yer bow, elf, to lead our way in, but I've got a hammer or two to spin into a bugbear's eye. Here's me thinking. Yerself, the elf, and Danica will lead us in. The two of ye are the fastest and should get yer chance at the boss. Cadderly will come next, watching both sides to see where he's most needed."

Cadderly realized that Ivan had politely told him to keep out of the way—not that he minded.

"Me and me brother'll take up the back end," Ivan went on. "That way ye won't need to be worrying that a bugbear will be crawling up yer backside."

Elbereth studied the drawing and found little to complain about concerning Ivan's plan. It seemed solid enough, though the elf was somewhat surprised that the dwarf had made allowances for him to personally battle

Ragnor. Elbereth had presumed that Ivan would want that glory for himself.

"Suppose Dorigen is still there," Cadderly interjected, still not thrilled with the whole idea.

"Then we can do even more harm to our enemies," Elbereth replied.

"Many of my fighting styles are designed to deal with wizards," Danica added, offering Cadderly the consolation that he obviously needed. "As in my previous encounter with Dorigen, I believe the wizard will have little in her repertoire to harm me."

"Unless you are busy battling bugbears or some other monsters," Cadderly retorted. "Then you might prove an easy target for one of Dorigen's lightning blasts."

"It'll be up to yerself," Ivan decided. "Keep yer watch for the wizard. If ye see her, then knock her down with yer fancy bow."

"I don't have it anymore," Cadderly said.

"Then use yer stick, or that toy ye dance at the string's end," said Ivan.

"Dorigen has my crossbow," Cadderly said, on the verge of panic.

None of the others seemed to share his apprehension about that fact. In unison, they looked to Ivan to continue with his plotting.

"She has my crossbow and some of the magically loaded darts!" Cadderly said again, even more anxiously.

"If Dorigen is more concerned with that weapon than with her repertoire of spells, we'll be better off," Danica said, her calm tone mocking Cadderly's concern.

"We'll just hope she's not as good a shot with the thing as yerself, lad," Ivan added. Similarly unconcerned, he went back to his plan. "I'm thinking that twilight would be the best time to go, when the light's down a bit but before the darkness takes advantage from our human friends."

Elbereth looked to Danica, who nodded her accord.

"When ye're done with the brute boss, ye'll have me and Pikel to take ye back out again," Ivan explained to Elbereth. "We'll cut ye a path ye could ride yer horse through."

"That we do not doubt," Danica said, and even Elbereth, so angry at the dwarf just a short while before, made no sarcastic comments.

"We're off then," Ivan said, taking up his great axe. He motioned with his arm for Elbereth to take up the lead.

The group moved quietly into position under the widespread boughs of a pine tree and waited while the last of the daylight faded. Cadderly sat on the western edge of the shadows, trying to get every last moment of light as he worked hard over an open book. At first, Danica thought he was still trying to translate the book of Dellanil Quil'quien, but then she saw that he held *The Tome of Universal Harmony* instead.

"There are spells that might be of use," Cadderly explained in answer to her inquisitive glance.

Danica's expression revealed her surprise. She had never seen Cadderly attempt any clerical magic beyond simple spells of healing, had never really considered him that manner of priest.

"I have spent my life in the order of Deneir," Cadderly protested, drawing a slap from nearby Ivan and a profound "Sssshhh!" from Pikel.

Cadderly turned back to the book. "There is a spell of silence," he whispered, "which might hinder Dorigen if she appears in the battle and attempts her magic."

He could tell that Danica wasn't convinced, and he couldn't honestly find the words to argue against her look. Cadderly had performed minor ceremonies before, had once created a font of holy water—in which he had immersed the bottle containing the dreaded chaos curse—but in truth, he had never put much store in spells. He was a Deneirrath, a disciple of Deneir, the god of art and literature, primarily because he had been raised among that sect at the Edificant Library and because Deneir's edicts so befit Cadderly's intelligent and kind nature. Cadderly had spent nearly as much time with the priests of Oghma, god of knowledge, and secretly considered himself a true priest of neither—to Headmaster Avery's ultimate frustration.

"Time to go," Ivan whispered.

Cadderly quickly perused the spell of silence one last time, hoping that if the need arose, he would find the strength to use it. Full of trepidation—should he have tried to study spells of healing instead?—he slipped the tome back into his pack beside Dellanil's book.

They started off cautiously for the sloping, grassy incline that led to the tent-covered ridge. Danica stopped them a short distance out and disappeared into the brush, returning a few moments later.

"Sentry," she explained when she came back to them.

"Bugbear?" Elbereth asked.

"Goblin."

"Dead goblin," Ivan muttered, giving Danica an appreciative wink.

Pikel added a happy, "Hee hee."

They came to a halt crouched in a line of thick brush just below the enemy camp. The grassy slope was teasingly quiet. A couple of bugbears wandered along no apparent course, and through the open flaps of one of the side tents, the companions could see others milling about. But it was the topmost tent, on the crest of the ridge, that held the companions' attention. Somewhat smaller than the other two tents, it was by far the finest and left little doubt where the enemy leader, if this was indeed Ragnor's camp, would be located.

"Now or not at all," Ivan whispered to Elbereth. The elf turned to the dwarf and gave a determined nod. Then Elbereth looked to Danica and they burst from the brush and began their wild charge up the hill.

Head low, arms and legs pumping in perfect harmony, Danica quickly outdistanced the elf. She hit the first two bugbears before they could guess that they were under attack. Knees and elbows flew wildly then so did the bugbears, which tumbled to the grass with little desire to return to face the frenzied woman.

Elbereth charged past Danica as the second bugbear flew away, the elf bearing down on a third monster, similarly surprised but with time enough to ready a long spear with which to meet the attackers.

The elf prince's focus went beyond the creature, to the flap of the fine tent he knew was Ragnor's. He hardly noticed the spear thrust his way.

His fine sword whipped across, snapping the bugbear's crude weapon before it got near its mark. Elbereth ran right by the stunned bugbear, sticking his sword into its knee as he passed so that it couldn't follow him up the hill.

The unfortunate creature, clutching at its wound, unwittingly remained in Danica's path as she followed the elf. Hardly slowing, she launched a perfectly synchronized kick with her running strides, catching the bending monster in the chin and laying it straight out on the ground.

The felled beast noticed another human running past a heartbeat later then it felt the heavy stomp of dwarven boots. The last thing the bugbear saw was the swift descent of a huge axe.

Alarms rang out all through the encampment, and the two side tents opened up, with many bugbears and several goblins spilling out onto the grassy hill.

"More than we thought!" Ivan bellowed.

Cadderly held his spindle-disks and his walking stick close, hoping he wouldn't be forced to use them. He looked around frantically, expecting and fearing that Dorigen would make her appearance, and tried to keep the spell of silence in his thoughts through the growing tumult around him.

Danica and Elbereth widened the gap ahead of Cadderly, and Ivan and Pikel were fully engaged in combat right behind him. He turned then turned back, and looked all around as the bugbears—even more poured from the tents—began to surround the small group.

Q

Neither Elbereth nor Danica paid any heed to the events behind them. Their goal was in plain sight, and their strides quickened when a burly, brutish monster stepped from the fine tent. Both knew at once that it was Ragnor come to meet them, huge and terrible and with that telltale single tusk sticking up over his lip.

Standing at the very top of the ridge, the ogrillon grinned wickedly and beckoned them on.

Danica realized they would not get to him, though. A group of three bugbears closed from the side, and the monsters' angle would put them between their leader and the attackers. Danica was confident that she could outdistance them if she ran full stride, but Elbereth would have no chance of getting to Ragnor.

"Run on!" she cried to the elf as she veered to the side to meet the interceptors.

She started in high, forcing the monsters to raise their spears, then dived to the grass and slid sideways, clipping their feet and sending all three tumbling down around her.

C

Elbereth's first instincts were to go to her, caught in the middle of such powerful enemies, but the elf continued his course, realizing that Danica had made the move for his benefit and reminding himself that their lives were not important when weighed against the potential gains of destroying Ragnor.

If the ogrillon was afraid, he didn't show it.

Elbereth came fast and hard, his sword weaving and thrusting, using his momentum to get in strikes too quickly for Ragnor to defend.

Blood oozed from the monster's shoulder. Another gash lined one cheek. Still Ragnor grinned, and Elbereth's charging advantage quickly played itself out.

It was the ogrillon's turn.

C

Cadderly had never seen such brilliant teamwork before. The dwarf brothers held the higher ground, but that still didn't bring them close to eye level with gigantic bugbears, and they were outnumbered two to one.

That hardly seemed to matter.

Ivan cut a crossing swipe with his axe, not close to hitting the mark. A bugbear waded in behind them then Cadderly understood the dwarf's attack to be no more than a feint, drawing the monster in. Pikel suddenly broke from his own fight and followed up his brother's swing with a low thrust from his tree-trunk club.

The lunging bugbear's knee snapped backward— Cadderly thought that it resembled the gait of an exotic bird he had once read about—and the monster fell away, writhing in agony.

Ivan, meanwhile, had not been idle. He went with the momentum of his powerful cut, stepping beside his dipping brother and taking Pikel's place with the other two monsters. The surprised bugbears hardly seemed to comprehend what had happened—the dwarves' movements were so in harmony—and they didn't understand the difference in that dwarf's fighting style. They kept their arms extended, a proper style for defending against Pikel's wide-armed club swings, but thoroughly useless against Ivan's sheer ferocity.

The dwarf charged inside their long reach, butting with his antlered head, biting, kicking with his heavy boots, and waggling his double-bladed axe through a series of short chops.

One of them was down, the other running away, before Cadderly had even remembered to draw a breath.

"Oo!" Pikel howled with appreciation seeing his brother make such quick work of the two, and purposely turning his back on his remaining bugbear in the process.

"Behind you!" Cadderly cried, not knowing that the dwarf knew what he was doing.

The bugbear raised its spear over its head and leaped, but Pikel dipped low and rushed backward, slamming his back into the monster's knees. The bugbear barely caught its balance and didn't go headlong over the dwarf, but it would have been better off if it had. Pikel dropped down to one knee, held his club on its narrow end, and drove it straight up between the bugbear's legs, heaving the creature from the ground.

By the time the bugbear came back down, still standing but quite winded, Pikel was behind the monster and had realigned his grip on the club. The dwarf stepped into his swing with all his bulky weight, slamming the bugbear in the lower back.

The breathless monster tried to howl, and when that didn't work, it settled instead for slumping to its knees, clutching its blasted back and watching the world spin.

"Wish we had the time to finish a few of these," Ivan grumbled as he and Pikel moved higher up the hill.

Many more bugbears came at them from both sides, and cries of alarm continued to sound, and not just on the grassy slope.

Cadderly clutched his weapons and continued his scan for Dorigen, though he was beginning to understand that the missing wizard was the least of their problems.

Q

Every bugbear strike seemed to be just an inch behind the scrambling woman, and whatever contorted position Danica had to put herself into to avoid the attacks, she seemed quite able to launch her own.

One bugbear yelped in glee, thinking it had finally caught up to its prey, only to catch Danica's foot squarely in the face.

Danica sprang to her feet, a bugbear kneeling before her. She envisioned it as a block of stone and slammed her head into the monster's chest. Ribs—a dozen, perhaps—snapped apart, but they did so with a single sickening *crack*.

Then there were two.

Q

"One more elf head for my trophy wall!" Ragnor laughed.

Elbereth got his shield up to block the ogrillon's heavy sword, but his arm went numb under the sheer weight of that incredibly powerful blow.

"You'll look fine next to your kinfolk!" Ragnor boasted, wiggling his elf-ear necklace for his adversary to see.

Thinking Elbereth distracted by the gruesome sight, Ragnor stepped in. Elbereth, horrified indeed, managed to skip back from the ogrillon's strike, though he slipped on the thick grass and nearly went to one knee. He came up fast instead, stepping within Ragnor's follow-up attack and driving his sword into the ogrillon's thigh. A fine counter, except that Ragnor's free hand grabbed the elf as he passed, and with tremendous strength, hurled Elbereth backward and to the ground.

The heavy sword sliced at him but buried itself halfway to the hilt into the soft ground as Elbereth rolled aside.

The elf climbed back to his feet as Ragnor withdrew his sword. Elbereth took a quick glance around and saw that all sides seemed to be caving in on his companions. If he was to gain any semblance of a victory, he would have to strike Ragnor quickly. When he took a quick survey of the ogrillon, though, that didn't seem likely. Speed and agility were on Elbereth's side, but Ragnor could take anything Elbereth could throw his way. Defeating the brute would require time, plenty of time, to wear the heavier monster down, nicking and jabbing until Ragnor's blood ran from a hundred grazing wounds.

"Damn you," Elbereth muttered, and with all his world at stake, the valiant elf launched himself at Ragnor. He hacked once with his sword then, when he was too close to use the long blade, punched fiercely with the weapon's gem-encrusted hilt.

Q

"No time!" Ivan bellowed, seeing that his plan could not succeed with so many bugbears, goblins, and a host of newly-arrived orogs appearing from all around the base of the ridge. He turned to Pikel and winked. "Second choice!"

"Oo oi!" Pikel heartily agreed.

Cadderly was about to ask what "second choice" might mean, when Pikel rushed right up to him, and right through him, barreling along up the hill with the stunned young scholar firmly in tow.

Q

Ragnor and Elbereth held their deadly embrace. The elf's punches had bent the ogrillon's porcine snout every which way and lines of thick blood covered the monster's face. Still Ragnor maintained his fiendish grin.

Finally, one huge hand clamped onto the back of the elf's neck, and Elbereth was hauled out to arm's length. They were still too close for any effective sword strikes, but Ragnor's sword arm, held at the wrist by Elbereth's shield hand, hovered dangerously above the elf's head. Elbereth feared that the ogrillon would overpower him and drive his sword hilt down onto Elbereth's head.

The elf's fears trebled as Ragnor pushed a hidden catch on his weapon's crosspiece and a second blade, a gleaming stiletto, protruded from the bottom of his sword, its wicked tip just an inch from Elbereth's head.

Elbereth struggled wildly, kicking Ragnor repeatedly about the knees and groin. The ogrillon only grinned and forced his huge arm down.

Something slammed into Elbereth's side. He saw the sudden confusion on Ragnor's face then the world went flying about him. He hit the waist-deep river hard, twisting an ankle and a knee in the process then he understood, for he heard Ivan griping and water gurgling.

"You pulled me from my battle!" Elbereth roared as he grabbed his sword. "I could have—"

"Died," Ivan finished for him, though that wasn't exactly what the elf had had in mind. "Stop yer whining, elf," said the dwarf with a derisive chuckle. "And get me helmet, would ye?"

Elbereth blustered and growled, looking for a retort. To Ivan's obvious surprise, though, the prince reached over and scooped the half-floating helmet from the water, even hopping a few steps downstream to recover one of the antlers, which had come loose.

Cadderly flew over the precipice next, backstepping, his scrambling feet barely able to keep up at the end of Pikel's thick club. Both man and dwarf hit the river just a few feet from their companions. Cadderly came up spitting a stream of water and sputtering in shock. He kept enough wits about him to pull his precious pack above the water and fish out his short, stunned companion's head.

Pikel tried to squeak his thanks but wound up sending a stream of water into Cadderly's eye instead. The dwarf shrugged meekly and smiled.

"There she is!" they heard Ivan cry, and they looked up to see Danica spinning over the edge. The incredible monk half-ran, half-fell down the bank, grabbing for root-holds with one hand but holding her other arm, her wounded arm, tight against her body. Somewhere in the fight, Danica had reopened the arrow wound, and the sleeve and side of her tunic were stained crimson.

She managed her controlled descent, though, coming lightly into the water at the river's edge and easily outdistancing the two bugbears that pursued her. The monsters came on stubbornly, gingerly searching for handholds as they made their way down.

A hail of arrows whistled out of the trees beyond the far bank, every shot scoring a direct hit on the vulnerable monsters. Danica had to duck aside as the two hairy forms came crashing down.

There would be no cheers from the companions, though, for another arrow whistled from the trees, burying itself into Ivan's leg and sending the startled dwarf spinning to the ground. Before Ivan could begin to recover, fine swords landed heavily on his shoulders, one against either side of his thick, but quite vulnerable, neck.

"Uh-oh," muttered Pikel, who understood the misperceptions enough to slip behind the cover of Cadderly's body.

SIXTEEN

ANCIENT WISDOM

H old! Hold!" Elbereth cried, splashing from the river and shoving aside the two elves holding swords to Ivan's throat. "He is no enemy!"

The proclamation caught Ivan by surprise. "Thank ye, elf," he said, grimacing in pain with every word. The black-shafted arrow was nearly halfway through his thickly muscled thigh.

The two elves, thoroughly flummoxed, dipped their shoulders under Ivan's arms and hoisted the dwarf the rest of the way from the river.

"Away, and quickly!" one of them said. "The enemy will cross after us if we remain in the open."

None of the weary band had to be asked twice to leave, especially since they could still hear Ragnor above the din of the rushing waters, back out of sight over the ridge, wildly bellowing orders to his soldiers.

Elbereth, most of all, looked back at that ridge. Never before had the elf prince been bested in battle, yet for all his complaining at Ivan, Elbereth had to admit that if the dwarf had not torn him from the fight, Ragnor would have killed him.

The elf prince left the river with that dark thought in mind.

The elves' encampment wasn't formally a war camp. Rather, it was an area where the shadowy boughs of every tree seemed to hold an archer, grim-faced and ready should the enemy attempt to cross the river.

Elbereth and his companions were met in a small clearing by welcome faces, Shayleigh and Tintagel, two elves that the prince had feared slain at Daoine Dun. They offered no smiles as they walked over to join the companions. They frowned at the sight and smell of the dwarves.

"It is good that you have returned," Shayleigh said, her melodic voice more somber than Elbereth ever remembered hearing it. He stared long and hard at her, just then beginning to understand the depth of the defeat at Daoine Dun.

"Many have died," added Tintagel, similarly reserved.

Elbereth nodded. "Who tends the wounded?" he asked. "Lady Maupoissant's arm requires a new dressing and my—" he looked at Ivan curiously for a moment— "my friend has taken an arrow."

Ivan's eyes widened at the elf prince's proclamation of him as a friend.

"Wow," breathed Pikel.

"Bah! It's nothing, elf," Ivan growled, but when he pulled away from his supporters and tried to take a step, he nearly swooned from the pain and found that the leg would not support him.

Danica was beside the dwarf in an instant, propping him with her good arm. "Come," she said, straining a smile. "We will go to be tended together."

"Two old and broken travelers, eh?" chuckled Ivan.

"Not as broken as the enemies we left behind," Danica pointed out. She noticed that Shayleigh and Tintagel had not relinquished their frowns, and she nearly growled at them as she and Ivan walked past.

"The dwarves are to be treated as allies," Elbereth ordered, "for that they are, and let no elf consider them otherwise."

"By whose command?" came a voice from the side, which Elbereth recognized as his father's before he ever turned to regard the king.

"Have you taken command of the forces?" Galladel snarled, moving to his son. "Is it your right to choose our alliances?"

Danica and Ivan stopped and turned to watch. Cadderly and Pikel didn't blink, but Cadderly dropped a hand on Pikel's shoulder to keep the dwarf calm as the elf king walked close by them.

Elbereth wasn't convinced that his father's outburst was even worthy of an answer, but he knew that the trouble would only increase if he didn't face Galladel then and there.

"I did not believe we were in a favorable enough position to refuse help," he said.

"I never claimed to help ye, elf," barked Ivan, wanting to put the whole thing back into a perspective that his dwarf sensibilities could accept. "Me and me brother came to watch over Cadderly and Danica, not yerself!"

"Oo oi!" Pikel agreed.

"Indeed," said Galladel, setting his stern glare upon one brother then the other. "Do watch over Cadderly and Danica, then, and keep out of the People's way."

"Father—" Elbereth began.

"And I will hear no arguments from you, Prince of Shilmista!" Galladel shouted. "Where were you when Daoine Dun was overrun? Where were you while the People were slaughtered?"

For the first time since he'd met Elbereth, Cadderly thought the prince looked very small. The young scholar looked past the elf to Danica, and saw that a wetness rimmed her almond eyes. No jealousy came over the young scholar, though, for he shared Danica's sympathy.

"Go off again, if you so desire," growled Galladel. "Then, perhaps, you will not be forced to watch our final moments, the destruction of our ancestral home."

The elf king wheeled about and disappeared into the brush.

Elbereth stood long and silent in the deepening shadows.

"They'll not attack at night," Tintagel offered to the companions, hoping to break the grim mood.

"Darkness favors goblins," Cadderly said, more to continue the conversation than to argue the point.

"Not in Shilmista," the blue-eyed elf wizard replied, forcing a smile. "Our enemies have learned to fear the darkness here. They attack only during the day. Such was the case at Daoine Dun. . . ." Tintagel's voice trailed away as he mentioned the fateful battle.

Elbereth said nothing. He didn't lower his face, refusing to dip his proud chin, as he slowly walked away.

Q

The night was unusually chilly for late summer, and Cadderly was allowed a fire far back from the front lines. He took up his light tube and the book of Dellanil

Quil'quien and began his task at translating, determined to do what he might to help the elven cause. He became distracted soon after, though, by a night bird's melodic cries a short distance away.

A thought came over Cadderly. He placed the ancient book down and recalled the spell of silence he had memorized earlier that day. It was not an easy spell, and Cadderly had known all along that casting it would challenge him. While he was glad that Dorigen had not appeared in Ragnor's camp, he almost wished he'd found the opportunity to take that challenge.

"Why not?" the young scholar mused.

Cadderly slipped away from the fire, narrowing the light tube's beam to better locate the bird. He recited the runes exactly, not sure of his inflection, but confident that he would omit no words from the prescribed chant. Several heartbeats passed then Cadderly felt a strange energy building within him.

It gathered strength and urgency, called for him to let it loose. And he did so, uttering the last syllable with all the determination he could throw into his voice.

He paused a moment. The night bird went silent—all the forest was quiet.

Cadderly clenched his fist, victorious. He went back to the ancient book, feeling better about the role he might play in the coming battles.

His enthusiasm was stolen soon after, though, when Danica approached his fire. The young woman's lips moved in greeting, but no words came from her mouth. She looked around, confused. Cadderly knew what was wrong, and he dropped his face into his hands.

His sigh, too, could not be heard, nor could the crackle of the fire, he realized. Grabbing a stick, he wrote,

"It will pass," in the dirt and motioned for Danica to sit beside him.

C

"What happened?" Danica asked a few moments later, when the noise of the flames had returned.

"I have once again proved my uselessness," Cadderly replied. He kicked his pack, containing *The Tome of Universal Harmony.* "I am no priest of Deneir. I am no priest at all. Even the simplest spells roll awkwardly from my lips, only then to fall upon targets I do not desire. I tried to silence a bird and quieted myself instead. We should be glad that the wizard did not appear at the last battle. We all would have died if she had, though no one would have heard our final screams."

Despite Cadderly's grave tone, despite everything around her and the pain in her injured arm, Danica laughed aloud at that thought.

"I'm afraid to call for even the simplest healing spells," Cadderly continued, "knowing that they would probably deepen a wound, not close it."

Danica wanted to comfort him, to tell him that he was the most intelligent man she had ever met and the highest regarded young priest in the Edificant Library. But she found no sympathy for his problems, not with the weight of doom hanging heavily in Shilmista's ancient boughs.

"Self pity does not become you," she remarked dryly.

"Self truth," Cadderly corrected.

"So it may be," argued Danica, "but an irrelevant one now."

"All my life—" Cadderly began.

"Has not been wasted," Danica interrupted before the

young scholar could sink lower into despair. "All your life? You have just begun to live."

"I had thought to live it as a Glyphscribe, a priest of Deneir," Cadderly lamented, "but that doesn't seem to be my course."

"You cannot know that," Danica scolded.

"Agreed," came a voice. They looked up and were surprised to see Kierkan Rufo approaching the fire.

Danica had nearly forgotten about the man, and seeing him again brought back many unpleasant thoughts. Cadderly obviously sensed her anger, and he put a hand on her shoulder, surely fearing that she would spring at Rufo and throttle him.

"Some of the highest-ranking Glyphscribes are inept at spellcasting," Rufo went on, taking a seat on a log opposite the low fire and pointedly avoiding Danica's cold stare. "Your friend, the headmistress, for example. Even the simplest spells often fail when uttered by Headmistress Pertelope."

Rufo's angular features seemed sharper in the flickering shadows, and Danica detected a tremor in his voice.

"How can that be true?" Cadderly asked. "Pertelope is a leader among the order. How could she have attained such heights as Headmistress of the Edificant Library if she cannot perform the simplest spells?"

"Because she is a scholar, as are you," Rufo replied, "and in Deneir's favor, do not doubt, even if that favor does not manifest itself in the form of spells. Headmistress Pertelope is no pretender to her title."

"How do you know this?" Danica asked, and she had many other questions she wanted to ask of Rufo, particularly concerning his interactions with Dorigen.

"I heard Avery talking once," Rufo replied, trying to sound casual, though his monotone voice quivered with every word. "And I have been attentive since." He leaned back on his bony elbows, again trying futilely to appear calm.

Passing moments did little to dissipate the tension. Still, Cadderly seemed relieved to hear Rufo's claims about Pertelope.

Rufo stood stiffly. "I'm glad you've returned," he said, his voice somewhat strained. From his pack he produced Cadderly's silken cape and wide-brimmed hat, the latter a bit crumpled. "I'm . . . glad," Rufo said again. He half-bowed and started away, nearly tripping over the log as he went.

"Surprised to see us, do you think?" Danica remarked when Rufo was beyond hearing distance. "Certainly our friend was a bit nervous."

"Kierkan Rufo has always been nervous," Cadderly replied, his voice sounding relaxed for the first time since he had discovered the failure of his spell of silence.

"You think it's a coincidence, then," Danica muttered. "And is it a coincidence that Dorigen knew of him?"

"She may have learned of Rufo from the same source that told her of us," Cadderly reasoned. "The imp?"

"Indeed," the young woman agreed, and her wry tone shifted the connotation of Cadderly's own words to sound like an accusation against their companion. "Indeed. . . ."

Q

Cadderly awakened to the sound of battle shortly past dawn. He fumbled about his pack for his spindle-disks, grabbed his walking stick, and rushed away. The fight was over before he ever got close, though. The elves successfully beat back yet another enemy probe.

Despite the success, though, neither Danica, Elbereth, nor the dwarves seemed pleased when Cadderly came upon them.

"I-I'm sorry," the young scholar apologized, stuttering. "I was asleep. No one told me . . ."

"Fear not," Elbereth replied. "You would have had little role in the fight. Our archers turned the enemy back before very many of them even got across the river."

"And them that did wished they'd turned back!" added Ivan, seeming none the worse for his wounded leg. He pointedly held out his bloodied axe for Cadderly to see. Pikel, meanwhile, was busily pulling a clump of goblin hair from a thin crack in his club.

Cadderly didn't miss the appreciative stare Elbereth cast the dwarves' way, though the elf obviously tried to mask the look.

"Go and gather your strength now," Elbereth said to Danica, then he looked around to indicate that his words were meant for all of them. "I must attend council with my father. Our scouts will return this morning with more complete estimates of the enemy's strength." The elf bowed and was gone.

Ivan and Pikel were asleep almost immediately after they returned to Cadderly's small camp. The dwarves had been up all night, showing some of the more receptive elves how to construct a proper barricade, complete with cunning traps.

Danica, too, stretched out to rest, and Cadderly, after a quick meal of tasty biscuits, dived back into the book of Dellanil Quil'quien. His translating had gone slowly through the wee hours, and he thought he had discerned the meaning of just a single rune. A hundred more arcane symbols remained a mystery to him.

Elbereth came to see them later that morning, accompanied by Tintagel and Shayleigh. The prince's grim expression revealed much about what the returning scouts had reported.

"Our enemy is more disciplined and organized than we had believed," Elbereth admitted.

"And the enemy wizard returned this morning," added Shayleigh. "She sent a line of fire from her hand, shrouding an unfortunate scout. He is alive, but our healers do not expect him to survive the day."

Cadderly reflexively glanced over to his pack, to *The Tome of Universal Harmony*. What healing secrets might he discover there? he wondered. Could he find the strength to help the wounded elf?

He looked away, ashamed, admitting that he could not. He was no Glyphscribe. He had established that fact the night before.

"What of allies?" Danica asked. "Has the Edificant Library responded to our call?"

"There has been no word of outside help," Elbereth replied. "It is believed that the library could not muster sufficient force anyway, even if they could arrive in time."

"Where does that leave us?" Cadderly asked.

"Galladel speaks of leaving Shilmista," Elbereth said past the welling lump in his slender throat. "He talks often of Evermeet, and says that our day in Faerûn has passed."

"And what do you say?" Danica asked, her question sounding almost like an accusation.

"It is not time to go," the proud elf answered. "I will not leave Shilmista to the goblins, but . . ."

"But our hopes here are fast fading," Shayleigh finished for him. Cadderly couldn't miss the edge of sadness in her violet eyes, a somber look that had stolen her vigor and heart for the fight. "We cannot defeat so large an enemy. Many goblins will die, it is true, but our numbers will continue to dwindle until we are no more."

To his own surprise, Cadderly broke the ensuing silence. "I have begun the translation of Dellanil's book," he said. "We will find our answers there."

Elbereth shook his head. "You have little time," he explained, "and we do not expect as much as you from the ancient work. The magic of the forest is not as it used to be—in that regard, I fear, my father is correct."

"When will he decide our course?" Danica asked.

"Later this day," replied the elf prince, "though I believe the meeting is just a formality, for the decision has already been made."

There was no more to be said, but so much more to be done, and the three elves took their leave. Danica fell back to her blanket, squirming about in a futile attempt to find some sleep, and Cadderly went back to the ancient book.

He studied on, frustrated by two simple runes that appeared on nearly every page. If those two could take so much of his time, how then could he hope to complete the work in a single day?

He moved the book aside and stretched out, exhausted and defeated, filled with loathing for his own inadequacies. Cadderly the Priest? Apparently not. Cadderly the Fighter? Hardly. Cadderly the Scholar?

Perhaps, but that talent suddenly seemed so very useless in the real and violent world. Cadderly could recount the adventures of a thousand ancient heroes, tell of long-dead wars, and inscribe a wizard's lost spellbook after having seen it only once. But he couldn't turn the black tide from beautiful Shilmista, and none of his other talents really seemed to matter anymore.

Sleep did finally take him, mercifully, and in that sleep came a dream that Cadderly could not have expected.

He saw Shilmista under the light of an ancient sky, under starlight of violet and blue and crisp yellow rays, filtering softly through the thick leafy canopy. There danced the elves, ten times the number of Shilmista's present host, led in song by the greatest of the elves' kings.

The words were strange to Cadderly, though he fluently spoke the Elvish dialect common to his day. Stranger still came the reaction of the forest around the elves, for the trees themselves reverberated with Dellanil's song, answering the elf king. Only a slight breeze wafted through the ancient vision of Shilmista, yet the great limbs bent and swayed, synchronous to the graceful movements of the sylvan folk.

Then the vision was gone and Cadderly sat up, awakened by Ivan and Pikel's thunderous snores. The young scholar shook his head and lay back, hoping to recapture that lost moment. His dreams were fading fast, only a blur, but he remembered the serenity, and the magic, acutely.

His eyes popped open wide and he scrambled for the black-bound book. Those unknown runes greeted him once again, but Cadderly threw aside his notes and logical, practiced techniques. Instead, the young scholar used his emotional revelations, felt as Dellanil had felt in his dreamy vision, and sent his soul dancing as the elves and the trees had danced, their song sounding within him.

C

"Get out!" Kierkan Rufo growled, banging his arm against a tree trunk. "I did as you demanded, now leave me alone!"

Rufo glanced around, nervous, fearing that he had spoken too loudly. The elves were everywhere, it seemed, and Rufo had no doubt that any one of them would gladly put an arrow into him if they ever discovered the source of his dilemma.

He was alone in the forest, physically at least, and had been since his departure from Cadderly and Danica the previous night. Rufo could find no sleep—the imp's voice in his head would not allow that. Already the man appeared haggard, haunted, for he could not be rid of Druzil's telepathic intrusions.

What have you to lose? purred the imp's raspy voice. *All the world will be your gain.*

"I don't know what they're planning, nor would I reveal it to you if I did," Rufo insisted.

Oh, but you would, came Druzil's confident reply. *And you shall indeed.*

"Never!"

You have once betrayed your friends, Kierkan Rufo, Druzil reminded him. *How merciful would the elf prince be if he learned of your weakness?*

Rufo's breath came in short gasps. He understood that Druzil's question was a direct threat.

But think not of such unpleasantness, Druzil continued. *Aid us now. We will prove victorious—that is obvious— and you will be well rewarded when the battle is won. Scorn us, and you will pay.*

Rufo didn't realize his own movements, was oblivious to the sharp pain. He looked down in shock to his hand, holding a clump of his matted black hair.

SEVENTEEN

A DESPERATE ATTEMPT

O ur sincere pardon," Danica whispered when she and Cadderly entered the small glade beyond a thick grove of pines that blocked the outside world. The elf leaders—Galladel and Elbereth, Shayleigh, Tintagel, and several others that Danica and Cadderly didn't know—had gathered there. Their faces were grim, and though Galladel said nothing about the interruption, both friends could see that the elf king was not pleased by their intrusion.

"I have translated the work," Cadderly announced, holding up the book of Dellanil Quil'quien for all to see.

"Where did you get that?" Galladel demanded.

"He found it at Daoine Dun," Elbereth explained, "and has it now with my permission." Galladel glowered at his son, but Elbereth turned to Cadderly. "You have not had time to read the entire tome," the elf prince remarked. "How could you possibly have translated it?"

"I have not," Cadderly replied guardedly. "I mean . . ." He paused to search for the correct way to explain what he had accomplished, and also to calm himself under Galladel's imposing stare.

"I have deciphered the meanings of the connotations, of the ancient runes," Cadderly continued. "The symbols pose no more difficulties. Together we can read through the work and see what secrets it might provide."

Some of the elves, Elbereth and Shayleigh in particular, seemed intrigued. Elbereth rose and approached Cadderly, his silver eyes sparkling with a hint of renewed hope.

"What value do you expect to find within those pages?" Galladel asked sharply, his angry tone stopping his son in midstride.

An expression of confusion crossed Cadderly's face, for the young scholar certainly hadn't expected that reaction.

"You bring us false hope," the elf king went on, his anger unrelenting.

"There's more," Cadderly argued. "In this work, I have read a most remarkable account of how King Dellanil Quil'quien awakened the trees of Shilmista, and of how those trees crushed an invading force of goblins."

With the parallels to their present dilemma so obvious, Cadderly didn't see how that news could be met with anything other than joy. But Galladel seemed less impressed than ever.

"You tell us nothing we do not already know," the elf king snapped. "Do you think that none among us has read the book of Dellanil?"

"I thought the runes ancient and lost to understanding," Cadderly replied. Danica put her hand on his shoulder.

"Lost now," Galladel replied, "but I, too, have read the work, centuries ago when those runes were not so uncommon. I could decipher them still, if I had the mind and the time to do so."

"You did not think to awaken the trees?" Elbereth asked his father in disbelief.

Galladel's glare bored into his impertinent son. "You speak of that act as though it were some simple cantrip."

"It's not a spell," Cadderly put in, "but a summons, a calling to awaken the powers of the forest."

"Powers that are no more," Galladel added.

"How can you—?" Elbereth began, but Galladel cut him short.

"This is not the first war that has come to Shilmista since I began my reign," the elf king explained. He seemed old and vulnerable, his face pale and hollow. "And I read the account of Dellanil's battle, as you have," he offered to Cadderly with some apparent sympathy. "Like you, I was filled with hope on that long ago occasion and filled with belief in the magic of Shilmista.

"But the trees did not come to my call," the elf king continued, drawing nods of recognition from two other aged elves sitting by his side. "Not a single one. Many elves died repelling the invaders, more than should have, I fear, since their king was too busy to join in their fight."

It seemed to Cadderly as if the aged elf's shoulders sagged even lower as he recalled that tragic time.

"That is a summons for another age," Galladel said, his voice resolute once more, "an age when the trees were the sentient sentinels of Shilmista Forest."

"But are they not still?" Shayleigh dared to interject. "Hammadeen bade us to hear their warning song."

"Hammadeen is a dryad," Galladel explained, "much more attuned to the flora than any elf ever could be. She can hear the song of any plant, anywhere in the world. Do not allow her cryptic bidding to bring you false hope."

"We have few options," Elbereth reminded his father.

"The summons will not work," Galladel insisted, his tone showing clearly that he considered the conversation at an end. "You do have our thanks, scholar Cadderly," he said, somewhat condescendingly. "Your efforts have not gone unnoticed."

"Come," Danica whispered into Cadderly's ear, pulling him by the hand back out of the glade.

"No!" Cadderly replied, twisting from her grasp. "What will you do?" he snapped at Galladel. He approached the elf king, sitting directly across the glade, pushing right by the shocked Elbereth on his way.

"I have heard many admit that the force opposing Shilmista is too great for the elves to defeat," Cadderly went on. "I have heard that no help will arrive in time or in sufficient numbers to save the forest. If all that is so then what will you do?"

"That is what we have gathered here to discuss . . . privately," the stern elf king replied.

"Then what have you decided?" Cadderly shot back, not backing down in the least. "Are you to run away, leave the forest for the invaders?"

Galladel stood and met Cadderly's determined stare with one equally unyielding. Cadderly heard Danica rushing to corral him then heard, to his surprise, Elbereth intercept her.

"Most will go," Galladel admitted. "Some—" he spoke the word callously and looked pointedly at Elbereth as he uttered it—"wish to stay and fight, determined to hinder and punish the enemy until they have joined their kin in death."

"And you will go . . . to the Edificant Library?" Cadderly asked. "Then away west from there, to Evermeet?"

Galladel nodded. "Our time in Shilmista, in Faerûn, has passed, young priest," he admitted, and Cadderly could see that the words pained him deeply.

Cadderly was not unsympathetic, and he didn't doubt the truth of Galladel's claims, but there were other ramifications to their actions that the elves apparently had not considered, most prominently the fate of the rest of the Southern Heartlands.

"As an emissary of the Edificant Library, I can assure you that you and your People will be welcomed there for as long as you wish to stay," Cadderly replied. "But as one who has seen what befell the library, and now Shilmista, I must beg you to reconsider your course. If the forest falls, then so, too, shall the men of the mountains, and of the lake and city to the east. The enemy must not be allowed so easy or so complete a victory."

Galladel seemed on the verge of exploding. "You would sacrifice us?" he growled, his face only inches from Cadderly's. "You would give the lives of my People, that a few *men* might survive? We owe you nothing! Do you believe it is with light hearts that we surrender our homeland? I have lived in Shilmista since before your precious library was even constructed."

Cadderly wanted to argue that Galladel's own claims proved that Shilmista was worth fighting for then, and that every possibility, even an attempt to awaken the trees, should be exhausted before the elves fled their homes. The young scholar couldn't, though. He could find nothing to throw against Galladel's outrage, nothing to diminish the elf king's ire. When Danica again came to him and pulled him toward the glade, he did not resist.

"I thought I could help them," he said to her, not looking back at Galladel.

"We all wish to help," Danica replied. "That is our frustration."

They said nothing more as they walked slowly away and heard an argument raging behind them within the ring of pines. When they were back at the campsite with Kierkan Rufo and the dwarf brothers, the weight of the world seemed to bow Cadderly's shoulders.

They were surprised later, when Elbereth, Shayleigh, and Tintagel came to join them.

"You are certain that you have the runes deciphered?" Elbereth asked, his jaw firm and eyes staring hard at Cadderly.

"I am certain," Cadderly replied, jumping to his feet, suspecting what the bold elf prince had in mind.

The expressions splayed across the faces of both Shayleigh and Tintagel revealed their discomfort.

"What was the council's decision?" Danica asked of Elbereth. She rose beside Cadderly and looked hard at the elf prince.

Elbereth didn't retreat from her gaze. "By my father's word, the People will depart the forest," he admitted. "We surrender the ground in exchange for our lives, and never shall we return."

"It was not an easy decision for Galladel to come by," Tintagel offered. "Your father has witnessed the deaths of many elves these last days."

The statement stung Elbereth, as Tintagel, obviously not pleased with Elbereth's intentions, apparently had hoped it would.

"Their deaths will have been in vain if the enemy is handed Shilmista," the elf prince declared. "We have options still, and I will not leave until they are exhausted."

"You plan to awaken the trees," Cadderly reasoned.

"Oo oi!" piped in a happy Pikel, who dearly wanted to see such druidlike magic.

All three elves cast a disconcerting look the round-shouldered dwarf's way.

"Oo," Pikel chirped, and he lowered his eyes.

"With your help," Elbereth said to Cadderly, "we shall recapture the magic of days long past. We shall turn the forest against our enemies and drive them back to their mountain holes."

Cadderly was excited by the thought, but he saw that he and Elbereth, and perhaps Pikel, were the only ones holding out much hope.

"Your father does not believe that," Danica reminded the prince.

"He will not approve your actions," added Shayleigh.

"How can we leave until we have tried?" Elbereth asked. "If we fail, then we shall go along with Galladel's plans, and what have we lost? If we succeed, if the forest comes to life, if great trees walk beside us as allies . . ."

Tintagel and Shayleigh managed somewhat hopeful smiles. Danica looked to Cadderly, doubting, but ready to support him in whatever manner he required.

"I'm ready to show you the words," Cadderly said. "Together we shall find the song of Dellanil Quil'quien and implore the trees to our side!"

The three elves took their leave then, and Cadderly, visage set firm, took up the ancient book and opened it to the appropriate passage.

Danica wanted to tell him of the futility, wanted to warn him of the dire consequences his failure might have on the elven host's already weakened morale, but looking at her love sitting so stern and determined as he pored through the book, she could not find the words.

None of them noticed Kierkan Rufo quietly slip away.

Q

The elves will depart? came the telepathic voice, revealing the imp's excitement. *What defenses will they leave behind? And what of young Cadderly? Tell me of Cadderly!*

"Leave me alone!" Rufo screamed back. "You have gained enough from me. Go and question another." The man could sense the imp's distant laughter.

"The elves will depart," Rufo admitted, hoping to mask the more important news with something the enemy would discern soon enough in any case.

And that's all? came the expected question.

"That's all," Rufo replied. "A few may remain, just to slow your advance, but the rest will go, never to return."

And what of Cadderly?

"He will go with them, back to the library," Rufo lied, knowing that to reveal anything else would invariably lead him into the middle of another conspiracy.

Again came the reverberations of the imp's distant laughter. *You have not told me all,* came his thoughts, *but you have revealed more than you intended simply by trying to hide that which you cannot. I will be with you, Kierkan Rufo, every step. And know that your unwillingness to*

*cooperate will be revealed once our conquest is complete, once
you face my mistress. I assure you that she is not a merciful
victor. Go and reconsider your course and your untruths.
Think of the path that lies ahead for Kierkan Rufo.*

Rufo felt the connection break, then he was alone,
stumbling through the woods, a haunted man.

Q

Danica was glad of the change that came over Cadderly, whatever the outcome of their desperate attempt.
She knew that Cadderly was a sensitive man, frustrated
by the violence that had been forced upon him and by
the destruction of so many wondrous things, both in
beautiful Shilmista and back in the Edificant Library.
Danica didn't doubt Cadderly's willingness to fight back
however he could. They stood in the same glade that the
elves had used earlier for council, wanting their attempt
to be private in case it failed, as Galladel had predicted.
Watching Cadderly and Elbereth in their preparations
for the ceremony, the young scholar tutoring the elf on
particular inflections and movements, Danica almost
allowed herself to believe that the trees of Shilmista
would awaken, and that the forest would be saved.

Tintagel, Shayleigh, and Pikel, beside Danica, seemed
to hold similar, though unspoken hopes. Ivan merely
grumbled a stream of complaints, though, thinking that
they should all be out "clobberin' orcs" instead of wasting
their time calling to "trees that ain't got ears!"

Several other elves appeared when Elbereth began the
song, an even-paced, melodic chant that reverberated
under the mystic evening canopy.

Pikel nearly swooned and began a dance, graceful by
dwarven standards, but a bit strained in an elven wood.

Still, Tintagel and Shayleigh couldn't help smiling when they saw the would-be druid, his green-dyed, braided beard bouncing about his shoulders with every twirl.

Then Galladel stepped between Shayleigh and Danica, his scowl threatening the magical aura as surely as would a goblin attack.

"Do not disturb them, I beg you," Danica whispered to the elf king, and to her surprise, he nodded gravely and remained quiet. He glanced over to Pikel and frowned, then turned his attention back to his son, who was fully immersed in the ancient song.

Danica watched the elf king's eyes well with tears, and she knew that Galladel looked upon an image of himself centuries ago, that he recalled that time when he had failed to awaken the trees at the cost of many elves' lives.

Elbereth's song reached out to Shilmista. Danica couldn't understand the words, but they seemed fitting for the forest, almost otherworldly and even more purely elven than *Daoine Teague Feer* had seemed. Those elves, and many had come, gathered around the small glade's fringes, did not even whisper among themselves—did nothing but listen to their prince's enchanting call.

A wolf howled somewhere in the distance. Another took up the call, and another in response to that.

Then, too suddenly it seemed, Elbereth was done. He stood in the center of the glade, Cadderly moving beside him, and they, and all those around them, waited with held breath for Shilmista to respond.

There came nothing, save the howl of the wolves and the lamenting keen of the evening wind.

"Trees ain't got ears," Ivan muttered after a long while.

"I told you it would not work," Galladel berated them, the anticipation of the moment stolen by the wide-eyed dwarf's comment. "Are you finished with your folly? Might we get along with the business of saving our People?"

The look Elbereth gave Cadderly showed only remorse. "We have tried," the elf prince offered. "At least we have tried." He turned and walked slowly away to rejoin his father.

Truly perplexed, Cadderly stood in the middle of the glade, moving the beam of his light tube across the text of the ancient book.

"It was worth the attempt," said Danica as she and the dwarf brothers came over to join him.

"Worthy indeed," came a tittering voice that they recognized at once.

In unison, they turned and spotted Hammadeen the dryad standing beside a pine opposite from where Galladel and the others had just departed.

"What do you know?" Cadderly demanded, heading for the dryad. "You must tell us! The trees did not respond to the call, and you know the reason."

"Oh, they did hear!" Hammadeen replied, clapping her hands happily. She moved behind the pine and was gone, reappearing a moment later behind another tree many feet from the volatile young man. "They did!"

"Have they begun their march upon our enemies?" Cadderly breathed, hardly daring to believe.

Hammadeen's laughter mocked his hopes. "Of course they have not!" the dryad chirped. "These trees are young. They have not the power of the ancients. You are in the wrong place, do you not understand?"

Cadderly's crestfallen look was matched by Danica's and Pikel's expressions. Ivan just grumbled something, huffed, and stormed away.

"But the trees in this part of the forest have heard the elves' song," Hammadeen offered to brighten their mood, "and they are pleased by it."

"Lot o' good that'll do 'em," the departing Ivan chided.

Danica echoed the thoughts of the remaining three perfectly when she whispered, "How pleased will the trees be to hear the crack of orcs' axes?"

Q

Hammadeen stopped laughing and faded into the pine.

The four companions were on the trail south later that same night, joined by Kierkan Rufo. Many elves accompanied them, though the fair folk did not walk the straight trails, as Cadderly and his friends had been told to do. Rather, they dipped in and out of the shadows to the sides, wary though weary, and those who were not riding often kept to the trees, crossing silently among high and intertwined branches.

Shayleigh found the travelers and dropped from her horse to walk beside them, but her presence did little to comfort them, particularly when it became apparent that she couldn't look Cadderly in the eye.

"They are fighting again, behind us," the elf maiden said, "as it shall be all the way out of Shilmista."

"Stupid orcs," Ivan muttered, and that was the only response forthcoming from the group.

"This time it would seem King Galladel was correct," Shayleigh went on.

"We had nothing to lose," Cadderly replied, a bit more sharply than he had intended.

"But we did," said Shayleigh. "Word has spread of our failure. All the elves know that Shilmista will not rise beside them. Our hearts are heavy. Few will remain beside Elbereth as he continues to hinder the enemy."

Both Cadderly and Danica started to say something, but Ivan promptly diffused their stubborn enthusiasm.

"No, ye won't!" the dwarf insisted to the two of them. "Ye won't be staying, nor will me or me brother."

"Oo," said Pikel sadly.

"This ain't our place," Ivan roared on. "And there ain't a thing we can do now to slow them monsters down! Too many of the damned things!"

Shayleigh left them then, and Danica and Cadderly couldn't even muster the strength to bid her farewell.

EIGHTEEN

A WOOD WORTH FIGHTING FOR

Danica noticed a change in her companion during their long and dismal walk. It started with Cadderly glancing all around, staring into Shilmista's shadows, his gray eyes rimmed with wetness. But the tears never came. Instead they were replaced by an anger so profound the young scholar could hardly keep his breathing steady, could hardly keep his fists unclenched.

He dropped out of the retreating line and pulled his pack off his back, offering no explanation to Danica, Rufo, or the dwarf brothers as they moved beside him.

"A bit of reading for the road?" Ivan asked, seeing Cadderly take out the ancient book of Dellanil Quil'quien.

"It should have worked," Cadderly replied. "The words were spoken correctly. Every syllable was as King Dellanil spoke them centuries ago."

"Of course they were," said Danica. "No one in all Shilmista doubts the sincerity of your attempt or that your heart was for the forest."

"Flattery?" Cadderly barked at her, his voice more full of anger than it ever had been toward his love.

Danica backed away a step, stunned.

"Oo," moaned Pikel.

"Ye've no right to be speaking to the lady that way," Ivan said, slapping his axe loudly against his open hand.

Cadderly nodded in agreement but would not let his embarrassment steal his mounting determination. "The summons must work," he declared. "We have nothing else—Shilmista has no other hope."

"Then we have nothing at all," Ivan replied. "Ye heard the wood sprite yerself. Ye're in the wrong place, lad. Shilmista will not come to yer call."

Cadderly looked around at the trees that had deceived him, searching for escape from the apparent finality of the dryad's claims. A thought struck him then, one so simple but it had not occurred to any of them.

"Hammadeen didn't say that," Cadderly told Ivan. The scholar turned to include the others in his revelation.

Danica's head tilted curiously. "The dryad's words were direct enough," she argued.

"Hammadeen said we were in the wrong place," Cadderly replied. "We took that to mean that Shilmista was the wrong place. Hammadeen said the trees heard the call. How wide an area was she speaking of?"

"What are ye babbling about?" Ivan demanded. "What other 'area' might there be?"

"Think of where we were when Elbereth read the incantation," Cadderly prompted.

"The clearing," Ivan replied at once.

"But the trees around that grove!" Cadderly said. "Think of the trees."

"I'm not for telling one tree from another," Ivan protested. "Ask me brother if ye're wanting to know—"

"Not what sort of trees they were," Cadderly explained, "but their age."

"The camp was surrounded by young growth," Danica realized. "Even the circling pines were not so tall."

"Yes, too young," Cadderly explained. "Those trees weren't alive when Dellanil intoned the ancient words, not alive even when Galladel tried to awaken the wood. They didn't exist when magic still filled Shilmista's air."

"Would that matter?" Danica asked. "A spell—"

"This isn't a spell," Cadderly interrupted. "It's a call to a once-sentient forest. The new trees might still speak so that a dryad would hear, but they have lost the ability to walk beside the elves. But the oldest ones, the ones from Dellanil's time, may not have."

"If any of those remain," Danica stated.

"Not likely," Kierkan Rufo had to add, fearing that Cadderly's newest revelations would keep them all in the forest longer than the man desired.

"Oh, but there are," came a voice from the side. An elf that none of them knew rose from the brush just a few feet away and smiled at Ivan's glower and the others' stupefied expressions.

"Pardon my eavesdropping," the elf said. "Your conversation was much too interesting for me to interrupt, and I only speak now to tell you that there are indeed trees in Shilmista from the days of King Dellanil: a grove of huge oaks, west of here. The place is called Syldritch Trea, the Most Ancient Trees."

"Did King Galladel go to Syldritch Trea when he failed in his attempt at the summoning?" Cadderly asked, already suspecting the answer but eager for confirmation.

The elf thought for a moment then answered, "No, I do not believe he did. But neither was King Dellanil in Syldritch Trea when he called the trees."

"Bring Elbereth, I beg, and hurry," said Cadderly, ignoring the elf's last statement. "Shilmista's day may not be past."

The elf nodded curtly and was gone, disappearing into the surrounding brush in the blink of an eye.

"Ye cannot be thinking . . ." Ivan began slowly.

"Indeed I can," Cadderly replied.

"He just said that Dellanil—" Danica started to protest.

"Don't presume anything about the ancient forest," Cadderly interrupted. "Perhaps, in that time, the trees called to each other after Dellanil began the enchantment. Perhaps the trees spread the summons throughout Shilmista."

Ivan's look reflected his doubts. Even Pikel, so hopeful when they'd first tried to awaken the trees, frowned.

"It will work," Cadderly growled at them with such determination that even Ivan did not try to tell him differently.

Danica hooked his arm for support and gave him an approving wink.

Q

Elbereth arrived a short while later, accompanied by Shayleigh and Galladel. The three had already heard of Cadderly's latest revelation, and Galladel seemed displeased.

"Syldritch Trea," Cadderly said as soon as they arrived, giving the pessimistic elf king no time to quash his momentum. "The summons will work in Syldritch Trea."

"You cannot know that," Elbereth replied, though the elf prince appeared intrigued.

"And we cannot afford to waste precious time," King Galladel added. "You have seen the despair your false hopes have given us, priest. It would be better now for all concerned—if you continued on your way home."

"Home. . . ." Cadderly echoed, aiming his remark at Elbereth. "Quite a concept, that. A place to be defended, perhaps. At least, that's what I, who have never had a true home, was once told."

Danica winced and gave Cadderly's arm a jerk as Elbereth stormed over to stand before them.

"What do you know of it?" the elf prince demanded. "Do you believe it is with light hearts that we leave Shilmista?"

"I don't believe you wish to leave at all," Cadderly replied, not bending an inch under Elbereth's cold glare. "And perhaps you need not. Perhaps—"

" 'Ware his twisted tongue!" Galladel cried. "I understand you now, *n Tel'Quessir,*" the elf king roared, wagging an accusatory finger Cadderly's way. "You have come to encourage us to continue this hopeless battle, to sacrifice us, that your own precious home might be saved."

"The library is not my home," Cadderly muttered, but his words were lost in the ensuing explosion of protests aimed at the king from Ivan and Danica, a "Hey!" from Pikel, and even a few stern words from Elbereth.

When things quieted again, Cadderly gave Galladel's accusation not another thought. He looked at Elbereth, and at Elbereth only, as he made his case.

"The summons must work," he said. "I believe in it with all my heart. This is no ruse, no deception to encourage sacrifice. It's a hope that your home will not fall under our monstrous enemy's shadow, that the elven dance will continue in this forest throughout my lifetime at least."

"Syldritch Trea lies to the west and north," Elbereth replied. "To get there, I will have to cross the enemy lines once more, and far deeper this time. If the summons does not work. . . ."

"You'll not go alone," Cadderly vowed, and he shot a glance Galladel's way.

"He'll not go at all!" the king growled.

"What say you, Elbereth?" Cadderly continued, holding the prince's gaze from his father's scowl. "Back on the paths of the Snowflakes you told me you would fight for Shilmista, that you would kill every invader without mercy. I have no home but I will go with you, fight with you and die with you if that must be, on this last chance for the forest."

"As will I," Danica asserted.

"Seems we're going for another walk, me brother," Ivan piped in, and Pikel's head wagged in approval.

Elbereth looked around at all of them, his smile growing wider with each passing heartbeat.

"You have given me hope, *Sha'Quessir,*" he said to Cadderly. "I will read the words in Syldritch Trea, and let the forest decide its fate."

"And yours," Galladel snarled. "What will you do when the trees do not awaken? You will be caught in the open and vulnerable, surrounded by our merciless enemies. I hoped I would not live to see my son perish, but never would I have imagined that his death would come from his own foolishness."

Shayleigh, for so long biting back her increasingly bitter thoughts, broke her silence at last. "Not foolishness," she cried. "Courage. Many will go with you, Prince Elbereth, entrusting their lives to your hopes and to the forest."

"That would not be wise," Elbereth replied, but for purely practical reasons and not because of any doubts he had concerning the ancient summons. "A small band might slip through without a fight."

"Then we shall meet your return," Shayleigh promised. "With the trees of Syldritch Trea beside us, we will drive the enemy from our land!"

"I am still King of Shilmista," Galladel, standing some distance from the conspirators, reminded them.

"You wish to come along and read the summons?" Cadderly asked, for he knew well that Galladel had no desire to do any such thing. Beside him, Danica gasped at his impudence.

"I could strike you down for that, human," Galladel growled at him.

"I don't think so," Ivan remarked, his axe bouncing prominently on one shoulder.

"And you, dwarf," spat the elf king. "When this is ended—"

"Aw, shut yer mouth and get in line behind yer son," Ivan snapped.

Galladel cast a murderous glare at all of them, turned, and stormed away.

"How dare you speak to the King of Shilmista like that?" Danica scolded Cadderly, amazed, though obviously not as upset as her words made her sound.

Cadderly looked away from her, to Elbereth, more interested in what the prince thought. Elbereth said nothing, but his nod was one of approval.

"You have inspired my father's hopes as well," Elbereth said. "I do not doubt that King Galladel will be among those awaiting our return from Syldritch Trea, waiting to fight beside the forest itself to rid our land of the foul invaders."

The elf prince and Shayleigh followed Galladel away then, with many plans to be made.

Q

Kierkan Rufo didn't know what to make of Danica's approach, or of her grim visage. Sensing another telepathic intrusion from the wretched imp, Rufo had wandered off alone, away from Cadderly and the others.

"And so I shall return to the library alone," the man said meekly to the approaching woman, "to tell of your bravery, and of Cadderly's, and to hope that all goes well in this ancient grove of oaks, this Syldritch Trea that the elves speak of so reverently."

"Your hopes for our success had better be sincere," Danica replied. "You're coming with us."

Rufo nearly toppled at the announcement. "I?" he balked. "What use could I be? I am hardly a fighter and am not . . . knowledgeable of the woodlands . . . in any way."

"It's not for your value that I insist you come," Danica explained. "I fear the consequences of leaving you here."

"How dare you speak such words?" Rufo groused.

"I dare not hesitate to speak them," Danica retorted. "I don't trust you, Kierkan Rufo. Know that, and know that you shall accompany us."

"I will not!"

Rufo didn't even see her move, but suddenly he lay on his back, looking up at the stars with a burning pain behind his knees. Danica bent over him and scowled.

"You will not be left behind, " she said. "Understand that, for the sake of your very life."

Q

By the time the sun began its ascent in the east, Elbereth, Shayleigh, and two score of other elves had found their way back to Cadderly and his companions.

"It is decided," the elf prince announced. "We three— you, Danica, and I—shall go to Syldritch Trea."

Pikel cleared his throat.

Elbereth looked to Cadderly and Danica.

"They did save your—our—lives," Cadderly reminded the prince. "And I would honestly feel safer with the brothers beside me."

"Why would you wish to come along?" Elbereth asked Ivan. "This journey could prove ill-fated, and even if it is not, the gain will mean little to you."

"Me brother likes trees," Ivan answered without the slightest hesitation.

Elbereth shrugged hopelessly, and Cadderly thought he saw the elf quickly dismiss an appreciative smile. "Then we five shall go—"

"Six," Danica corrected.

Even Cadderly turned on her curiously.

"Kierkan Rufo insists that he come along," Danica explained. "He fears being left alone in the forest with only the elves, whom he does not understand."

The notion seemed absurd—Rufo had already been left with the elves—but when Cadderly looked to the man, he was nodding, if somewhat reluctantly.

"Six, then," said Elbereth.

"None of yer own folk got the belly for it?" Ivan asked.

"Perhaps when all of this is ended, I should get in line behind Elbereth and King Galladel," Shayleigh answered, before Elbereth could explain. She tried to cast a threatening glare but couldn't hold it in the face of Ivan's amused chuckle.

"The People will be there," Elbereth explained. "All of them. Even my father. They'll be near us, unseen in the boughs. They will give us the cover we require to allow us to get through to Syldritch Trea, and they will be ready to begin the final battle when the summons is complete.

"You must understand the risks," Elbereth continued, mostly to Cadderly. "If the trees do not come to my call, then many, perhaps all, of Shilmista's elves will die. In light of that, tell me again of your confidence in the ancient words."

"If the trees do not answer, then my life, too, will be forfeit," the scholar replied in defense of his claims. "As will Danica's, which I treasure above my own."

Danica glanced sidelong at Cadderly. He didn't return the look, intent on Elbereth, but she knew he understood her approval of the change that had come over him.

They set off immediately after their morning meal, the company of six with a host of elves slipping all around them, clearing their path.

Kierkan Rufo was not pleased, though he was smart enough to keep his complaints silent. Merciless Danica had left him no choice, and so he had come along.

So, too, in Rufo's mind, had Druzil.

Q

Dorigen got the news of the elves' departure not too long after. She sat in her tent in Ragnor's camp, trying to decide what course to take.

"They tried once before to awaken the trees," Druzil reminded her, hoping to ease her obvious torment. "Why should we believe their luck will be any better this time?"

"We would be wise to fear anything involving that young scholar and his resourceful friends," Dorigen replied.

"We can catch them," Druzil said, eagerly rubbing his plump hands together.

Dorigen shook her head. "Not again."

Druzil's bulbous eyes narrowed. "Have you lost your courage along with your barbarian lover?"

Dorigen's answering glare stole the bite from the absurd remark. "My wisdom has grown with my failures," she corrected. "Our last defeat cost me much prestige in this camp, and in Ragnor's eyes. I doubt the ogrillon would lend me the soldiers to capture that crew—and that number, I fear, would be considerable."

"He's just a boy," Druzil remarked, "and his friends as unlikely a group of heroes as ever there was."

"He is a boy who nearly destroyed you in mental combat," Dorigen reminded him, "and whose friends include an elf prince and a woman able to dodge lightning. Must I remind you of the mighty dwarves as well? Ogres, a dozen orogs . . ."

"Enough, enough," Druzil conceded, not wanting to hear the disastrous battle recounted. "I only hoped that we might discover some method to regain our advantage. Their course might prove dangerous to us all. I had thought to lessen—"

"You're correct," Dorigen interrupted, rising with determination from her seat. "This is too important to be concerned with the petty squabbles of Castle Trinity."

"You're going to Ragnor?" Druzil asked. "What of the young priest?"

"I am," Dorigen answered. "As for Cadderly, we two will look for a way to take him, as we had originally planned. If that way cannot be found, then he will die with the rest of them."

She left the tent in a rush, leaving Druzil to sit alone on the small table with his private thoughts.

"People. . . ." the imp muttered.

NINETEEN

When you pass the duskwood tangle, get down to the left, came Druzil's telepathic instructions. *The soldiers have been instructed not to harm you.*

Kierkan Rufo looked around anxiously, fearing that the cold sweat on his forehead would give him away. The others seemed unconcerned with him. They were all nervous, even Ivan, crouching and crawling along with the undeniable knowledge that monsters lurked all around them. They heard the cries of battle somewhere behind them and to the north, and they knew that Shayleigh and Tintagel were hard at work, keeping the pressure off their secretive band.

Rufo pondered the reference to the tangle of duskwood trees. Elbereth had mentioned the place just a short while before, saying that they would get beyond it soon.

Rufo was running out of time.

Q

Danica crawled along, her crystal-bladed daggers held tightly in her hands. She saw Elbereth to the side, similarly crawling, making for a goblin guard twenty feet from the two Danica had chosen as her targets.

It had to be done swiftly and quietly; they could smell the goblins in the woods around them and wanted to avoid a fight if at all possible. An unfortunate three were in their path, though, and the companions had no time to go around them. Skirmishes were becoming too common around the group, echoing from both sides and behind. Shayleigh, Tintagel, and the other elves soon would be hard-pressed as the enemy closed in on that section of the forest, and Elbereth's party had to get to Syldritch Trea without delay—to the misfortune of three goblin guards.

Danica looked over to Elbereth, who had taken position just a few feet behind his goblin. The elf nodded for her to go first, and Danica agreed, since her task would be more difficult.

She clutched her daggers, feeling the golden tiger sculpture in one hand and the silver dragon in the other. Crouching low, she crossed her wrists in front of her at waist level, with the dagger blades pointing up and out.

The goblins, backs to her, were only two strides away, talking easily, suspecting nothing.

Danica leaped between them. They managed to gasp just once before the monk, in a single movement, snapped her arms out wide, driving the daggers up under their chins. The goblins twitched; one got its hand weakly up to grab Danica's wrist.

A cry to the side turned Danica around. Elbereth's goblin stood facing her, its weapon dropped and its arms held out wide. The creature jerked, its face contorted in confusion. Elbereth's sword came bursting out the front of the doomed creature's chest.

Danica and Elbereth nodded to each other and dropped back into the brush, holding their positions for a few moments to ensure that no other monsters were about. Together they rejoined the others and explained that the way was clear.

"We should make the duskwood tangle without further delay," Elbereth explained. "Syldritch Trea is less than a mile to the west of that."

Elbereth paused, and a curious expression crossed his face as he regarded Kierkan Rufo, who stood trembling, with sweat rolling down his face.

"What is it?" the elf asked.

"If ye've not the belly for it—" Ivan began, but Danica hushed him.

"I cannot get him out of my thoughts," a frantic Rufo admitted. The man looked around, his beady, dark eyes darting desperately, as though he expected all the monsters of the Realms to descend upon him. "He knows of our plans," Rufo explained, trying in vain to keep calm. He stuttered through a few jumbled words then his control blew away. "He knows!" Rufo cried, and his volume sent the others into defensive crouches. "I have doomed us all!"

"Quiet him!" Elbereth whispered, and he slipped out a few steps to ensure that no enemies were nearby.

Danica and Cadderly took Rufo's arms and eased him to a sitting position.

"Who knows?" Cadderly prompted, eyeing Danica, whose scowl gave Cadderly the distinct feeling that she would soon break Rufo's head open.

"It's not my fault," Rufo declared. "I tried to resist him—the imp!—with all my strength."

"Uh-oh," Pikel muttered, echoing all their thoughts.

"You have tried to resist the imp, but you cannot," Cadderly prompted. "In what way? You must tell me."

"In my head!" Rufo replied, finally taking care to keep his voice to a whisper. "The imp follows my thoughts, learns things from me, no matter how hard I resist."

Cadderly looked at Danica, his face twisted in confusion.

"I have never heard of such a thing," he said. "Dorigen's imp is telepathic. That much I learned." He turned back on Rufo. "But to invade your thoughts, and remain there without your consent?"

"If you're lying. . . ." Danica threatened, wagging a fist in Rufo's direction.

"Unless," Cadderly mumbled, scratching his smooth chin and thinking of any old stories that might give him an idea of what was going on. When he looked back to the others, he saw that they were staring at him, waiting.

"Have you ever seen the imp?" Cadderly asked Rufo.

"Once," the man admitted.

"And did the imp give you something to carry?" Cadderly asked. "A personal item, perhaps? Or did he touch you, or handle any of your possessions?" He looked to Ivan and Pikel and nodded.

"W-what?" was all Rufo could stammer before the dwarves grabbed his ankles and laid him out on the ground. They then began systematically stripping the man, holding up each possession for Cadderly to see, and when he shook his head, the item went flying. Pikel was about to rip Rufo's tunic open when the dwarf spotted something.

"Oo oi!" Pikel squealed, realizing that his find might be important.

"What ye got there?" Ivan asked, and when his eyes widened also, Cadderly and Danica moved over for a look.

"Where did you get that amulet?" Cadderly asked. He figured that their search was at its end, for the amulet, edged in gold and centered with a fabulous emerald, was far beyond Rufo's meager means.

"What amulet?" the man replied, perplexed.

"This one," Cadderly explained. He unpinned the thing and held it up for Rufo to see.

Even Danica couldn't doubt Rufo's sincerely confused expression. Without a thought, Cadderly handed the amulet to Ivan, and the dwarf, with a wink to his brother, produced a frog from his pocket and pinned the amulet to a loose fold in the creature's skin.

"That'll keep the imp-thing guessing," the dwarf explained. " 'Course now I'll be needing to catch me a new supper!"

"This allowed the imp to invade your thoughts," Cadderly explained above the quiet chuckles of Danica and the two dwarves. The young scholar was certain of his guess and continued with some confidence. "Without it, you are free—unless you choose to let him back in."

"And you would not do that, would you?" Danica asked, suddenly grim. She grabbed Rufo by the shoulder and roughly spun him around to stare into her glowering face.

Rufo pulled free and tried to regain some measure of his dignity. "I have admitted my weakness," he said. "Surely I cannot be blamed—"

"No one is blaming you," Cadderly answered, speaking more to Danica than Rufo. "Now, you said you have betrayed us. What do you know?"

"The tangle of duskwood trees . . ." Rufo said. "I was instructed to keep out of the way when the enemy attacks you there."

Cadderly looked to Elbereth, who, satisfied that no enemies were in the area, had come back to stand beside them.

"Have you heard?" the young scholar asked.

Elbereth nodded gravely. "The forest is strangely quiet," he replied. "I had suspected that some mischief was afoot." His unyielding stare bored into Rufo. "Now I understand. How much did you tell the imp?"

Cadderly wanted to calm the elf, but he understood that Elbereth's fears went far beyond the safety of their little group. All of the elf's kin had come west and would be dangerously exposed if the enemy knew their movements.

"I don't know," Rufo replied, lowering his gaze. "It is . . . was, difficult to mask . . ."

"We must assume that Druzil learned quite a lot from Rufo," Cadderly put in grimly, "about our whereabouts and the position of the elven force." Elbereth's wince made Cadderly pause a moment. "Should one of us go back and find your people and warn them of the danger?" the young scholar offered.

Elbereth thought it over for a moment, sincerely torn. "No," he answered at length. "The best we can do for the People is to finish our business quickly. We can go around the duskwood tangle and avoid the ambush, though that course will cost us some time."

"And time lost will surely cost more elves their lives,"

Danica had to add, her unblinking gaze not turning from Rufo.

"I did not wish to come along," Rufo started to protest. But he couldn't maintain his anger and turned away then finished meekly, "I knew the imp would follow."

"Pity us if you had stayed behind," Danica spat, "for then we would never have learned of your betrayal."

"Enough of this," Cadderly demanded. "We cannot change what has transpired, and we mustn't waste our time arguing."

"Agreed," said Elbereth with an approving nod. "We will turn south, then back to the west when the course is clear. And you," he said to Rufo, his eyes narrowing, "if the imp somehow finds its way back into your thoughts, speak at once!"

The elf started off then, with Danica falling into line right behind. Rufo went next, flanked by the dwarves, who eyed him suspiciously with every step.

Cadderly hesitated a moment before joining them. The frog Ivan had pinned still sat on the ground at the young scholar's feet. Cadderly knew he was taking a chance as he reached down and removed the amulet then pinned it under a fold of his own cloak, but it was a risk he decided to take. He had confronted Druzil once before, and had won that contest. If the imp tried to make contact with Rufo again, Cadderly would be waiting for him.

Danica and Elbereth spotted several enemy guards crouched in the brush and veered to keep out of harm's way. They wanted no more extraneous fighting if they could help it, suspecting from Rufo's disclosure that the enemy had set a sizable force for the ambush.

Cadderly felt the telepathic intrusions.

What's taking so long? came the thoughts that the scholar knew belonged to the imp. *The soldiers are in place and grow impatient.*

In response, Cadderly conjured an image of the place where they'd discovered the amulet, a short distance east of the duskwood tangle. He could only hope that Druzil wouldn't recognize his thoughts as different from Rufo's, and he breathed a little easier when the imp's next communication came to him.

Good, Druzil told him. *You're near the ambush point. When your companions get moving again, stay close to them until you see the duskwood trees then get low and to the side. Mistress Dorigen would like to speak with you again.*

Then, abruptly, Druzil was gone from Cadderly's thoughts. The young scholar clenched hard on the amulet.

"Cadderly?" he heard distantly. His eyes popped open—he hadn't realized they were closed—and he saw his companions standing around him, staring at him curiously.

"It's nothing," he tried to explain. Elbereth grabbed his hand and forced it open.

"You should have been rid of this vile item," the elf scolded.

"I don't fear the imp," Cadderly replied.

His confident smile gave the others some measure of relief. That smile disappeared suddenly when Cadderly looked at Rufo, though, given the new revelations concerning his tall companion. There was more than one meeting with the imp.

So you have met Dorigen? Cadderly wanted to ask, but he kept his thoughts private, fearing that revealing what the imp had inadvertently revealed would cause trouble the party could ill afford.

"Let us go on," Cadderly bade. "We've fooled our enemies. They still sit, anticipating an ambush at the duskwood tangle, but they grow impatient."

Elbereth took the lead, Danica following on his heels, and Cadderly and the others in a pack behind.

"Ye didn't happen to bring along me frog?" Ivan asked hopefully, rubbing his belly. Cadderly only smiled and shook his head.

Elbereth turned back to the west a short while later, the elf hastening them along and slipping in and out of the shadows to the side and ahead with obvious urgency. They came down one slope into an area with less undergrowth than usual. Thick oaks dominated the area, and though they were not much larger than the other trees of Shilmista, Cadderly could sense their age, and could sense, too, a brooding sentience. It was as if he were being watched from all sides and from above.

He knew they had come to Syldritch Trea. He moved over to one of the oaks and felt its rough bark, toughened by the passing years, the birth and death of many centuries. What tales those trees might tell him, and Cadderly believed that they could indeed, if he had the time and patience to pause and listen.

Pikel, too, seemed caught in the enchantment of this most ancient grove. The dwarf called out, "Oo!" several times as he hopped happily from oak to oak. He hugged one so tightly that, when he turned away, his hairy face was creased by imprints of the tree's bark.

"We have come to Syldritch Trea," Elbereth announced, though he could see that his companions, with the possible exception of Ivan and Rufo, had already realized that. Danica nodded, and scrambled up the tallest oak she could find. She looked back to the east to see what storms might be brewing.

Cadderly took out the book of Dellanil Quil'quien, handling it with renewed reverence, for the tome seemed to hold much more meaning in that ancient place. He looked to Elbereth, his jaw set firmly, and opened the book to the ancient summons. He felt again the sheer power of the trees, their inner life, and he knew beyond doubt that he had done right in convincing the elf prince to come to Syldritch Trea.

He knew, too, the truth of his words when he again declared to those around him, "It will work."

C

Temmerisa reared and Shayleigh dropped from her saddle. Around her she saw only trees, but she knew from memory that no trees should have stood in that place.

"Tintagel?" she called softly. In response, one of the trees shifted form, becoming the elf wizard, who stepped out to greet Shayleigh.

"Well met," Tintagel answered, smiling in spite of their dire situation.

Shayleigh returned the grin and looked around at the unnatural trees. "How many?" she asked.

"A score and seven," the blue-eyed wizard replied. "It is my most powerful spell and one that should catch our enemies by surprise. Do you like my work?"

Shayleigh imagined the astonishment on the passing orcs' and goblins' faces as twenty-seven illusionary trees reverted to their true forms as elf warriors. Her widening grin answered Tintagel's question.

"How go the other fronts?" the wizard asked.

Shayleigh's smile disappeared. "Not well," she admitted. "Our enemies have gone farther south than we believed. And those monsters in the east have learned of our movement and are sweeping back toward the west. We have scouts searching now to see if those southwest of here are moving east to join them, or if we still have an escape route open to us."

Tintagel considered the grim news. When they had formulated their plans to come out near Syldritch Trea, they had known their success would depend on secrecy. But the enemy had somehow anticipated their movements, and that boded ill indeed.

The tension didn't lessen a short time later when several elves rode up, King Galladel at the lead.

"The south is blocked," the king proclaimed in a superior tone. "Our folly in coming here is revealed to us in full."

Shayleigh didn't turn away under the her king's accusing stare. Only a few of Shilmista's elves, most notably Galladel, had argued against the action, but so determined were most of the People, Shayleigh included, that the king had finally agreed to the desperate plan.

Even with the enemy moving to surround them, Shayleigh held firm to her belief that they had done the right thing in trusting in Shilmista's magic. Shayleigh believed, too, that her dear forest was worth dying for.

"We will find the weakest point in their advancing line," Galladel reasoned. "If we move fast and hard, perhaps we might break through."

"When we came out here, we knew that our success would depend on Elbereth's call to Syldritch Trea," Tintagel reminded them. "If we had not the courage to see that through, then we should not have come out at all."

Galladel glared at him. "We are barely a hundred strong," he said, "with only a handful of horses. Our enemy's force numbers in the thousands, with giants and ogres among their ranks."

"Let the battle begin then," Shayleigh added. "Let our enemies come on, every one. When it is ended, Shilmista will again belong to the elves!"

"When it is over," Galladel growled, "Shilmista will be no more."

TWENTY

WHEN MAGIC FILLED THE AIR

What is the delay? came a telepathic call, but Cadderly didn't have time for the imp's intrusions. He dropped the amulet to the dirt and placed his foot over it then took up Dellanil's book and continued his scan, double-checking his translation before uttering the words to Elbereth.

Where are you? came Druzil's call again, but it was distant, and Cadderly easily pushed it aside. Still, the young scholar recognized the desperation in Druzil's thoughts and knew the clever imp would not easily give up.

"We must hurry," Cadderly implored Elbereth. "Our enemies will soon understand that we've traveled around them."

Elbereth rubbed his hands slowly across the bark of the nearest oak, gathering strength from the wood's solidity. He was the most nervous of the group. If the summons failed, all of them would likely lose their lives, but Elbereth stood to lose even more. The basis of his existence, the magic of Shilmista, hung in the balance. If the trees failed to answer his call again, his father's dismal belief—that magic no longer filled Shilmista's clear air—would be proven true, to the dismay and doom of all of Elbereth's People.

Cadderly held the book open before him. "Are you ready?" the young scholar asked.

"Flames in the east!" came Danica's call from the high boughs of a nearby tree. Her companions on the ground heard the branches rustling as Danica made a swift descent. "A force approaches swiftly."

Cadderly nodded to Elbereth, gaining the elf's attention. *"Seide plein una malabreche,"* the scholar began.

Elbereth held his hands out wide to the wood and walked around the nearest oaks as he echoed the words. *"Seide plein una malabreche."*

"Come along," Danica whispered to the dwarves, and somewhat hesitantly to Rufo. "We'll keep the enemy at bay while Cadderly and Elbereth complete the calling."

"Oh," moaned a disappointed Pikel.

"What's an Elbereth?" Ivan asked, but his wry smile quickly diffused Danica's sudden frown.

They took up positions along the perimeter of Syldritch Trea, hoping that their friends would finish before the enemy arrived. None of them had to voice their fears of the consequences should the summons fail.

Q

The great white horse carried Shayleigh effortlessly, springing over patches of brush and gliding between the tightly packed trees. Shayleigh reined in Temmerisa many times, not wanting to outdistance King Galladel and the seven other riders. The great horse heeded her commands, though the maiden could sense from the rippling muscles in Temmerisa's shining white neck that the horse wanted to run strong and hard.

A host of orcs trailed the troupe, rushing wildly, hungrily, in pursuit, hooting and howling. A hundred strong, they numbered as many as all the elves remaining in the forest, and their evil kin, many times their number, were all around them. Soon, the orcs believed, that small band would be surrounded and the slaughter would begin.

So the orcs believed, anyway, and so Galladel and Shayleigh and the other elves wanted them to believe.

Shayleigh led them into a wide expanse of low shrubs and young trees. The riders took extra care to avoid the saplings there, practically walking their mounts and taking no heed of the orc force fast closing from behind.

The elves came to the opposite edge of the expanse, where the forest darkened once more under the canopy of older growth, and urged their horses into the shadows. Just a short way in, they reared and turned around.

Oblivious to the danger, the stupid orcs charged through the open area.

Tintagel waited until all the baited monsters had come within the perimeter of his devious trap. Then the wizard stepped from his tree form and uttered a triggering syllable. A score and seven other "trees" reverted to their true forms and the elves stepped into the middle of the orc host. They cut into the unsuspecting creatures from every angle, each elf felling several of the foul beasts before the orcs began to comprehend what had happened.

Shayleigh held Temmerisa back no longer. The mighty steed burst out of the shadows and trampled an orc, and the warrior atop it bent low in her saddle, her golden hair flying wildly behind her and her gleaming sword hacking at any monster that strayed too near.

Galladel and the others charged right behind, circling the perimeter of the clearing, killing all those orcs that thought to flee. The wretched creatures dived and rolled, tried to run, but ultimately had nowhere to go.

Elven bows twanged mercilessly, and elven swords bit deep into orc flesh.

It was over in moments, and orc bodies covered the open expanse. None of the elves held any notions of victory, though, and not one of them smiled. They knew the battle was just beginning. Cries of another fight sprang up somewhere to the east, and farther north the enemy had started fires. The season had not been too dry, and the fires didn't rush through the forest, but they were fueled by the prodding of many, many monsters.

Another group of elves, flushed out by the flames, sprinted by, hulking orogs in close pursuit. Shayleigh didn't look back to her king for instructions. For the fiery elf maiden, the appropriate course was easy to discern.

"Take to the shadows!" Shayleigh cried, and most of Tintagel's contingent had already started for the trees, knowing that to get caught in the open was to die. Amid all the confusion of the expanding battle and swirling smoke, she saw a new enemy to strike. "Come, Temmerisa!" she called, and the spirited mount, apparently in complete agreement with her courageous rider, broke into a wild charge in pursuit of the orogs.

One of the other riders moved to follow Shayleigh, but Galladel held him back.

"We eight shall stay together," the king said. "The fight will come in full, and if Elbereth does not awaken the trees, our course will be whichever way is quickest from Shilmista's bloody boughs."

The other riders could tell by Galladel's grim tone that their king did not hold out much hope for his son's attempt. And at that dark time, with the forest thick with monsters and smoke, cries of battle erupting from every direction, and hundreds, perhaps thousands, of enemy soldiers moving to surround them, not one of Galladel's cavalry companions could muster the courage to dispute the king's fears.

Q

"Teague!" Cadderly cried.

"Teague!" he heard Elbereth repeat.

The young scholar inadvertently glanced over his shoulder, hearing the fighting not too far away.

"Concentrate!" he growled, more to himself than to Elbereth, and he forced his gaze down into the book of Dellanil Quil'quien and looked for the next phrase in the woodland summons.

"Teague!" Elbereth echoed several more times, growing nearly as frantic as Cadderly.

The People were dying while he danced about an oak grove, and he could not ignore that his sword was needed just a few hundred feet away.

Cadderly saw that the elf prince was slipping from the trance. The young scholar dropped the book—somehow guessing that he would not need it, that the ancient words had become a part of him, or rather, that their meaning had become so crystal clear to him that he could follow the path of their cant from his heart alone.

"W-what're ye doing . . . ?" he heard Ivan stammer.

Kierkan Rufo added something Cadderly could not discern, and Pikel piped in with "Huh?"

Cadderly blocked them all from his mind. He rushed over to Elbereth and grabbed the elf prince's hands, tearing one's stubborn grasp from Elbereth's sword hilt.

"Teague immen syldritch fae," the young scholar said.

Whether it was his tone or his grave expression, he couldn't tell, but he knew then that he had gained Elbereth's full attention, that by his demands, Elbereth had put the closing battle out of his thoughts. Elbereth took up the chant, and Cadderly continued, keeping a few words ahead of the mesmerized elf.

The young scholar felt a power budding within him, an awakening of his soul and a strength he never suspected he possessed. His words came faster—too fast for anyone to possibly keep up.

And yet, Elbereth, pulled along by a similar inner urgency, caught in the throes of building magic, repeated with perfection each of the phrases Cadderly uttered, matched the young scholar's timbre and inflection as perfectly as a mountain echo.

Then Elbereth and Cadderly spoke as one, the words, the summons, coming from both their mouths in unison.

It was impossible, Cadderly knew. Neither of them knew the phrases well enough to recite them from memory. But the young scholar had no doubt that their words rang perfectly, that they spoke exactly as Dellanil Quil'quien had spoken on a mystical day centuries before.

They neared the end, and their phrases slowed as the final runes built within. Cadderly grabbed Elbereth's hands, looking for support, unable to contain the power.

Elbereth, equally terrified, held on with all his strength.

"A intunivial dolas quey!" they cried together, the words torn from their hearts by a power that consumed their minds and left their bodies leaning heavily against one another. Together they slipped down to the thick grass.

Cadderly nearly swooned—in truth, he wasn't certain whether or not he'd blacked out for a moment—and when he looked to Elbereth, he saw that the elf wore the same expression of weariness and confusion. Their companions were all around them, even Kierkan Rufo, wearing a mien of concern.

"Ye all right, lad?" Caddery heard Ivan ask, and the young scholar wasn't really certain how he should answer.

With the dwarves' help, Caddery managed to get back to his feet while Danica and Rufo helped Elbereth stand. The forest was quiet save for the continuing din of distant combat.

"The summons went unheard," Elbereth groaned after many long moments had slipped by.

Caddery held his hand up to stop the elf from continuing. He remembered the sounds of birds in the trees before the summoning, but there were none. It could have been his and Elbereth's shouting that had scared them off, or perhaps they had taken flight from the approaching melee, but Caddery thought differently. He sensed the stillness of Syldritch Trea to be a prelude, a deceptive calm.

"What do you know?" Danica asked him, moving to his side. She studied his face a moment longer then reiterated, "Caddery, what do you know?"

"Do you feel it?" Cadderly finally replied, looking around at the great oaks. "The mounting energy?" Hardly taking note of his own actions, he bent down and picked up the amulet, slipping it into a deep pocket. "Do you feel it?" he asked again, more insistently.

Danica did feel it, an awakening, a growing sentience all around her, as though she was being watched. She looked to Elbereth, and he, too, glanced about in anticipation.

"Oo," Pikel remarked.

"What is it?" Ivan growled, uncomfortable. He took up his axe and hopped in circles, eyeing the trees with suspicion.

Behind Kierkan Rufo, the ground trembled. The man spun to see a gigantic root tear up through the ground. There came a rustle as the branches of a huge oak began to shake, and the sound increased, multiplied, as several other trees joined in.

"What have we done?" Elbereth asked, his tone reflecting both amazement and trepidation.

Cadderly was too entranced to answer. More roots came up through the ground; more branches shook and bent.

Ivan seemed on the verge of exploding, holding his axe as though to rush over and chop down the nearest tree. Next to him, Pikel hopped up and down in glee, thrilled by the growing display of druidic magic. The round-shouldered dwarf grabbed his nervous brother's weapon arm and wagged a finger back and forth in Ivan's face.

The companions didn't even notice that they were all moving closer together, back-to-back.

The first tree, the one behind Rufo, broke free of the ground and took a sliding stride toward them.

"Do something!" the terrified man said to Elbereth.

All fear had left the elf prince. He jumped out in front of Rufo and cried, "I am Elbereth, son of Galladel, son of Gil Telleman, son of Dellanil Quil'quien! War has come to Shilmista, a great force not seen since the days of my father's father's father! Thus I have summoned you, guardians of Shilmista, to march beside me and cleanse this, our home!"

Another great tree moved over to join the first, and others followed suit. Elbereth took up the lead, thinking to head straight for the battle, but Ivan patted the elf's shoulder, turning him around.

"Fine words, elf," the obviously relieved dwarf offered.

Elbereth smiled grimly and looked to Danica, who stood quietly beside Cadderly. Both the young scholar and the woman understood the elf prince's tentative intentions from the look on his face, and almost in unison, they smiled and nodded their agreement. Elbereth returned the smile and pulled Ivan beside him at the lead of the column. Together they started off, unlikely allies. Pikel, more interested in the continuing spectacle of the moving trees than in anything that lay ahead, came behind.

Kierkan Rufo looked around anxiously, apparently unsure of where he fit in. As he seemed to come to trust that the great oaks meant him no harm, his horror of the trees began to wane and it was as though he found his place in it all. He climbed one of the oaks, moving as high as he could—higher, Cadderly figured, than a goblin could throw its spear.

Cadderly continued to hold Danica back as the woodland column, some dozen or so ancient trees, slipped past.

"Dorigen knew where we were going," he explained as the thunder of the tree's steps diminished. "And for whatever reason, she wants me as her prisoner."

Danica motioned to a shadowy hollow to the side, and she and Cadderly took up a watch there, agreeing that they would set out after Elbereth and the others if the wizard did not appear in the next few moments.

Q

A group of orogs stared curiously at the spectacle, not sure of what to make of the approaching oaks. They jostled each other and scratched at their scraggly hair, pointing and lifting spears the trees' way in an almost comic threat.

They understood more—at least that the gigantic trees were not friendly to their cause—when they saw an elf and two dwarves hop down from the closest tree's lowest branches. The orogs took up a unified hoot and one launched its spear, but they still didn't seem to fathom how they should react to such a display.

Ivan, Pikel, and Elbereth charged at them, eager to begin the fight.

The lead tree's reach was longer, though, and it sent huge branches crashing down upon the beasts, battering and thrashing them. A couple of orogs slipped away, out of range, and ran straight off, not daring to look back.

"Aw, this ain't about to be much fun!" Ivan roared—by the time he and his two companions reached the orogs, not a single one of the beasts could offer any resistance. "Except fun to watch!" Ivan quickly added, noticing an orog high in the air, kicking futilely against the stranglehold one branch had put around its neck.

The surly dwarf grabbed Pikel by the arm. "Come, me brother!" Ivan yelled. "Let's find a goblin head to cleave!"

Pikel looked back longingly to the moving oaks, not wanting to part from them. But there were indeed many monsters about, and it didn't take Ivan long to convince his equally fierce brother that the game had just begun.

Elbereth watched them sprint off into the shadows, falling over a small band of goblins. In just a few heartbeats, the two remaining goblins were running fast into the forest, Ivan and Pikel hot on their heels.

The elf prince managed a weak smile, and managed, too, to hope that the day might yet be won.

TWENTY-ONE

LONG LIVE THE KING

"The battle begins in full," Danica whispered in Cadderly's ear. "We must go."

Cadderly held her in place, and pulled her lower into the shadows. He sensed something, a presence, perhaps, and knew instinctively that danger was about. Unconsciously, the young scholar dropped a hand into a pocket of his traveling cloak and closed his fingers around the tiny amulet.

"Druzil," he whispered, surprised as he spoke the word. Danica looked at him curiously.

"The amulet works both ways," Cadderly realized. "I know the imp is nearby. And if the imp is about. . . ."

As if on cue, Dorigen stepped into the clearing in the wake of the passing trees. Cadderly and Danica crouched lower, but the wizard was obviously intent on the increasingly distant spectacle of the marching trees.

Danica pointed to the west then started stealthily away, circling behind the wizard. Not daring to speak a word, Cadderly held up the amulet to remind her that

Dorigen's devilish henchman was probably also in the area, and probably invisible.

"What have you done?" Dorigen cried, and Cadderly nearly fainted from fear, thinking that she was addressing him. Her narrow-eyed gaze remained locked on the moving trees, though.

She thrust her fist out in front of her and cried, *"Fete,"* the Elvish word for fire. A jet of flame roared from Dorigen's hand—Cadderly thought that perhaps it came from a ring—a burning line that stretched across the yards to engulf the last tree in the procession.

"Fete!" the wizard repeated, and the flames did not relent.

She moved her hand, shifting the angle of the fire to immolate the tree. The great oak turned its cumbersome bulk around, inadvertently setting small fires on the trees beside it. It reached out with a long root for Dorigen, but the wizard lowered her hand in line with the root and burned it to ashes.

So horrified at the sheer wickedness of Dorigen's destructive actions, Cadderly couldn't draw a breath. He looked to his right, the west, for some sign of Danica, praying that his love would come out and stop Dorigen's carnage. But while Danica was indeed concealed in the brush behind the wizard, she couldn't easily get to Dorigen. Three orogs had moved out of the shadows and taken up a defensive position behind and to either side of the wizard.

The tree crackled and split apart, falling into a flaming heap. Dorigen stopped her attack, but kept her fist clenched, trying, it appeared, to make out another target through the smoke and flames.

Cadderly knew he could not allow that to happen.

Q

Dorigen extended her fist again and started to utter the triggering rune, but she stopped, distracted by a curious sight off to the side. A beam of light emanated through the brush and from the shadows, rocking slowly back and forth. Keeping her fist extended, the wizard slowly moved over to investigate.

Her expression turned to one of curiosity as she neared the shadowed hollow. A cylindrical tube, the source of the light beam, rocked along the inner edge of a light blue, wide-brimmed hat that had been placed on its side. Dorigen didn't recognize the hat, but she had seen the cylindrical object before, inside the pack belonging to the young priest, Cadderly.

Dorigen realized that she was vulnerable, knew that she should be wary of the Deneirrath, but pride had always been her greatest weakness.

Q

A short distance away, low behind the trunk of a tree, Cadderly unscrewed his feathered ring, pulled back the ram head of his walking stick, and inserted the dart. He took great care to keep it out of the sunlight, but he was less than confident as he pursed his lips against his blow-gun and drew a bead on Dorigen.

"Where are you, young priest?" Dorigen called. She turned to signal to her orog guards, then flinched as something small and sharp struck her on the cheek.

"What?" she hissed, pulling free the feathered dart. She nearly laughed aloud at the puny thing.

"Damn," Cadderly groaned, seeing her still standing. Dorigen yawned then, and wiped bleary eyes.

Cadderly knew his chance was slipping by. He jumped from the side of the tree and rushed at his enemy.

Seeing their mistress endangered, the orogs howled and charged to intercept the young scholar. They found Danica instead, though, and each tasted a foot or a fist before it realized what had happened.

But Dorigen didn't seem to need her guards. Her fist, still clenched, pointed to greet Cadderly—he could see the onyx ring she wore on that hand. He couldn't possibly get to her in time, and he had no other weapons to strike with from a distance.

Dorigen began to speak—Cadderly expected the words to fall over him like the pronouncement of doom.

Q

"Where will you hide, elf king?" Ragnor roared above the ring of steel and the cries of the dying.

Galladel reined in his horse and wheeled around, as did the others of his cavalry group.

"There!" one of the elves shouted, pointing to a break in a line of bluetop trees.

There stood Ragnor in all his evil splendor, his bottom tusk sticking up grotesquely over his upper lip and his elite bugbear guards fanned out in a semicircle around him, their sharp-tipped tridents gleaming wickedly. Galladel led the charge, the seven other riders bravely at his side.

The elf king pulled up short, though, knowing that he and his troops could not get through Ragnor's defensive ring. Somehow, Galladel realized, he would have to get to the ogrillon, would have to strike a decisive blow in the lopsided battle.

"You are Ragnor?" Galladel cried in a derisive tone.

"He who hides behind his minions, who cowers while others die in his name?"

The ogrillon's laughter defeated Galladel's bluster. "I am Ragnor!" the beast proclaimed. "Who claims Shilmista as his own. Come, pitiful elf king, and pass your crown to one who deserves it!" The ogrillon reached over his shoulder and drew his huge, heavy broadsword.

"Do not, my king," one of Galladel's escorts said to him.

"Together we can crush their ranks," offered another.

Galladel put his slender hand up to quiet them all. The king thought of his past failures, of the time he had failed to awaken the trees at the price of many lives. He was weary and wanted only to travel to Evermeet. But noble, too, was the King of Shilmista, and he saw his duty clearly before him. He spurred his horse ahead a few strides, ordering his escort to stay back.

Ragnor's bugbears parted, and Galladel's charge was on. He thought to bury the ogrillon, smash straight in with his powerful steed and crush the invader. His plans came to a crashing end as a huge boulder, hurled by a giant in the shadows, caught his horse on the flank and sent the poor, doomed beast spinning to the ground.

Galladel's escort roared and charged, but the bugbears and the giant moved quickly to block them. When Galladel pulled himself from the pile and regained his feet, shaken but not seriously injured, he found himself alone, faced off against mighty Ragnor.

"Now the fight is fair!" Ragnor growled, steadily advancing.

Galladel readied his own sword. How much larger the brutish ogrillon seemed to him, with his horse lying dead at his side.

Q

Cadderly fully expected to be fried long before he got to Dorigen. The wizard began to utter the triggering rune, but yawned instead as the sleep poison continued to work its insidious way inside her.

Cadderly didn't hesitate. He charged straight in, launching a roundhouse, two-handed swing with his walking stick that caught Dorigen on the side of the head and blasted her to the ground. In all his life, Cadderly had never hit anything so hard.

Dorigen lay still at his feet, eyes closed and blood trickling from a cut the ram's head had torn along her ear.

The sight unnerved Cadderly, sent his thoughts spinning back to the tragic events of a month before. Barjin's dead eyes hovered over the young scholar as he looked down at Dorigen, praying that she was still alive.

Q

Danica uttered no such prayers for the first orog she had felled. She had hit the beast squarely in the throat and knew that its windpipe was crushed and that it soon would suffocate. The other two fought savagely, though, despite the wounds Danica had inflicted. Wielding finely crafted, razor-edged swords, they soon had the young woman backing steadily away.

A sword cut just above her head as she ducked. She kicked straight out, connecting with the monster's thigh, but had to back off as the other monster pressed her savagely. One, two, and three, came the creature's wicked swipes, each missing the scrambling woman by no more than an inch.

Then Danica was up again, balanced on the balls of

her feet. The orog she had kicked lagged behind its companion in the pursuit, and Danica found her opening.

The single orog thrust its sword straight at her. Faster than the weapon could get to her, Danica fell into a crouch, nearly sitting upon the ground, then came up hard and angled in toward her attacker, the fingers of her right hand bent in tightly against themselves. Her left arm led the way, brushing aside the orog's sword, leaving the monster defenseless. Her deadly right arm, coiled tight against her chest, snapped in through the opening, slamming her open palm into the hollow of the orog's chest with every ounce of power the young woman could throw into it.

The beast hopped two feet from the ground and landed back to its feet, breathless, then it fell dead.

The remaining orog, moving in on the young woman, looked at its fallen companion curiously then abruptly changed its course, howling and hooting, scrambling for the trees.

Danica started to follow then dropped to her knees in surprise as something whistled past her, just a few feet to the side. The dart hit the orog in the back and exploded, throwing the creature face down on the ground. It gasped once for breath that would not come then lay still.

Danica looked back to see Cadderly, his crossbow, reclaimed from the unconscious wizard, in his hand. Standing over Dorigen, he seemed a terrible thing to Danica, his visage stern and angry.

Danica guessed what emotions tore at poor Cadderly. She understood the guilt and confusion that had brought him to that point. But it was no time for weakness.

"Finish her," Danica instructed. She glanced around quickly to ensure that there were no more enemies nearby then ran after the departing trees, where the larger battles had been joined.

Cadderly looked down at the unconscious wizard, clearly disgusted at what he knew he must do.

Q

When he had led the procession from Syldritch Trea, Elbereth had thought to keep his forces together and cut a wedge through the enemy lines to rejoin the People. As the prince came upon the scene of battle, though, he saw the folly of his plans.

There was no line to cut through, and no clear group of elves to rejoin. Chaos ruled in Shilmista, a wild scramble of elf and goblinoid, walking trees and giantkin.

"Good fighting, elf!" were the last words Elbereth heard from Ivan, circling back out of the trees with Pikel, as the elf prince sprinted off to the side to engage a bugbear moving along a patch of brambles.

By the time Elbereth had finished the creature, the trees had moved past and split up, many going for the fires burning in the north or for the cries of battle in the east, and the dwarves were nowhere to be seen. Too busy to go in search of them, Elbereth sounded his horn, a call that he hoped would soon be answered.

Temmerisa appeared in moments, flying like the wind, with Shayleigh holding tight to the steed's reins. The horse ran down one goblin then leaped over several others as they crawled through the thicket.

"The trees!" Shayleigh cried, her words choked with hope and astonishment. She looked back over her shoulder to an oak that pounded down a host of monsters. "Shilmista has come alive!"

Shayleigh dropped from the saddle. "Take Temmerisa," she said quickly to Elbereth.

"The horse is in fine hands," Elbereth replied, refusing the bridle. "I only called to ensure that Temmerisa and his rider were still about."

"Take him!" Shayleigh implored the elf prince. "Find your father. I have heard whispers that he alone faces Ragnor, and if that is true, he will need his son beside him!"

Elbereth needed to hear nothing more to convince him. He grabbed the bridle and swung up into the saddle. "Where are they?" he cried.

"The line of bluetops," Shayleigh replied.

Elbereth pounded through the forest. He saw dozens of small encounters where his sword might have been of use, but he had not the time. Galladel facing Ragnor! The thought lodged in Elbereth's throat and stuck his heart like a sharp pin. He recalled his own painful encounter with the powerful ogrillon, a fight he would have lost. And Elbereth was more highly regarded as a swordsman than was Galladel.

Elbereth ducked under a low branch and pulled Temmerisa in a tight turn through a narrow gap between two maples, then urged the horse into a long leap across a patch of brambles. He could feel the lather on Temmerisa's muscled neck, could hear the proud steed's lungs straining to pull in the air needed for such exertion.

Another leap, another turn, then a straight charge, and Temmerisa seemed up to the task, running hard, sensing his beloved master's urgency.

Elbereth caught sight of the giant out of the corner of his eye, saw the hurled boulder rushing in. He yanked hard on Temmerisa's reins, turning the horse aside, but not fully out of harm's way. The white stallion went down under the force of that impact, but came right back up, stubbornly, and continued on his way.

"We will pay back that beast," Elbereth promised, slapping his precious steed's neck. Temmerisa snorted, lowered his great head, and charged on.

Ivan and Pikel tried as best they could to stay in the vicinity of the marching trees. Every orc or goblin the dwarves encountered slowed them, though, while the oaks walked right through, scattering horrified monsters wherever they went.

The dwarves heard elves cheer from all around, though they saw few of Elbereth's kin. Not that they minded, the brothers were more interested in spotting enemies than in finding allies they didn't really believe they needed.

Then the trees were far beyond them, fanning out in their steady march, and the Bouldershoulders were all alone.

"Uh-oh," Pikel remarked, suspecting what was to come. Sure enough, dozens of humanoids appeared from their concealment in the wake of the passing trees, dozens of monsters with no apparent targets other than the dwarf brothers.

"Get yerself ready for some fighting," Ivan said to Pikel.

The words were hardly necessary. Pikel smashed one orc even as Ivan spoke.

Then Pikel grabbed his brother and scrambled to the side, under the low-hanging, thick boughs of some pines. Ivan understood his brother's intent, and wisdom, as soon as the monsters closed in on them, for the close quarters and low visibility favored the out-numbered dwarves.

Still, almost everywhere that Ivan swung his axe, blindly or not, he found some monster waiting to catch it and a dozen others in line behind, ready to step in.

Q

Safe in his high perch, Kierkan Rufo thought himself quite clever. He had no intention of playing any role in the horrific battle beyond that of observer, and in that regard, he thoroughly enjoyed watching the pitiful gob-lins, orcs, and orogs flee before the incredible power of his moving oak.

He changed his mind when the oak stumbled upon a different enemy: two giants that were not so cowardly and not so small. The tree shuddered violently as a boul-der slammed against its trunk. It swung a branch at the nearest monster, connecting solidly, but the giant, instead of falling dead, grabbed the limb and twisted.

Above, Rufo heard the sharp crack of living wood and thought he would faint away.

Another branch swung in to pound on the monster, but the second giant got in close to the trunk, grab-bing on with frightening strength. The giant heaved and pulled, and the huge oak swayed to one side then the other.

More branches descended over the more distant giant, battering and lashing it. The monster caught a few boughs and snapped them apart with its huge hands, but the beatings were taking a heavy toll. Soon the giant fell to its knees, and soon after that, the oak pounded it to the ground.

Another thick branch, the lowest on the great tree, wrapped around the trunk, encircling the tugging giant in an unbreakable hold.

Kierkan Rufo found himself cheering the tree on as the giant fought for breath. Rufo thought the battle won, thought his oak could finish its foe and move on, hopefully to safer and smaller opponents.

The gasping giant slumped as low as it could get on its thick, trunklike legs then heaved for all its life, pushing up and to the side.

One of the oak's roots bent back on itself, and the tree went down in a heap, never to rise again, clutched in a death grip with its doomed destroyer. More branches wriggled in to ensure the giant's fate.

Rufo was sure that one of his legs had been broken, though he couldn't see it. The leg was pinned under a huge tree branch. He thought of crying out then realized the stupidity of that. Many more enemies than allies were around to hear him.

He scooped away some dirt, digging a shallow pit, then he pulled as many small, leafy branches over him as he could and tried to lay very still.

Q

Danica came into the chaos with her mouth hanging open in amazement. Never had the young woman witnessed such destruction. She saw the tree go down with the giant then another tree went down, farther in, under a press of bugbears.

Danica looked back behind her, worried for Cadderly. She couldn't protect him—she didn't really believe she could protect herself. With a resigned shrug and one longing glance back to where she'd left him, the young woman set off, knowing she would have no difficulty finding an enemy to hit.

A resounding "Oo oi!" turned her head to a grove of thick pines. A bugbear rushed out, followed by a flying club. The weapon took the creature in the legs, knocking it to the ground. Before it could rise, Pikel ran out, collected his club, and splattered the bugbear's head against the ground. The dwarf looked up at Danica, his white smile shining within the layer of gore that covered his face.

Despite the madness and danger all around her, Danica returned his smile and winked at the dwarf, and both she and Pikel suspected that it would be a wink of farewell.

Pikel disappeared back into the pines, and Danica bent low and took out her twin daggers. Then the young monk went a-hunting.

Q

Cadderly fumbled with *The Tome of Universal Harmony*, trying to find some answers that would offer him escape from the task Danica and the insane situation had placed upon his shoulders. Dorigen lay still below him, groaning softly every now and then.

More important was the growing roar of the battle. Cadderly knew he could ill afford to delay much longer, that he should join in the fight beside his friends, and that even if he didn't, the melee would likely come to him all too soon. He had his retrieved crossbow reloaded—only five darts remained—and lying ready atop the fallen wizard.

The pages of the great book seemed a blur to him. In his frantic state of mind, he could hardly read the words, much less discern some value in them. Then he was pulled from the pages all together, distracted by a distinct sensation that he was not alone. He spent a brief moment concentrating on that feeling, focusing his thoughts.

Slowly, Cadderly reached down and took up the crossbow. He spun, letting his senses guide him where his eyes could not, and fired.

The explosive dart slammed against the trunk of a sapling, blasting the tree apart. Just to the side of it Cadderly heard a sudden flap of leathery wings.

"You cannot hide from me, Druzil!" the young scholar cried. "I know where you are!"

The sound of beating wings faded away into the forest and Cadderly couldn't prevent a grin of superiority from crossing his face. Druzil wouldn't bother him again.

Dorigen groaned and began to shift her weight, groggily trying to get up to her elbows. Cadderly turned the crossbow down at her and loaded another dart.

His eyes widened in shock at his actions. How could he think of killing the defenseless woman, and how could he think of using his damning weapon to commit the foul deed? His breath came in gasps. Barjin's eyes stared at him from the shadows.

He dropped the bow and took up the book, closing it and grasping it tightly in both hands.

"This is not what you had in mind when you gave this to me," he admitted, as though he were addressing Headmistress Pertelope, then he slammed the heavy tome on the back of Dorigen's head, again dropping her flat to the ground.

Cadderly worked frantically, before the wizard recovered again. He pulled three rings from Dorigen's hands: first her signet ring bearing the design of that enigmatic

Talonite sect, then one of gold set with a shining black onyx—the one Cadderly suspected had loosed the magical flames—and the last of gold set with several small diamond chips. The wizard's robe came off next. Cadderly stuffed it into his backpack. He found a slender wand slipped under a tie in Dorigen's undergarments, and fumbled through any pouches or pockets in her remaining clothing, making certain she had no more magical devices or spell components.

When he was done, he stood staring at the helpless woman, wondering what to do next. Some spells, he knew, required no physical components, and others used small, common items that could be found almost anywhere. If he left Dorigen like that, she might still play a role in the continuing battle, might wake up and kill any of them, kill Danica, perhaps, by uttering a few simple syllables.

Outraged by that thought, Cadderly grabbed his walking stick and laid the wizard's hands out to the side. Grimacing as he swung, he smashed Dorigen's fingers, on both hands, repeatedly, until her hands were black and blue and wickedly swollen. Through it all, the drugged and battered wizard only groaned softly and made no move to pull her hands away.

Cadderly gathered his possessions, placed the bandoleer with the remaining darts over his shoulder, and started away, not having any idea where he should go.

Q

At last Elbereth spotted his father, fighting in the small clearing against Ragnor. The elf prince knew it would take him some time to circumvent the many other melees in the area to get near Galladel, and he knew, too, that Ragnor was fast gaining an advantage.

He watched his father try a desperate, straightforward strike. Ragnor caught the elf king's arm and sent his sword in an overhand chop, which Galladel stopped by grabbing the ogrillon's wrist. It all seemed horribly familiar to Elbereth. He wanted to scream a warning, wanted to destroy himself for not telling his father of the ogrillon's favorite tactic.

The stiletto popped from Ragnor's sword hilt, straight down at Galladel's vulnerable head, and still Elbereth could only watch.

They continued their struggle for another moment before Ragnor freed his huge arm and plunged it down.

And suddenly, so suddenly, Elbereth was King of Shilmista.

TWENTY-TWO
VISIONS OF HELL

The mighty stallion stormed in, bravely bearing its rider toward the enemy leader. Bugbears stepped out to intercept, but Temmerisa lowered his head and plowed straight through them, scattering them like falling leaves.

Temmerisa stumbled, the great horse's forelegs tangled in a falling bugbear. A trident, thrown from the concealing brush, entered Temmerisa's side, finishing the proud horse's charge. Down Temmerisa went, whinnying and thrashing from the poison that had tipped the devilish weapon.

Elbereth rolled free of the tangle and looked back in horror as his proud steed stilled.

But when the elf prince looked around, he saw that his path was clear all the way to Ragnor.

"Come along, elf," the ogrillon spat, recognizing Elbereth from their earlier encounter. "I have beaten you before. This time I will kill you!" Just to spur his opponent on, Ragnor kicked the elf king's corpse at his feet.

For all his confidence, though, the ogrillon was shocked at the sheer wildness of Elbereth's charge. The reluctant king's sword whipped and hacked furiously, cut in on Ragnor, and stubbornly came back in after the ogrillon barely managed to parry the first strike.

"I avenge my father!" Elbereth cried, slashing away.

Confident Ragnor smiled wickedly and thought, The elf king was this one's father? What victories I will pile up this day!

Elbereth's furious assault went on and on, and Ragnor remained on the defensive. The ogrillon was a veteran of a thousand battles. He knew that the younger elf's rage would play itself out and soon give way to exhaustion.

Then it would be Ragnor's turn.

Q

By the time Cadderly got in sight of any of the fighting, he had passed the scarred remains of the earlier melees. Blasted trees and bodies lay all around him. The cries of the dying seemed a macabre game of ventriloquism with too many bodies about for the young man to discern the source of any single cry.

One goblin grabbed his ankle as he passed. Instinct told him to fire his crossbow at the monster, but he realized that the goblin, blinded from a sword slash and near death, had grabbed him out of fear, with no thought of attacking. Cadderly pulled his leg free and stumbled away, having neither the courage to finish the creature, nor the time to tend its mortal wounds.

In the distance, another of the walking trees tumbled, buried under the bulk of a hundred monsters. Most of those creatures were already dead, tangled in strangling branches, but those that weren't hacked wildly at the fallen oak. An elf rushed to the tree's defense, taking down two orogs before he was buried by the others and ripped to pieces.

Cadderly didn't know which way to run or what to do. For the young scholar, who had lived his whole life in the sheltered library, all of it seemed like some vision of the roiling Hells.

He heard soft weeping in a nearby tree and saw Hammadeen in its boughs, her shoulders bobbing with her sobs.

Another groan came from a goblin dying in the shadows, and another shriek split the air from somewhere in the unseen distance.

Cadderly ran on, circling the humanoids still hacking at the fallen tree. He wanted to find a hole and hide in it, but he knew that to stop moving meant death.

He crossed through a tight copse of duskwood trees—the duskwood tangle that he and the others had avoided on their way to Syldritch Trea, he assumed—and came into a small field of chest-high blueberry bushes, dotted by occasional trees. Suddenly the fight was all around him.

At the tree line across the field, a force of goblinoids tried to penetrate the stiff defense of a group of elf archers, and in several places combatants rolled around in the blueberry bushes, all together hidden from Cadderly's view. He heard them, though, and saw the bushes tremble with their vicious struggles.

Cadderly worked his way through the brambles, went down a slope, and came around to the backside of a hill. There he froze, stunned by yet another sight.

"Great Deneir," the stunned young priest muttered, hardly conscious that he had spoken.

Cadderly had seen ogres before, and had nearly swooned at the size of the huge monsters. But when he saw his first giant, nearly twice the height of an ogre, and he would guess ten times an ogre's weight, Cadderly, standing in its shadow, felt puny indeed.

Fortunately, the giant's back was to Cadderly and the creature was busy gathering rocks, probably to throw at the elves in the tree line. Cadderly would have been wise to walk past, but he reacted out of terror.

He fired a dart into the giant's backside.

"Hey!" the monster roared, rubbing its burning buttocks and turning around.

Cadderly, having realized his drastic error, had already taken flight and turned just once to fire another dart. That one caught the monster squarely in the chest, but the giant hardly flinched at the ensuing explosion.

The priest put his head down and sprinted for the safety of the trees, hoping that no elf would mistake him for an orc and shoot him down. He didn't look back again at the giant, guessing correctly that it had taken up the chase.

The giant laughed stupidly, surely thinking the human an easy catch, but its expression changed considerably when the two dwarf brothers popped up from the bushes beside it. One sliced into the back of the monster's hamstring with an axe, and the other crushed the giant's kneecap with a club.

The behemoth veered and tumbled down, and the Bouldershoulders were atop it before it ever stopped bouncing.

"Nice high ground to make a stand," Ivan remarked to Pikel, burying his axe into the giant's neck.

"Oo oi!" Pikel heartily agreed, striking the giant on the back of the skull with his tree-trunk club.

"Was that Cadderly that came running by?" Ivan asked. Pikel looked to the dark trees and nodded.

"Good bait, that one!" Ivan roared.

The conversation ended when a group of orogs crashed through the brush and charged at the exposed dwarves.

Q

A blinding flash ripped through the shadows. Cadderly heard several goblins squeal then he spotted the source of the lightning bolt, a familiar and welcome face.

"Tintagel!" he called, rushing to the elf wizard's side.

"Well met, young priest!" the blue-eyed elf replied sincerely. "Have you seen Elbereth?"

Cadderly shook his head. "I just came onto the field," he explained. "Dorigen is down." He displayed the rings he had taken from the wizard and the wand sticking from under his belt. "Might these be of—?"

"Down!" Tintagel cried, pushing Cadderly aside as a spear narrowly missed them both.

The elf threw out one hand and uttered a spell. Magical bolts of energy erupted from his fingertips, swerving unerringly through the trees and diving behind one large trunk. Out the other side fell a dead bugbear, its hairy body singed in several places from the magical attack.

"Elbereth," the wizard said again to Cadderly. "I must get to him, for it is said that he battles Ragnor!"

"He does," said a dryad's melodic voice to the side.

"Where are they?" Cadderly demanded, moving toward Hammadeen.

The dryad shied back against the tree, and Cadderly suspected that she meant to vanish.

"Do not go, I beg," the young scholar pleaded, mellowing his voice so as not to frighten the skittish creature. "You must tell us, Hammadeen. The fate of Shilmista rests in your hands."

Hammadeen did not reply or move, and Cadderly had to look hard to sort her out from the tree bark.

"Coward!" Cadderly growled at her. "You claim to be a friend of the forest, but you will do nothing in its time of need?"

He closed his eyes, concentrating on the tree hiding the dryad. Strange and marvelous emotions came over him as he attuned his senses to that tree, and he recognized the paths the tree had opened for Hammadeen's escape.

"No!" Cadderly growled, reaching for the tree with his thoughts.

To Cadderly's amazement, the dryad reappeared, looking back at the tree as though it had somehow betrayed her.

"They fight in the grove of bluetops, to the southwest, and not so far," the dryad said to Tintagel. "Do you know the place?"

"I do," Tintagel replied, eyeing Cadderly sidelong. "What did you do?" he asked after the skittish dryad had fled.

Cadderly stood dumbfounded, having no idea how he might reply.

The elf wizard, so very familiar with the forest, his home, conjured an image of the bluetop grove and recalled the words of another spell.

"Watch over me," he said to Cadderly, and the young scholar nodded, knowing the wizard would be vulnerable while casting. Cadderly took one of the two remaining darts from his bandoleer and cocked his crossbow.

A door of shimmering light, similar to the one Cadderly had seen Dorigen step through, appeared in front of Tintagel. Cadderly heard a familiar rustle as another nearby bugbear heaved a spear.

The young scholar spun around, picked out the target crouching in some bushes, and fired, blasting the monster right out the back side of the brush. There was no joy in Cadderly, and his satisfaction was soon lost, for when he turned back, he found Tintagel slumped, the spear buried deep in his side.

Cadderly cried out to him, grabbed the elf close, and having nowhere else to go, leaned forward, taking them both through the shimmering door.

Q

The giant groaned loudly, and Pikel broke away from his fight with an orog just long enough to smack the fallen behemoth on the back of the head. Seeing its opponent diverted, the orog tried to leap up onto the giant's back. Pikel's club caught it in midflight, dropping it back to the ground some distance away in a writhing heap.

The dwarves fought back to back, as they had atop the dead ogre in Dorigen's camp. Only the dwarves were even higher, standing taller than the orogs they battled, and the creatures had a considerable climb in trying to get at their enemies. Half the orog band of ten lay dead beside the giant, and not one of them had gotten close to standing toe-to-toe with the dwarves.

The brothers Bouldershoulder were truly enjoying themselves.

A commotion from the tree line made both dwarf and orog glance to the side. Out came Danica, running like the wind, a mixed group of orcs, goblins, and bugbears close behind her. Two of the orogs broke away from their fight with the dwarves and moved to cut her off.

An arrow got one in the chest, a second arrow thudding in a heartbeat later, just an inch from the first. The remaining orog made the mistake of looking to the side, to the elf maiden in the shadows of the tree line.

Feet first, Danica soared through the air, connecting with a double kick into the distracted orog's chest. It flew away, disappearing under the blueberry bushes, and did not reappear.

Danica was back up and running in an instant.

"I'll cut ye a path!" Ivan promised.

He leaped from the giant, right between two orogs. His axe whipped left and right, and his promise was quickly fulfilled.

"Good to see ye, Lady Danica," Ivan said, offering his gnarly hand.

They went back up together, joining Pikel as he clobbered the last orog. New enemies were not far behind, but the mixed band of humanoids found their ranks thinned as they charged. Arrows soared out from the tree line, scoring hit after hit.

"Shayleigh," Danica explained to the admiring dwarves.

"Glad she's on our side," Ivan remarked. Even as he spoke, another arrow soared out, hitting a goblin in the side of the head and dropping it dead on the spot.

"We cannot stay here for long," Danica told the brothers. "The area is in turmoil. Goblins and giants are everywhere, it seems!"

"How are the trees doing?" Ivan asked.

"Yeah," Pikel concurred excitedly.

"The trees have caused tremendous losses to our enemies," Danica answered. "But they are few, and fewer still since several have been brought down and several more battle the fires our enemies have started. The elves are scattered, and many, I fear, are dead."

"To the woods, then!" Ivan bellowed.

He leaped down again and charged into the approaching host, swinging so ferociously that more monsters turned and fled than remained to fight him. Danica nearly laughed aloud, and she pulled out her daggers, whipped them into the nearest target, and charged down, Pikel going right beside her, to join Ivan.

They were back under the trees in moments.

Q

Cadderly loaded his last explosive dart as he came through the other side of Tintagel's shimmering gate, carefully laying the wounded elf wizard at his side. He spotted Ragnor and Elbereth in the throes of a titanic struggle just a few yards away.

He spotted Galladel, too, dead in the dirt at their feet.

Cadderly had no doubt as to where he wanted to place his last dart, and told himself that he would feel no remorse for blowing a large hole in Ragnor's ugly face.

A charging bugbear changed Cadderly's plans.

The young scholar had no time to think, he just swung around and popped the dart into the hairy monster's belly when it was only a stride away. The bugbear lurched violently and stumbled past, tumbling face down in the dirt.

Cadderly looked to Tintagel, lying helpless and writhing in agony. He wanted to tend to the elf wizard, to get the spear out of Tintagel's side at least, but he saw clearly that Elbereth could not hold out for long against the powerful ogrillon.

"I vowed that I would die beside you," the young scholar whispered.

He thought for a moment of searching his pack, of getting out the flask of oil of impact and trying to load another dart, but realized that he had no time. Reluctantly, Cadderly dropped his useless crossbow and took up his walking stick and spindle-disks, thinking them ridiculous against a foe as obviously powerful as Ragnor. He reiterated his vow to Elbereth one last time and charged in beside the elf prince.

"Why are you here?" Elbereth demanded breathlessly when Cadderly rushed up. The elf ducked a quick cut of Ragnor's heavy sword, one of the few offensive strikes the ogrillon had taken.

Cadderly understood immediately the course the fight had taken. Elbereth was plainly tired, couldn't even seem to catch his breath, and Ragnor showed a dozen nicks and scratches, none of them deep or serious.

"I said I would fight beside you," Cadderly replied.

He stepped ahead, motioned with his walking stick, and threw out his spindle-disks. Ragnor blocked the attack with his forearm, curiously eyeing the strange but hardly effective weapon.

"You have powerful allies, elf prince," the ogrillon laughed derisively.

Cadderly struck again with the spindle-disks, and the ogrillon didn't even bother to throw up his arm, taking the blow squarely on the chest and laughing all the while.

Then Elbereth came on wickedly, his fine sword darting to and fro, and sometimes straight ahead. Ragnor showed considerable respect for that weapon, and while the ogrillon was fully engaged, Cadderly grabbed his walking stick in both hands and connected on Ragnor's elbow.

The ogrillon winced in pain. "You will die slowly for that!" he promised Cadderly, while furiously parrying Elbereth's cunning stabs and slashes. "Slowly. . . ."

Cadderly looked to his weapons as if they had deceived him. He knew he couldn't really hurt Ragnor, no matter how clean his blow, but he knew, too, for Elbereth's sake, that he must try to do something.

He waited and watched the fight's ebb and flow, staying back in the hope that Ragnor would pay him even less attention over the next few moments.

If Ragnor was at all concerned about the young scholar, the ogrillon didn't show it.

Elbereth's blade spun in circles around Ragnor's then poked ahead, into the ogrillon's arm. Ragnor growled, but if Elbereth was the faster swordsman, Ragnor was the tougher. The ogrillon went on the offensive, repeatedly hacking with his huge broadsword. He connected on Elbereth's shield, the sheer force of the blow splitting it and throwing Elbereth to the ground.

Cadderly knew he had to act then or watch the elf prince be cut apart. He dropped his walking stick to the ground and yelled wildly, taking two steps toward Ragnor and leaping onto the ogrillon's arm. The young scholar caught hold stubbornly, his arms around the ogrillon's neck and both of his legs locked tightly around one of Ragnor's.

Cadderly was neither a small man nor a weak one, but powerful Ragnor hardly swayed from his path toward the elf. The ogrillon glanced to the side incredulously, and Cadderly hung on for all his life.

Ragnor would have finished Cadderly then, except that Elbereth jumped back to his feet and wasted no time in returning to the attack. With Cadderly clutching and tugging and generally distracting Ragnor, Elbereth's cunning maneuvers scored even more hits.

"Off!" the ogrillon howled.

He drove Elbereth back with a vicious flurry then slipped his free arm around Cadderly's, breaking the young scholar's grip. Ragnor's strength was frightening indeed, and a moment later, Cadderly found himself flying through the air.

TWENTY-THREE

Back in the shadows of the trees, Ivan and Pikel hardly had trouble finding enemies. Goblins and orcs popped up from the undergrowth all around them, drooling and hungry for battle.

True to their dwarf heritage, the Bouldershoulder brothers promptly went berserk, clubbing and slicing with wild abandon, and though they had been fighting steadily for some time, neither showed any signs of weariness. Goblins flew every which way, launched by Pikel's heavy club, and Ivan, with a mighty overhead chop, sliced one orc nearly in half.

Through all the fury of that first melee, Danica rested back behind the brothers, gathering her energy for when she would inevitably be needed. Cadderly dominated the young woman's thoughts in that lull. Danica had found no time before that to consider where the young scholar might be and she feared he'd met a gruesome end. Her duty was clear to her, though, and she would not sway from it. More than ever, Danica had to trust in Cadderly to take care of himself, had to keep her focus on the desperate struggle for Shilmista.

No matter how many times Danica reminded herself of that fact, her heart still longed to find Cadderly.

The last orc's head flew off into the bushes. In the respite, Ivan turned and noticed the despair in Danica's almond eyes.

"Don't ye worry, lass," the dwarf told her. "We'll save ye a few in the next fight."

Danica's face crinkled at the words, revealing to the dwarf that he'd misjudged the source of her sadness.

"It's yer Cadderly, then," Ivan guessed. "Where'd that one get himself off to, anyhow?"

"I left him," Danica admitted, looking back over her shoulder to the west, toward Syldritch Trea.

A boulder plummeted through the tree branches, narrowly missing the three companions. In response, one arrow after another flew out from the side, zipping back in the direction of the berry bushes.

"Giant!" Shayleigh called, appearing from her hiding spot and stringing yet another arrow. "I've hit it three times, but still it comes on!"

She drew back and fired, and the companions watched the arrow fly through the leafy tangle to thud into what seemed like a moving mountain. Another huge form shifted beside the first.

"Two giants!" Ivan bellowed with excitement.

Danica grabbed Ivan and Pikel, as they started past her on their way to engage the giants.

"No doubt with a host of escorts beside them," the fiery young woman explained. "Don't be so foolish," she scolded. "You're much too valuable to us—to me."

"Oh," Pikel replied rather sadly.

Shayleigh popped another arrow into the approaching giants then caught up with Danica and the dwarves.

"We must be gone quickly," Shayleigh said.

"You three go on," Danica bade them. "I'll search for Cadderly."

"The priest is with Tintagel," Shayleigh replied. "Fear not, for if any can keep him safe in the fight, it is the wizard."

The news did brighten Danica's mood. Knowing that Cadderly was beside one as seasoned and wise as Tintagel eased her fears that her love had been abandoned to make his way alone in that forest of horrors.

"The four of us, then," Danica offered with determination.

"Oo oi!" was Pikel's reply.

"Woe to any monsters that cross our path!" Shayleigh vowed.

She spun and launched another arrow at the mass of approaching giants, just for good luck, and together the fighting foursome sprinted off into the shadows, formulating plans as they went.

Q

Without his shield, Elbereth could only grasp his sword hilt in both hands to deflect Ragnor's mighty blows. The ogrillon was finished with defense, determined to end the fight and move on to fresh kills. He cut a two-handed swipe straight across at Elbereth's chest, stepping into the blow so that the elf couldn't back away and would have to use his sword to parry.

Elbereth's weapon rang loudly under the force of the blow, vibrating for many moments. Elbereth's arms went numb, and he had to struggle just to hold his grip on the sword. Ragnor launched a second strike, identical to the first.

Elbereth knew that to similarly block that blow would tear the sword from his hands. He threw himself straight back instead, tumbling to the ground.

Ragnor attacked furiously, thinking the fight was won.

Elbereth's agility and speed crossed the ogrillon up, though, for the elf suddenly twisted and whipped his sword across, swift and low, stinging Ragnor's shins and abruptly halting the ogrillon's charge.

Elbereth was back up again, wary and keeping his distance as Ragnor, spitting curses and limping only a little, advanced steadily.

Cadderly groaned and forced himself up to his elbows, knowing that he, and especially Elbereth, could ill afford any delays. The young scholar had landed hard from Ragnor's throw, and had lost his breath in the tumble.

He looked at Elbereth, weary and sorely outmatched, and knew that Ragnor would soon add a second elf king to his day's kills.

"Back to the fight," Cadderly vowed, but he didn't even manage to get to his feet before he felt the wetness along the back of his neck. Thinking it blood, Cadderly put a hand over it and scrambled to remove his pack.

He breathed a sigh of relief when he saw that the moisture came from his pack, not his own body, but then he nearly swooned when he realized the only possible source.

Slowly, carefully, the young scholar untied and opened the pack and removed the cracked flask. He shuddered to think of what might have happened if his landing had shattered, and not just cracked, the container of volatile *oil of impact*. He looked up to the high branches of the bluetop trees and imagined himself hanging up there, twisted and broken from the horrendous blast.

Cadderly glanced at Ragnor then back to the flask, and a wicked smile found its way across his face. He carefully removed the top half of the cracked container then scooped his spindle-disks inside, cupping his hand to get as much of the remaining liquid as he could.

When Elbereth's back went against a tree, both the elf and the ogrillon realized that the running game had ended. Bravely, Elbereth launched a series of vicious thrusts, a few getting through to poke at Ragnor, but none solidly enough to keep the huge monster at bay.

Elbereth barely ducked in time as the ogrillon's sword smashed in, chopping a sizable chunk from the tree. Elbereth managed yet another hit as Ragnor tore his blade free. The ogrillon winced and swung again, shortening up on his stroke so he would connect with the elf, or nothing at all.

His blade flew freely as Elbereth dived to the ground, the overmatched elf's only retreat.

"Now it is done!" Ragnor proclaimed, and Elbereth, cornered and on the ground, could hardly argue.

Ragnor saw Cadderly coming in fast from the side, the young scholar's arm cocked and the curious—and useless—weapon readied for a throw. The ogrillon, sword high for a killing strike, paid the young scholar no heed, didn't even lower one arm to block the attack.

Cadderly growled and threw all his weight and strength into the throw. The spindle-disks slammed against the side of Ragnor's barrel-like chest, and the force of the explosion spun the ogrillon around to face Cadderly squarely.

For a moment, Cadderly thought that Ragnor was running backward, away from him, but then the young scholar realized that Ragnor's feet, pumping helplessly, were several inches off the ground.

Ragnor's arms and legs continued to flail as the ogrillon tried to slow his flight. A branch bent then cracked behind him, and he came to a sudden stop, impaled through the backbone against the tree. Ragnor hung there, a foot from the ground, a scorched hole in one side of his furry leather tunic—and in the skin underneath—and his legs lifeless below him. He felt no pain in those limbs, felt nothing at all. He tried to plant his feet against the tree, that he might push himself free, but alas, his legs would not heed his call.

Stunned beyond words, Cadderly looked down to his weapon hand. There hung the cord, shortened by half and its end blackened. Of the rock crystal disks, there was nothing to be found except a single scorched flake on the ground where Ragnor had been standing.

Similarly amazed, Elbereth rose to his feet. He looked at Cadderly for a moment then took up his sword and stomped over to Ragnor.

The world was a blur to the burly leader of the invading forces. Ragnor had to forcibly thrust out his chest just to draw breath. Still, the stubborn creature held fast to his sword, and he managed to raise it in a semblance of defense against Elbereth's determined approach.

Elbereth swatted the blade once, then again, driving it aside. The elf's sword slashed across the ogrillon's eyes, blinding Ragnor. Wisely, Elbereth stepped back as Ragnor's fury played itself out in a series of vicious cuts.

Cadderly thought Ragnor a pitiful thing as the blinded ogrillon continued to slice wildly at the empty air. Ragnor began to tire, and Cadderly looked away as Elbereth stepped back in. He heard a growl then a groan.

When he looked back, Elbereth was wiping his crimson-stained blade and Ragnor hung near death, one hand twitching pitifully at the hole Elbereth had cut through his throat.

Q

"Stupid things," Ivan whispered, looking ahead across a small clearing to the group of mixed humanoids and giant-kin.

The dwarf and his three companions had easily back-tracked to get behind the two giants, several orogs, and numerous goblins that had been pursuing them. One of the giant's movements appeared strained, the creature having caught several of Shayleigh's arrows.

"Bring them in," Ivan said with a wink to the elf maiden then he and Pikel slipped out of the tree line into the deep grass of the lea.

Shayleigh looked to Danica. The elf was not timid by anyone's standards, but that group of monsters seemed a bit too powerful for the small band to handle.

Danica, clearly similarly concerned but perhaps better understanding the dwarves' prowess, nodded grimly and motioned for Shayleigh to continue.

Shayleigh raised her great bow and took aim for the already wounded giant. She put a second and third arrow into the air before the first ever struck its mark.

The first hit the giant at the base of its thick neck. The monster howled and grasped at the quivering shaft, and the second arrow whipped in beside the first, pinning the giant's hand in place. By the time the third arrow hit, just below the first two, the giant was on its way down. It fell to its knees and held unsteadily there for a few moments then dropped into the grass.

The rest of the monstrous band let out a common shout of outrage and spun around, charging wildly back across the lea. Shayleigh promptly dropped one ferocious orog, putting an arrow between its bulbous eyes.

"Take to the trees," Danica instructed her. "Shoot for the lesser monsters. Be confident that the dwarves have a plan in mind for the giant."

Shayleigh looked to the grass where Ivan and Pikel had disappeared and smiled, surprised to learn that she, too, had come to trust a couple of dwarves. With agility befitting an elf, Shayleigh found a handhold and pulled herself into the branches of the nearest tree with remarkable ease.

Q

With its great strides, the remaining giant came ahead of its smaller companions. It heaved a boulder Danica's way, and the nimble monk barely dodged it as the rock took down a small sapling.

An arrow from above cut down a goblin.

Danica looked up and winked her appreciation to Shayleigh. Then, to the elf maiden's amazement, Danica stormed ahead, right at the approaching giant.

As the lumbering creature raised its huge club, Danica whipped her two already bloodied daggers into its face. The giant roared in outrage, dropped its club, and grabbed at the stuck weapons. Danica veered, smiling as Ivan and Pikel popped up from the grass, hacking and bashing at the monster's thick legs.

Q

The confused giant didn't know which way to turn. Ivan chopped at one of its legs, cutting out wedges as though he were felling a tree, but the pain in the monster's face demanded its attention. Finally, the giant mustered the courage to tear out one of the stubborn daggers, but by then it was too late for the leg, and the creature toppled to the side.

Ivan rushed past the monster toward the oncoming orogs, and Pikel headed for the giant's head to finish the job. The giant got a hand on Pikel as he neared its face, and started to squeeze. Pikel wasn't overly concerned, though, for he was close enough for a strike and Danica's remaining dagger, deep in the monster's cheek, offered a positively marvelous target.

Q

As Danica broke to the side, so too did a group of three orogs. Danica continued to veer, allowing the monsters to stay close enough so that they wouldn't give up the chase. Soon, the monk had nearly completed a full circuit, heading back for the same trees she'd just exited. Orog swords nipped at her heels, but Danica was confident that she could keep just ahead of the stupid things. She heard a yowl of pain and surprise behind her, and a gasp after that, and knew that Shayleigh had begun her work.

Danica dived headlong, twisting as she rolled, to come up facing the charging orogs. The closest beast, glancing back at its companion, who had taken two arrows, turned back just in time to catch Danica's fist on the chin. A sickening crack resounded above the din of battle, and the orog's jaw broke apart. When the creature at last settled on the ground, the bottom half of its jaw was aligned more with its left ear than with the upper half of its mouth.

The remaining orog spun and took flight. It managed to get a few strides away before Shayleigh's next arrow pierced its thigh, slowing it enough for Danica to rush up and bury it.

Q

Ivan waded into the horde of goblins and orogs with typical dwarf finesse. The dwarf butted with his horned helmet, bit where he could, kicked with both feet, and generally whipped his axe to and fro with such ferocity that the entire band of monsters had to give ground steadily. Those that could not retreat, caught between the dwarf and their own companions, most often hit the ground at about the same time as their severed extremities.

The downside to Ivan's tactics, in addition to the weariness that inevitably would accompany such a wild display, was that Ivan was all but blind to the events around him. And so the dwarf was off his guard as one orog managed to slip in behind his tirade. The creature, timing its attack between axe slashes so as not to get caught in a follow-through, stepped right up to the dwarf and let loose a wicked downward cut with its heavy club that Ivan couldn't begin to dodge or deflect.

"Yuck," Pikel remarked as soon as he realized that his head-bashing had become rather redundant.

The giant's grip had relaxed by that point, and Pikel stepped purposely away from the gruesome thing that had once been the creature's head. The dwarf seemed to consider retrieving Danica's dagger, which was buried in giant flesh with the tip of its point poking out the other side of the huge head, but clearly decided that if Danica wanted it back, she would have to get it herself.

That business done, Pikel crawled over the giant's chest to join his brother, and let out a squeaky warning just as the orog's club descended on Ivan's head.

"Ye called?" Ivan replied then added, "Ouch!" almost as an afterthought.

He spun to clobber the orog, but kept on spinning, around and around, finding no bearings until his cheek came to rest on the cool grass.

The orog howled in victory, a cry of glee cut short by Shayleigh's next arrow and even more so by Pikel's fury. The dwarf imitated the orog's own tactics, but while the orog's club had sent Ivan in a spin, Pikel's bash dropped the creature straight down in a heap with its legs straight out to the sides and its head lolling about on a useless neck.

Pikel wanted to hit the thing again, and again after that, but he had no time, for the remaining monsters had descended over helpless Ivan.

"Ooooo!" the dwarf bellowed, following yet another arrow into the throng.

Goblins flew every which way—even powerful orogs prudently leaped aside—and in mere moments, Pikel straddled Ivan's prone form.

Danica hit the group from the side a moment later, with equal fury, and Shayleigh dropped another orog, sinking an arrow right through its eye.

The monsters broke ranks and scattered.

Pikel remained defensively over his brother while Danica took up the pursuit, tackling an orog and rolling over it in the grass. Shayleigh fired off several shots, but realized to her dismay that she could not down all of the monsters before they found the safety of the trees.

The monsters' hoots of relief as they made the tree line were short-lived indeed, though, for out of those same shadows came a host of elves. In a few moments more, not a goblin or orog remained alive on that blood-soaked field.

Ç

Cadderly stood staring as Elbereth came over to join him. The world had gone mad, Cadderly decided, and he had been fully caught up in that insanity. barely a month before, the young scholar had known nothing but peace and security, had never even seen a living monster. But everything had gone upside down, with Cadderly—almost by accident—playing the role of hero, and with monsters, so many monsters, suddenly very real in the young scholar's life.

The world had gone mad, and Elbereth's forthcoming congratulations, the mighty elf's thanks for a blow that had defeated a monster beyond innocent Cadderly's wildest nightmares, only confirmed the young scholar's suspicions. Imagine, Cadderly winning where Elbereth could not—where King Galladel, lying dead at their feet, could not!

There was no pride in the young scholar's thoughts, just blank amazement. What cruel trick fate had played on him, to drop him so terribly unprepared into such a role, and into such chaos. Was that what Deneir had in store for him? If so, did Cadderly really want to remain the Scribe of Oghma's disciple?

Elbereth's startled look turned the young scholar around. Ragnor's remaining elite guard, half a dozen mighty bugbears wielding tridents dripping with a substance the two companions could only assume was poison, charged at the two, not so far away, certainly not far enough for Cadderly to escape.

"And so we die," he heard Elbereth mutter as the elf lifted his stained sword, and the young scholar, weaponless and weary, had no words to deny the proclamation.

A blast of lightning abruptly ended the threat. Four of the bugbears died on the spot, and the other two rolled around in the dirt, scorched and crippled.

Cadderly looked to the side, to Tintagel, bravely propped against a tree, wearing a smile only occasionally diminished by throbs of pain. Cadderly and Elbereth ran to their friend. Elbereth started to tend the wound, but Cadderly shoved the elf aside.

"Damn you, Deneir, if you do not help me now!" the young scholar growled.

It didn't take someone knowledgeable in the healing arts to see that Tintagel's wound would soon prove fatal. Where the elf had found the strength and presence of mind to release the magical strike, Cadderly would never guess, but he knew that such courage could not be a prelude to death.

Not if he had anything to say about it.

Elbereth put a hand on his shoulder, but Cadderly muttered and slapped it away. The young scholar grasped the spear shaft, still deep in Tintagel's side. He looked up to the blue-eyed elf, who understood and nodded.

Cadderly tore the spear out.

Blood gushed from the wound—Cadderly's fingers could not begin to hold it in—and Tintagel swooned and stumbled to the side.

"Hold him steady!" Cadderly cried, and Elbereth, a helpless observer in the spectacle, did as he was told.

Cadderly futilely slapped at the pouring blood, and actually held in Tintagel's spilling guts.

"Deneir!" the young priest cried, more in rage than reverence. "Deneir!"

Then something marvelous happened.

Cadderly felt the power surge through him, though he did not understand it and hardly expected it. It came on the notes of a distant, melodious song. Too surprised to react, the desperate young priest simply hung on.

He watched in amazement as Tintagel's wound began to mend. The blood flow lessened then stopped all together. Cadderly's hands were forced aside by the magically binding skin.

A long moment passed.

"Get me to the fight," a rejuvenated Tintagel bade them. Elbereth threw a hug on his elf friend, and Cadderly fell to the ground.

The world had gone mad.

TWENTY-FOUR

PACK OF WOLVES

Hammadeen's hand stroked Temmerisa's muscled flank, tenderly touching the bloodied white flesh around the garish, three-holed trident wound. The great horse hardly moved in response, only snorted now and again.

"Can you do for Temmerisa what you did for me?" Tintagel asked Cadderly.

The young priest, retrieving his walking stick, shrugged helplessly, still not even certain of exactly what he'd done for Tintagel.

"You must try," Elbereth bade him. Cadderly saw the sincere grief in his friend's face and wanted dearly to say that he could mend the horse's wounds.

He never got the chance to make the attempt, though, for Temmerisa gave one final snort then lay very still. Hammadeen, tears in her dark eyes, began a soft song in a tongue that none of the companions could understand.

Cadderly's vision blurred and the forest around him took on a preternatural edge, a surrealistic, too-sharp contrast. He blinked many times, and many more when he looked at Temmerisa, for he saw the horse's spirit rise and step from his corporeal body.

Hammadeen spoke a few quiet words in the horse's ear, and both she and the spirit walked slowly away, disappearing into the trees.

Cadderly nearly fell over as his vision shifted back into the material world. The young scholar didn't know how he could apologize to Elbereth, didn't know what in the world he might say to the elf whose father and prized steed lay dead at their feet.

Tintagel started to offer condolences, but Elbereth wasn't hearing any of it. The proud elf looked at his father then at Temmerisa then rushed away, stained sword in hand. Cadderly propped up the injured wizard, that they might follow.

A pair of orcs were the first monsters to have the misfortune of crossing Elbereth's path. The elf's sword moved with sheer fury, tearing through the creatures' meager defenses and slicing them down before Tintagel and Cadderly had the opportunity to join in.

And so they went on through the forest, Elbereth leading, his sword an extension of his rage, cutting a swath through the monstrous ranks.

Q

"The trees fight at Deny Ridge," an elf told Shayleigh. "A great force of our enemies has taken the high ground."

"Then we must take it back," Shayleigh replied.

She and the other elf looked around, counting heads. Including the dwarves and Danica, their numbers totaled twenty-three, but while the other elf had reservations, Shayleigh, with full confidence in her n Tel'Quessir companions, only smiled and started away to the south.

By the time they'd come within sight of the ridge, a dozen more elves, one a wizard, had fallen into their ranks, relieved to see some semblance of organization amid the chaos.

Deny Ridge was aptly named, Danica noted, staring at it from the tree line across a small, grassy break. From that side, the ground sloped upward at a steep pitch for a hundred feet, climbed straight up a rock face for thirty more, then sloped another hundred feet or so through thick grass to the top. According to Shayleigh, the other side, where the goblinoids battled the remaining sentient trees, was even more defensible, being a rocky, almost sheer drop from top to bottom.

The band could hear the fighting, and could tell from the sounds that the trees were having a hard time of it. Goblinoids lined the top of the ridge, using burning torches as their main weapons. Several archers were among their ranks, eagerly tying rags to their arrows, lighting them on the torches, and shooting them down into the attacking trees.

"We must get up there, and quickly," Shayleigh said, pointing to the left, to still another band of monsters making their way to join their comrades atop the ridge. "If our enemies are allowed to hold this ground, more will come beside them and they will have an unbeatable base from which to conduct their conquest."

"Two, three hundred of the things up there now," Ivan replied. "Ye might find getting to the top a bit of work. But still. . . ." the dwarf mused, and he wandered off toward his brother.

"Have you any ideas?" Shayleigh asked Danica and another elf by her side.

Danica looked at the dwarf brothers, engaged in a private conversation, pointing this way and that. Ivan was doing most of the talking, with Pikel nodding eagerly, or shaking his head vehemently and piping in an "Oo," or an "Uh-uh," every now and then.

"They will find a way if there is one," Danica explained to the confused elves.

Ivan stomped over a few moments later and announced that he and Pikel had done just that.

"Get us down to the right," he said. "And we're going to be needing plenty of ropes."

Ivan wet one finger and held it up. Pikel pointed behind them and Ivan nodded his confirmation that the wind was favorable.

Shayleigh and Danica understood none of it but had nothing better to go on. On the maiden's command, the entire band of elves moved silently through the trees down to the right as Ivan had instructed. They managed to produce five lengths of fine cord, which Ivan declared long enough for the task.

"Set some of yer friends about, looking back to the woods," Ivan instructed. "If we get caught here by some more goblins making their way in afore we make the top, then the game's up. But put yerself and yer archer friends, and that wizard elf, too, in line for shooting to the ridge top. Me and me brother'll make it to the rocks easy enough. After we get up on them, we'll be needing yer help."

"What are we to do?" Shayleigh asked, somewhat hesitantly, for others of the band had expressed some concern about being led by dwarves.

"Ye'll know," Ivan said slyly. He looked at Pikel. "Ye ready?"

Pikel hoisted the coiled lengths of cord over his shoulders, stuck a small hammer between his teeth, and responded with an enthusiastic, "Hroo hoi!"

From one of the many pouches on his wide belt Ivan produced a similar hammer and several iron spikes. His nod sent the brothers off and running, up the first grassy slope toward the rock break.

Shayleigh, Danica, the elf wizard, and half a dozen archers took up positions along the tree line, their flanks and rear guarded by the remainder of the elf fighters. Whispers circulated among the ranks, most in admiration for the brave, if foolish, dwarves.

Ivan and Pikel picked their careful way up the rock face, apparently still unnoticed by the monsters atop the ridge.

Just under the lip of the cliff, the dwarven hammers rang out, driving spikes to hang down the five lengths of cord.

"Are we to charge and climb?" Shayleigh asked Danica, wondering if the time to act had come.

It was clear that Shayleigh thought that the plan was not such a good one, for the elves, though they might make the top of the rocks, would still be out in the open with more than a hundred sloping feet between them and their enemies.

Danica held her hand up to calm Shayleigh. "Ivan and Pikel aren't finished," she replied with some certainty, though she, too, still hadn't quite figured out what the brothers had in mind.

Danica's guess soon proved correct, for Ivan and Pikel were far from finished. Pikel swung himself over the rocks first, coming onto the higher grassy slope. Immediately the goblins spotted him and let out a unified hoot. Pikel dived for the cover of a boulder, but wasn't quick enough to dodge the first arrow.

"Ow!"

The dwarf grimaced and pulled the shaft from his hip—not too serious a wound. Pikel looked back to the trees then peeked back up the slope. He smiled despite the pain when the first elven arrow took out the archer who'd hit him, sending the goblin flying over the back side of the ridge.

Ivan came up over the rock face next, hollering, *"Dwarven brigade, charge!"* at the top of his lungs and in the Goblin tongue. Pikel ignored his wound and rushed out beside his brother.

"What are they doing?" Shayleigh asked. "And why did he cry out the attack in Goblin?"

Danica seemed similarly stunned for just a moment, until she noticed the goblins' reactions. The creatures atop that section of the ridge went berserk, it seemed, many of them rushing down toward Ivan and Pikel and heaving their flaming torches down the hill.

"Dwarves," Danica muttered above the din of twanging bowstrings as the elves let loose on the suddenly open targets. "In all the wide world, there is nothing a goblin hates, or fears, more than dwarves."

"Oh, fine trick!" the elf wizard cried, and he rushed from the trees to get into range, and sent a volley of magical bolts from his fingertips, dropping two of the closest goblins.

Ivan and Pikel were no longer hanging around for the battle. As the flaming torches flew thick around them, the dwarves headed back for the rocks, caught two of the ropes they had hung, and swung out below the ledge.

The goblins' mirth at the apparent rout—from their viewpoint, only two of the wretched dwarves had even shown their ugly faces—lasted only as long as it took the dimwitted creatures to realize that the fires begun by their own hurled torches were swiftly making their way back up the slope.

"Follow the flames!" Ivan roared, hearing the startled screams from above. Then he added quietly to Pikel as they made their way back over the lip, "Goblins been around for a hundred, hundred years, and they ain't learned yet, when things get tough, that fire burns up!"

"Hee hee," came Pikel's reply.

With incredible agility and swiftness, Danica and the bulk of the elven force got to the hanging ropes and climbed to the top of the rock face, while Shayleigh, her archers, and the wizard remained behind to continue their own assault.

The fires led their way to the ridge top, clearing a path in the goblin lines. Monsters fell all over each other, and many were pushed over the cliff on the back side of the ridge in an effort to get away from the fast-moving blaze.

The fuel soon consumed, the fires died away as quickly as they'd started, leaving the elves holding a high spot atop the ridge. Enraged goblins came at them from both sides, outnumbering the small band ten to one, determined to recapture the lost ground.

"Forward!" Shayleigh instructed, knowing that she and her archer companions would have to get closer to provide any real aid in the desperate battle. The handful of elves sprinted up the first slope and took to the ropes.

Ivan, Pikel, and Danica centered the defensive line on the right, the short side of the ridge. The three worked with their typical harmony, complementing each other's movements and biting so fiercely into the goblin lines that many elves were freed up to join their kin on the other flank, where the bulk of the enemy force remained. It was a tenuous position indeed for the defenders, and every elf that fell left a large hole for the enemy to get through.

Danica thought the fight would be lost, especially after Shayleigh's band came up over the rock face, only to be met in close quarters and hard pressed, with their backs to the cliff, by another group of goblins.

"Should we be planning a retreat?" Danica asked Ivan.

"Never said it'd be easy," was all the dwarf replied as he chopped down a goblin that had come too near.

Then a strange cloud, greenish and thick, appeared over the ranks of goblins, just a few feet from Danica and the dwarves. The companions couldn't see under the opaque layers of that cloud, but they could hear the goblins gagging and choking. One miserable creature stumbled out, too intent on grasping at its churning belly to even realize its doom as Ivan and Pikel simultaneously smashed it down.

Most of the goblins that managed to escape the sickly vapors went out the back side of the cloud, angling down the slope, away from the fight. They found little running room, though, for there waited Elbereth, stern and mighty, and his sword worked tirelessly on the startled and weakened creatures.

Then the magical cloud dissipated, leaving more than a dozen goblins exposed and helpless on the ridge top. Ivan and Pikel started for them, but furious Elbereth got there first, hacking and slashing his way through. Without a word of greeting, the grim elf passed the dwarves, Danica, and the first rank of elves. He crashed through the faltering elven line defending the left flank and threw himself headlong into the pressing goblin throng.

No goblin sword or spear seemed to harm him. He didn't sway an inch from his path. In just a few furious moments, goblins ran from his terrible blade and the elves rallied behind him.

With the right side of the ridge swiftly cleared, Ivan and Pikel led several elves down to aid Shayleigh and the archers. Danica did not accompany them, for she saw someone else, a friend she could not ignore.

Q

Cadderly and Tintagel braced themselves for trouble as those goblins who had escaped both the cloud and Elbereth's fury rushed down at them. Tintagel muttered a quick spell, and Cadderly stood amazed as several images of himself and the wizard appeared, making their band of two seem like many. The goblins, already panicked and with the high ground fully lost, came nowhere near the unexpected throng, veering instead into the tree line to run away screaming.

Then the goblins were gone, and Danica was with Cadderly, and for both of them for just that quick moment, the world seemed right once more.

All across Deny Ridge, the battle became a rout. With Elbereth in the lead and Shayleigh and her archers freed once more, the elves and the dwarf brothers plowed the goblins away, crushing and scattering them. Ivan and Pikel turned one band around at the base of the ridge, and drove the stupid things into the waiting branches of four enraged oak trees.

It was over in short order, and Deny Ridge belonged to Elbereth.

Q

"Ye give me half a day, a dozen elves—including yer hurt wizard there—and move them trees where I tell ye, and I'll hold this place for a hundred years, and a hundred more after that if ye need me to!" Ivan boasted, and after the dwarf's exploits in leading the charge up the hill, not an elf in the camp doubted his words.

Elbereth looked at Cadderly.

"The trees will move as we bid," the young scholar answered with confidence, though he wasn't quite certain how he knew that to be true.

"The ridge is yours to defend," Elbereth said to Ivan. "A fine base from which our hunting parties might strike out."

"And your strikes will not be blind," Cadderly announced, looking to the nearest of the oak trees. "Will they, Hammadeen?"

The dryad stepped out a moment later, confused as to how the young scholar had seen her. No human eyes, not even elf eyes, could normally penetrate her camouflage.

"You will guide the elves," Cadderly said to her, "to their enemies and to their wayward friends."

The dryad started to turn back to the tree, but Cadderly cried, "Halt!" so forcefully that Hammadeen froze in her tracks.

"You will do this, Hammadeen," Cadderly commanded, seeming suddenly terrible to all watching the spectacle.

Amazingly, the dryad turned and nodded her compliance. Cadderly nodded, too, and walked away, needing some time alone to try to decipher all the surprises that were meeting him at every turn. How had he seen the horse's spirit? He hadn't asked, but he knew instinctively that Elbereth and Tintagel had not seen it. And how had he known that Hammadeen was in those trees?

Furthermore, how in the world had Cadderly so commanded the wild dryad?

He simply did not know.

Q

All through that night and the next day, while Ivan and Pikel set the defenses of Deny Ridge, small bands of elves—"packs of wolves," Ivan called them—slipped out into Shilmista. Following Hammadeen's guidance, they struck hard at the disorganized enemy. More elves were discovered in the woods, or found their own way to the new camp, and soon Elbereth's forces had systematically sliced holes through the encircling monsters.

Cadderly remained at the ridge beside Tintagel and the other wounded, though Danica was quick to join Shayleigh and set out on the hunt. It didn't fall upon Cadderly to strive for the level of healing power he had needed to save Tintagel, and Cadderly thought that a good thing, for he didn't believe the healing powers would ever flow through him with such intensity again.

He knew that something was happening around him, or even to him, but he didn't want to depend on some unknown power, for he certainly didn't understand it.

Q

The first real test of Ivan's defenses came late the next afternoon, when a band of more than two hundred monsters, ranging from skinny goblins to hill giants, set their sights on reclaiming the high ground. Only a score of elves were on the ridge beside Cadderly and the dwarves at that time, but that number included both wizards. After an afternoon of vicious fighting, more than half of the monsters lay dead and the rest had been scattered to the woods, easy pickings for the "packs of wolves" that roamed the forest.

Not a single elf had died in the fight, though two had been nicked by giant-hurled rocks, for the battle had never come to hand-to-hand range. Cunning dwarven traps, volleys of arrows, magical strikes, and the four towering oak trees slaughtered the enemy before they ever got past the steep rock face halfway up the ridge.

By Ivan's estimation, the most difficult part of the whole fight was in cleaning up the fallen goblinoids when it was all over.

"I'd forgotten that one," Ivan remarked to Cadderly, pointing to the tree line as darkness began to fall over the forest. Out of the trees came three elves and a companion whom Cadderly, too, had forgotten in the commotion of battle.

Kierkan Rufo leaned heavily on a staff, and even with the stick, still needed the support of one of the elves. The man's leg was not broken, as he had feared, but it was badly bruised and twisted and would not support his weight. He instructed his escorts to take him to Cadderly, and after several moments struggling to get past the natural obstacles of the ridge, Rufo plopped down in the grass beside Ivan and the young scholar.

"So nice of you to look over me," Rufo, in a foul mood, remarked.

"Bah, ye took to the trees, way up, to keep out of the fight," Ivan retorted, more amused than angered.

"High ground!" Rufo protested.

" 'Hide ground' would be a better way to name it," Ivan replied.

"Hee hee hee."

Rufo didn't need to look over his shoulder to know that the laugh belonged to Pikel, walking behind him.

"Could you at least get me something to eat?" Rufo growled at Cadderly. "I have spent the last day under the limbs of a fallen oak, miserable and hungry!"

"Hee hee hee," came a distant answer.

Q

Danica and Shayleigh returned a short while later. Neither of them was overjoyed to find Kierkan Rufo in the camp. The man defiantly pulled himself to his feet beside Danica.

"Another supposed friend," he spat. "Where was Danica Maupoissant when poor Rufo was in need? What alliances are these, I ask, when companions care nothing for each other's welfare?"

Danica looked from Cadderly to Ivan to Pikel as the man continued his tirade.

"You are all to blame!" Rufo fumed, his anger gaining momentum.

Danica curled up her fist and gritted her teeth.

"You are all—"

With that, Rufo fell to the ground, out cold.

Danica's shrug was not an apology for her blow, just an admission that her behavior in slugging Rufo might have been a bit impulsive. She expected Cadderly to berate her, but the young scholar could not, not against the wave of approval coming in from all around her.

Q

When the friends came upon Elbereth later that night, they found him smiling more than they had seen in many, many days.

"The news is good," the elf explained. "More than seventy of the People are known to live, and that number might increase, for nearly a score of elves are as yet unaccounted for and Hammadeen has told us that a battle was fought back in the east. And the paths farther to the east, through the Snowflake Mountains, are open once more, for a contingent of priests has arrived from the Edificant Library. Guided by the dryad, one of our hunting parties has joined the group, and even now they make their way to Deny Ridge."

"We are still badly outnumbered," Shayleigh put in, "but our enemy is disorganized and confused. With both Ragnor and Dorigen dead—"

Cadderly's sudden grunt stopped her and turned all eyes toward the young scholar.

"Dorigen is not dead," he admitted. The looks all around him turned sour, but the most painful retort to Cadderly, by far, was the sharpness of Danica's tone.

"You did not finish her?" the young woman cried. "You had her down and helpless."

"I couldn't."

"I'm doomed!" Rufo wailed. "Dorigen will see to our end—to my end, you fool!" he yelled at Cadderly.

"Are ye looking for another nap?" Ivan asked him, and Rufo realized from Danica's scowl that he would be wise to remain silent.

But Kierkan Rufo did have an ally.

"Fool indeed!" roared Elbereth. "How?" he demanded of Cadderly. "Why did you let the wizard escape?"

Cadderly couldn't begin to explain, knew that his admission of compassion would not be appreciated by the new elf king. He was truly amazed at how quickly Elbereth had apparently forgotten his actions in the battle, in Syldritch Trea and against Ragnor, and in saving Tintagel.

"Dorigen cannot use her magical powers," the young scholar offered weakly. "She is sorely wounded and stripped of her magical devices."

Cadderly unconsciously dropped a hand into his pocket to feel the rings he'd taken from Dorigen. He had considered giving them and Dorigen's wand to Tintagel, to learn if they might aid in the fighting, but he had dismissed the notion and resolved to check out the dangerous devices himself when he found the time.

Cadderly's claims did nothing to alleviate Elbereth's anger. "Her presence will bring unity to our enemies!" the elf growled. "That alone dooms Shilmista!" Elbereth shook his head and stalked away, Shayleigh at his side. The others, too, dispersed, Pikel sadly, leaving Cadderly and Danica alone by the campfire.

"Mercy," Cadderly remarked. He looked at his love, and caught her brown eyes in a gaze that would not let go. "Mercy," he whispered again. "Does that make me weak?"

Danica spent a long moment considering the question. "I don't know," she answered honestly.

They stood quietly, watching the fire and the stars for a very long time. Cadderly slipped his hand into Danica's and she accepted the grasp, if somewhat hesitantly.

"I will remain in the forest," she said finally, dropping Cadderly's hand. Cadderly looked at her, but she didn't return the stare. "To fight beside Elbereth and Shayleigh. The priests will arrive tomorrow, so it's rumored. Likely they will stay a few days to forge pacts with the elves, and some might remain to fight on. But most, I assume, will return to the library. You should go with them."

Cadderly found no words to reply. Was Danica sending him away? Had she, too, perceived his compassion as weakness?

"This is not your place," Danica whispered.

Cadderly took a step away from her. "Was Syldritch Trea my place, then?" he grumbled coldly, as angry with Danica as he'd ever been. "And have you heard of how mighty Ragnor met his end? Or have you forgotten Barjin?"

"I don't question your value," Danica answered, finally turning to regard him, "in this fight, as in anything. You will find no comfort in the continuing battle for Shilmista, just more violence, more killing. I don't like what that will do to you. I don't like what it's done to me."

"What are you saying?"

"There is a coldness here," Danica replied, poking a finger to her heart. She crossed her arms in front of her as if to ward off a wintry blast. "A numbness," she continued. "A fading of compassion. How easily I told you to kill Dorigen . . ." She stopped, choked by the admission, and looked away.

Cadderly's visage softened with sincere pity.

"Go away," Danica begged. "Go back to the library. Go home."

"No," Cadderly replied. "That place was never my home."

Danica turned back and eyed him curiously, expecting some revelation.

"This is not my place, that much is true," Cadderly went on, "and I have little fight left in me, I fear. I will leave with the priests when they depart, but to the library only long enough to retrieve my belongings."

"Then where?" Danica's voice hinted, just a tiny bit, of desperation.

Cadderly shrugged. He wanted desperately to beg Danica to come away with him, but he knew that he must not, and that she would refuse in any case. It struck them both then that this was farewell, perhaps forever.

Danica embraced Cadderly and kissed him hard then moved back and pushed him away.

"I wanted to stay beside you when the fighting began in earnest," she said, "after the trees had come to life. But I knew I couldn't, that the situation would not allow me my wishes."

"And so it is now," Cadderly said, "for both of us."

He ran his fingers through Danica's strawberry-blond hair, matted and tangled from so many days of battle.

Danica started to kiss him again, but changed her mind and walked away instead.

Cadderly remained at Deny Ridge for five more days, but he did not see her again.

EPILOGUE

Q

"Y ou should have stayed in the forest," Aballister said, pacing the length of his small room at Castle Trinity.

Dorigen wisely kept her stare locked upon him. Unlike Barjin's demise, the defeat in Shilmista had brought a somber mood to the head of Castle Trinity, a real fear that his plans for conquest might not be so easily accomplished. He still had more than three thousand soldiers at his command, and many more might be salvaged from the tribes returning to their mountain homes, but Shilmista was lost, at least for the time being, and the new elf king was determined and valorous. Dorigen had heard, and recounted for Aballister, many tales concerning mighty Elbereth's exploits in the battle for the wood.

"You should have stayed!" the older wizard growled again, more forcefully.

"I would not remain among such treacherous rabble with my fingers broken," Dorigen answered, holding up her bandaged hands. "Do you really believe that I would have been safe among goblins and orcs?"

Aballister couldn't deny the truth of her observations. He had seen firsthand what wild goblinoids might do to a woman.

"Without you to guide them, Ragnor's army is no more than scattered bands," he reasoned, "easy targets for the organized elves and this new king they hold so dear. We will be months in recovering our losses."

"The goblins will find a leader amongst them," Dorigen replied.

"One loyal to us?" Aballister asked.

"We still have time before the onset of winter to go back and set things in Shilmista to our advantage," Dorigen snapped back at him, not conceding an inch regarding her decision to leave. "The elves are not many, no matter how well organized and how well led they might be. For all their gains now, they'll surely have a long road in ridding Shilmista of the dark plague Castle Trinity has dropped upon it."

"You should have stayed."

"And you should have watched out for your son!" Dorigen rejoined before her better judgment could overrule her actions.

Druzil, perched on Aballister's desk, groaned and folded his leathery wings around him, certain that his master was about to blast Dorigen into little pieces.

Nothing happened. After several moments of silence, Dorigen, also fearful, realized that she had hit a sensitive area, one where even mighty Aballister felt vulnerable.

"Cadderly," the wizard mumbled. "Twice he has wandered into my way—and I had thought myself rid of the boy. Well, the first inconvenience could be forgotten. I wasn't so certain I wanted Barjin to conquer the library in any case," the wizard admitted. "But this! No, Cadderly has become too much a threat to be tolerated."

"How do you intend to end that threat?" Dorigen asked. She could hardly believe the coldness on Aballister's face when he spoke of his long-lost son.

"Boygo Rath has some helpful connections in Westgate," Aballister answered, his thin lips curling up in a wicked smile.

Dorigen winced, suspecting what the wizard had in mind.

"You have heard of the Night Masks?" Aballister asked.

Dorigen winced again at the mention of the assassins guild. Of course she had heard of them—everyone from the Dragon Reach to Waterdeep had heard of them. She nodded, her expression openly revealing her disbelief that Aballister would be wicked enough to hire such a band to kill his own son.

Aballister laughed at that incredulous expression. "Let us just say," he remarked, "that Cadderly, too, will soon hear of them."

Dorigen took the news with mixed feelings. She was angry with Cadderly, to be sure, for what he had done to her, but she could not ignore the fact that the young priest easily could have killed her. She shrugged her thoughts away and reminded herself that it was none of her affair, that what transpired next was between Aballister, Boygo, and Cadderly.

And the Night Masks.

Q

"Them goblin things are to be dancing in the trees tonight when they hear that ye're a dead one," Ivan remarked, cutting an easy swipe with his great axe.

"More likely, they shall sing of the death of a dwarf," Elbereth retorted, easily backing from the lazy swing. He rushed in behind the swipe, looking for an opening, but Ivan's defenses were back in place before the elf got within reach.

"What's an Elbereth?" Ivan taunted, white teeth shining through his yellow beard.

"I shall use that phrase for your epitaph!" the elf roared, and he played his sword through a dazzling display of feints and thrusts, ending up with its point sinking through Ivan's armor, toward the dwarf's chest.

Ivan fell back and blinked stupidly.

"Oo," moaned Pikel from the side, a sentiment echoed by Shayleigh, Tintagel, and many of the other gathered elves, including even Elbereth.

"Ye killed me, elf," Ivan grunted, his breath coming hard. He stumbled backward, barely holding his balance.

Elbereth lowered his sword and rushed in, terrified at what he'd done. When he got two steps from Ivan, bending low to examine the wound, he noticed Ivan's lips curl up in a smile and knew he had been deceived.

"Hee hee hee," came a knowing chuckle from the side.

Ivan turned his axe sideways and thumped Elbereth on the forehead, sending him tumbling backward. The elf threw his weight into the roll and came back to his feet some distance away. He watched curiously as two images of Ivan Bouldershoulder steadily closed.

"Ye think yer skinny blade'd get through me dwarven armor?" Ivan huffed. "Silly elf."

They joined in melee again, Ivan taking the lead. Elbereth learned his lesson well, and he used his superior speed and agility to parry Ivan's attacks and keep out of the dwarf's shorter reach. Every time the cunning elf found an opening, he slapped the side of his sword against the side of Ivan's head.

He might as well have been banging stone.

After many moments, the only somewhat serious wound came when Ivan tripped and inadvertently dropped the head of his heavy axe on Elbereth's toes.

A sound spread around the perimeter of the battle, where nearly the entire elven camp had by then gathered:

"Hee hee hee."

Q

Cadderly looked out the open window, beyond the rooftops of Carradoon, toward Impresk Lake, but his thoughts were many miles away, back in the forest he had left a month before. The morning fog rose from the still water, and a distant loon uttered its mournful cry.

Where is Danica now? Cadderly wondered. And what of Ivan and Pikel?

The young scholar dearly missed his friends and lumped that emptiness into the same void he'd discovered when he realized that the Edificant Library was not his home, and never had been.

He had gone back to the library with Headmaster Avery, Kierkan Rufo, and a score of other priests after leaving Shilmista. Avery had begged him to stay and continue his studies, but Cadderly would not, could not. Nothing about the place seemed familiar to the young scholar anymore. He couldn't help but view the library as a lie, a facade of serenity in a world gone mad.

"There are too many questions," Cadderly had told the headmaster. "And here I fear that I will find too few of the answers."

So young Cadderly had taken his purse and his walking stick, and all the other possessions he had considered worthwhile, and left the library, doubting he would ever return.

A knock on the door broke the young scholar from his contemplations. He moved across the small room and cracked open the portal just enough to retrieve the breakfast plate that had been left for him.

When he'd finished his meal, he replaced the plate outside his door, leaving a silver coin as a tip for obliging Brennan, son of the innkeeper of the Dragon's Codpiece. Cadderly had asked for his privacy and the innkeeper had given it to him without question, delivering his meals and leaving him alone.

The calls in the street began again shortly after, as Cadderly expected they would. Carradoon was being roused for war; a force was quickly being mustered to organize a defense of the town. At first, the call was for soldiers to go to the aid of the elves in their noble battle for Shilmista, but the latest reports had changed that. Shilmista was secured, it seemed, with most of the scattered goblinoids fully on the run.

Still the force in Carradoon swelled, and restrictions, including a curfew, had been placed on the town.

Cadderly didn't enjoy the rising level of anxiety, but he thought the town wise in making preparations. The evil that had inspired Barjin's attempt on the Edificant Library and Ragnor's invasion of Shilmista was not fully defeated, Cadderly knew, and it would no doubt soon descend over Carradoon.

Cadderly didn't close his window against those calls. The wind coming off the lake was comfortably cool and gave him at least some tie to the outside world. Reverently, the young scholar took out his most valuable possession, *The Tome of Universal Harmony,* opened it on his small desk, and sat down to read.

Too many questions filled his mind.

FORGOTTEN REALMS

Ed Greenwood
Presents

Waterdeep

BLACKSTAFF TOWER
STEVEN SCHEND

MISTSHORE
JALEIGH JOHNSON

DOWNSHADOW
ERIK SCOTT DE BIE
APRIL 2009

CITY OF THE DEAD
ROSEMARY JONES
JUNE 2009

THE GOD CATCHER
ERIN M. EVANS
FEBRUARY 2010

CIRCLE OF SKULLS
JAMES P. DAVIS
JUNE 2010

Explore the City of Splendors through the eyes of authors
hand-picked by FORGOTTEN REALMS world creator Ed Greenwood.

They engulf civilizations.
They thrive on the fallen.
They will cover all trace of your passing.

THE WILDS

THE FANGED CROWN
Jenna Helland

THE RESTLESS SHORE
James P. Davis
May 2009

THE EDGE OF CHAOS
Jak Koke
August 2009

WRATH OF THE BLUE LADY
Mel Odom
December 2009

FORGOTTEN REALMS

The *New York Times* BEST-SELLING AUTHOR

RICHARD BAKER

BLADES OF THE MOONSEA

". . . it was so good that the bar has been raised.
Few other fantasy novels will hold up to it, I fear."
—Kevin Mathis, d20zines.com on *Forsaken House*

Book I	Book II	Book III
Swordmage	**Corsair**	**Avenger**
	March 2009	March 2010

Enter the Year of the Ageless One!

TRACY HICKMAN
Presents

The Anvil of Time

The Sellsword
Cam Banks

The Survivors
Dan Willis

Renegade Wizards
Lucien Soulban
March 2009

The Forest King
Paul B. Thompson
June 2009

The lost stories of Krynn's
history are coming to light.

DRACONIC PROPHECIES

JAMES WYATT

From acclaimed author
and award-winning game
designer James Wyatt, an
adventure that will shake
the world of EBERRON.

STORM DRAGON
AVAILABLE NOW IN PAPERBACK

DRAGON FORGE
IN PAPERBACK APRIL 2009

DRAGON WAR
IN HARDCOVER AUGUST 2009

Everything you thought you knew
about MAGIC™ novels is changing…

From the mind of

ARI MARMELL

comes a tour de force of imagination.

AGENTS OF ARTIFICE

The ascendance of a new age in the planeswalker
mythology: be a part of the book that takes fans
deeper than ever into the lives of the Multiverse's most
powerful beings:

Jace Beleren™
a powerful mind-mage whose choices now will forever
determine his path as
a planeswalker;

Liliana Vess™
a dangerous necromancer whose beauty belies a dark
secret and even darker associations; and

Tezzeret™
leader of an inter-planar consortium whose quest for
knowledge may be undone by his lust for power.